PRAISE FOR KELLEY ARMSTRONG

"Armstrong is a talented and evocative writer who knows well how to balance the elements of good, suspenseful fiction, and her stories evoke poignancy, action, humor and suspense."
The Globe and Mail

"[A] master of crime thrillers."
Kirkus

"Kelley Armstrong is one of the purest storytellers Canada has produced in a long while."
National Post

"Armstrong is a talented and original writer whose inventiveness and sense of the bizarre is arresting."
London Free Press

"Kelley Armstrong has long been a favorite of mine."
Charlaine Harris

"Armstrong's name is synonymous with great storytelling."
Suspense Magazine

"Like Stephen King, who manages an under-the-covers, flashlight-in-face kind of storytelling without sounding ridiculous, Armstrong not only writes interesting page-turners, she has also achieved that unlikely goal, what all writers strive for: a genre of her own."
The Walrus

ALSO BY KELLEY ARMSTRONG

A Stitch in Time time-travel gothic series
A Stitch in Time
Ballgowns & Butterflies (novella)
A Twist of Fate
Snowstorms & Sleigh Bells (novella)
A Turn of the Tide
Ghosts & Garlands (novella)

A Rip Through Time mystery series
A Rip Through Time
The Poisoner's Ring

Haven's Rock mystery series
Murder at Haven's Rock

Standalone Horror
Hemlock Island

Standalone Thrillers
The Life She Had
Wherever She Goes / Every Step She Takes

Past Series
Rockton mystery series
Cursed Luck contemporary fantasy duology
Cainsville paranormal mystery series
Otherworld urban fantasy series
Nadia Stafford mystery trilogy

Young Adult
Aftermath / Missing / The Masked Truth
Otherworld: Kate & Logan paranormal duology
Darkest Powers/Darkness Rising paranormal trilogies
Age of Legends fantasy trilogy

Middle Grade
A Royal Guide to Monster Slaying fantasy series
The Blackwell Pages trilogy (with Melissa Marr)

A CASTLE IN THE AIR
A STITCH IN TIME
BOOK IV

KELLEY ARMSTRONG

Cover Design by Cover Couture www.bookcovercouture.com

ISBN-13 (hardcover): 978-1-989046-73-9
ISBN-13 (paperback): 978-1-989046-72-2
ISBN-13 (ebook): 978-1-989046-71-5

INTRODUCTION

*If you're new to my **A Stitch in Time** stories—or if it's been a while since you've read one—here's a little introduction to get you up to speed. Otherwise, if you're ready to go, just skip to chapter one and dive in!*

There's a time stitch in Thorne Manor, hereditary summer home to the Thornes of North Yorkshire. As far as we know, Bronwyn Dale was the first to pass through, traveling from the twenty-first century to the nineteenth, where she met William Thorne when they were both children. Later, as a widow, she returned to find William still there. They're now married with two daughters, living in Thorne Manor and dividing their time between the modern world and the Victorian one.

Before Bronwyn returned to Thorne Manor, Rosalind Courtenay—the wife of William's best friend, August—accidentally went through the time stitch into the modern world, where she was trapped for four years, separated from August and their young son, Edmund.

Rosalind returned home and reunited with her family, including her sisters, Portia and Miranda. Miranda had her own adventure in the stitch, going backward in time by accident and meeting Nicolas, a French marquis's son enlisted as a privateer. In the holiday novella *Ghosts & Garlands*, Miranda finally went to the twenty-first century. While there, Miranda and Nicolas encountered the ghost of a young highwayman,

Colin Booth. Colin had been murdered over a priceless French clock, and he now haunts a museum trying to get it back. Miranda promised to take money to his family in the early eighteenth century.

Now Miranda and Nicolas are making good on that promise. Except they haven't returned, which means it's Portia's turn to have her grand adventure through time.

I am about to step through time, and I am terrified. I literally stand at the precipice, having determined the exact spot on the floor where the time stitch lies, the toes of my boots a scant inch outside it.

My sister is on the other side, and she needs help, and no one can provide it except me, because our elder sister is thousands of miles away, along with her fellow time-travelers. I am the only person here who knows about the stitch—and the only one who knows that Miranda and her husband, Nicolas, passed through it.

I am also the only one in our family who has not taken this leap. That includes my infant niece, who regularly travels from our time—the nineteenth century—to the twenty-first. I have said I have no interest in making the journey. That is a lie. I have said I simply do not have the time. That is less of a lie, but in truth, it is preposterous to say I could not afford even an afternoon to see another world.

I am afraid of what lies before me. It represents chaos. An upheaval of everything I know. Visit another world? I'm still struggling to find balance in my own.

I am unsettled by what lies beyond because Miranda embraces it, and my sister is chaos in human form, wild and impetuous and bold and all the things I cannot afford to be. I am a woman trained as a doctor and passing as a nurse, and the only way I manage that is by keeping my head down, giving no one cause to notice me.

Yet none of that matters if Miranda needs me, and the only reason I still hesitate is . . .

Fear.

Fear that I am not what she needs in this moment.

Two weeks ago, Miranda and Nicolas leaped through this stitch to fulfill a promise made at Christmas. The Sight runs in our family, and while my own experience with it is . . . complicated, Miranda sees and can communicate with the dead, and she promised a young man's tormented spirit that she would help his family.

To do that, Nicolas and Miranda had to go to the eighteenth century. Before they left, we learned everything we could about the historical period and the young man's story, because this was no ordinary young man. He'd been a highwayman who'd been murdered by Scarlet Jack, a vigilante posing as a fellow highwayman.

While Miranda did not expect to encounter trouble—they only planned to visit the dead boy's family—something has happened. She was due back three days ago, and I have waited as long as I dare.

I lift my satchel from the floor. I have spent the past three days rushing about preparing for my own trip while hoping it would not be needed, that Miranda and Nicolas would stagger out of the stitch, exhausted but safe, Miranda bubbling with a new story to tell.

That has not happened, and so I am here, wearing one of my two newly made traveling dresses that will fit the *robe à la française* style, with a tightly laced bodice, deep square neckline and pleated skirt. Instead of a corset, I ought to be wearing stiff stays that pull my shoulders back and thrust my chest forward, but I do not quite know how to achieve that, so I have made do as best I can. At worst, I will be considered unfashionable, and I hardly care about that.

Thankfully, my visit will predate the era of powdered and puffed hair, and I only pin mine up while adding a simple cotton cap appropriate to the time. Curling one's hair is also appropriate, but mine is already curly enough that I need only to let a few tendrils hang. My boots ought to be pointed at the toe, so I have selected ones as close to that as possible. I also ought to wear makeup, and while that thought intrigues me, I would not know where to begin, so I must hope that it is not expected of a woman traveling. In my satchel, I have only items that are—if not completely correct for the time—correct enough that I may only seem a little odd, which is nothing new for me. I have left nothing to chance. I will enter the early eighteenth century with a plan and everything I need to pass as unnoticed as I do in this world.

I am about to step through when I realize I have forgotten to remove my spectacles. I do not actually need them to see. They are only part of "passing unnoticed," along with dowdy clothing and a downcast glance. In a place like Thorne Manor, where I am comfortable, I do not wear the spectacles or the dull clothing and certainly not the downcast gaze, but I was in town today and quite forgot to remove the spectacles on my return.

I set them atop the letter I have left for Bronwyn and Rosalind. Then I lift my foot toward the—

Wait.

What if Miranda didn't end up where she needed to be? It is not as if she can point to a date on a calendar and go there. She trusts that the stitch will take her where she needs to be, and so far, it has, but what if it did not?

And what is to say that I will end up in the same time she's currently in?

The others travel between our time and Bronwyn's, like a rail line with only two destinations. It is different for Miranda. Why would it also be different for me? What if I end up trapped in the future, as Rosalind did the first time she stepped through?

No, I cannot do this. I am being overly impetuous and must think it—

A yowl startles me, and I spin to see Bronwyn's calico cat, Enigma, leaping straight at me. I stagger back in surprise. The cat hits me, slamming me backward, and I fall flat on my rear, satchel still clutched in one hand.

"Enigma!" I say. "That is most unacceptable . . ."

I trail off.

The cat is gone.

The entire room is gone, and I am sitting on the floor in an empty one, dust swirling around me.

I have fallen through the stitch.

I have crossed time.

I leap to my feet and wheel to look at the spot where I landed, at the mark I left in the dust.

That's the spot. Step back into it and return—

No, I can curse that blasted cat for knocking me through, but I also know that I owe her a plate of fish for giving me the push I needed. If I go back, even just to test that I can, I might never summon the courage to return.

One look around tells me I am where I need to be. While the room itself is devoid of any furnishings that would tell me the time period, the fact that it has been left empty has also led to dust, and in that dust, two sets of fading footsteps cross from me to the door.

Miranda and Nicolas came through, left this room and did not return. That means I am in the same world as they are, and so it does not matter what the actual time period is.

I am where I need to be.

❧

If this were one of my sister's novels, she would tell how her heroine prowled the house, taking in everything and wondering at it all. But this is me, Portia Hastings, the overly practical and overly somber middle sister. I have a goal in mind and no time to tarry. I have done quite enough of that today, and if I linger, I shall put myself impossibly behind schedule. Also, I do not particularly wish to linger. Oh, I am certain this world contains wonders, but I will see them in passing as I make my way toward the goal of my imperiled sister.

When Miranda invited me to join the planning for their trip, she pretended to be in need of my research skills and attention to detail. In truth, I think she secretly hoped to entice me into joining the mission itself. She expected it would be like helping plan another's exotic voyage. How could I not long to join it? One would think that after years of me not being the least tempted to join Miranda's adventures, she would know better. But I suppose I cannot blame her for hoping she might still light a spark inside me.

There *is* a spark inside me, and it is very easy to light. Tempt me with knowledge. That is what I seek. Miranda does the same, but her curiosity is far more scattershot. She simply wants to know. Anything. Everything.

She is a sponge soaking up all new information. I want to know that which will allow me to help my patients.

There is only one thing before this that has lured me in the direction of that stitch: the promise of medical knowledge from the future. Yet I soon realized I did not need to make the voyage myself. Like me, Nicolas is a doctor by training if not by certification—in his case, a pirate ship and the looming presence of a guillotine ended his plans for a complete medical education in France. Now he has access to the medical knowledge of the future, which he happily shares with me.

I pause only long enough to ensure there is no one at home. The house is indeed closed up and looks as if it has been for more than a season. All that means is that I do not need to worry about bumping into a very surprised ancestor of Bronwyn's husband, Lord William Thorne.

I know this house well, and so I make my way directly to the front door. Within minutes of coming through the stitch, I am outside of Thorne Manor and striding toward the path that will take me to Whitby.

Having helped my sister prepare for this trip, I know exactly where she intended to go, and I know how they intended to get there, so I need only follow in their footsteps. Once I left the house, I lost the guide of those prints in the dust and must rely on their metaphorical prints, following the route I helped them plan.

I need to head deeper into the Yorkshire moors, east toward Whitby. The easiest way to get there would be to take a coach from High Thornesbury. But as Miranda and Nicolas realized, High Thornesbury is too tiny for strangers to simply appear in without everyone wondering where you came from. We couldn't even determine whether High Thornesbury *has* a coach stop in this period. So they had planned to walk to Whitby, knowing they'd find one there.

Whitby is not a short walk. It is nearly ten miles. That is why I wore comfortable boots and brought food. I had planned to stop for a picnic on the moors, but I am running later than I expected, having underestimated the walking time and overestimated my own sense of direction.

By the time I reach Whitby, it's midafternoon. It will be only a few hours by coach to my destination, meaning I will arrive in time to find lodgings, if there are lodgings to be had. If not, I am prepared to spend the night in whatever shelter I can find. That is the advantage to being practical. I may not be the most spontaneous person, but nor do I shrink at the idea of sleeping in a hay barn.

Practicality also means I do not shrink from using cold stream water to tidy myself. When I am presentable, I find a high spot from which to observe the town. I have been in this world for hours now, and I still am not certain what year it is . . . or even which century. Yes, that sounds ridiculous, but I have been crossing through the moors. Any farmhouses I spotted were simply that—farmhouses, with no distinguishing features that would place them in the eighteenth century, the nineteenth or even the seventeenth.

Once I have found the highest perch I can manage in boots and skirts, I pause to observe. At first glance, Whitby looks much like the one I know, complete with the harbor and the gothic abbey on the opposite hill. It is only on closer inspection that I see the differences—a building I do not recognize, another building I cannot find. It is also significantly smaller.

When I draw closer, I can truly see that I am well before my time. There is no train, not even the old horse-drawn one. The ships are different, too, and there are far fewer of them. Far fewer, too, than in the Whitby where Nicolas lived at the end of the eighteenth century. Most of all, though, the people are different. Their dress differs, to be sure, but I expected that from my research. In my time, Whitby is a thriving destination for seaside vacations, and I see little of that here, the grand hotels and such not yet built.

As I make my way to the inn from whence the coach departs, I pass a stand selling various sundries, including newspapers, the best way to discover the date. There is only one paper, and it is much rougher in design than the ones I'm familiar with. The price, though, is not significantly less than I would expect to pay in my time.

I buy a copy and then walk far enough that no one will see me staring intently at the date . . . perhaps with a look of surprise.

There is no surprise. I have arrived in the spring after the young highwayman perished. In other words, Miranda came out of the stitch exactly when she expected to. She had hoped that Fate might bring her back a year earlier, *before* the boy died. Yet Fate seems to decide which wrong it wants Miranda and Nicolas to right, and in this case, it was not to save the boy, but to ensure his destitute family received the money he'd given his life for. And now it has helpfully brought me to the same year to help them.

Before I go to climb the inn's rough steps, I lift my skirts, and I'm momentarily unbalanced when that requires far less effort than it would in my time. I'm wearing a traveling dress, but in this era, our research indicated that I only needed a chemise, petticoats and a very small pannier under it. I am also wearing drawers, which would not be found in this era, but I could not bring myself to forgo them.

My dress is dowdy, as it would be in my time. That is not my preference, but it is excellent for blending in. When I look around, I see a lack of the vibrant colors I would expect in my time, and most of the pretty pastels are reserved for women younger than my twenty-nine years. There are many floral prints and plenty of lace and bows that I eye rather longingly.

I am dressed correctly, though, as I can tell by the woman and her daughter who enter the inn ahead of me. They are both very finely attired, looking rather out of place in the provincial lodgings. Another couple alighting from a coach are also dressed well. This must be one of the better accommodations in town then.

I head to the counter and tell the clerk that I wish to buy a ticket for the next coach heading northwest through Ravensford. He frowns at me and says, "You missed today's coach, miss. It left an hour past."

I keep my face expressionless, as I inwardly chastise myself. An hour? In other words, I would have caught it if I had not gotten lost on the moors. Or if I had not insisted on surveying the town first and buying a newspaper.

"I will buy a ticket for tomorrow, then," I say. "And I will also require a night's accommodation."

When the man hesitates, I steel myself for him to ask who else will join me in the room. My husband? Parents? Elderly relative? Miranda has said that the Victorian restrictions on a woman's freedom of movement are largely a product of our own era, particularly outside the cities. Is it different in this time period? The man's expression suggests not, which means I might indeed be seeking a hay barn for the night.

"There is no coach tomorrow, miss. Nor the next day, either. It'll be three days hence."

I stare at him. "Three days?"

"If you wish to travel to York or Leeds, there are coaches in the morning. You can likely catch one to Ravensford from there instead. Not much call for travel from here to there."

I hadn't considered this. If Whitby is not yet a popular holiday destination—nor even a popular port—then travel would indeed mostly be to the larger centers.

"I can sell you a ticket to Leeds," the man says. "That would be best. Go to Leeds, and then take a coach going through the smaller towns, like Ravensford."

"How much is the ticket to Leeds?" I ask.

He tells me. It is less than half of what I would pay in my own time. That gives me another option.

"I am in rather desperate straits," I say. "My sister is about to have her first child, and she telegraphed to say she is having difficulties. I am trained in midwifery. Perhaps I could hire a private coach?"

The man looks dubious. "You appear to be traveling alone, miss."

"Yes, I am." I channel the same attitude I use whenever anyone questions my right to be in a medical lecture. I lift my chin and cloak myself in the self-importance of my male colleagues. "As I said, my sister is in urgent medical need. I did not have time to find a proper traveling companion."

"I understand, miss, and I am not questioning that. It's just that . . ." He lowers his voice. "There are some proper coaches for hire, but they're all away, and the ones that remain are . . ."

"Ah," I say, softening my tone. "They are not the best conveyance for a woman traveling alone."

"Yes, miss. Not the best conveyances or the best . . . conveyors."

"I understand."

I think fast. Ravensford is nearly thirty miles from here. I could walk, but it would take two days. Perhaps I could hire a horse? I am not certain my riding skills are up to that. I'm still thinking when a voice behind me says, "Did I hear you're going to Ravensford, dear?"

I turn to see the woman I'd followed into the inn. Her daughter has taken their packages inside, and the woman must have been waiting behind me to speak with the clerk. I quickly step away from the desk.

"So sorry, ma'am," I say. "Please go ahead. My business can wait."

"Oh, I am not in any hurry, dear. I just overheard that you seem to be heading in our direction and are unable to procure a coach. We pass through Ravensford, and we'll be leaving in an hour or so, if you'd care to join us."

"Oh." I hesitate. I urgently need to get to Ravensford, but to travel with a stranger? Is that different in these times? Better? Worse?

"I . . . I would not wish to inconvenience you, ma'am," I say.

She smiles knowingly. "Which is a polite way of saying you do not know us at all and, as a young lady traveling alone, you must be careful." Before I can protest, she turns to the clerk. "David? You know us, yes? Could you provide an introduction?"

He straightens. "Of course. This is Mrs. Marion Ward. Her husband owns a shipping line, and they stay with us regularly."

"A *small* shipping line," Mrs. Ward says with a smile. "We have a country house ten miles past Ravensford, and my husband insists we stop in Whitby for business each time we come up." She turns her smile on the clerk. "Which I do not mind, as I adore the coast." She turns back to me. "There is no need to decide just yet. I was just going to ask David for a pot of tea before we leave. Would you join me for that, and we can get to know one another properly?"

W ith the desk clerk having vouched for Mrs. Ward, I do not need time to make up my mind. Still, I do join her for tea. She seems very kind and well mannered, with subtle inquiries about me and my family that I do not begrudge her. That is the way of things in my world, and I am certain it is the same here. We are judged not by who we are but from whence we came.

No, that isn't entirely true. It *does* matter who you are, in the sense that if I were an "unsuitable" woman, no family connections—short of royal ones—could save me. I mean that I am otherwise judged by my family. Do I have noble or genteel blood? If not, do I at least come from respectable people . . . and by *respectable*, they mean people of both repute and money.

My father was a doctor, a respected member of a very respectable profession. As for money, there was little of that. To be a wealthy doctor means to treat only those who can afford it. That was not my father, nor is it me. I skim over that by playing my best card—my brothers-in-law. My eldest sister is married to an earl's son and my youngest to a French marquis's son. Both are younger sons, to be sure, without titles themselves, but what matters is the lineage . . . and if such "respectable" families welcomed daughters-in-law from my family, well, I must come from very good stock indeed.

As I said, such inquiries are normal in my world, and so I do not begrudge Mrs. Ward the asking, or the answers . . . until I realize why she asked, which I don't discover until I'm in the coach with her and her daughter, waiting to leave.

"Oh, and here is my husband," she says, opening the door to greet him.

Mrs. Ward introduces me to Mr. Ward, and then another figure appears . . . that of a man about my own age.

"And my son," she says, with such satisfaction that I understand exactly why I have been invited along. "Georgie? This is Miss Portia Hastings. She is from London, going to help her younger sister with her first baby. Her sister is married to a French marquis's son. Isn't that exciting? And her older sister is married to an *earl's* son."

I cringe, and I also feel a rush of annoyance. I'd said earlier that I understood Mrs. Ward's interest in my family. That was when I presumed she was only making certain she hadn't impulsively invited an unsuitable woman to share a coach with her daughter. Now I understand why she'd been asking, and I cannot help but wonder, if I had avoided the questions, would that invitation have evaporated?

Oh, I'm so terribly sorry, Miss Hastings, but we don't seem to have any room in the coach after all.

I need this ride, however awkward it might be, and I take comfort in the fact that "Georgie" only glances at me and grunts. Yet another spinster his mother is trying to foist on him, too old by far.

Mrs. Ward makes small noises of distress at his lack of interest, but then the coach is pulling away, and it is too late to deposit the rejected potential bride on the roadside. Also, Mr. Ward starts talking, and I would like to think he is saving me from a strained situation, but it is soon apparent that he simply likes to talk—about himself. His business and the trials and tribulations thereof, all due to the "laziness" and "ineptitude" of his workers.

Hours pass. His daughter falls asleep first. Then his wife. Mr. Ward takes no offense and only switches his attention to his son, who is gazing out the window with such obvious disinterest that I'm impressed in spite of myself. How lovely to be an only son, secure in the knowledge that you will inherit the family fortune without even pretending to respect your father.

Eventually, Mr. Ward runs out of grievances to share and promptly falls asleep, leaving me safe to turn my attention to the window. It's early dusk, blanketing the moors in silence and dove-gray light, the perfect complement to the purple heather. I gaze out, and let time pass as I forget all my obligations and my worries, and I imagine lying on the heather, staring up at a star-dappled night sky, inhaling the rich smell of the moors. Precious moments of peace and quiet, nothing pulling at my attention. Moments to truly bask in the glory of the world around me and—

"I ought to offer my congratulations."

I startle and look at Georgie, smirking at me.

"Pardon?" I say.

"My congratulations on fooling my mother. Admittedly, it is not so difficult a task, as much as she likes to think herself a perceptive creature. I am debating whether to tell her the truth. I will promise to wait until you are gone in return for"—he flashes his teeth—"considerations."

"Whatever you think you know—" I begin.

"To believe such a story shows how desperate she is for me to wed. An exceptionally attractive woman . . ." His gaze travels down me. "Traveling alone? Unmarried at your age. You must be nearly five-and-twenty."

I could laugh at that, but I only press my lips together.

He continues, "With an earl and a French marquis in the family, you could be the foulest-tempered shrew, and you would still have your pick of husbands. Therefore, you are lying about your brothers-in-law. Still, no woman who looks like you should be unwed at such an advanced age. You may be hiding in that hideous dress, but I am quite certain your tastes run to far more extravagant attire."

I blink in surprise. Yes, I do have a weakness for pretty things, be they bright colors or lace trim or crisp ribbons. Left to my own devices, I would walk around in dresses that—as Miranda jests—Rosalind could use as models for her fancy cakes. The problem with such dresses is that they make me seem silly and frivolous.

It does not help that, as this lout is pointing out, I am considered conventionally attractive, which means my features follow a rather dull symmetry, with a disappointing lack of striking characteristics. If I were a dress, I would be one that is perfectly styled and perfectly boring, pleasing to the eye but not surprising in any way. In other words, I would be a dress that I myself would not want to wear. How much more interesting to be an averagely attractive woman with stunning eyes or a strong nose or anything that makes one look twice and say more than "She is very pretty."

Losing myself in my thoughts, I forget that it was a very odd and perceptive comment for Georgie to make. I miss the next thing he says and only rise from my preoccupation when I see him leering at me.

"Hmm?" I say.

"I am correct, am I not? That you prefer extravagant attire, both in your dress and under it?"

"I beg your pardon?"

"Oh, do not play the miss with me. I know what you are." He winks. "I am from London, after all. I have an account at both Marguerite's and Juliet's."

I have no idea what he's talking about, and I only stare.

"Shall I spell it out?" He leans toward me, whispering, "You are a W-H-O-R—"

I jerk back, my gaze going to his father, sleeping beside him, and his mother and sister beside me.

"They are sound asleep, and I will not share your secrets, as I promised, in return for"—he smirks—"considerations."

"I am not a . . ." I choke on the word, and I sputter, and even as I do, I feel rather foolish for my prurience. I long to be Rosalind at this moment. She would have a sharp rejoinder, putting the young man in his place. Or Miranda. Dear Lord, I shudder at how Miranda might handle this. She'd play along, and I almost wish I could do that . . . except that playing along in this could lead to a terrible sort of trouble.

"I am unmarried because I have an occupation," I say, finally, finding my voice and chilling it as I meet his eyes with an equally icy glare. "I was engaged—for three years—to a young man who died fighting abroad."

Where ever did that come from? Part of it is true. I was engaged for years. Also, I did lose him after he went abroad . . . and fell madly in love with another.

I try not to be resentful of Reginald's betrayal. Try and fail miserably, and I must find some of that outrage now, because Georgie doesn't laugh at my lie. He hesitates and then rolls his shoulders, as if throwing off the unacceptable discomfort of potentially being wrong.

"You still cannot expect me to believe you are unmarried, with such a face and figure." His appraisal now rakes over me, as if my own body can be used as evidence against me.

"Perhaps I am not romantically interested in men," I say.

Where did *that* come from? Moreover, how do I manage to say it without blushing? I am quite pleased with myself, though, and I fully expect him to be rendered speechless, perhaps even blush himself.

Instead, he only shrugs and says, "Romance need have nothing to do with marriage. It rarely does."

In other words, he did not take my meaning at all, and I'm gathering the courage to be plainer when he says, "Whatever the answer, your story is rubbish, my dear. Rushing madly to the side of your sister in . . . Where are you going again?"

"Ravensford."

His head jerks up. "Ravensford?"

"That is what I said."

He thumps back against the seat, laughing loud enough that his sister briefly stirs. "Oh, you are going to join the horse race. Or should I call it a mare race?"

He snickers at his own unfathomable joke. When I don't react, he says, "Lord Sterling, Earl of Ravensford?"

I still do not react, having no idea what he means.

"The earl needs money and a wife," he says. "Fortunately, for a man with such an old and esteemed title, the two often come together, which is exactly what he hopes, being rather"—he lowers his voice, as if saying a profanity—"destitute."

Georgie leans back before continuing. "Seems the old chap is in danger of losing his lands. His aunt has arranged a ball, during which all the prospective maidens will be paraded before him, like the prize fillies they are. Although, if the situation is as dire as I hear, they'd stand a greater chance of catching his eye if they ride in on pots of money."

He guffaws, and his sister stirs again but still doesn't wake. He jerks his chin her way. "Mama is trying to convince Father to take Eloise to the ball."

I glance at the girl, who looks barely old enough to wear a corset. "Surely she is not of age."

"Sixteen. Too young to wed, but not too young to form an engagement, which Lord Sterling might agree to if it came with a generous loan. As for you . . ." That raking gaze again. "If you thought to catch his eye with your face and figure and a modest dowry, you had best turn back now."

"I am going to visit my sister," I say. "I have no dowry, which means I would be of no interest to Lord Sterling. Now, if you are finished insulting me, sir, might I ask a favor?"

"Your wish is my command, my lady." He feigns a half bow. "Whatever could you want of me?"

"Silence," I say. "I would like sil—"

A noise sounds outside the coach, and one of the horses lets out a neigh of alarm as the driver pulls them to a sudden stop.

Please tell me there is a sheep on the road. It is the Yorkshire moors. There are always sheep on the road, and the fact that I have not already been saved from Georgie by a stray ovine is disgraceful.

Through the window, I can see that it is now late dusk, with a full moon lighting the moors. I cannot, however, see what has stopped us.

Whatever it is—sheep, dog, conveniently fallen tree—the sudden stop has the desired effect of waking the Wards, the elder Mr. Ward startling up with "What's that?" and Mrs. Ward clutching her breast with "Oh, heavens!"

I take the door handle, and I have it halfway open when Mrs. Ward says, "My dear, what ever are you doing?"

"Escaping," I mutter. Again, that is not like me at all, but it is as if I have realized I am in a world where no one will ever see me again. I can do and say what I wish without fear of how it will reflect on my family or me.

I climb from the coach and—

Oh!

I find myself staring into a pair of amber-gold eyes.

That's when I see the mask covering the lower half of his face.

And then I see the gun.

3

T he man—I still see nothing but those arresting eyes—wears a black kerchief over his nose, covering the lower half of his face. He also holds a flintlock musket, which is pointed at my midriff.

"Get back on the coach," he growls.

I stare, not quite comprehending what is happening. Then another male voice—lighter and almost jovial—says, "Ignore my companion's rudeness, miss. While I am loath to say this and deprive my eyes of such beauty, I must insist that, yes, you retreat to the safety of the coach."

"Why?"

I keep my gaze on the first man, whose eyes narrow and then open again as he nods.

"She's simple," the first man says to the second.

"I am most certainly not *simple*," I say. "I only do not understand . . ."

And then realization strikes. We are on an empty road through the moors, in a fancy coach, which has been stopped by armed and masked men.

"Highwaymen," I whisper.

"We prefer knights of the road," says the second man. He speaks with a clear Yorkshire accent, but it's lighter than I'd expect from the region.

I must have fallen asleep on the coach. I finally got Georgie to stop talking, and I fell asleep with the others. That is the obvious explanation. I am on a mission to help my sister, whose own mission involves highwaymen. And so I am dreaming that we've been stopped by highwaymen.

"Miss?" the second one says. "I really do need to insist you get back into the coach."

I reach up to my throat and unclasp the necklace there. It is a simple piece, far from my favorite and lacking any sentimental value.

I hold out the necklace to the first masked man. "Take this. It is all I have, as I am traveling alone and have only caught a ride with these people. There is a little travel money in my bags, but I would ask that you allow me to keep that." I lower my voice. "The gentlemen on the coach will have more. Particularly the younger. He is a boor, and you ought to take him for everything he has. His papa will give him more."

The man stares at me with those remarkable eyes. I waggle the necklace in front of his masked face.

"Well, take it," I say. "I wish to stretch my legs while you complete your business here."

"You may keep your necklace, miss," the second one says. "But I really must insist that you—"

"What is the meaning of this!" says a voice behind me.

I glance over to see Georgie fairly leaping from the coach.

"Oh, decided to join us, did you?" I say.

"I was asleep."

I make a most unladylike noise. "No, you were cowering until you realized they were being reasonable and mistook that for weakness."

The second highwayman chokes on a laugh. I finally glance over at him. He is somewhat smaller than the first man, who is tall and broad shouldered. The second is fair haired, the first dark, both with their hair tied at the nape of the neck, worn much longer than is the fashion in my day. The second called the first his "companion," but I suspect the relationship is closer than that, given the resemblance in their broad foreheads and eyes. Cousins? Brothers, even?

I am examining the scene as if I am awake, yet haven't I already decided I'm dreaming?

Am I still certain of that? I rather hope so, as I have just told two highwaymen that I am ignoring their demands. I have also been most ungracious to Georgie, though, to be quite honest, if this is not a dream, I will be less horrified by that than I ought to be.

I look at each man in turn. They haven't moved or spoken, as if frozen in a tableau, which should indicate this is indeed a dream. Yet they are not immobile. The younger highwayman is still recovering from his laugh; Georgie is still recovering from my sharp words, and the older highwayman is glowering at me as if I am the cause for this going sideways.

I suppose I am, aren't I? And I suppose I am also mistaken, and it is not a dream after all. We really have been set upon by highwaymen.

"Miss?" the younger one says. "Keep your necklace, and if you do not wish to climb back inside, please step away from the coach. Our business is with Mr. Ward and his family."

"You know who we are?" Georgie asks.

The younger highwayman rolls his eyes. "No, we simply sit on this empty road for hours in hopes that more than a farmer's cart will pass. We know who you are, and we know that you can afford to pay the toll."

"Toll?" Georgie says.

"He is being metaphorical," I say with a sigh. "You must pay him so that we may continue on our way. Have you never been set upon by highwaymen before?"

"Certainly not."

"Then you are overdue in paying your road tax." The younger highwayman sweeps off his tricorne hat with a mock courtly bow and then holds it out to Georgie. "Pass this around inside. We prefer money, and if we get enough of it, we will not require your valuables."

Georgie makes no move to take the hat. The younger highwayman is several feet from him, holding it out, and Georgie just stands there with his hands shoved into his pockets.

The younger one sighs and steps toward Georgie, his voice broadening into a deeper Yorkshire brogue. "Take the hat, lad, and we will not need to bother your family inside the coach."

Georgie lifts his chin, meeting the other man's gaze. The older highwayman rocks forward, as if to intervene, but at a look from his compatriot, he settles for a warning growl.

"Here," I say, with a step toward the younger highwayman. "I shall take the hat and pass it inside. His mother and young sister are within, and if they can stay there, that is best."

Georgie's left arm flies out to ward me off.

"Then take the bloody hat," I mutter.

Georgie puts out his left hand for it. The younger highwayman takes another step. Georgie yanks his right hand from his pocket, and I see why it was hidden there . . . and why he wanted the highwayman moving closer.

"Knife!" I say.

I twist to stop Georgie, but the older highwayman knocks me out of the way. There's a gasp and a curse and then a snarl of rage, and by the time I recover my footing, Georgie is on the ground. The older highwayman has one boot on the young dandy's chest and the muzzle of his musket under Georgie's chin. I turn to the younger highwayman. He's reaching for something on his chest, and it takes a moment for me to realize it is the handle of a small knife, the blade embedded in him.

"Don't remove it!" I say.

I hardly expect him to listen, but he stops, and his gaze lifts to mine.

"I am trained in medical care," I say. "Do not remove it, or it shall bleed more."

The coach door flies open, Mr. Ward leaning out. "Georgie?" His gaze swings to the first highwayman. "Unhand him, you cad. *Now.*"

The older highwayman raises his musket to point at Mr. Ward. The older man stumbles back and seems about to close the door.

"Give him the hat," the highwayman growls to me. "He is to fill it with everything they have, and if I do not think it enough, I will give his son an injury matching my companion's."

I pick up the hat from the ground and hand it to Mr. Ward. "Do it."

The old man sputters.

"Georgie injured his compatriot," I say. "He will not hesitate to do the same to your son. To your *heir*." I meet his gaze. "Your *only* heir."

"And perhaps I will aim lower," the man growls. "Ending the possibility of *continued* heirs."

Inside the coach, Mrs. Ward twitters and gasps. Mr. Ward snatches the hat from me and snaps, "You will pay for this, girl."

"She did nothing," the highwayman says. "If you wish to blame someone, blame your son."

"For not wishing to fatten the pockets of scoundrels?"

"Why not?" the highwayman meets his gaze. "He does it when he works for you."

The younger highwayman makes a noise in his throat, and the older one glances over quickly, concern darkening his eyes.

"I am fine," the younger man says, his voice strained. "However, if we can finish this with minimal delays for sermonizing, I would appreciate that."

The highwayman shoves his gun muzzle back under Georgie's chin and says to Mr. Ward, "I will count to thirty."

Mr. Ward disappears into the coach.

"May I look to your companion's injury?" I ask the older highwayman.

"Please," the younger one says. "And don't ask him. He'll let me bleed to death as he decides whether you can be trusted not to murder me."

The older man curtly nods and returns his gaze to the coach. I hurry to the younger one and help him lower himself onto the road, propped against the coach wheel.

I examine the wound, and I am torn between relief that the injury is not worse and distress that it is still more severe than I hoped. The knife has a small blade, and only half of it is embedded in the man's chest, which is good. Yet that half had the bad luck of finding a spot between his ribs. Thankfully, Georgie apparently has little knowledge of anatomy and struck on the right side, well away from the man's heart.

Once the man is seated—out of sight of his companion's watchful gaze—he allows himself to wince. "It is bad, isn't it?" he says.

"It would have been worse if you had removed the blade."

His eyes crinkle slightly, as if he's smiling weakly beneath his mask. "You are avoiding the question."

I finger the edges of the wound. "Very carefully inhale for me. Do not make any sudden movements."

His long and slow inhalation makes him wince, but he manages it.

"The blade has not pierced the lung. That is good. But the placement does mean that I will need to remove it before it does."

"Twenty-nine," the older highwayman calls. "Thirty."

The coach door swings open. Ward climbs out with my satchel in hand, hanging open. He shoves the hat at the highwayman and curls his lip at me, making it clear where the coins have come from.

"Oh, no, no, no," the younger highwayman rasps. "We want *your* money. Not hers. I think we made that clear."

"I do not care," I say. "There is no time for argument—"

The older man grabs the hat and tosses it aside, coins tinkling to the hard-packed road. Then he yanks Mr. Ward aside and climbs into the coach, ignoring Ward's bleats of protest. More sounds of protest rise within, but they're equally weak, and moments later, the man emerges with a wad of notes in one fist and necklaces dangling from the other. Without a word, he pushes Ward perfunctorily against the coach, empties his pockets and takes his jewelry.

The highwayman starts to give Ward a push toward the coach, only to haul him back by his collar and look at me. "I presume you do not wish to continue traveling with them?"

"Why, yes," his companion says. "Surely she would like to be shoved out at the first crossroad, left on the moors in the dead of night." He looks at me. "We will see that you arrive at your destination, miss."

"Provided you treat my compatriot first and that he survives."

The younger highwayman rolls his eyes. "Pay him no mind. He is fond of barking, but rarely bites." At a noise from his compatriot, he sighs. "I said *rarely*, not *never*. Now stop growling, or she shall begin to wonder whether she has encountered a barghest on the roadside."

The older highwayman releases Ward.

"Wait!" I say as Ward climbs into his coach. To the highwayman, I gesture at his injured compatriot propped against the wheel. He lets out a curse and shouts to the driver to hold up, but Ward, safely inside, shouts the opposite, and the older highwayman fairly dives my way. We both take hold of his injured companion just as the coach rocks forward.

"We shall report you to the authorities!" Georgie calls out the window as they ride away.

"Please do!" the younger man calls back. "I am the damnable Lord Sterling, Earl of Ravensford. Please see to it that he—*I* am arrested at once."

Georgie makes a rude gesture as the coach rolls off.

"I am going to remove your shirt," I say to the younger man.

"I should hope so, as my injury is on my chest."

I nod, hoping my flush isn't apparent. I am accustomed to a world where I do indeed need to warn male patients before I disrobe them, sometimes even having them protest and attempt to cover themselves as best they can, which makes a proper examination most frustrating. It seems it is indeed different here, and the younger man does not bat an eye when I remove his bloodied shirt.

"I appreciate your kindness, miss. Given that we held up your coach, you have been both generous and equanimous."

I arch my brows at him. "You did meet my fellow passengers just now, did you not? I was quite ready to jump out and flee into the moors on my own."

"How ever did you end up with them?"

I turn to his companion, and I am about to ask for water when the man thrusts a waterskin at me. I nod my thanks and wet a clean part of the discarded shirt as I tell my story—from my pregnant sister to the lack of coaches and Mrs. Ward's offer.

The older man grunts. "She thought you seemed a possible match for that young lout."

"Indeed. I wish I had realized it as quickly as you. Fortunately, he was not interested, as he presumed I was telling tales and was actually . . ." I clear my throat, uncertain of the right words and not convinced I could use them even if I was. "A lady who trades in her affections."

"What?" the older man's eyes darken over his mask, his voice lowering to that growl.

"I set him straight," I say as I clean his companion's skin around the knife handle. "Then he decided I was heading to some sort of bride-choosing ball for a Lord Sterling." I look at the younger man. "Is that the one you mentioned?"

"It is." He regards me. "*Is* that your intent?"

"Certainly not. I am hardly in the market for a husband, and even if I was, this Lord Sterling apparently requires a sizable dowry. I have none."

"Good," the younger man says. "You do not wish to be caught up in that nonsense. Nor married to Lord Sterling."

"You did not seem overly fond of him."

"He is a brute. Rude, uncouth and an utter tyrant. Anyone living under his roof deserves nothing but sympathy."

His companion moves forward. "Did you say you needed that knife out of him?"

"I do," I say. "I have cleaned the area in preparation."

"She can do it," the younger man says. "She is the physician's assistant after all and—"

His companion wrenches out the knife.

4

B y the time I have the younger man bandaged, I know the two are siblings, as the younger one slipped up and called the elder "brother." I also have names, or at least things I may call them. The younger brother is "Jay," and the older is "Bee." I presume those are initials, but when I say so, Jay only jokes that Bee is his brother's highwayman name, in deference to his stinging demeanor, to which his brother retorts that Jay is for "popinjay." I do not ask further, understanding that I should not wish to know their actual names, under the circumstances. I give them Portia for mine, and Jay declares that an excellent choice, after Shakespeare's Portia, a woman who took on the role of a typically male profession, much as I am with my medicine.

"Where were you traveling?" Jay asks as I finish binding his wound.

I hesitate. I do not know where these two are from, but I suspect it is nearby if they seem to know Lord Sterling, and so I dare not say Ravensford, in case they might expect to know my "pregnant sister."

When I hesitate, though, Jay misinterprets and says, "And that was a most intrusive question. Apologies, Miss Portia. We will not inquire into specifics regarding your sister and her family, as you ought not to give them to two men who held up your coach."

"I do not mean to be rude," I say.

He laughs. "You are being far too polite already. I know what we are, and we do not pretend to be otherwise. We will, however, take you wherever you need to be—"

"No," Bee says. "We will not."

"Again, ignore him. One of us can claim the title of gentleman thief. The other is a common scoundrel." He gives his brother a look. "But even he will recognize that we cannot leave you—"

"Of course we will not leave her here," Bee says. "I mean that we are taking her nowhere tonight."

"Ah, yes, it is very late."

"I hardly care about the hour," Bee says. "I care that you have been badly injured and she is the one caring for you, which she will continue to do until I relieve her of those duties."

"You cannot—" I begin.

"He *will* not," Jay says firmly, with a hard glare at his brother.

"I will compensate her for her time."

"I do not want your money," I snap. "My sister needs my help—"

"And I will release you as soon as possible."

I look him in the eye. Then I turn and stride along the road.

"Does that truly seem wise?" Bee calls after me.

I turn. He gestures to the musket on the ground.

"Oh!" I say. "I completely forgot about that."

"I thought you might have."

"Thank you for the reminder," I say.

I bend and pick up my satchel and my money. Then I turn and resume walking.

He waits until I get another ten paces and then bellows. "Are you mad, woman?"

I look pointedly from him to the musket, still on the ground. "No, I do not think I am. You are not threatening me with that. You are threatening me with the threat of that, and I am calling your bluff."

Even from here, I can see his eyes blazing over his mask. "That is most unwise."

"Is it? I think not. In fact, I think, if you were seriously threatening to shoot me, your brother would be objecting, and he is not, which means I have correctly assessed the situation."

Bee turns a glare on Jay, who only lifts his hands. "I'm not doing anything."

"That is the problem," Bee says.

"May I suggest another tactic?" I say. "Repeat after me. Miss Portia, I appreciate what you have done for my brother, and I wonder if there is any way I might be able to convince you to see him safely through the night, after which I will ensure you are taken to a coach that can convey you to your sister's side, and if you believe my brother is in need of additional medical attention, I will pay for a proper doctor . . . with some of the funds that I have just *stolen*."

At a noise from Jay, I shake my finger his way. "Stop laughing. You will set your wound bleeding again."

"Then I would suggest you stop making me laugh."

"Then I would suggest you tell your brother to take my suggestion."

"Oh," Bee says. "That was a *suggestion*, was it?"

"No, you are correct. It was not. It is an ultimatum. Either you agree to my sensible solution, or I force you to shoot me in the back. It is most unfair of me, I know."

Bee rises to his feet. He takes one slow step toward me and then another. He keeps approaching, his entire demeanor radiating menace. I hold my ground until he is right in front of me. Then I lift my chin to look at him.

"I note that you do not have the musket," I say.

"Oh, I don't need that."

"Are you threatening me with physical violence, sir? In return for warning your brother of the knife and then tending to his wounds? You are going to throw me over your shoulder and carry me off, in recompense for saving your brother's life?"

"That depends."

"Depends?" I say, struggling to keep my voice from rising in outrage. "Whatever could that depend on?"

"Whether my brother's life is still in danger. If I believe it is, I would not hesitate to carry you off to tend to him. Yes, it is outrageous behavior toward one who has been helpful thus far, but if your leaving places him in the same position he was in when the boy pulled that knife—the threat of death—then I do not see how you have saved him, and so I would owe you no such consideration."

Now I am the one glaring at him. I am indeed outraged but also . . .

What if someone tried to kill Miranda, and the person who could save her tried to walk away?

"Your brother will not die," I say.

"Am I to take the word of a stranger on that? A stranger who has reason to lie, only wanting to leave?"

"I do not want to leave tonight. I believe I made that clear. I am willing to stay if you promise to release me in the morning."

"He does," Jay calls. "You have my word."

"And you have mine," Bee says, "*if* his condition does not worsen."

"If it does, then I shall stay with him while you fetch a doctor."

"The local doctor is away—"

"Then you'll fetch another," I say. "Stop being obstinate and combative."

Jay calls, "You might as well tell him to stop breathing."

"Well, he will be less obstinate and less combative if he wishes you to live as much as he claims he does."

"Fine," Bee snaps. "You have my word. Now stay with him while I fetch the horses."

杓

ADMITTEDLY, I THOUGHT BEE WAS OVERREACTING TO HIS BROTHER'S INJURY. Yes, the wound was troubling, but Jay was not in shock nor showing any signs of breathing distress. He was alert and in good spirits. Yet I remind myself that a doctor must always listen to those who know the patient, even when they seem overcome by excessive fears. Bee knows his brother. He knew he was putting on a good show, and that is obvious when we reach our destination and Jay nearly falls off the horse.

By the time we get Jay inside the building—a cottage they use as a local hideout—he's clearly in pain and struggling to stay conscious. Sleep is the best thing for him. I insist he give up the fight, and he eventually concedes.

"We need to remove that mask," I say. "He ought not to sleep in it, in case he has breathing problems. That is the greatest risk he faces if the blade struck a lung."

I can't see the lower half of Bee's face, but given the look in his eyes, his jaw sets most firmly at that.

"I do not care what he looks like," I say with half exasperation and half annoyance. "I care that I may not hear if his breathing becomes labored. The mask is already making it sound labored, as you can hear."

"Fine, but I am not removing mine."

"Having no need or desire to see what lies beneath it, that is perfectly fine with me."

His eyes narrow to slits. "What is that supposed to mean?"

If I were not so exhausted, I might actually laugh at his expression, as if he is terribly insulted that this woman—to whom he has been nothing but rude—isn't eager to see what he looks like.

"I mean that I am not trying to see your faces so that I may report you to the authorities," I say. "Perhaps that is selfish of me, not wishing to get involved, but I have other concerns."

"Your sister."

"Very much my sister," I say. "That is all that matters to me at this time. My sister and her husband."

"I thought your sister was with child. That does not concern her husband."

I realize my mistake, but I cover it with, "Does it not? What if my sister dies in the childbed? He would most certainly care about that. Or if his child dies, he will care about *that*. All three of them are my concern, and if I reported you and your brother, I would be delayed from running to my sister's side." I meet his gaze. "More than I already have been."

"You will be free in the morning."

I notice that he does not add "if my brother is well." I only remove the kerchief from Jay's face. Then I set to work treating his wound properly.

I do not notice my surroundings for at least an hour, as I clean Jay's wound better now that we can boil water on the hearth.

There are many things I have learned from twenty-first-century medicine, but this is perhaps the most important: the dangers of infection. In my time, there are many explanations for sepsis, including the belief that pus is a sign of healing. That is not to say everyone believes it. Even my father, practicing medicine a quarter century ago, had noted that clean wounds healed better. What I have now is the confidence that a theory is indeed correct, and that perhaps the single best thing we can do for an open wound is also the simplest: keep it clean.

I use both hot water and a bottle of gin, and I try not to worry when Jay does little more than shudder at the alcohol touching his wound. At least he is not writhing in agony. To Bee's credit, while he does lunge forward with each sign of his brother's pain, he does not question my treatment.

Once I am certain the wound is clean, I stitch it up. I have the needle and sutures for that in my bag—knowing my sister and her husband, I packed an emergency medical kit. Bee doesn't question, apparently presuming the needle and thread are sewing supplies. Nor does he question me sewing the wound.

Once all that is done, I rise from beside the rough bed where Bee put his brother, and I look around. It is indeed a tiny cottage, with a single room, two small beds, a table with two rough chairs and a hearth.

I am still looking about, too tired to even process what I am doing, when Bee shoves a cup at me and says, "There's not much to eat, but I'll fix something."

I shake my head, and again, I swear I see his jaw tense under the mask.

"Poisoning you would hardly be in my best interests," he says. "At least not before you've saved my brother."

I look up sharply, and there's no obvious sign of humor in his eyes, but I still get the sense that was meant to be a joke.

"I did not suspect poison," I say. "I am simply too exhausted to eat."

"Then drink." He shoves the cup at me. "It's clean water. There's brandy, too."

"Brandy?" My brows shoot up.

Now there is the definite hint of humor in his eyes. "The best French brandy. Taken from a smuggler."

"You do not only rob coaches then?"

"He was in one. Just because a man can afford a fine coach doesn't mean he is not a thief. In fact, most are, in their way."

"Like the Wards." I take the water cup and sip it. "Is that what you do then? Rob the rich?"

"And give to the poor?" He snorts and shakes his head. "Do you want the brandy or not?"

"I shouldn't. I need to be alert in case your brother has trouble tonight."

"Then if you won't eat, at least get some sleep. I'll sit up with him."

⚜

I SLEEP SOUNDLY FOR SEVERAL HOURS BEFORE I SNAP AWAKE WITH A realization.

Miranda and Nicolas came here seeking to resolve a matter involving highwaymen.

I am now with two highwaymen . . . from the same region.

Yes, I ought to have realized this before, but I'd been caught up in the robbery and then Jay's injury while maintaining the story about my pregnant sister . . . to the point where I'd mentally obscured why Miranda and Nicolas were truly here.

They were taking money to the family of a dead boy, who had been a highwayman, and he'd been killed by someone with a vendetta against highwaymen. So I have reason to fear that Miranda and Nicolas's disappearance is connected to highwaymen.

I glance over at Bee, sitting in a chair pulled up to his brother's bedside. He has his back to me, and I wonder whether he's fallen asleep, but then he rolls his shoulders.

I know where to find the young highwayman's family. That's where Miranda and Nicolas were heading. Yet something has gone wrong. Miranda and Nicolas are in trouble, and that trouble would most logically be connected to the boy's demise. They have run afoul of either Colin Booth's highwaymen comrades or the fake highwayman Scarlet Jack, who'd murdered him.

Either way . . .

Should I be quick to disassociate myself from these men?

What if *they* are responsible for Miranda and Nicolas's disappearance?

I would like to say I cannot imagine it, but that ensnares me in a dangerous trap, one created by all the writers who reinterpreted old highwayman stories as heroic tales of gentlemanly criminals.

It does not help that Jay seems ripe inspiration for such tales, kind and gallant and, yes, handsome, with his fair hair and sparkling eyes. Even Bee has not been truly "criminal" in his behavior. Short tempered and ill tempered, but still fair, in his way.

I would not like to discover these two have harmed my sister and her husband, yet I cannot dismiss the possibility. Also, while they may not have done it, they could know who did. Their local community—such as it is—cannot be large. Surely they would know who Colin Booth associated with, and they would also know of this Scarlet Jack.

I cannot ask Bee now. Even if I framed it as casual interest, he would be suspicious. It seems his nature. But while I do need to leave as soon as I can, there is advantage in this unexpectedly auspicious meeting.

With any luck, I will discover that Miranda and Nicolas have only been unexpectedly delayed at the Booth home. If they found the family in dire need of something they could provide—from doctoring to thatching a roof—they would stay. I hope that is the answer, but if it is not, then I have made a valuable association here.

5

Morning comes, and Jay is neither as well as I might hope nor as poorly as I might fear. He is awake and breathing well, and the wound seems clean, which is the most important thing. He is weak, and it pains him to move, but as I tell Bee, that is to be expected.

"I can leave instructions for wound care," I say. "The doctor—"

"Is away, as I said. Gone to London to visit his daughter. Also, he is a charlatan. I would not trust him to care for my horse."

"He is a trained doctor," Jay says patiently. "London educated—"

"And a fool who believes there is nothing that cannot be cured with bleeding. It is his only trick, and it is a poor one. He is also a pompous jackass. Can you imagine telling him that a woman said you must keep the wound clean? He'd likely gather dirt from the garden and rub it in just to prove her wrong."

"*You* can ensure his wound is kept clean," I say. "I will show you how, and I have no doubt that you will see to it, whatever this doctor says." I meet Bee's gaze. "I must go."

His jaw works, the mask moving with it.

"She must, Ben," his brother says.

Bee is too deep in thought to catch the slip, but I mentally file it away. Ben. Short for Benjamin? Useful, if I need it.

"She must go," Ben says. "But that does not mean she must stay gone."

"And how would that work?" Jay says gently. "You need to return home, and I must accompany you."

"You cannot move. I will do what I must at home, which is all the more reason we require her assistance, as I should not leave you alone for long." He turns to me, those golden eyes cool as if working hard to overcome his pride. "I understand the situation with your sister. What I propose is that you go to her, and if she is not in urgent need, you return to help with my brother until he is past the worst of it. I realize that is an inconvenience, but I will repay you, Miss Portia."

Jay makes a noise of warning, but Ben ignores it and keeps his gaze on me. I'm almost glad of my epiphany last night—that I should not be too hasty to leave these men behind. Otherwise, I would have struggled, knowing I should refuse while hating to do so when Ben is making a reasonable request out of desperate concern for his brother.

"I am not at death's door," Jay says.

"I recognize that, which is why I am willing to let Miss Portia leave."

"Willing . . ." I murmur.

"Careful, brother," Jay says. "I think the word you want is *happy*. You are *happy* to let her leave."

Ben snorts. No, he isn't happy about it at all, and the fact he is "willing" is as much as I can hope for.

This is why I do not like complicated men. Give me a simple one any day.

Like Reginald, whispers a tiny voice in my mind.

I shift my weight in discomfort. Yes, Reginald *had* been simple in his tastes, very easy to get on with, our relationship as smooth as still water, so effortlessly navigable.

Boring, that voice whispers again.

I bristle, but I cannot deny it. In the end, yes, Reginald found me boring, found our relationship stultifying. He met someone more interesting and married her within days . . . after postponing our engagement for three years.

Now you are being obtuse, the voice whispers. *I did not say you were the boring one.*

"I agree to your terms," I say, before my mind can wander further into memory. "You will take me where I need to go, and if my sister does not need me, I will return. If her need is urgent, I shall send a message to notify you."

"This is not a London town house," Ben says. "You cannot send a message here."

He has a point, blast him. Even if I could tell a messenger where to find this cottage, I should not. And he certainly isn't going to tell me where to find his home.

He continues, "I will take you where you need to be. Then we shall meet again at an agreed-upon time and place."

Jay says, "And if you tell him that your sister is in urgent need, he will not attempt to stop your leaving." He looks at his brother. "In any way."

Ben grumbles under his breath but only says, "Prepare yourself to leave. I do not wish to be gone overly long."

❦

WE DEPART WITHIN THE QUARTER HOUR. AS I SUSPECTED, BEN ENSURES THAT I do not see where the cottage is located in relation to the town of Ravensford, where I insist on being deposited. He blindfolds me and walks me through the forest. Riding would be quicker, but do I really want to ride double with this man?

I . . . feel I should not answer that, for the sake of my dignity and pride.

We walk at a brisk pace, and when he removes my blindfold, we are nearing a road. I look over to see he is still masked. That is, I presume, another reason why we do not simply ride along the roads. He is keeping me from knowing precisely where the cottage is located, and he is keeping himself from being spotted by anyone who might wonder why he is riding in broad daylight while masked.

"Head east along this road, and you shall reach the village."

When I don't answer, he steps into the path of my vision, which had been fixed in the distance.

"What is that?" I say, a little breathlessly as I step to see around him again.

Atop a rise, two black towers soar above the treetops. Below, I can make out what appears to be the wall of a . . . castle?

"Head along this road—" Ben repeats.

"I asked a question. What is that?"

"Ravensford Keep," he grunts. "Now—"

"A castle?"

"A *keep*," he says. "The walls are in ruins, and the rest is set to follow at any point."

"Why is it black?"

He waves a hand. "Some siege from long ago, when the fields were set ablaze."

"It is breathtaking."

"No, it is the remains of an old and ugly soot-stained castle. Now—"

"You said Ravensford Keep. That would be the ancestral home of Lord Sterling. I presume he does not live there if it is in such poor condition."

A grunt that I could take either way.

"No," I say slowly as I think it through. "He is looking for a wealthy bride to restore his family fortunes, which presumably include the keep, so he might well live there." I gaze at the black towers again, starkly beautiful against the gray sky. "I would find it difficult to abandon such a place."

"I suspect you would change your mind after a night within those walls. You'd scarcely make it until morning before being driven out, if not by the icy drafts, then by the skittering rats or the flitting ghosts."

I stiffen. "Ghosts?"

He gives me a hard look. "Do not tell me you are one of those, Miss Portia. I took you for a woman of sense."

"A woman of sense can take an interest in drafty castles or flitting ghosts."

"And skittering rats?"

"One would need to be a woman of great sense—and gravity—to take an interest in those. My own interest would be in getting rid of them. I would suggest Lord Sterling concentrate on that before bringing in a bride."

"I shall pass along the message," he says dryly. "Now, if you are quite done gawping at decrepit ruins . . ."

"I was admiring. Not gawping."

"Head along this road to Ravensford. It is but a half mile or so. If you look, you can see smoke over there."

He points out the tendrils, as villagers cook their breakfasts and ward off the morning chill.

Ben continues, "I will meet you here at noon. If you do not arrive, I will return at two. If I still do not see you, I will come looking." He meets my gaze. "I do not think you wish that."

"It is possible, sir, to request a thing without pinning threats to the tail of it."

"It most certainly is." Those amber-shot eyes bore into mine. "When it *is* a request."

"There is a saying in my part of the world. One catches more flies with honey than vinegar."

"And why ever would I want to catch flies?"

I choke on a sudden laugh at that. He does, of course, have a point, even if he is willfully ignoring *my* point.

"I will make every effort to be here at noon," I say. "Not because I am afraid of your retaliation if I do not, but because I am concerned for your brother and do not wish you to leave him longer than necessary. If I am delayed, I will be here at two. If I am not, then something terrible has befallen me, and I appreciate your insistence on coming to my aid. It is most kind of you."

Now he's the one snorting what could be a laugh. "All right. If you are not here at two, I shall find you, and you may consider it a rescue. Reasonable?"

"Reasonable." I nod my chin. "Good day to you, sir."

A grunt that I will interpret as "and to you, as well." Then he turns on his heel and heads back into the forest.

❧

THE LOCATION COLIN BOOTH GAVE MIRANDA AND NICOLAS WAS A SMALL farm a mile outside of Ravensford. If I recall my history correctly, we are in a time when such farmers would likely have been tenants—the land belongs to Lord Sterling, who lets them rent it for a significant portion of the farming income. Such arrangements still exist in my time, but they were even more common here, being the only way for the gentry to maintain the increasingly huge swaths of land that made up their holdings.

I do not walk directly through Ravensford village. I have no need of that. There'd been enough food at the cottage for breakfast, and I am not quite certain how out of place I might seem, as a woman on her own, having appeared seemingly from nowhere. It is a rather small village. Tidy and pretty, but even from a distance, signs of disrepair are evident. As I walk farther, I see the possible cause of the economic conditions. While the land here is most suited to animal husbandry, there are crops, yet the fields lie empty, and the ground is a dusty brown. It is spring, yet I do not see flowers and leafy trees. I see brown. Everywhere, I see brown.

Drought.

The area has been stricken by a severe drought. That means Lord Sterling would not have the farm income he expected, and even if he is as brutish as Jay said, one cannot squeeze water from a stone. His castle is falling apart. His lands are parched and barren. His livestock will not be able to graze. His roads are plagued by highwaymen, taking advantage, I suspect, of his inability to hire men to clear them out. Is it any wonder he is looking for a wealthy bride?

While the picture Jay painted makes me ill inclined to favor the Earl of Ravensford, I must credit Lord Sterling for being clear with his expectations. He is not looking to trick some wealthy family by slipping down to London, waving his title about and hoping to snare a girl who dreams of living in a castle. He is clear about what he wants, and if the bride-seeking ball is to be held here, he is also clear about what his bride is getting. A castle in ruins and land dying from lack of rain. He is offering a purely practical business arrangement, and as a purely practical woman, I must grudgingly commend him for his honesty in that.

The drought might also explain why Colin Booth felt that joining a gang of highwaymen was his only hope for feeding his family. That erases much of the credit I'd just given Lord Sterling. Yes, the weather is outside his control, but has he let his farmers fall so destitute that they turned to robbery? One must presume he is not dining on cooked rats from that castle of his, and so it is inexcusable.

By the time I reach the Booth cottage, I have worked myself into a lather of outrage. Then I stop and stare at a situation far worse than I could have envisioned.

I open my satchel and pull out the book where I jotted all my notes, including where to find the Booth cottage. Right here, at the crossroads where, as Colin's ghost told Miranda, "you cannot miss it."

He had described his home as being the only one on the crossroads. A thatched cottage with a "bit of land" that we presumed was acreage for farming. Instead, judging by the crumbled stone wall, that "bit of land" is only large enough for a garden. Or it would be large enough, but there isn't a single shoot rising from the parched earth.

That isn't the shocking thing. We'd presumed the Booths were tenant farmers by the fact they did not live in town. We knew Colin's father was dead, and so it was only him, his mother and four younger sisters. Seeing the house now, if they *had* been farmers, that must have ended with his father's death, leaving them unable to continue growing crops and thus unable to lease more than their home and little garden from Lord Sterling.

No, the shocking part is the condition of the house. It is not merely old or even merely in disrepair. It is quite literally falling down. The roof is caved in, and there are holes in the walls.

Jay was correct. Lord Sterling is indeed a brute. If he is *not* dining on roast rat, then he has no excuse for anyone on his land living like this, in a cottage that could be made livable with some materials and a few days' labor.

As I approach the tiny house, I see something that suggests the reason my sister has been delayed. There are tools in a wooden carrying box set at the corner of the house, along with a small ladder.

Miranda and Nicolas came to deliver money and made the same assessment I just did: that a bit of work could make this cottage at least livable. They have stayed to do that work for a widow who has lost her son, likely the person who had done such repairs. In other words, Miranda and Nicolas are taking on the earl's tasks as their own. If it sets them behind schedule, well, it is not as if they had immediate obligations waiting on the other side of the stitch. Everyone is away except Miranda's middle sister, who will surely be too busy to even notice their prolonged absence.

I walk to the door and rap smartly. Then I wait. When I knock harder, the door swings open. Foul smells swirl out on a cloud of dust, and my hand flies to my mouth and nose. I push the door open farther. It is dark inside, save for light coming through holes in the roof. The smell seems to be rotted food and an overflowing privy bucket.

I start to step inside when a voice says, in a thick Yorkshire accent, "You do not wish to be going in there, miss. The smell'll never come off you."

I turn to see a man in rough working clothes, with a cap on his head and dirt streaking his face. In one hand, he holds a prying bar, and that might have me taking a step back if my gaze did not go to the box of tools.

He continues, "If you've come from the ladies' charitable society, you need to tell them to stop sending you poor lasses. Like I told the other one, there's no one here."

"Is this the home of Mrs. Booth?"

"Aye, it was, but she's been gone since before the snow flew. That's the smell. He came and drove her out for not paying her rent. Didn't give her and the wee lasses time to do more than pack a bag."

Lord Sterling. They could not pay their rent, and he cast them out.

I look at the prying bar. "And now you are repairing the cottage for the next family?"

"No, ma'am. I am taking it down. Just like all the others. Clearing the land for the master's sheep."

I am about to ask another question when my mind tugs back to what he said when I first arrived. "You said the ladies' charity already sent someone else?"

"Aye. A fortnight ago."

When Miranda would have arrived.

"I was not aware the agency sent another," I say. "Perhaps I know her. Could you describe her?"

"Right pretty lass. Yellow hair, like your own. Plump, my wife said. Well fed, I'd say."

That sounds like Miranda.

"She had an escort, too," the man says. "Dark-skinned fellow. African, my wife said."

Nicolas is from Martinique, but I understand the man's meaning, and it leaves no doubt that my sister and her husband were here.

"That is most vexing," I say. "The society has quite enough poor families to tend to without doubling their efforts. I do hope they haven't accidentally given us the same list. Do you know where she was headed next?"

"To find Mrs. Booth and the lasses. The lass was most concerned for their welfare and wished to know whether we had any idea where they might have gone. I said Mrs. Booth had a sister in York, and that's where she'd head. Her sister is a milliner, married to a cooper. I do not know the name, but the lass said that was quite enough. She would find them."

And she will. That is the true reason for Miranda's delayed return. She did not run into trouble here, except for the sort that comes with discovering the person they came to help is gone . . . and likely in even greater need of the money they brought. Miranda and Nicolas would have set out on that trail right away, tracking the family to York, where they would need to find Mrs. Booth's sister.

I thank the man for his help. When I am sufficiently far from the house, I pause to collect my thoughts under a massive chestnut tree. Then I check my pocket watch. It is nearly eleven. I can return with Ben to see how Jay is faring, and then, I suppose, if he is well enough, it is time for me to return home.

My adventure is at an end.

When disappointment prickles at the thought, I shake it off. I have traveled into the past. I have been set upon by highwaymen and lived to tell the tale. That is enough of an adventure for anyone. At least, it is enough of an adventure for me.

I have things to do at home. So many things. There is no room in my life for chasing fancies, and if I feel a whisper of regret at that, then I chalk it up to exhaustion and a stray flash of whimsy. It will pass. It must.

6

I am waiting inside the forest when Ben arrives, coming from the direction of the cottage where he left his brother. When he is close enough to communicate, I say, "How is he?"

Ben slows and eyes me over his mask.

"What?" I say. "I asked after your brother's health."

"You asked quite readily after it. I know my brother can have that effect on women, and I had hoped you had not fallen prey to it. If so, you will be sadly disappointed. He is not in the market for a wife."

"And I am not in the market for a husband," I say. "Only a handsome man to spend the night with. Once he recovers, of course. Is he also not in the market for that?"

I have no idea where those words come from. And how I manage them without a stammer or a blush. Indeed, they trip jauntily off my tongue, leaving Ben blinking and speechless.

"Oh, bother," I say with a dramatic sigh. "He does not wish that, either? Then I have quite wasted my time. It is so hard to find dashing young highwaymen to rescue. All that time practicing my medical craft. And for what? Naught, I tell you. Naught but a cold bed and colder nights."

"You are jesting," he says.

"No, I am mocking you. Do I seem in desperate need of a husband?"

He hesitates, and now I'm the one narrowing my eyes.

"You are not young," he says. "And you are traveling alone. I wouldn't say you are in *desperate* need, but my brother is both handsome and charming."

"And a highwayman. I should hope I could do better than that, if I were looking for a husband, which I am not. I asked after your brother because he is my patient." I walk past Ben. "Presuming he has not perished, you will want to get back to him, not stand here being silly with me."

Ben strides up beside me. "I am never silly."

"Oh, you are very silly. You only believe you are not, which is worse. It comes dangerously close to making you a fool."

He says something under his breath, which I do not catch and presume I am not supposed to.

"My sister does not require my immediate care," I say as I walk. "She has gone to York. So I shall tend to your brother for a little longer, but I really must leave as soon as I can. To that end, I would appreciate advice on the best way to travel to York."

"By coach."

I look over my shoulder and give him a withering look. "I mean advice on where and how to catch it."

"Let us drop the charade, Miss Portia."

I slow, but before I can say anything, he continues past me, still talking. "You have a sister. I do not doubt that. But she is not anywhere near Ravensford. I am well enough acquainted with the people of this region to know there is no woman with child who could possibly be your sister. In the event I was mistaken, I made inquiries this morning, before returning to my brother's side."

"You *investigated* the story of a woman you have *forced* to tend to your brother? When you yourself are a highwayman hiding behind a *mask*?"

"I need to know who I am dealing with."

"As do I."

He keeps walking until he must realize I have stopped. He turns and scowls, as if I am a child digging in her heels unreasonably.

"I did not ask why you are here, Miss Portia. I only said that we can abandon this charade of a pregnant sister. Simply tell me where you need to go, and I will ensure you arrive there with no questions asked."

"That is what I was doing," I say, trying not to grit my teeth. "Telling you where I need to go. York."

"Then you shall go to York." He waves for me to get ahead of him, as if to ensure I do not flee. I grudgingly obey, and we continue on.

"However . . ." he says.

"Of course," I mutter.

"Of course what?"

"Of course there is a *however*. You have more to say. If you are reminding me that I must tend to your brother before leaving, I believe I said that I would."

"No, that is not it. I am only going to say that if you are—despite what you claimed—here for the bridal ball, you oughtn't to pretend otherwise. Subterfuge does not become you."

"Do I dress as if I come with a rich dowry? Did you notice my wealthy parents accompanying me?"

"You obviously have a little money, from what Mr. Ward tried to steal. As I am certain you have seen a mirror in your life, you know that you could entertain reasonable hopes of wooing a man who might have hoped for a larger dowry."

"Despite my advanced age?"

"You are not old. Simply older than the average marriage prospect. Being in possession of some money and a beautiful face, you might have come hoping to convince Lord Sterling that he does not require such a large dowry."

"And if so, you are here to tell me he will not be swayed."

"I do not know the man well enough to say. I only mean that if you intend that, you can say as much."

I continue walking as I shake my head. "I assure you, on my life, that I did not come for this Lord Sterling."

"But perhaps, having heard of the ball . . ."

"No," I say sharply. "I learned quite enough about Lord Sterling this morning. I pity the woman who marries such a monster."

Silence. Then, when he speaks, his tone is half confusion and half wariness. "What do you think you learned about him?"

"Enough," I say. "I understand that his lands are in the midst of a drought, and that will explain why he needs a bride. I even credit him for being clear what he is offering and what he expects. But what he is doing to his people is indefensible. Your brother was right. The man is a brute. Worse, in my opinion. Now, can we cease this topic of conversation? Tell me how your brother has fared this morning. That is far more important than Lord Bloody Bastard Sterling."

Ben is silent long enough that I am about to look back when he begins, "My brother's condition is unchanged, I fear."

"At least it is not worse. We shall see how he is when I arrive."

⬥⬥⬥

Jay is as his brother described. No better and no worse. Seeing him, I am less concerned than Ben seems to be. Jay has no infection or breathing issues. He is weak, but mostly, he is restless. This is not the most pleasant of lodgings, and like most patients, he wishes to go home. I agree. As there is no medical reason to keep him here, he should go home where he can be comfortable, with everything he needs at hand.

I would say "Ben disagrees," but that makes it sound like a civilized debate. Ben does not allow debate on this. He sees a very valid reason not to move Jay—his brother's injury—and so Jay will stay another night. As for any conveniences from home, Ben will bring them. Jay said that Ben has business to attend to. I presume that means he must take the stolen goods to an associate who will sell them. It could also mean he has a legitimate job, one that keeps people from wondering how he puts food on his table.

Either way, Ben needs to go home for the rest of the day and will return this evening with whatever Jay requires. Also, whatever I require. Not that he offers that—it's Jay who insists. I say that I will eat whatever is brought, and the only other thing I would ask for is soap, if they can spare it. That is not sarcasm. While I understand soap is cheap in the twenty-first century, it is expensive in my time and a luxury in this one. Ben doesn't blink at the request. He only makes a remark that seems to indicate I am indeed in need of it. I ignore that. If I am in need of it, he is in greater need. At least *I* have used some of the warm water for washing.

Ben is not quick to leave. He hovers, like an overanxious parent, until Jay threatens to get out of bed and kick him out the door. Ben has business to attend to, and the sooner he gets to it, the sooner he can return with decent food.

I change the bandages on Jay's wound, which also gives me a chance to clean it again. Earlier, Ben suggested he'd gone into the village to check my story, but it seems his real purpose was getting fresh cloths for cleaning and binding his brother's wound. He also purchased willow bark, and after the wound is dressed, I brew some for Jay. He drinks only half of it before falling asleep, which is truly the best thing for his injury.

I spend the next couple of hours cleaning the cottage. I have nothing else to do. I cannot go outside and risk Jay waking. I cannot rest and risk falling asleep. I will admit, with some guilt, that this is one reason I much prefer doctoring to nursing. Nursing involves a great deal of sitting at a bedside, and I am terrible at that. When I must do it, I bring a satchel of books to keep myself occupied. Here, I can only clean.

The cottage is in better condition than I might have expected from a highwaymen's hideout. But I have already concluded that the brothers are not like Colin Booth, forced into criminality by desperation. Instead, they seem dangerously akin to the highwaymen of legend. At least, Jay does. His manners and speech tell me he does not come from a family of tenant farmers. He is educated, and likely of my own social class. I will not speculate on why they have chosen such a life. My task, as a doctor, is to help where I may and not judge which patients deserve my care.

The point is that the cottage is not a filthy hovel. If it had been, I'd have pushed harder to move Jay elsewhere. Still, it could use cleaning, and that is what I do. I'm finishing when I realize I ought to have started with the hearth. I am taking a load of ash outside when I catch sight of someone moving through the trees.

I pause, thinking Ben must have returned, but the figure is moving too stealthily, as if trying not to be seen.

I consider ducking back inside but remind myself that I am sheltering a wounded highwayman, and a hasty retreat would seem suspicious. Instead, I pretend not to have noticed the movement and continue forward to dump the ashes.

The person lurking in the trees goes still. I can make out enough of a figure to know it is a tall and bearded man. While getting a sidelong look his way, I dump the ashes. Then I shake the dust from my skirts.

When I half turn back—being careful not to put the stalker at my rear

—I call toward the cottage, "Are you planning to hunt for our supper, or do you expect a deer to fall at our doorstep?" Then I mutter, "Lazy sod," under my breath as I stalk back.

Once inside, I slam the door in feigned annoyance, while also hoping to rouse Jay. He's already propped up and blinking at me.

"Did I dream that you told me to go hunting for our dinner?" he croaks, his throat dry.

I motion him to silence and bring a cup of water. As he sips it, I say, "There is a man skulking in the forest."

"Skulking?"

"Lurking with questionable intent."

The corners of his mouth quirk. "Oh, I know what the word means. It just rarely has a use in everyday speech."

"It does in this instance. It is a man with a hunting rifle. Poaching on Lord Sterling's land, I presume, which I would not interfere with, but he is taking too great an interest in this cottage."

Jay shakes his head. "There is no poaching in Ravensford forests."

Because I presume Lord Sterling deals with it harshly, even when his people are desperate.

"Can you describe the fellow?" Jay asks.

I do, and that sets Jay cursing.

"He is Carleton's man," he says.

"Carleton?"

Jay waves off an explanation as he glances toward the window. "I have told Bee that this cottage isn't safe, not when Carleton's men can see the smoke."

"He is looking for you and your brother then. To arrest you."

"He is looking to do whatever he can to us, which means this is a fine mess. I presume you were making it sound as if you were living here with some layabout."

"Well, you *are* laying about."

That makes him laugh and then wince at the pain, and I remind myself not to say anything in jest.

"I could attempt to frighten him off," I say. "Head out for some purpose and spot him and make a womanly fuss."

Jay shakes his head grimly. "He has a gun, and I'll not presume he wouldn't use it."

"If he thinks I am hiding a highwayman in my cottage."

"Even if he thinks you are not."

Jay reaches for his mask beside the bed.

"But if you are wearing that," I say, "and he peeps in the window . . ."

"If he peeps in the window and sees me without it, he will draw a conclusion I can ill afford."

"He knows you then. As your true self."

"Yes."

I help Jay put on the mask. Then I go to the window and look out. After a few minutes, I return.

"He does not appear to be there."

Jay attempts to pull himself upright, only to wince in pain, and I dart forward to stop him.

"I need to get out of here," he says. "I do not trust the fellow has left for good, and if he returns and insists on entering, my brother and I are undone."

"If he insists on entering, there is a musket in the corner."

"Can you fire it?"

I hesitate.

"I cannot," he says. "Not in my condition."

"You cannot leave, either," I say. "Not in your condition."

His eyes flash in a way that tells me he shares at least a little of Ben's stubborn streak.

"You cannot—" I begin again.

"I can leave the cottage, though," he says. "Help me outside and to a spot where we might hide until Bee returns." When my own jaw sets, he meets my eyes. "Please."

7

I have helped Jay out of the cottage, taking my satchel so the intruders will not find it. My plan is to find him a resting spot while I search for a hiding place. I'm settling him against a tree when voices ring out.

"It's over here," a man says. "That damnable cottage. I told you someone was using it. There is a woman inside."

"A woman?" another man says. "Then Sterling has loaned it to one of his peasants. The man . . ." I do not catch the rest, but two other voices laugh.

At least three men are approaching, intent on investigating the cottage. I look down at Jay. We're barely fifty feet from the front door, and not at all well hidden.

Jay lifts a hand for me to help him up. We need to get someplace—

A dog barks. We both go still, our gazes swiveling in that direction.

"Hounds," I whisper. "They have brought hounds."

I take Jay's hand and quickly get him to his feet. He tries to walk on his own, but I force his arm around my shoulders. He points, and we make our way in that direction as quietly as we can manage. When I veer left, Jay stops me and leans to my ear.

"Avoid dead underbrush," he says. "It will crackle. Follow my lead. There is a stream this way, and it will hide our trail from the dogs."

"Not the first time you have been tracked by hounds," I whisper.

He only smiles. I let him lead the way, but we make it only a few more steps before one of the men shouts.

"It's empty!"

Jay curses and moves faster, and I resist the urge to slow him. Behind us, the men's voices rise. The cottage is empty. The occupants have fled. Set the hounds on them. They need a scent. No time for that. Just set the hounds on them.

A dog bays. Another joins in.

"Where is the stream?" I whisper.

"Not far," Jay says, but his tone tells me it is not near either.

We move much faster than I'd like for him, but those hounds are baying behind us and the men are shouting and I cannot hear or see a creek. I stumble on a vine and quickly catch myself. I should have brought the musket. While I am not certain I could use it, it would be something. Better yet, I should emulate Miranda and carry a knife.

Why am I not carrying a knife?

I headed into the unknown, alone, knowing I might find Miranda and Nicolas in dire straits, and I did not even equip myself with a knife.

Because I know the damage one can do.

I am trying to heal a man suffering from the damage a knife can do.

I still need one, despite my concerns. If we cannot outrun these men, then I must defend us, and what am I going to do, grab a branch and swing it at them?

I will if I need to.

And then I smell water. If asked whether I would recognize such a scent, I'd have scoffed at the thought. But I do. I smell the nearby creek and then hear the burble of it.

"Finally," Jay croaks, in a voice so weak that my head snaps up.

"I am fine," he says. "Just winded. Once we're to water, we can get to safety."

I nod and let him lead us a little faster. We only need to cross the water . . .

That is not what he said, as I realize once we are wading in the creek, up to mid-calf in fast-running water. The dogs cannot follow our trail through water, but they will first presume we simply crossed and check for the trail to resume on the opposite bank. We must walk through it.

Fight our way upstream, against a strong ice-cold current, while wearing boots because we had no time to remove them.

My feet are soon numb. When I begin to shiver, Jay whispers, "Just a little farther."

I shake my head. We must go as far as we can manage. The hounds have not yet reached the stream, and the burble of it covers our floundering. When I glance back, I can no longer see where we came in, with the bends of the winding creek.

We must walk in this as far as we can. No, we must walk as far as *Jay* can. I will put this decision in his hands.

"There," he says, his breath coming hard as he lifts one arm to point weakly. "Around that corner."

Ahead are rocks. Once we pass them, I help Jay out, my arm still around him. His foot slips on the wet stones. I start to fall with him, and it is all I can do to catch my own balance so I do not land on him. He goes down with a yowl of pain, cut short as he shoves his fist into his mask and stops himself.

I help him up and out of the stream-bed. I get him as far as I dare—into a thick grove of trees along the creek—before lowering him to the ground. The moment he's sitting, blood begins to leach through his shirt. I unbutton the shirt to see the stitches have ripped open.

"How close are we to the road?" I ask.

He doesn't answer.

"Not close, then," I mutter. "Not close enough."

"Getting to the stream meant moving away from the road. It is perhaps three-quarters of a mile. Through the thickest part of the woods."

I curse, making him give a weak smile.

"I can manage it," he says.

"You cannot, and you will not. What you will do is tell me where to find your brother."

He hesitates.

"Enough of this nonsense," I snap. "I do not care who you are. If you do not trust me by now—"

"I do. It's only . . ." He shakes off his objection. "The road is that way." He points. "Find it, and turn south. You will see two black towers."

"Ravensford Keep."

"Yes, my brother is there."

"He works at Ravensford Keep?"

"You will find him in the stable or the fields. Do not speak to anyone along the way. Just find Bee and bring him here."

"I will."

ॐ

I RUN THE WHOLE WAY TO THE ROAD, IGNORING MY SLOSHING BOOTS AND THE spots where the skin within them rubs raw. I must reach Ben before Carleton's men find Jay. I run with my drenched skirts held high. One advantage to somber travel dress? Dirt and dampness do not show from a distance, and so I can hurry along the road without fear of being mistaken for a corpse who has dragged herself from a watery grave.

Fortunately, I pass no one along the way. Soon I near the castle—yes, I am going to insist on calling it that, however much Ben grumbles. I refrain from gaping at it, or even taking a closer look, and instead, I veer around the back. As Jay predicted, his brother is busy at work, chopping firewood. He is dressed in coarser clothing than his highwayman garb, and his shirtsleeves are rolled up to reveal forearms well accustomed to hefting an ax.

He is also not wearing his mask, and I realize this may be a greater intrusion than knowing where he is employed, but there is naught I can do for it. In truth, while the mask had covered the specifics, it had still given me a good idea of what lay beneath. A strong Romanesque nose and a stronger jawline, the muscles undoubtedly firmed by all that tensing and setting his jaw.

Yesterday, I had bemoaned the fact that I have a very conventional sort of face. Too symmetrical by far, the sort that does not linger in the mind beyond an overall impression of what fashion considers beautiful. Before me, I see a perfect example of the opposite: a face that is not at all conventionally handsome but absolutely arresting, strong features at odds with beautiful amber eyes and a wide, full-lipped mouth.

I am nearly upon him before he seems to sense me there and turns, ax lifted. When he sees me, his fingers tighten around the handle.

"It is your brother," I say. "He told me where you work."

"Where I . . . ?" He looks at the ax, and his hands loosen their grip. With a grunt, he sets it down, leaning against the stable. "Yes, I am employed by Lord Sterling, and if you breathe a word of that to anyone—"

"Abandon that sentence, or I shall be the one issuing threats. Namely, that if you continue them, I will not tell you where to find your brother."

"Find my . . . ?" His eyes darken. "You let him leave the cottage?"

I quickly tell him what happened, and his brusque nod agrees that we had no choice but to depart. When I explain why I left Jay behind, another of those nods suggests this was correct.

"Take me to him," he says.

"That is what I am doing. But you ought to be armed."

"I can fetch a musket. Come. You can wait over here."

He leads me toward a blackened tower, this one standing free, the walls flanking it long gone.

"There," he says. "You wanted to see the towers."

"Can I climb up it?"

He looks over sharply, as if trying to gauge whether I am joking. I keep my expression smooth, giving him no hints.

He shakes his head. "I have no doubt you will do as you like. But if you fall and perish, I only ask that you do not haunt the keep."

"Why not? From what I hear, Lord Sterling could use a good haunting."

"He has quite enough of that."

Ben mutters something about superstitious nonsense as he continues steering me toward the tower. We are almost to it when a voice rings out.

"Lord Sterling!"

Ben grips my elbow and moves me faster. As he does, a puzzle piece falls into place, and with it, my heart sinks.

"Lord Sterling!"

The man's voice comes clearer, and I glance over to see a man with a walking stick approaching, a gleaming black coach parked in front of the castle.

Ben seems prepared to keep moving and play out this charade for as long as he can. Then he slows, and that strong jaw sets as his fingers tighten on my elbow.

"Benedict!" the man calls. "I know that is you, however you might dress. What *are* you wearing?"

"Go to the tower," Ben—Benedict—whispers roughly to me. I am about to dig in my heels when I realize why he wants me hidden. Up close, it will be obvious that I am wet and filthy . . . as if I waded through a stream while fleeing hounds hot on my trail.

I whisk up my skirts with a sniff, as if I have been dismissed, and I flounce off to the tower.

I reach the tower, and there's part of me that wants to keep walking. "Ben" is Lord Benedict Sterling, the Earl of Ravensford. The man who ran the Booths off their land.

But it is not Lord Sterling who concerns me right now. It is his younger brother. If I storm off, I leave Jay in the woods, where Benedict cannot find him. No, I must see this part through. Then I shall leave.

I duck through a doorway and find myself inside a tower that is far less ruinous than I expected from the outside. There is a stairway in decent repair, and I do indeed climb it, seeing no reason not to. At the top, a hatch opens into a small room even tidier than the cottage, swept and scrubbed, with rugs and a makeshift hearth and chimney. Furs are draped over a wooden chair, and a table sits beside it, with a book resting open.

Before I can see the book's title, the men's voices draw me to the window. Both stand near the foot of the tower. The newcomer looks to be in his fifties and is dressed well, with that silver-tipped walking stick.

"What do you want, Carleton?" Benedict says.

Carleton. Whose men set us running from the cottage.

"I came to warn you that someone is using your old gamekeeper cottage," Carleton says. "One of my men accidentally wandered into your part of the forest and stumbled upon it."

"Accidentally wandered into it?" Benedict says. "Please explain how that works when my forest does not join yours?"

"He mistook one forest for the other," Carleton says smoothly. "When he saw the cottage, he realized his error, and he was about to withdraw when he noticed someone was staying there, and he knows you can no longer afford a gamekeeper."

"I no longer require one, as a gamekeeper's primary purpose is to keep people from hunting my game, and I do not consider it mine. The deer belong to whoever requires them."

"Such lofty ideals, Sterling. Come speak to me again when you have no deer left, your farmers having eaten them all."

"They understand that if they do that, there will be no more next year or the year after. The principles of conservation are part of hunting, and I trust them to understand that."

"You really are a fool, aren't you?"

"I most certainly am, such a fool, in fact, that I do not care one whit if someone is living in my cottage, and I must insist that you leave them be. Also? Stay out of my forest."

"Your tone, Sterling—"

"It is one of heartfelt concern, Carleton. As I have said, people hunt those woods, and I would not wish your man to be shot. Now, if that is all—"

"My man saw a woman there. A most fetching woman with golden hair, not unlike the one you just shooed into that tower."

There is a pause, long enough that I tense. *Think of something, Benedict. Anything—*

"I would suggest you mind your own business, Carleton." Benedict's voice has dropped to that distinctive warning growl. "I know you find it most difficult, but here, I really must insist."

"I am *concerned* for you, Sterling. As your neighbor. My man saw a woman trespassing in your cottage, and then I spied her here. Lord knows what kind of heart-wrenching tale of woe she has told you—"

"I was the one in that cottage," Benedict says. "I was there with a widowed friend, and now she is here with me, and *that*, Mr. Carleton, is none of your bloody business."

"You mean she is your mistress?"

"Yes. And if we sought out privacy for her visit, that is—again—none of your business."

That is his story? Claiming I am his *mistress*?

Well, I did mentally wish for him to come up with an excuse. Any excuse. Also, I am not in my time, and I do not know this Carleton fellow and will never see him again. Benedict may tell him whatever he likes. I will even go along with it, if that helps.

"True," Carleton murmurs. "Who you bed and where you bed them is indeed none of my business. But it might be the business of your future wife."

"As I have not chosen a wife, I do not think she will care who I dallied with before our engagement. I am thirty-five years old. She'll hardly expect me to have never known a woman before her. Her concern, rightly, will be my behavior afterward, and once I am engaged, my lady friend knows we must part ways."

I swear I *hear* Carleton roll his eyes. "You wear your honor like a golden cloak, Sterling, when it is one of lead, weighing you down and making you most dull. You are marrying for convenience. You hardly need to give up your mistress for that, and you will not need to if you marry my daughter."

"Did you not just berate me for having a mistress when I plan to wed soon?"

"I was needling you. It is such fun to see you growl and glower. Now, I came to speak to you about the woman in the cottage, but understanding the circumstances, I will say no more about it and instead turn this visit to business matters. Namely, my daughter. Call off this ridiculous bridal-hunt ball and wed the chit. You could not hope for better. Or richer."

"Get off my land," Benedict says, clearly through gritted teeth. "Now."

Carleton laughs. "Or you shall call Juno to chase me off again? Where is that old hound? Oh, that's right. Dead. Even your faithful hound has deserted you."

"Get off my—"

"I am leaving. Have your silly ball, Sterling. You will see the choices and realize I am offering the best one."

I watch until Carleton begins to leave, and then I hurry down the steps, nearly bashing into Benedict at the bottom.

"What an odious man," I say.

Benedict only grunts. Then he looks at me standing two steps up and on his eye level.

"I presume you have something to say about this?" he says when I don't speak.

"About the fact you are the Earl of Ravensford . . . and also a highwayman? About the fact you allow your farmers to hunt your forest . . . and yet also drive them off for unpaid rent?"

"Drive them off? Who said—"

"It does not signify," I say as I try to squeeze past him.

"Of course it bloody well signifies. You accuse me of evicting tenants during the worst drought in two centuries. Explain yourself or—"

"Or we shall stand here, discussing it, while your brother bleeds to death?" I wave toward the door. "We need to go."

"Then you will explain on the way."

"If I must."

"Yes, you must."

"Fine."

W e are walking as fast as we can. Or as fast as Benedict can walk, which means I am fairly running to keep up. It is not until we reach the forest path—where we must slow for the dense trees—that he says, "Explain."

"My sister is not with child, as I claimed. She came with her husband on a mission, delivering money to a family in dire need of it. When she did not return as expected, I came after her, fearing trouble."

"Trouble delivering money in Yorkshire?"

"Is that so hard to believe? There seems to be a problem with highwaymen. Not that you would know about that."

He grunts and pushes aside branches as we pass.

I continue, "I went to the family and discovered they'd been evicted. They seem to have gone to York, and presumably, my sister followed."

"Evicted? There are two families who left recently, but I did not send them off, and if anyone says otherwise, they are lying. Even if I were monstrous enough to evict tenants during a drought, what would be the point? I can hardly find others to take their cottage, on account"—he glares back at me—"of the bloody drought."

"Their cottage is not being re-let. It is being torn down for grazing."

He lets out a string of curses.

"Such colorful profanity," I say. "I suppose you will still insist I am mistaken, despite seeing the cottage in the midst of being dismantled."

"No, you are correct, but— Where is this cottage, and who owns it?"

"It is at the crossroads west of the village. Owned by—"

"Widow Booth. Yes. I know the family. I had not realized they'd left, and I am sorry to hear it. That is not my land. It belongs to Mr. Carleton."

I frown. "So close to the village? I have seen maps of the area, and the Earl of Ravensford's lands extend well beyond that."

"They did," he mutters. "Now they belong to that . . . What did you call him? Odious man. No, that is too kind. He is a bastard."

I hesitate, working it through. Then it dawns. "You had to sell some of your lands."

"Not important," Benedict grunts. "I'll get them back, and I am sorry for the Booths. They deserved better."

I do not know what to say to that, and so I say nothing and continue following him to his brother.

⚜

We reach Jay, whose name is actually Jude. Jude Sterling. Benedict gives Jude the briefest version of what has transpired, and I see no point in expanding on it. I care only about getting Jude back to Ravensford Keep.

I restitch Jude's wounds while Benedict brings water from the stream. Once Jude is stabilized, Benedict half supports and half carries him to the road. There, Benedict has me stand guard as he hurries his brother across it. We are soon within the remains of the keep walls. Ahead, the keep itself is as dark as its walls.

"There is no one within?" I say.

"We have a housekeeper and a groom," Jude says when Benedict doesn't answer. "They have gone to visit their son. That is why Ben had to return to feed the animals."

I stare up at the looming keep before us. "Two servants for such a place?" I say, before I realize why the staff would be so small. "I apologize. I know you are in financial straits, and that is the obvious answer."

"That and the ghost," Jude says with a tiny smile. "We could afford a maid to help our housekeeper, but the phantom will not let us keep one."

I look over sharply at Benedict. "You mentioned a haunting, and you implied you were joking."

"Ben never jokes. He just doesn't believe there *is* a ghost."

"Do not tell me you are afeared of spirits, Miss Portia," Benedict says. "Oh, wait. Please do not tell me you have seen them yourself."

"Do you know one of the traits I find most despicable in people? Mocking the experiences of others. If you have not experienced a thing— whether it is ghosts or poverty or being treated as lesser because of your sex—then you ought not to mock others for it."

Jude starts to say something, but I move forward to open the door for them. It isn't the massive front doors but a smaller side entrance, and it is unlocked. I step inside into darkness and hold the door as they enter.

"There is a lantern on the table to your left," Jude says. "If you wouldn't mind lighting it, Miss Portia. We do not fill the hall lamps."

I find and light the lantern. Then I motion for them to lead the way, and Benedict continues supporting his brother down the hall. When I offer my help, he says, "Hold the lantern."

"But thank you," Jude says. "For your kind offer. That is the part he wished to add."

"You do not need to cover for your brother's rudeness," I say. "Lord Sterling may not be the monster I expected, but the change of perspective does not alter his actual personality. He can be as rude as he likes. I am here to ensure my patient—you—recovers, and he will not frighten me off."

"No, that is the worst of it," Jude says. "He is not trying to frighten you off. He *wants* you here. He is simply unable to do anything to ensure it."

"Beyond threatening to keep me from leaving?"

"Exactly."

Benedict glowers over. "If you two are quite finished—and Miss Portia is still offering her assistance—she could open that door on the right."

I move ahead of them to do that. The door opens into blackness. I step inside with the lantern and light the oil lamp near the door.

My experience with castles is that, for all their grand appearance, actually living in them is quite a different thing, with cavernous drafty rooms. This chamber is neither cavernous nor drafty, but a proper—if somewhat medieval—bedroom, with tapestries on the walls and thick rugs underfoot.

I light a second lamp, and the bed appears, and it is a beautiful piece of carved furniture with a decent mattress. Benedict arranges his brother on it as I start a fire in the hearth. I am not certain whether coal heating is yet common, but I see no sign of it here. The hearth is clean and prepared, and I quickly get the fire going.

"There are no guest quarters," Benedict says.

"Hmm?" I say, rising from the fireplace.

"No guest quarters. No room for you to sleep in."

"If you wish me to leave, you need only to say I am no longer required. I would appreciate directions and some aid in leaving—"

"Jude is not ready for you to leave, and you have admitted you do not need to."

"Ben . . ." Jude says.

I lift a hand to Jude. "You do not need to play the role of mediator or interpreter. I am only attempting to understand your purpose, Lord Sterling, in telling me there isn't a room for me. If it wasn't a hint to leave, then I presume it means I should expect rustic sleeping arrangements, such as a cot in the kitchen. Or in here, to tend to your brother."

"No, I mean that you will need to sleep in my bed."

I pause. "That seems a very convoluted way to accomplish such a goal. If you wish to bed me, Lord Sterling, you need only to ask. I would refuse, but I will not judge you for asking."

Jude bursts out laughing, and Benedict starts to sputter.

"I did not mean—" Benedict says.

"Oh, I know," I say. "I was needling you. You mean that I will take your quarters while you sleep elsewhere. I could argue that you do not need to do that, but I am here to assist your brother, with no expectation of compensation, and so I will accept a proper bedroom, even if it means taking yours."

"We *will* compensate you," Jude insists.

"I am still needling your brother. I do not wish compensation."

"Then why bring it up?" Benedict mutters.

"To make my point. In lieu of recompense, I will accept being treated as a proper guest." I wave at the door. "You may prepare your quarters for me while I tend to your brother. Also, I am famished and would appreciate an early supper, as I missed my lunch."

"Anything else?"

"A glass of wine would not be amiss, if you have it. Brandy would do."

"I might come to wish I had offered compensation instead."

"Too late." I shoo him toward the door. "Now go. Bring food."

⚜

"I WILL STOP MAKING EXCUSES FOR MY BROTHER," JUDE SAYS AS I CHECK HIS wound.

"You really must," I say. "You are not his keeper. Nor the intermediary between him and the world."

"I know. I just . . ."

"Don't want me to think overly ill of him?" I rebandage his wound. "I can see by his treatment of you and his concern for his people that he is not an ogre, however much he snorts and growls like one."

"He is a good man. A truly good man. One overloaded with responsibilities. I will not pretend he was different before our father died. Benedict has always been brusque and stubborn and difficult."

"But it is worse now that he has so much on his mind." I button his shirt back up. "My parents died when my eldest sister, Rosalind, was eighteen. I remember how it affected her. Then she was lost to us for a few years, and I had to step into that role. I took my responsibilities a little too seriously, given that my younger sister, Miranda, was no longer a child. I can only imagine the weight of having tenants relying on you. So I understand what your brother is experiencing. It is an explanation of his temperament but not an excuse for it. I promise that he will not inadvertently drive me off, but I will not let him get away with bullying me."

"As you shouldn't. I try not to mediate the situation. You are both quite capable of butting heads and surviving the encounters."

"And if you insert yourself to cushion the blows, the only one who will be hurt is you. Rest and recuperate. That is your job here, Mr. Sterling."

"Jude, please."

"Then I will insist on Portia, without the title of miss."

"Portia, then." He lies back on the pillows, and I am about to move away when he says, "You must have questions. I know that we misled you as to who we are, and we owe you answers, which you will not get from Benedict."

"I do not wish to pry, but there is one rather obvious line of inquiry."

"Why is an earl robbing coaches?" A dry chuckle. "Yes, that is the obvious question. The answer is rather . . . convoluted."

"Is it? I have heard of Scarlet Jack, rumored to be a gentleman posing as a highwayman to clear these roads of them."

Jude shakes his head. "Benedict is not Scarlet Jack, if that is what you are asking. Nor am I. We do not know who Scarlet Jack is, though we respect what he is doing, as these roads are dangerous indeed. We sit on the route between London and Edinburgh, yet we are situated in an empty stretch of the moors, making travelers easy prey."

I am about to comment on them respecting Scarlet Jack—given that he murdered young Colin Booth—but another part of his statement catches my attention more urgently.

"Your roads are dangerous because of highwaymen. Your *roads*, which you govern, being the local gentry. And yet you add to the danger by holding up coaches yourselves?"

Jude sighs. "I know . . ."

"I understand you are in dire straits, and perhaps this seems the answer—steal from wealthy strangers—but, and I am sorry to be harsh, I find that most short sighted."

"I suspect the term you wish to use is not *short sighted* but *morally reprehensible*. Yet what we are doing . . . it is rather more complicated than that, and perhaps, I hope, a little less repugnant. To explain, I must give some family history that may also answer questions you are too polite to ask. May I do that?"

"Of course."

He shifts to get comfortable. "Our mother died when I was very young. Benedict is seven years my senior, and there are no siblings between us. Our mother was an invalid, and so childbearing was difficult, and after Benedict was born, they . . . found ways to avoid more children. I was an accident. But when I was five, her frail health led to illness, and she died. While Mama was physically frail, she was, as my father said, the smartest person he'd ever met, particularly when it came to money. They often say that one should marry a person who complements oneself, and that's what they did. My father was a bright man, but when it came to money, he was hopeless. He was cheerful and charming and too trusting by far."

Jude slants a gaze my way. "If you hear Benedict say I take after my father, it is not entirely a compliment. It is also not entirely untrue. I am our father's son, with some of mother's head for finances, and he is our mother's son, with our father's robust health."

Footsteps sound in the stone halls, and we both go quiet, but they head in another direction.

Jude continues, "Neither Benedict nor I had any idea of the estate's financial situation. Our father hid that from us, encouraging us to go off into the world and make our way and not worry about what was happening at home. When he died four years ago, creditors surrounded the manor like ravenous wolves."

"Your father had been maintaining the illusion of money by borrowing it."

Jude's expression hardens, a sliver of his brother peeking through. "Borrowing is too pretty a word for it. He was betrayed by men he considered friends, led by Mr. Carleton, who summered here with his family. They offered to help with the management of his estates, which they did through an elaborate ruse whereby they stole his money and replaced it with borrowed funds. Then, at the opportune moment, they intended to swoop in and take his lands and title in payment. His death provided that opportunity, or so they thought. But Benedict was able to block their efforts by paying off the most onerous of the loans and keeping the wolves at bay by raising capital using whatever means necessary, including . . ." He waves a hand around the room.

"Living frugally in a ruined keep."

"Selling Sterling Hall to Mr. Carleton was the only way to raise enough capital to avoid losing everything else."

"Selling him the house *and* part of the lands."

Jude shakes his head. "No, the lands were another matter. Ben would never have betrayed our tenants like that. The loss of the land was part of a contract triggered by our father's death, but there is a codicil that will allow us to buy them back by year's end, at a prearranged price."

Which explains the bridal hunt. But if Mr. Carleton is already clearing those lands . . .

Again, I don't say anything. This isn't the time.

Instead, I say, "And then came the drought."

"At the worst possible time. We had only just paid off the debts and begun saving money to buy back . . ." He inhales sharply. "But one cannot control nature, and the important thing is the tenants. Instead of saving money, we began losing it. That's when I made a proposal." He smiles. "Because sometimes, being the reckless-dreamer sibling comes in handy. Those men who had betrayed my father and stolen our money managed to do so because they have connections in the region. My father knew and trusted them. They—and their shipments—pass through here regularly, and so I suggested . . ."

I cannot help but smile. "That you relieve them of their goods when they do."

"Judiciously, of course. No more than they can readily afford to lose, or they will find another route. That is the money we use to keep our tenants—and ourselves—from starving."

"So Mr. Ward was one of the men who took advantage of your father."

"One of many. When we learned he was passing through with his family, we were ready. We would not have taken your money. Once we understood you were but an accidental passenger, you were no longer fair game."

I remember everything Mr. Ward had said about his success and the impression I had, that it came at the expense of his workers and others.

"So are we slightly less morally reprehensible?" Jude asks.

I smile at him. "Slightly less."

Footsteps sound outside the door, and Benedict appears with a tray.

"Slightly less what?" he says.

"I was telling your brother that his condition is slightly less dire," I say. "Now I hope that tray bears food."

He mock bows. "Of course, my lady. Make yourself comfortable, and I shall serve."

9

After lunch, Jude falls asleep, and Benedict has work to do in the fields.

"I do not think your brother needs my constant care," I say before Benedict leaves. "He really does require rest more than anything, and he can achieve that best in a quiet room. Might I look about for another place I can sit?"

I expect an argument—either over leaving Jude's side or poking around the castle—but Benedict only grunts what sounds like assent and leaves. A moment later, he pokes his head around the doorway with an impatient wave. Clearly, I was meant to follow.

I do follow, but he strides down the hall without a backward glance, and I'm soon wondering whether I misunderstood again and he only meant for me to leave Jude's room. Then, just as I am about to head another way, he stops and turns.

"My chambers are here. If you wish to nap, I will change the bedding."

I peek in to find a tiny, stark room. A newly lit fire takes off the chill, but otherwise, there is an old bed and a dressing table and drawers and nothing more, not even rugs on the floor. Everything required in a bedroom and nothing that isn't.

"It will warm up," he says, "but it is not the most comfortable of rooms if you only wish to rest. There is the kitchen, where the fire is lit, and also a library, where it can be lit."

"The library will be most suitable. If you show me where it is, I won't wander farther."

"You are free to wander," he says. "Not much to see. Just empty, closed rooms, mostly. The only thing I ask . . ."

He strides off without another word, leaving me hurrying along to keep up with his long strides.

"The only area you may not explore is here," he says.

He stops before a heavy door, barred on this side.

"You must keep this shut," he says. "And do not venture beyond."

When I give him a hard look, he grunts, "What?"

"There is a barred door in a ruined castle, and the dark and moody lord of that castle is telling me I must not open it? You must have a taste for gothic fiction."

"For what?"

I remember the time period. "For stories of a gothic nature. Did I mention my sister is a writer of adventurous tales? Having spent my life as her first reader, I know well what lies beyond that door. Mystery and danger and possibly inconvenient relatives."

One thick brow lifts.

"Or an inconvenient wife," I muse. "Yes, that is it. You married once, in secret, but now you must wed again for money, and so you have locked your first wife in that tower."

He unbars the door and pushes it. On the other side, there is no more than four feet of hallway before the floor crumbles. Sunlight streams through cracks in the walls. Beyond it lies the rest of the hallway, complete with broken ceiling and fallen timbers.

"No wife," he says.

"Terribly disappointing."

"I'm sure it is."

I peer through the doorway. "She might still be there. In those distant rooms. You locked her away and destroyed the corridor to keep people out."

"Then how would I feed her?"

"You don't. She has perished, and her moldering corpse is locked away in one of those rooms."

"That turned dark."

"It was not already dark when you were locking up your wife to wed another?"

He looks down at me. "That depends. Perhaps my wife was a doctor's assistant, met through happenstance and married in haste, a beautiful and intelligent woman . . . who needled me at every turn, called me moody, accused me of mistreating my tenants and then made up wild stories about me murdering a wife and hiding her body. In such a case, I might be forgiven for locking her away."

"In such a case, you'd never get the chance to lock her away. Oh, you might try, but you would carry her into the ruined wing, only to wake up and find yourself locked within."

His lips give the faintest twitch. Is that a smile? Before I can be sure, it vanishes with a shake of his head.

"Goodbye, Miss Portia. I have chores to attend to. You will find the library over there." He points. Then he closes the door and swings down the bar. "Stay out of here. I would not wish the ghost of my former wife to become jealous, seeing another woman in the keep. I cannot be held accountable for anything she does."

⚜

THE LIBRARY IS AS COZY AS JUDE'S CHAMBERS. OR IT IS ONCE I HAVE THE FIRE blazing. It also has books, which I realize is the defined purpose of a library but, in my experience, is not always a requisite component of one among the gentry. This has cases filled with nothing *but* books, along with two blanket-laden chairs for reading them.

I find the fiction shelves and remove a copy of *Moll Flanders*, marveling at the newness of it until I realize it *is* new in this time. I settle in on one chair, tug a blanket over my legs and begin to read. I haven't passed the first chapter before something thumps in the hall.

"Lord Sterling?" I call.

No answer. I return to my reading. Another thump, as if a heavy footfall echoes along the corridor. With a sigh, I set down my book, head to the door, open it and lean out.

"Jude? There is a bell by your bed. You are supposed to use—"

Another footfall . . . from the other direction. I turn and find myself looking at that barred door, ten feet away. The sound comes again, and it is less of a firm footstep than a dragging one.

A shiver creeps up my spine.

I shake off the feeling. I was teasing Benedict about someone being locked in that ruined wing, and now I hear dragging footsteps there? It is a joke. Yes, Benedict doesn't seem the type for pranks—that would be more Jude's realm—but I haven't known him long enough to be sure of that.

I head to the door. "Lord Sterling? If that is you—"

Someone scratches on the door, and I fall back so fast I nearly tumble.

"Lord Sterling," I say, more sharply than I intend. "That is not funny."

Another sound, this one a loud thump from my left. There's a door there, and I open it to find an unused room. When another thump sounds, I hurry across the empty room to the window and look out to see Benedict over by the stables, chopping wood.

Could that have been the sound I heard? The chopping of wood?

No, I can just make out the thump of the ax, a distant and very different sound.

I slowly turn back to that barred door. It isn't Benedict in there. It isn't Jude, who would never make it this far without me hearing him. There's no one else in the keep.

No. That's a logical fallacy. Just because there isn't *supposed* to be anyone else here doesn't mean no one else *could* be in here. From what I saw of that wing, I'm sure there are open windows and even holes in the walls big enough to enter through.

The scratching comes again, and I remember what Jude and Benedict said about the castle allegedly being haunted. They've only been living in this glorious ruin for a couple of years. If someone wanted them gone, it would be the perfect setting to stage a haunting. And there are plenty of people who might want them to sell this castle and the rest of the lands, chief among them Mr. Carleton.

On the other side of the door, the intruder scrapes their nails in a long, slow scratch down the wood.

"H-hello?" I say, making my voice quaver as I move to the door. "L-Lord S-Sterling? Tell me that is you."

As I speak, I very carefully lift the bar, raising my voice when the hinge threatens to squeak.

The scratch comes again.

"It is you," I say, still tremulously. "I know it is and—"

I yank open the door, ready to crow in triumph as I spot the intruder.

No one is there. I'm standing in the open doorway, with nothing but that short stretch of broken hall before me. I dash along it, still certain I'll catch the culprit fleeing. Only I reach the end, where the floor gives away, and there is no one there. No one in the ruined hallway. No one outside beyond the gap.

There's no one there.

No one I can see.

I back up, slowly, until I am on the other side of the door. Then I stand there, looking through and listening, but all has gone quiet.

Ghost.

The word seems to whisper through the air, and I rub my arms. Then I bar the door and retreat to the library, shutting that door, too, before tugging my chair closer to the window, where the sunlight pours through and I hear nothing but the distant thump of Benedict chopping wood.

I wrap the blanket around myself and lean into that sunlight, lifting my face to feel it.

The Sight runs in my family. Miranda has it. She sees and hears ghosts and can communicate with them, and for her, it is simply part of her life, even sometimes a gift, as when she can help the dead find closure and peace. Rosalind has caught glimpses of ghosts, but only rarely. For most of my life, that was also my experience—very rare and fleeting glimpses.

That changed after Rosalind disappeared. It was the most anxious time of my life. When my parents died, my world crashed, but Rosalind was there to put us on our feet again. When she vanished, presumed dead, I understood a little of what she'd gone through with our parents —managing her own grief while keeping our world intact.

Rosalind disappeared and then my fiancé married another and I . . . broke. I could not keep even my own world intact, let alone Miranda's. But I faked it. Oh, I faked it very well. Stiff upper lip and carry on as if my life wasn't shredded in tatters around me.

That's when I encountered my first true ghost. I didn't see or hear it. I felt it—I was *attacked* by it.

I'd traveled to a medical symposium alone, Miranda having been otherwise occupied and unable to travel with me. I'd been staying in a lodging house, and I awoke in the middle of the night to a force attacking me.

I call it a force. I know it was a ghost, but that is not what I experienced. It is not what I have also experienced sporadically since that night. I catch glimpses or whispers and snatches of words. That is all. I cannot see the ghosts clearly. I cannot hear them clearly. And I cannot communicate with them. I am at their mercy, and they take full advantage.

All those encounters have been negative. I seem to attract only the angriest and most vindictive of spirits, who torment me because they can . . . or because they think I am refusing to communicate and help.

I haven't told Miranda about this. I haven't told anyone. It happens rarely, and I keep hoping it will stop. The spirits took advantage of my weakened mental and emotional state, and all I need to do is find my strength again. Find my footing again. Once I have that, they will go, and in the meantime, there is no need to worry my sisters.

That is why I reacted when Jude suggested the keep was haunted. I do not want to stay in a place where there are ghosts.

Oh, I could leave. But Jude needs me, at least for a little while longer, and it is not as if I am being beset by spirits. I heard footsteps. I heard scratching on the door. That is all.

A knock comes, loud enough that I jump. I steel myself and walk to the door. Then I fling it open. No one is there. Another knock, this one clearly at the barred door. I pull myself up straight, shoot a cold glare in that direction and then head into the hall, walking the other way.

I can handle this. I will take a bit of fresh air to clear my head, and then I will be fine.

10

Before I go outside, I check on Jude. He is soundly asleep, with the bell beside him. I add a note that I am stepping outside but should still be able to hear the bell. I am not overly concerned. He really is past the worst danger and needs only to rest, as I told Benedict.

I will, however, speak to Benedict before I walk around the castle grounds. If he is concerned about Jude being alone in the castle, I will return inside and walk later, once he finishes his chores.

I take the longer way, heading to the main doors for a look through this part of the castle. I pass the side door we entered and then the kitchen, heat from the fire warming the otherwise chilly corridor. The hallway soon opens into a massive room. I step in and lift my lantern.

I have danced in the ballrooms of many an estate house, but none were half as large as this. The banquet hall is perhaps the best-known part of a medieval castle. It is a place for feasting with hundreds of guests and then pushing the tables aside for dancing. The place, too, for showing the world who you are. The Earl of Ravensford, wealthy and noble landowner, *able* to entertain hundreds.

Now the cavernous room sits empty and long abandoned. There are at least four hearths and a raised platform at the front, where the Sterlings would sit like royalty. Dark shapes hang from the wall, and when I move toward one, the smell tells me what it is before I see it. Moldering tapestries. I raise the light and let out a gasp. It is an idyllic scene of fanciful creatures, unicorns and griffins and dragons, and I cannot even imagine the work that went into weaving such a thing on a loom. Regret stabs through me for what was lost here, gorgeous woven art left to rot when the family moved to the newer Sterling Hall.

Had they expected to still use this one for grand gatherings? Expected to and left the tapestries and then found their new home better suited to entertaining? Easier to heat, I am certain, with cozy bedchambers that overnight guests would doubtless prefer.

These tapestries had been left behind, and while I can mourn the loss of such incredible artistry, a hundred years ago, they'd have been little different than average art placed on a modern wall. Something to add a bit of color and interest and, in this case, insulation from the cold stone.

If only Benedict had been able to salvage the tapestries, he could have sold them for a significant amount. Not enough to buy back his lands, but at least to make up for losses the drought has inflicted.

I finger the nearest tapestry for a better look. Could they still be salvaged? Perhaps some of them? Repaired and taken to my world—or even to the twenty-first-century one—then the money returned to the Sterlings, an absolute fortune in this time?

I have been resisting the urge to figure out how to solve their financial difficulties. I do not know whether everyone sees decent people in trouble and wish to help. No, of course not everyone is like that, or the Sterlings wouldn't *be* in this situation, their father hoodwinked and robbed by his supposed friends.

But my sisters and I were raised by parents who'd rather have eaten porridge for supper than refuse to treat a patient who couldn't pay. I want to help the Sterlings, and I know that smacks of charity, which is uncomfortable. I also know that wild dreams are best left to Miranda. Even if I could salvage a tapestry or two, could I get it through the stitch? Could I get the money back again? Could *I* get back again?

I will think on all this later, though I realize that Benedict's plan is indeed the sound one. Marry a wealthy young woman who understands the situation and is not being fooled in any way. A business arrangement to suit all parties, ensuring a steady flow of income to support everyone who relies on the Sterlings.

And if I feel an odd twinge of . . . something at the thought of Benedict marrying for money? If I feel the nudge of regret that I do not have the money he needs—

And what? Marry Benedict myself? Giving up my life in the nineteenth century to wed a man I met a day ago? A marriage almost guaranteed to have one of us locking the other in a ruined tower?

Of course not. From all I can see, Benedict and Jude Sterling are good men, and I'd like to help them, which does not mean marrying Benedict, because I do not have the money he requires, and dear lord, would I really marry someone to be *helpful*? That goes much too far, and if I feel a pang thinking of his upcoming bridal-hunt ball, it is only a deeply hidden romantic side of me that hates to see someone marry for such wholly practical reasons.

I continue through the banquet hall to the main entrance. It is a massive pair of doors that I realize, belatedly, I could never open alone. Fortunately, there is a smaller door to the side, and I can exit through that one.

I step out into the sunshine, and I turn my face up to enjoy it before realizing this is the reason for the drought. Gorgeous weather for the Yorkshire moors, sunny and warm, not a cloud in the sky. Perfect for traveling and walking and sitting out enjoying the sunshine.

For farmers, though? For them, sunshine is like vegetables. Good and necessary for your body, but you need more for proper growth and health. The land needs rain, and when I peer out, I see dirt as dry as sand, any vegetation stunted and yellowed.

I also spot something else. A boy coming up the lane, pulling a cart with a crate on it.

"Hello, miss!" he calls, his voice barely audible over the squeak of the wheels.

He is no more than ten, his trousers and boots as dusty as the land around, his face not much cleaner, though his smile shines through.

"Hello," I say. "I presume you are here for Lord Sterling?"

"No, miss. I came to see you."

I hesitate.

He continues, "I heard there was a lady up at the castle. A friend of Lord Sterling's." He takes off his cap and slaps the dust out before returning it to his head. "That'd be you, wouldn't it? Mr. Carleton said she was a very pretty and proper widowed lady, and that seems like you."

Mr. Carleton.

He's telling the villagers that Benedict has a mistress at the keep?

I manage as friendly a smile as I can. "Well, that is most kind of Mr. Carleton to flatter me so. Yes, as there are no other guests here, he must have been speaking of me."

"Good. That is why I came. Because you are a lady on your own, and my mum says that isn't safe. That's what she always tells my sister. Don't go walking around the moors without Blackie."

"Without . . ."

"Blackie. Our hound." The boy walks over to the crate, which I now notice is wiggling . . . and whining. "What you need, miss, is a dog."

"I—"

"Lucky for you, I have them." He opens the crate to show a mass of wriggling puppies. "Our Blackie had a litter three fortnights ago, and I thought to myself, that lady at the castle, she's going to need a dog, and there's no better dog in the world than Blackie, so what would be better for the lady than one of Blackie's pups?"

"I . . ."

I trail off before I say I do not need a puppy, that I cannot possibly take one. I *can't*, given that I'm a mere visitor to this world. But then I see the boy's ragged trousers and hopeful smile.

I could tell him that I do not need a puppy, but I will pay for one anyway. Yet that is, again, charity, and I was raised to be very aware of when it would be welcome and when it would be an insult.

Didn't Mr. Carleton say something about a dog? That Benedict had lost his recently?

I know it is wrong to give someone a pet as a gift. I wouldn't do that. But . . .

I look at the puppies, almost a sidelong glance, as if they are a tray of sweets that I know I should not touch, even as they call to me.

I've never had a pet. Do I want one?

I am not in the habit of asking myself whether I want a thing that isn't a required part of my life. I do grant myself indulgences—hair ribbons and lacy corsets—but even those fill a necessary role, the frivolity sliver of the circle that encompasses my worldly needs.

Do I want a puppy?

The idea sparks a reaction almost like fear. As if the puppies are no longer sweets but dancing flames, enticing me closer when I know I should beat a hasty retreat.

What would I do with a puppy? How would I take it home? How would it fit into my life? I barely have time to look after myself, much less a pet.

Yet a traitorous tiny voice whispers deep inside me. It says that I could find a way, if I wanted. It is the voice of the little girl who would see a dog and feel an inner pang of longing while knowing better than to ever admit it, as there was no place for pets in our lives and my parents would hate to refuse me.

I look at these puppies, and I feel that same pang . . . one that oddly feels like the pang I had just earlier, thinking about Benedict Sterling.

A longing for something I cannot have.

I shake off the thought quickly. I am being ridiculous. Blame the strong sun melting my brain. I do not feel that way about Benedict Sterling. A puppy, though . . .

"Yes," I say before I can change my mind. "I believe I would very much like a puppy."

The way the boy's face lights up makes me want to buy all the puppies. Thankfully, even in my recklessness I am measured, and I stifle that impulse.

"How much are they?" I ask.

"Two shillings, miss."

"Only two?" I frown. "I thought you said your Blackie was the best of dogs."

"Did I say two? I meant three."

I nod. "That is more like it."

I move to the crate and bend to look at the puppies. The boy called them hounds, but they are shaggy. Hounds of the moors, bred for sheep-herding and hunting. Three are black and white. One is all black with four perfect white paws. As I lean down, that one launches itself at me, and I nearly fall back, ready to protect myself from attack. Instead, it has landed in my arms and is bathing my face in kisses.

I move the puppy to arm's length, and it leaps from them, landing on the ground and barking, forequarters bent in an invitation to play. I scoop it up again, noting as I do that it is female.

"Hmm," I say. "This one seems quite friendly and energetic. She is also the largest, and I presume you mean to keep her for yourselves, being such a fine specimen of a puppy. If that is the case, I understand, but if you might part with her, I would offer five shillings."

"You are right," the boy says solemnly. "She is the best of the litter. You have a good eye, miss, and you make a good bargain. I will let her go for five shillings."

He speaks the words with calm maturity, but I can see the look in his eyes, the tamped-down excitement as he scarcely dares hope I am serious.

"Five shillings," I say. I reach into my pocket and count them out.

"Thank you, miss," he says, words tumbling out as he tips his cap to me. "Thank you very much. Have a lovely day. Thank you."

He is already backing out with his cart, as if I might change my mind. The puppy whines, but I hold her close and pet her as the boy takes her littermates away. Then I turn back to the keep and—

"What the *devil* is that?"

Benedict stalks around the corner of the keep, ax still in hand.

"This?" I hold out the puppy. "A lamb. The dear boy brought back one of your lost lambs. Is it not the sweetest thing?"

I hold out the wriggling puppy. Benedict stares at it.

"That is a dog," he says slowly. "A puppy."

I widen my eyes. "Are you sure? The boy said it was a lamb, and I gave him five shillings for returning it."

Benedict stares at me.

I roll my eyes. "I know it's a puppy. You're the one who asked what it was."

"You paid five shillings—" He stops. "Wait. You *bought* a puppy?"

"Yes, I am terribly impulsive like that. I see puppies, and I must buy them. I have twenty at home."

"As you do not strike me as the impulsive sort, I must presume you are still jesting."

"I am. However, having never had a dog and having just bought one, perhaps I can no longer claim to be un-impulsive." I lift the puppy and look at her. "You are the second most impulsive thing I have ever done in my life."

"And the first?"

"Letting two highwaymen take me to their lair." I lower the puppy. "I did hear that you recently lost a dog, and so if you wish one, you may take her. If not, I will keep her. The boy seemed most hopeful of making the sale, and I hated to disappoint him. Nor did I feel right offering money without taking what he was selling, which happened to be . . ."

"Puppies. I suppose I should be glad you weren't moved to buy the entire litter."

"I considered it, but thankfully, it was only a temporary whim." I pause. "I don't suppose you would like a dog or three?"

He shakes his head and reaches for the puppy. I pass her over, and he holds her up under her forelegs, making both me and the puppy squirm.

"A bitch," he says. "Good size on her." He holds her in one arm, on her back like a baby, as he pokes and prods, running his finger down her limbs, examining her paws . . .

"She'll grow big," he says.

I resist the urge to ask, "How big?" but he answers anyway with, "Maybe eight, nine stone, given her dam. I think I know the sire. Irish wolfhound."

Nine stone? I try to think of such a dog in our London town house.

"Good, solid moor dog," he says.

Do you want her, then? I don't ask. I did offer the puppy to him, and he has not said anything either way. I am not certain what I want his answer to be, even if he does predict she will grow into a fair beast.

When he goes to check her teeth, she gives the smallest growl, tentative, as if testing.

"None of that," he says sharply. Then to me, "You must get them accustomed to being handled. Tail. Teeth. Paws. They will not like it, but if you let them have their way, you will lose a finger trying to help them if they are injured."

He gives the puppy a quick scratch behind her ears. "She'll do nicely."

"So you . . . want her?" I say, my voice as tentative as the puppy's growl.

"Let's get her inside and see what we have for her dinner."

And that did not answer my question at all.

J ude hears the puppy barking and uses that as an excuse for getting out of bed. I consider my options and decide on a weak argument rather than a firm one. If I take a firm stance, I must uphold it or patients will feel free to ignore future admonishments.

I do not know whether male doctors have the same issue. I have asked Nicolas, but he says that the answer, in his case, depends on whether his patient is a fellow person of color or not. With the latter, he must be firmer. I suppose that applies to me as well, as I have found male patients are quicker to decide I am not as reliable as a doctor of their own sex.

I do not get the sense I will have that issue with Jude. Still, I must assess the situation, and I decide that he is indeed well enough for short bouts of freedom from his bed. So I will allow that, with the warning that if he overdoes it, I'll send him back and put Benedict on bedside watch.

We sit in the kitchen, which the brothers seem to also use for dining and a general living space, the library reserved for quieter moments. That really is all they have reopened in the castle: the kitchen, the library, and the two bedrooms.

As we feed meat scraps to the puppy, Jude says, "Did Ben tell you about Juno?"

"Mr. Carleton mentioned something about a dog with that name who passed."

"Ben's dog. Lived to be nearly seventeen. A big black moors hound that followed him everywhere. Got her just before he left for the city, and we used to joke that it wouldn't be long before Ben sent her home. Juno was not a city dog. He never did, though. When I visited London, that blasted hound was right there, taking up the entire hearth and blocking the heat. And taking up half the road when we walked. I always said that's the real reason Ben took her. The dog would clear the way for him."

Benedict only grunts and gives the puppy another scrap.

"Didn't that boy's family take one of Juno's pups?" Jude says.

Another grunt.

Jude nods. "So this would be Juno's granddaughter. Fitting. Is she yours then?"

He directs the question to his brother. I glance over, but Benedict only stands and goes to the chopping block for more meat.

"You giving her a name?" Jude calls after him.

Benedict waves at me.

"Ah," Jude says. "You get to do the honors, Portia. What will it be? Boots, for her white paws?"

Benedict gives a derisive snort.

"Apparently, you get to do the honors," Jude says. "But someone holds the power of veto. What do you wish to call her?"

My first reaction is panic. Name this puppy? That is too great a responsibility.

And if *that* is too great, I had better hope Benedict takes her, as I am ill prepared for the responsibility of the dog herself.

"She is the granddaughter of Juno," I say. "Digging into my knowledge of Greek and Roman mythology, I am thinking Hippolyta. Queen of the Amazons. Lord Sterling said she would grow large, and she was the biggest and boldest in her litter."

"Lord Sterling?" Benedict grumbles as he brings over scraps of fresh meat. "I would take that as overly formal civility if I did not suspect you are needling me."

"Then you would be wrong. It is civility, and not overly formal, but simply a respectful acknowledgment of your title, pending permission to call you something else."

"Benedict," he says. "My name is Benedict. Or Ben. As for this one . . ." He bends to give her a scrap. "Hippolyta is a fair name."

Jude looks over. "He means it is an excellent one."

"I thought you vowed to stop playing translator?" I say.

"I will slip, now and then. As for the name, if I may be permitted an opinion, it is indeed excellent, though perhaps a bit much for such a young pup, much as our parents decided Benedict was too much for a young boy. Might I suggest that as her name but something shorter to call her?"

"Hippo?" Benedict says.

"I was thinking Lyta," Jude says.

Benedict glances at me.

I nod. "An excellent suggestion. Hippolyta, also known as Lyta." I bend in my chair. "What do you think, Lyta?"

The puppy barks and vaults onto my lap.

"Best cure her of that," Benedict says. "Or she'll be doing it when she's big enough to topple you."

"Says the man who never made his own dog stop crawling into his lap, even when she was so big you scarcely knew where the man ended and the dog began."

"Then I know of what I speak."

I pat Lyta. "She's fine for now. If I wish to curb the habit, I can do so later." I glance at the two men. "And in all the fuss of the puppy, I forgot there is something I must tell you. The boy did not come to see whether Lord—whether Benedict wanted a puppy. He came because of me."

"You?" Benedict's brows rise.

"Yes, apparently, Mr. Carleton has let it slip that you are entertaining a widow. Quite by accident, I'm sure."

Benedict lets out a string of curses. Even Jude's face darkens.

"The bastard," Jude mutters. "I know Ben suggested you were a widowed friend, which was" —a hard look his brother's way—"a ruse that should have had Portia's consent first. But setting that aside, a gentleman would have kept it a secret. A lout would not have openly mentioned it, but might have let it slip. It takes a right bastard to deliber-ately spread the story, and within mere hours, no less."

"Poisoning the well," I murmur. "When is the bridal-hunt ball?"

"Two days from now."

I stiffen, a little voice inside whispering, *So soon?* in a tone of dread I don't quite comprehend.

When I catch Jude studying my expression, I force myself to look merely contemplative.

"And if I am here, that poses a problem," I say. "The young women and their chaperones will arrive to hear that Lord Sterling—mere hours from searching for a bride—has a mistress ensconced at his castle home. That will not do. I must leave at once, in hopes you can remedy the misunderstanding before it is too late."

"No," Benedict says, the word coming fast and firm. "Jude still requires your assistance, and after that assistance has been graciously given, I would be a cad to turn you out."

"I would understand why," I say softly.

"I would not," he says. "It is out of the question. You aren't leaving."

Jude clears his throat.

When Benedict only turns a dark frown on him, Jude says, "He means you are not leaving, dear Portia, until you are quite prepared to leave, at which time he will assist you in any way necessary, in recompense for your kindness."

"I thought you were going to stop interpreting for me," Benedict says, as he steps over Lyta.

"I'm trying, but sometimes, I cannot help myself." Jude tilts his head, musing. "Unless that was not what you meant at all. Do you have some plan for persuading Portia to stay?"

"He has a locked wing of the castle," I say. When Jude lifts his brows, I continue, "He showed me the damaged wing with the barred door. I fear he means to keep me in there."

Jude sighs. "Have we not had this conversation before, Ben? You cannot keep locking women in ruined wings of your castle. Their haunting cries are becoming most difficult to explain to the townsfolk."

"If you two are quite done," Benedict says, "might I suggest we return to the issue at hand?"

"Yes," I say. "The issue being that Mr. Carleton has spread the story of your mistress across the town, and the arriving families are sure to hear of it."

"The solution," Jude says, "is clearly to convince them that Carleton misinterpreted, and Portia is actually here with me. As my mistress."

"No," Benedict says sharply.

"If Portia does not mind, I am willing to—"

"No."

"It will not help," I say to Jude. "Lord Sterling already claimed me as his mistress."

Jude's brows shoot up in mock surprise. "Has he? Well, things are progressing faster—"

Benedict shakes his head. "She means that I intimated she was my mistress, as you are already aware. I did not know what else to do, and the damage is done, so now we deal with it. We'll speak to Aunt Flora tomorrow."

"Aunt Flora is the one putting on the ball," Jude says to me. "It'll be held at her home, which is a far more suitable setting than this, and the ball was her idea so . . ." He shrugs. "She is in charge."

"As always," Benedict mutters.

"She'll know what to do," Jude says. "Ben is supposed to pay her a visit tomorrow, and he can consult with her on this problem."

⚜

EARLIER, BENEDICT HAD BEEN ABOUT TO CHANGE THE SHEETS IN HIS ROOM when he realized the fresh ones had not returned from the washerwoman. I said it was fine. I'd spent last night in a highwayman's hideout on a bed with only blankets and a straw mattress. He still insisted on taking the sheets out-of-doors and shaking them, and he would not accept help doing so. This morning, I had mentally remarked that the cottage was tidier than I expected. Now, seeing him shaking out those sheets and then wiping nonexistent dust from the bedroom furniture, I have a good idea who is responsible for the cottage's condition.

Benedict Sterling is a man of exacting standards, even if he must meet those standards through work considered beneath someone of his sex or station. I both admire him for that and truly begin to understand how dire their financial situation must be, if they cannot afford to hire someone to clean or cook or chop wood in the absence of their very small staff.

Having seen how diligently Benedict cleaned the blankets and sheets, when Lyta scrambles onto the bed, I hurry to remove her.

"Should I set a blanket by the fire?" I ask Benedict, who is still in the doorway. "I fear I have no experience with dogs." I pause. "Or did you want her in your room?"

We still have not ascertained precisely whose dog this is, and I fear asking for clarification. Lyta should be his. It is his house and his time period, and she is his recently deceased dog's granddaughter.

"She will sleep in whichever room she likes," he says, which does not answer the question at all. "If it bothers you to have her in your room, I'll take her to mine."

"It does not." I quickly add, "Unless you would prefer . . ."

"Here is fine. As for a blanket by the fire, that is your choice. She can sleep there or on the bed, whichever you like."

"If you would prefer her not to be on your bed—"

"It is your choice, Portia," he says with a snap of impatience. "Do not waffle like this. You clearly have opinions. State them, and be done with it."

I douse a spark of annoyance and say, evenly, "I ask because it is your room, and you may not wish dog fur and muddy paws on your bedsheets."

"That is why bedsheets are constructed of a material that can be washed. A most remarkable thing, is it not?"

I glower at him. "Just say you do not mind."

"Just say you would like the puppy in your bed."

"I . . ." I try for a tart response and find none, because even as he says those words, something in me shrinks back. Admit I'd like a puppy in my bed? Heavens, no. I want to duck and dodge and say it is up to Lyta and to him and to anyone except me, because I do not want . . . anything.

I want for nothing. I have no needs or desires or wishes for myself.

A memory flashes, from when I told Miranda that Reginald had asked for my hand.

"So you do love him?" she said.

"I like him very well."

Her brow furrowed. "You do not love him?"

I busied myself folding my napkin. "Oh, I'm sure I will. He is very kind and very easy to talk to. He treats me well, and he is in need of a wife."

"In need of a wife? You sound as if he's buying a new coach. What about you? Do you want to be married to him, above all others? What do you want?"

"He will make a very good husband, and I ought to have one."

Miranda threw up her hands and stormed from the dining room.

"Portia? What do you want?"

I startle, and it takes a moment before I realize that last line did not come from my memory. It is Benedict, standing there, frowning with what looks like concern.

"Are you all right?" he says.

"Quite." I put Lyta back on the bed. "If she wishes to be here, that will suit me."

"Good. Then I will see you in the morning." He pauses. "What time do you usually wake?"

"Whenever I am required."

That frown returns, and he peers at me so intently that I squirm.

"I will be in Jude's room with Jude," he says. "I wake at dawn, and if you are comfortable with me opening your bedroom door at such an hour, I will take Lyta out to do her business."

"I'm usually up early, but if you are earlier, she would likely appreciate that."

"All right then. Good night, Portia."

I cannot sleep, because the sheets smell of Benedict. That is not his fault. They are clean, and it is only the faintest smell and not an unpleasant one. It might be easier to sleep if it *were* unpleasant. The problem is that I keep drifting off to that scent of soap and sweat and . . . something else, something I cannot quite place. That scent sweeps me back to random moments of the day. Something Benedict said. Something he did. Some way he annoyed me. Some way he did not annoy me.

When the distant clock strikes one, I find a solution in the puppy, who smells of dog and not at all of Benedict Sterling. I lie twisted with my face near her, inhaling her puppy scent, and soon I am off to the land of dreams.

When I first hear Lyta whining, I am still in that dream realm. She is pressed against me, shaking and whimpering, and I am holding her close and telling her all is well. I know it is difficult to be separated from her family, but she is safe. Then cold fingers tickle over my cheek, and I startle awake to find myself clutching a bundle of fur that is indeed whining and shaking.

I quickly release Lyta, thinking I have startled her with my dream movements, but she scrambles back against me, curled up in a ball at my chest. I wrap my arms around her and whisper reassurances.

All is well.

She is safe.

An icy touch slides down my bare arm, and I twist so fast the poor puppy yelps. I apologize and stroke her and peer around the dark room. The window is ajar. That's what I felt. A breeze.

Still clutching Lyta to my chest, I slide from bed. My feet touch down on the old rugs, and I make my way to the window. I try to close it, but I can't while clutching the dog. I set Lyta down with a murmured apology, and she huddles against my bare feet.

I take hold of the window sash and—

It will not shut.

That is ridiculous. I opened it easily.

No, wait. I did not open it. Benedict had when he aired out the room, and I hadn't closed it.

The window must stick then. He'd be accustomed to it. I take the sash firmly in hand and pull hard, but it doesn't budge.

Benedict must have propped it up. I run my fingers under the opening, finding no obstruction—

The window slams down on my fingers. I let out a strangled gasp and fall back, but my fingers stay pinned. Panicked, I yank hard and they come free, but I fly back, tripping over Lyta and tumbling to the floor. The puppy scrambles onto my lap and whines frantically as she licks my face. I wrap one arm around her, ignoring the pain searing through my fingers.

As I hold Lyta close, a rap sounds behind me. The sharp crack of something striking the stonework. I scrabble around, still sitting and holding the dog. I can see the spot, but there's nothing there.

Another crack, and then another and another, the sound circling the room, as if someone is striding around it, smacking the wall with a stick. As it moves, I twist to follow, my heart hammering.

"I can't see you," I say. "I'm sorry. I cannot see you or hear you. I can hear what you do, but I cannot hear *you*."

Thwack. Thwack.

As those smacks draw closer, I struggle not to tense, not to cower and cover my head and whimper for the ghost to be gone, to leave me, please leave. Do not lash out in anger. Please do not—

Thwack. Thwack.

"I truly cannot hear you," I say as firmly as I can. "I am sorry. I know you wish to communicate with me. Somehow you realize I have a touch of the Sight. But it is only a touch. I cannot hear anything you say."

The sound stops back where it started. I look in that direction. Did the ghost hear me? They never seem to. I explain over and over—

A footstep sounds. My head jerks up. Benedict?

I push to my feet, Lyta under one arm. I take one running step toward the bed where I will . . .

Jump in and pretend to be asleep? Drowsily lift my head from the pillow when he asks what's wrong?

You heard a cry? A thumping? Why, no, I haven't the faintest idea what you could mean, Lord Sterling.

Another footstep sounds, this one clearly on *my* side of the closed door. I wheel, clutching Lyta, my arms crossed protectively over her small body.

Another step, as slow and deliberate as those blows on the wall. I throw off my terror and straighten.

"My name is Portia Hastings. If you can hear me, give a sign so we might communicate in some manner."

Another step.

"There are ways we could communicate," I continue, wincing as desperation creeps into my voice. "I could ask a question, and you could rap once for yes or twice for no."

Another step, this one so close that I must steel myself not to run away. I loathe the very impulse. I am not a woman who runs. I stand firm, even when I *ought* to flee. It is a Hastings trait, one that I have grumbled will someday get us killed.

And yet, when faced with a ghost, I want to flee, and I am shamed for it. I was raised to know that spirits exist and that we should help them whenever we can, as Miranda is doing for young Colin Booth. But my encounters are nothing like hers or my grandmother's. They are like this. Angry ghosts who wish to torment me for ignoring them, as if I am some wealthy lady who pretends not to see beggars at her town house gate.

"I cannot see you," I say. "But I know you are there, and I wish to help if I can."

My fingers still throb from that windowpane slamming on them, and a tiny, angry voice in me says that I do not wish to help at all. No more than I would wish to give money to a man who attacked me for my purse.

Still, I have treated patients who fought my ministrations, either through fever or frustration, and I never considered abandoning them. I must think of it that way.

"If you can hear me—"

Another step, this one a loud thump, right in front of me. I adjust my grip on Lyta, ignoring the pain in my fingers and schooling my expression to be kind.

"I will help you if—"

A hand strikes my cheek so hard that I reel back with a gasp. Lyta leaps from my arms, growling.

"No!" I shout.

Another blow, this one a wild strike to my shoulder that knocks me off-balance, but all I see is that Lyta is safely on the ground. She wheels, growling and snarling, and I run for her, certain she is about to be kicked. Instead, what feels like a boot strikes my calf, but I manage to keep my balance, grab the puppy and race to the door. I swear I feel fingers brush my hair, as if grabbing for it, just as I lunge into the hall.

I take one step to the right. Then I realize why I am heading that way. Benedict. I could tell myself I'm running to Benedict *and* Jude, but I know better. And if I was truly thinking of Jude, I would not do what I do next: spin and run in the other direction.

There is nothing Benedict can do to help me, and everything he can do to harm me. Not to strike out as this ghost has, leaving pain and bruises, but to inflict a deeper kind of damage. He can make me feel foolish, make me feel silly and hysterical.

Maybe I cannot stand up to a ghost, but I can stand up for myself—by handling this on my own. Get out of the house. That has always worked, and I dread the day it will not. For now, though, whenever I have encountered a ghost, I simply need to get out of its sphere. They seem trapped in a circumscribed area, and once I am past its boundary, I am safe.

As I run, though, I realize I have indeed done something foolish. The exit doors are in the other direction, past where Benedict and Jude sleep.

No, there is another way out. The ruined wing, with its cracks and broken windows.

Get to the ruined wing. Get out of the house.

I race down the hall, past the library and to that barred door. With Lyta under one arm, I throw open the bar and the door. Then I bolt through and along those few feet of hallway before the floor ends. I am about to leap over the gap when a wave of . . . something hits me. Something indescribable, as if my very marrow has turned to ice. My thoughts scatter in gibbering shrieks of terror. It is as if I stand outside my body, watching it react. My body turns on one heel and nearly falls, only to stumble and stagger back toward the door.

The *closed* door. Seeing that, enough of me returns that I am myself, but still wild with panic when I see that closed door.

There is no knob. No knob on the door. No way to get through it.

Turn around, a voice deep in my head snarls at me. *You are not trapped. Just turn around, and get out through the wing.*

But I can't. Something is behind me. Something that fills my veins with icy cold dread and fear. I need to get through this door. I need—

It opens under my fingers. Flies open, and I burst through, only to hit another obstacle, this one warm and solid. I don't care. It is still a wall, and I claw at it with my free hand, but something grabs my wrist, holding it tight.

"Portia!"

I rock back. I catch one glimpse of Benedict's face in the near dark, a sliver of it, hard and severe, and I see anger. I back up quickly, shaking him off and clutching Lyta to my chest.

"Let me pass," I whisper. "Please. Just let me pass."

"What the devil—?"

"Let me pass!"

He moves aside, and I shoulder by him and run down the hall, with Benedict on my heels, saying, "Stop, Portia. Damn you, stop and talk to me. Is there someone in the keep? I heard you cry out, and then I found you in— Stop running, damn it."

His hand lands on my shoulder, and I turn to throw it off, but his grip tightens. Panic flashes through me, and he must see it in my face, his gaze narrowing.

"Is there someone in the keep, Portia?"

"No, I just want . . ."

"You want what?" he says when I trail off.

"To leave," I blurt and then straighten, adjusting Lyta in my arms. "I must leave. Now."

"It is the middle of the night, Portia," he says slowly, his gaze uncomfortably locked on mine. "If there is no one else here, and I know that neither Jude nor I disturbed your sleep . . . Was it a nightmare?"

I want to say yes. Yes, I had a nightmare, and it has frightened me, and I no longer feel safe here and must leave.

I cannot form the lie. I only stand there, teeth clenched.

He continues, "If it was a nightmare, then perhaps a brandy? You can tell me about it if you wish, though I will not press. I know nightmares can be . . ."

He trails off. Then he goes very still, and his fingers lift to my cheek. Their touch stings where the ghost slapped me. When he speaks, his voice is a low rumble, rough with warning. "Who did this to you?"

I flinch and try to back up, but his hand tightens on my shoulder.

"There is a handprint on your cheek, Portia. I did not do it. Jude would not do it. I must ask again: *Is there someone else in—?*"

I straighten. "You are correct. I had a nightmare. I feel foolish now. I will take that brandy in the library, and you may return to bed."

"I am not returning to bed after finding my guest running through the halls in terror with a handprint rising on her cheek."

I turn toward the library. "I must have done it myself."

He catches my hand before I can escape. "Struck yourself in the face? You must think me a fool to believe such . . ." He trails off again. I turn, and he has my hand lifted, his gaze on the bruises rising on my fingers. His voice drops even more. "Who did this, Portia? If there is someone in my keep, I do not care what threats he uttered, frightening you enough to lie. You are safe, whatever he said to the contrary."

I set my jaw and say nothing.

"Damn it, woman, I am trying to protect you."

"You cannot protect me from this. It is impossible to protect anyone from something you do not believe in. What harmed me now seems to be gone, and so I will sit in the library and read until morning, when I will speak to Jude."

"Speak to my brother, because he will listen where I will not. Because what hurt you is something that I have called nonsense. A ghost."

"Yes."

"You were attacked in your sleep."

I glance over at him. "No, Benedict. I did not wake after being attacked by a human intruder and believe myself assaulted by a specter. I was awake when it happened. Fully awake. You do not believe in ghosts because you have never encountered any yourself. Therefore, they cannot exist, and anyone who says otherwise is deluded."

"I never said—"

"You dismissed the idea that your castle is haunted, when others have had experiences here."

"I . . ."

"Did you mock them to their faces? Or only behind their backs?"

Now he straightens, his face darkening. "I have never mocked anyone who claims to have encountered a spirit. I believe that they think they did."

"That they *think* they did. But they did not, clearly, because you have seen nothing."

"Ghosts are superstitious . . ." He wisely doesn't finish that and clears his throat instead. "I do not doubt their experiences, though I believe there are rational explanations."

"And the rational explanation for this?" I point at my cheek.

"I . . . I do not know."

"You have no theories? Or you are keeping them to yourself because I am distraught and do not wish to hear them? If it is the latter, then you are mistaken. I *do* wish to hear them."

He shifts his weight, looking for just the briefest moment like a schoolboy being called out for poor behavior. Then he clears his throat again. "I did consider the possibility you were attacked in your sleep. The keep is not as secure as it once was, and I feared someone may have set out to frighten you. Or to frighten me, as it is my room. However, you were awake when you were . . ."

"Struck," I say. "I was standing in the middle of the room, holding Lyta after being roused from bed by what felt like a cold touch. Not being one to jump to supernatural conclusions, I went to close the window. I could not. Believing it was merely stuck, I was fishing about to see whether you had propped it open when it slammed down on my fingers. I still thought the sash only fell by natural means. Then the rapping began, and footsteps came my way. I was slapped, pushed and kicked before I managed to escape."

"All right."

Anger boils in me. I cannot read his tone, but I feel like a small child throwing a fit over a monster under the bed while an adult, not wishing to make things worse by saying there is no monster, says simply, "all right."

I yank from his grip and march away.

"Portia." He strides into my path. "Tell me what I am doing wrong."

"You judged those who claimed to have experiences here, and now you are judging me for the same."

"I am—" He runs a hand through his hair, dark locks tumbling over a wide forehead. "I am not judging you." He pauses. "Well, not for this. For your taste in traveling companions, perhaps. For your taste in dogs, certainly."

I glare and start to turn the other way.

"That was a joke," he says. When I look back, he throws up his hands. "I am no good at any of this. Not jests. Not comforting. Not—" A wave of his hand. "Not saying what I mean. Never saying what I mean. Blast it. Perhaps . . . do you want to speak to Jude?"

"He is resting, which is imperative to his recovery. You do not need to speak to me, Benedict. Nor comfort me. Nor tease a smile from me. You are under no obligation—"

"See?" He waves his hands again. "My meaning is always either unclear or open to the worst possible interpretation." He lowers his voice to something like a mumble. "Which you seem particularly keen to latch on to."

"I am not *keen* to latch on to any interpretation, Lord Sterling. I am clarifying that I will be fine. The bounds of hospitality do not extend to comforting guests frightened by ghosts in your castle."

One brow lifts. "But if the ghost is in my castle, is it not my responsibility?" When the corner of his mouth quirks, I want to seize on that as proof of mockery. Then I remember what he just said. That I seem "particularly keen" to interpret his meaning in the worst possible light.

I sigh and shift Lyta from one arm to the other. "I am fine, Benedict. I am going to sit in the library awhile. You may do as you wish."

"What I wish is *not* to have a guest assaulted by a spirit in my home. To that end, I am staying up with you."

I open my mouth to argue, but I am suddenly exhausted.

"Do as you like," I say and head to the library.

The library fire is going, and I'm curled up in front of it with Lyta. I did not begin that way. I am hardly the "curl up on the floor" sort. But Lyta had seemed cold, possibly from the shock, and she did not wish me to leave her. So I am on the floor, where it is remarkably comfortable with a fur rug and a roaring fire.

I was promised brandy, but it is evidently not in the library, and Benedict has gone to fetch it. When he returns, he walks in and stops, his gaze on the empty chairs.

"I am down here," I say. "Lyta insisted."

He turns and gives a start. Then he stares, as if he cannot quite make me out in the gloom. I tilt my head to look up at him, but he keeps staring, and I begin to wonder whether my nightgown has shifted to reveal more than it should. No. It is properly draped and modest—I expected cool nights in the moors, so I selected a long-sleeved gown with a high neckline.

"Yes?" I say finally.

"You . . ." he begins.

"Yes?"

"Your hair," he says abruptly. "It is undone."

"I do not sleep with it bound."

"Yes, of course. I just had not noticed it before. It is . . . long."

I must bite back a smile at that. "That is what happens when it is not bound. It is difficult to put up if it is not long."

He nods, not seeming to know what to do or say next. I reach for one of the glasses of brandy, but he doesn't seem to notice. He finally draws back with what seems a forced laugh.

"I see you borrowed sleep attire from your traveling companions," he says.

I look down. "Why would you think that?"

"It is very . . ." He struggles for a word. "Bow-y."

"Bow-y?"

"It has a lot of bows. And frills. It rather reminds me of a fancy cake I saw once in France . . ." He trails off, catching my expression. "It is yours."

"It is very much mine," I say coolly.

He clears his throat. "Of course. It is pretty. I just did not expect it of you."

"You did not expect something pretty of me?" I lift my chin. "I happen to like pretty. Bright colors, lace, frills and, yes, bows. Yes, I am often forced to restrict my more 'frivolous' fashion to nightwear. I take my profession very seriously, and I cannot afford to look anything less than serious."

He nods. "I can understand that. You are very . . ." Another throat clearing. "That is to say, I can imagine it might be difficult to be taken seriously when you are so . . ."

"Bow-y?"

His lips twitch, and he relaxes. "Yes, that is what I meant."

"May I have my brandy now?"

"What? Oh, yes, of course."

He hands me a glass. When I go to sip it, Lyta rises, sniffing toward the glass, and I have to whisk it out of her reach. I laugh and look up at Benedict, my lips parting to say something, only to find him staring again. Staring in an even odder way now, his jaw slack, his expression almost . . . almost as if he has downed a glass of the brandy already and feels rather woozy.

"Benedict?" I say. "Are you well?"

"I . . ." He glances away sharply and squares his shoulders. "You need sustenance."

"Sustenance?"

"You have had a fright. You need food. There is bread in the kitchen that will soon go stale." He marches toward the door. "And fresh butter. I think there is also a bit of honey left. Yes, I am certain of it."

I am about to say I do not require bread—and butter and honey—but he is already gone. I stare at the door and then shake my head.

"Men can be odd, can they not?" I whisper to Lyta. "Most odd."

❮❯❯

BENEDICT BRINGS BREAD AND BUTTER AND, YES, HONEY, AND STUDIOUSLY avoids looking my way, and I rather begin to feel as if I am lounging in front of the fire in my drawers. That amuses me far more than it should, and I blame the hour. At night, everything can seem askew, particularly one's sense of perspective, and having Benedict carefully avoid looking at me while I'm very fully dressed makes me want to stretch out languorously and bat my lashes.

Once the bread is out, though, Lyta abandons me for Benedict, who feeds her scraps of crust. Do I catch him slathering butter and honey on those scraps? If so, I pretend not to notice. Once Lyta is over there, I have no excuse for staying on the floor . . . except that it is rather comfortable. But I begin to feel self-conscious and move into a chair, though I do still pull my feet under me and lay a blanket across my legs.

"I *do* think something happened to you tonight," Benedict says finally.

"Thank you, sir. That is most kind."

"Fine. Obviously, something happened to you, and I am struggling to . . ."

I do not need him to finish. It reminds me of the first scientist who saw tiny organisms under a microscope he had designed. He reported his findings, as a proper scientist, and was roundly mocked by his community. People in my time period still mock it. And by the twenty-first century, people will mock those who did mock, the existence of such organisms being a basic fact taught to schoolchildren.

It is difficult to accept what we have not experienced. It is even more difficult when we *cannot* experience it. At least, with such organisms, if one doubts them, one can look for oneself. Benedict cannot go in search of ghosts.

"You have never experienced anything here yourself, I take it," I say. He shakes his head.

"And Jude?"

Another shake.

"Yet others have," I say.

He hesitates.

"Talk, Benedict," I say with some exasperation. "You have no problem saying things that I may not wish to hear, so do not hold back now, when I am trying to comprehend the situation. A situation that"—I hold out my bruised fingers—"affects me."

Does he color a little at the reminder? It is hard to tell in this light. He does give a gruff, "Of course." Then he takes a gulp of brandy. "There have not been what I consider credible reports. It is nonsense beget by nonsense." He pauses. "I do not mean—"

"Say it in your own words, and I promise, this one time, that I will take no offense."

"This one time?"

"If you expect blanket absolution for saying offensive things, you have come to the wrong person. In fact, if I must be so bold—"

"No?" he murmurs under his breath. "Is *no* an option here?"

I continue, "I would warn that anyone who gives blanket absolution for saying offensive things is simply afraid of you, and you ought not to take their silence as proof that you aren't being offensive or that others are overreacting. Now, you said nonsense begets nonsense. By that, I believe you meant that stories spread. One person says it, and others echo it with even less credible experiences."

"Yes." He settles into his chair, relaxing. "My ancestors lived in the keep for generations. Jude and I were raised at Sterling Hall, but we spent countless hours here, both day and night, which we would not—as children—have confidently done if there'd been rumors of ghosts."

"There were not."

"There were not," he says emphatically. "Not beyond the sorts of tales that go with any castle. White ladies and black shucks and stories that even young children recognize as mere folktales."

"What changed?"

He sighs. "I suspect if I blame a woman, it will go poorly for me."

"Most likely, but it's too late to stop now."

"It began with a woman from the village, shortly before Jude and I moved back in. She lost her way coming home from market and took refuge in the keep. She was awakened by terrible noises, ran down the hall, through that barred door—which was not barred at the time—fell into the crack in the floor and seriously injured herself. Ever since then, people have claimed"—he waves his brandy glass—"all sorts of nonsense."

"Like being slapped by an invisible figure."

He misses my sarcasm entirely and says, "Nothing like that. Noises. Footsteps. Shadows that move. We had a devil of a time retaining a maid or even a hired hand for the stable. Eventually, Jude and I learned to do the extra work ourselves, which saved us money we did not have anyway, so we stopped looking for help."

"And your current staff? A housekeeper, yes? And her husband?"

"They came with us from Sterling Hall. They have seen nothing."

"Other members of your staff did?"

"The first stable hand swore he could not sleep for the noises, and so the maid quit with him—though she did not claim to have experienced anything herself. We tried another maid and stable hand, but they quit upon hearing the stories, despite—again—not experiencing anything themselves."

"All right," I say. "It does indeed sound as if there is a lack of credible sightings, which would be understandable. Ghosts do not appear to everyone who inhabits a place they haunt. One must have the Sight or some inkling of it."

"You have the . . . umm . . ."

"Do not look at me like that."

"Like what?" he says, a little too meekly.

"As if you are deeply disappointed that a woman who seemed relatively intelligent has spoiled the impression by speaking of things you believe to be mere nursemaid stories. No, I do not have the Sight. Not truly. My grandmother did, and my sister does, and if you do not believe it, then perhaps you can tell me how young Colin Booth died."

His brow knits at the change of subject. "Colin Booth?"

"The son of—"

"Yes, I know who he is. I have—had—known him since he was a child. He was murdered. Robbed in the moors while he was out looking for work."

"Murdered, yes. Out looking for work, no. Colin was a highwayman, murdered when he sought to turn in his compatriots for a reward."

Benedict stares at me. "Where ever did you hear such a tale?"

"From his ghost. Or my sister did. He became upset by the actions of his fellow highwaymen and agreed to turn them over to Scarlet Jack so they would see justice. He'd been promised a gold clock from his compatriot's ill-gotten gains. Scarlet Jack murdered him instead."

As I speak, I falter. Benedict's obvious skepticism has bitten deep. I'd slapped down Colin Booth's tale as if it were a winning hand of poker . . . only to hear just how ridiculous it sounded.

A tenant's boy was actually a highwayman? Who'd been promised a fancy clock? Only to be betrayed and murdered by the heroic Scarlet Jack?

"It is true," I say, a little quieter than I like. "You may not believe it, but it is true."

He says nothing.

He thinks me mad. No, worse. Madness is beyond one's control. He thinks me silly.

"Tell me about the clock," he says finally.

When I don't answer, he says, his voice firmer. "Tell me about the clock." Then a forced softening as he adds, "Please."

I relate what I can recall, both about the clock itself and its history.

"I know the piece," he says. "Carleton bragged about it."

"Mr. Carleton?"

Benedict nods abruptly. "Stolen goods, pilfered from France, as you said. Carleton bought it, and it was being brought here when the coach was beset by highwaymen. He offered a reward big enough that Jude and I considered trying to find the culprits ourselves."

He fingers the edge of his brandy glass. "There was a rumor that young Colin ran with a gang of highwaymen. We were concerned. Jude investigated, but before we had an answer, Colin was dead. Jude suggested . . . Well, he suggested his compatriots may have turned on him, making it look like a roadside robbery. I thought . . . I thought Jude was being dramatic."

It takes me longer than it should to realize Benedict is saying that he believes me. I brace for him to ask for details about where Miranda encountered Colin's ghost—I should have been more restrained with that story—but he does not.

Instead, he says, "So he was murdered by Scarlet Jack."

I hesitate. I have been intemperate, and now I must take care. I must see any potential holes in the story before he does.

"He was to meet Scarlet Jack," I say. "They had arranged a place. He heard a horse arrive, and then he was murdered. He said it was Scarlet Jack. That only means it was the man he'd arranged to meet, who had reached out to him as Scarlet Jack."

He nods. Then he stops and looks over sharply. "That is not me. Not Jude, either. Scarlet Jack, that is. You must be wondering."

"I did. Scarlet Jack is a fake highwayman, and you and your brother are, if not *fake*, then not exactly the usual sort. The rumor, as Colin relayed it, is that Scarlet Jack is a nobleman. Jude assured me it is not either of you."

"It is not," Benedict says firmly. "Scarlet Jack does operate in the moors but not near Ravensford. We keep this particular area clear ourselves. As highwaymen, we do not attack our prey within five miles of the village, and as the local landowners, we keep the local roads clear for our people and their trade. That is the one thing we can do for them." Bitterness tinges his voice. "Which is all to say that Colin's gang operates north of the village, on the route to Edinburgh, and that is also where Scarlet Jack might be found." He rubs his mouth. "Which, if he murdered the boy, means he is not the ally we hoped."

"Yes."

Benedict stretches his long legs. "You say your sister went to repay the money Colin's mother expected?"

"She did."

"Colin told her where to find the clock?"

I hesitate. The clock is in a museum . . . or it will be in a few hundred years. Miranda is taking money to Mrs. Booth, but I am not certain how to say that after suggesting I did not come from money myself.

"No," I say. "He has no idea where to find the clock, but he set a price on it, and she is attempting to pay his mother a portion of that."

"What did he think it worth?"

"Ten pounds."

Benedict shakes his head. "Then he truly had no idea of its value. It is worth a hundred times that."

"And presumably, it is still in the possession of his gang?" I say. "No, wait. I believe Colin had it when he met Scarlet Jack. That means Scarlet Jack must have it. That is what you are thinking, is it not? If you could find the clock, pay Colin's family the ten pounds and then sell it?"

He considers. Then his shoulders slump. "That would not be right, not to the Booths or the French. If it were merely stealing from Carleton?" He doesn't smile, but his eyes light. "That would be another thing."

"If you did know where to find it," I say, "I would say that repaying the Booth family double what Colin expected would be reasonable, if you also found a way for them to return here, if they wished. As for the French?" I shrug. "What do the wealthy do with such baubles except put them on a shelf to brag about? You and Jude would do better."

"Hmm." He considers and then rolls his shoulders. "That would suppose I had some inkling where to find the clock, which I do not. I do not even know whether Scarlet Jack took down that particular gang. It seems Colin died before he betrayed them, but that does not mean Scarlet Jack did not already have that information. I will see what his activity was, around the time—whether any highwaymen were turned over for justice—but with the ball in two days . . ."

He goes quiet, retreating into his thoughts. He means that it is too late for anything to save him from an unwanted marriage. It does strike me as odd to see a man in such a position. I always think of women being forced to consider marriage for reasons beyond personal choice. But men can find themselves in the same position, and probably do, more often than I would have realized.

I had been engaged to a man who did not love me. A man who had settled for me, much as I had settled for him. Compared to Benedict's situation, my reason had been so trivial that it now astounds me. I had been prepared to commit myself to Reginald because he was in need of a wife. I felt I could fill that role and being married would make my life easier.

Oh, it hadn't been as calculated as it sounds. I did not agree to his proposal thinking, *Well, a husband* would *be convenient.* I simply did what countless young men and women do. Find someone to share their life with because that is what we are supposed to do. Like leaving home and finding an occupation.

I could have been content with Reginald. We were compatible, and we enjoyed each other's company, and he was a decent person. It is a very low threshold to pass, and yet Benedict can scarcely *hope* to pass it with his future spouse. Perhaps that shouldn't be important—the majority of couples in my time do *not* pass that low threshold. Yet the thought of that for his future fills me with a sadness I do not dare analyze except to say that he has struck me as a man who deserves better.

I sip my brandy, brushing back my hair when it falls over my shoulder. I can feel his eyes on me, and when I glance over, he straightens. Then he says, "And that clock has nothing to do with the current situation, which is that you were attacked in my home. You said your sister can communicate with ghosts and discover what they want."

I nod, still half-lost in my odd melancholy.

He continues, "I would not ask you to communicate with any spirit that has assaulted you, but if it said something, if this is a matter that could be rectified . . ."

I almost smile at that. He has moved past his disbelief by reframing this as something he understands. A problem to be solved. Ah, so ghosts do exist? And I have one, which has attacked my guest? How can I get rid of it, to ensure no other guests suffer her fate? A matter of hospitality, as if ridding his castle of rats.

"I cannot communicate with them," I say. "Which I think is the problem. Somehow, they realize I have an inkling of the Sight, and they become enraged with me for ignoring them. It must be like finding themselves lost at sea and spotting another boat, only to have it ignore their distress calls."

"Hmph. That is a generous assessment. Attacking in frustration would be understandable as a last resort. Yet here it seems to have been the opening volley." He shifts his glass to his other hand. "What do you normally do in such situations?"

I shrug and stare into the fire. "Nothing. They only began in the past few years, and they are rare, so I have not yet devised a method for dealing with them other than to vacate the premises."

He stiffens. "You *do* mean to leave then. Tonight."

I shake my head. "Not tonight. The haunting has ended, and I am not returning to bed. Jude ought to be recovered tomorrow, and I will not need to worry about tomorrow night."

His hand tightens on his glass. "Because you will be gone." He straightens. "But ought we not to do something about the ghost? Could your sister speak to it? While it may not bother Jude or me, others have complained, and the woman who was frightened by it *was* injured."

"I . . . I am not certain Miranda could help. I could certainly ask, but I would need to catch up with her in York, if she is still there. And I presume you will not be living in the keep after you are wed."

"I do not yet know my plans," he says, a little too abruptly. "I should like this problem cleared either way. We will send word to your sister in the morning. She can attempt to communicate with this specter and accompany you home afterward. In the meantime, I will ensure you are not bothered again."

I have no idea how he is supposed to do any of that. Get a message to Miranda in York when we only know that she *may* have followed the Booth family? Who *may* have gone to an unnamed sister there? And how exactly would he ensure I am not "bothered" by an entity he can neither hear nor see?

"It is settled," he says, though I haven't spoken a word. "Now, if you wish to sleep, you may return to your room, and I will stand vigil."

At my bedside? I don't say that. It's a moot point, as I said I have no intention of returning to bed. It is nearly dawn. As for tomorrow night, I suspect his aunt is about to tell him to get me—mistress or not—far away before the ball.

"I am not returning to bed," I say. "You should, though. You—"

"No," he says. "I will stand vigil wherever you choose to be until morning."

"You do not need—"

"I will."

❧ 14 ❧

I do not recall falling asleep in the library, but I obviously do, because the next thing I know, I am waking with a puppy curled on my lap and a book dangling from my hand. I quietly lay the book on the table. At a noise beside me, I give a start, the ghostly encounter from last night flashing back, only to remember I am not alone.

"Lord Sterling," I say with a yawn.

"Mmm, no. Not unless you have murdered my dear brother for some imminently murderable transgression. And, to be quite honest, if you need any reason *not* to kill him, I really would rather not inherit his title, given the onerous responsibilities."

I smile over at Jude, sitting where Benedict had been. "I will try to remember that. But you ought to be in bed."

"I could say the same for you. I heard about your night."

"Hmm."

"So we really do have— Apologies. That was rude of me. Your cheek looks terribly sore. Does it hurt?"

I shake my head.

"And your fingers?" He shifts in his chair to lean my way and winces. "Those are even nastier bruises. How do they feel?"

"Stiff." I yawn again as I flex them. "I will not be playing piano anytime soon, which is best for all, really."

He smiles. "We have Benedict for that."

My brows rise. "Your brother plays?"

"Enviably well. He will refuse if you ask, though, so you must trick him into it. I would suggest a dare. He is ridiculously susceptible to dares." Jude looks over again. "Now that I have asked after your health, I can return to my earlier question. We have a ghost?"

"So it seems."

"That is most"—he composes his features into a mask of solemnity—"alarming."

"Which is not at all what you wished to say. But yes, you have an actual haunted castle."

"Temporarily," he says. "Benedict has already gone into the village to send a message to your sister. Well, first, that messenger also needs to find your sister, but my brother has gone from sneering at any mention of ghosts to barreling out of here at dawn in hopes of exorcising this one. It is suddenly *most* urgent to deal with this thing he did not believe in mere hours ago."

"He is concerned it will hurt others, and as host, he would feel responsible."

"Ah, is that the reason for the urgency? Such a congenial host, my brother. Always thinking ahead, to the scores of guests we have . . . Wait, no. In the two years that we have been here, we have entertained exactly one guest. Hmm. And, I suppose, that since he is trying to bring your sister here, you no longer need to leave? You must wait for her? How convenient."

I barely hear him. I'm thinking how Benedict's plan is for naught. I will be on the first coach out after their aunt gets wind of this arrangement.

I stretch and rub my eyes. "I need to check your bandages and make breakfast. Oh, the dog. I must take her out to do her business first."

"Benedict did that before he left. He also . . ." He waves to the table, where a cold breakfast of bread, cheese and boiled eggs waits, along with a pot of tea. "Such a good host."

I catch a whiff of the tea, and my stomach rumbles.

"I should tend to your dressings first," I say.

"And let the tea go cold? Absolutely not. Eat. Drink. Then you can fix me up."

☙❦☙

I HAVE CHECKED JUDE'S WOUND, WHICH IS HEALING EXCEPTIONALLY WELL. Well enough that there will be no excuse for me to stay after their aunt sends me on my way. I won't think of that. For now, it is only important that he is recovering, and I must admit that he is recovering so well that I cannot insist he return to bed. I can, however, insist he not exert himself.

Within the hour, I can see that my restrictions will be a problem. When I declare I am taking Lyta for a walk, Jude insists on accompanying me. We negotiate to letting him sit on the steps and watch me perambulate about the gardens with the puppy.

I say "perambulate about the gardens" ironically. There are no gardens. No lawn either. The front of the castle is a parched expanse of dirt, the ground so trodden by centuries of horse hooves that I suspect even without a drought, there is only a persistent bramble or two.

The problem is that Lyta needs more than perambulating. She has been a sweet lap puppy all night, and now she is a bundle of energy, running at me and barking and running away.

"She misses her brothers and sisters," I say as I walk toward Jude with Lyta nipping at my heels. "She has no one to chase her."

"I could—"

"Absolutely not." I peer down at the puppy, zipping back and forth at me. There is really only one thing to be done, the decision made far easier by the fact I am not in my own time or place. I can be whoever I wish here—it will not follow me home.

I hike up my long skirts, and I run. Lyta lets out a yelp of pure joy and chases. Then I whip about and chase her. I am running through the courtyard, making an absolute fool of myself, when Benedict stalks around the outer wall, his face stormy.

I catch only a glimpse of him as I'm running. Before I can halt, he pulls himself up short and stares at me.

"She needed a run," I say, panting and laughing as I scoop up the wriggling puppy.

He just keeps staring, and I can no longer see his expression as it is hidden by shadows from the wall.

I quickly tug at my bodice and lift a hand to my hair, only to realize it is a Medusa's mess, the exertion having given every lock permission to escape.

"I look a fright, I know," I say. Then I realize the real problem. "And I ought not to be out here at all, in case someone comes around. They'll be wondering whether the earl has a madwoman for a mistress."

"No one will come," he says shortly as he strides from the shadows. "Do not concern yourself with that. I certainly am not. I am far too busy concerning myself with this." He waves a piece of paper toward the front doors.

"Do you see this?" he calls to Jude as he stalks in that direction.

"Hard *not* to with you waving it about," Jude says. "A letter, I presume?"

"A command. She commands *me*." Benedict stands near Jude, still waving it. "Can you believe this?"

"First, I would need to read it, which requires you to stop signaling angels with it."

"Angels?" Benedict snorts. "She-devils, more like."

"From Aunt Flora?" Jude says mildly.

"She knows about Portia."

Jude winces. "We should have foreseen that. I presume she knows not only that we have a woman staying here but that she is supposedly your mistress?"

"Of course. Now she is demanding an audience."

"Well, you were supposed to join her for lunch, so it's not that—"

"She wants—no, insists—that Portia come along." He waves the letter again, paper snapping. "She commands our *guest* to appear before her."

"I will send my regrets," I say. "I must tend to Jude. I presume you will explain the true situation, that Jude was injured, and I am merely nursing him. Or do you fear she will not believe it?"

Jude seems to be fighting to contain a laugh. "Oh, she will believe it. Ben could tell her you were the victim of a shipwreck, somehow washed up on his doorstep, a hundred miles from the sea, and she'd find that more plausible than Ben having a mistress."

Benedict scowls at him.

Jude reaches over to clap his brother on the shoulder. "Yes, yes, you have been far too busy for any of that. Far too busy for anything." He looks at me. "That said, we should all go. The three of us."

"What?" Benedict says. "Absolutely not. You are injured—"

"Aunt Flora will send her coach."

"I will not allow Portia to be summoned as if she is a tenant farmer's wife."

"Portia? Do you object to going?"

"I am not afraid to face her," I say. "Nor am I offended by what I presume to be simply a forcefully worded request. However, it is up to you both."

"No," Benedict says. "I will not cede to her whims and fancies on this."

"It is neither whim nor fancy," Jude says, in that same mild way. "She is the sponsor of your bridal-hunt ball. If you are doing anything that might prove an embarrassment, that *is* a concern of hers. Now, if I know Aunt Flora, that coach will arrive within the hour. We should all prepare."

"For battle?" Benedict grumbles.

Jude sighs. "For lunch, dear brother. For lunch."

⚜

JUDE IS RIGHT. I SCARCELY HAVE TIME TO READY MYSELF BEFORE THE COACH arrives. Of course, "readying myself" also means making a travel dress presentable for a formal luncheon. As I do not have time to alter the dress, I must outshine the drab garb on my own. I cannot recall when I have last made such an effort with my appearance. Most times, it is the opposite. The last time I primped and preened . . .

Oh.

It was the night Reginald returned from his trip abroad. Even before he reached land, he'd sent a message to meet him most urgently for dinner upon his arrival. I thought he'd missed me, and I remember how that made me feel, tingling with a hope for something I hadn't realized I even lacked. Reginald could not wait to see me. Tucked deep under my very sensible self, I'd entertained a vision of him whisking me into a dark corner and kissing me with the sort of passion my sister wrote about in her risqué stories.

Instead, he'd introduced me to his new bride.

He hadn't even told me in private. He'd had her there, pretending I was a dear friend instead of the woman he was supposed to marry. Did he expect me to sit through that dinner smiling and acting as if nothing were wrong? Of course he did. That was the Portia he knew. She'd understand. She might even be happy for him. She certainly wouldn't throw the celebratory wine in his face and storm out like the jilted fiancée she was.

Ever since that night, I have been ashamed of my reaction. I don't know what came over me. Now, though, as I hurry down the halls of Ravensford Keep, I look back, and I'm oddly satisfied. I remember Reginald's expression, and I'm . . . dare I say, pleased?

"Benedict?" I say as I step outside, where he stands with his back to me, no doubt scowling at the coach.

He turns and . . . Am I hoping for a reaction? I have, after all, made a concerted effort to look my best, and when I make that effort, I am accustomed to a reaction. Even Reginald—on seeing me that night—had faltered, and there is a tiny shred of vanity in me that hopes he felt a whisper of regret.

Last night, Benedict had stared at me in front of the fireplace, and again this morning running with the puppy. I did not interpret either as a stare of admiration. They could not be—I'd been a mess. If anything, it would have been a stare of mild horror. It hadn't *looked* like horror. Quite the opposite, in fact, if I am being honest. But now that I have scrubbed and brushed and primped, do I expect some positive reaction? Yes, I do.

And I get nothing. No, that is not entirely correct. His gaze sweeps over me, and his lips tighten, just a little. Is that disapproval?

I'm still walking toward him, looking down at my dress for any sign of an obvious problem. The travel dress was chosen for its simplicity, unlikely to stand out in another era. My hair is done more elaborately than usual, in a style I'd seen in Whitby. Again, we are not yet in the day of powdered wigs—at least not in Yorkshire—and we are past the time of mile-high baroque styles. The word for the day is "curls." Even more curls than I already possess, which required a makeshift heated rod and ingenuity to achieve without proper tools and fixatives.

I had a necklace in my things, and I'm wearing that. My cheek is bruised, but I'd found a beet in the kitchen and applied some juice to the opposite cheek for color, in hopes of mitigating the damage. I'd also put some on my lips. After all, makeup is acceptable in this time.

There is nothing wrong or inappropriate in my attire.

So why the scowl?

At footsteps behind me, I turn to see Jude hurrying along the hall. He has changed into more formal attire, like Benedict, both of them dressed in linen shirts, breeches, leather shoes, long collarless coats and tricorn hats.

Jude sees me, takes my hands and holds me at arm's length, as if to get a better look.

"How did you take less time than me to prepare and you look like that?" he asks. "It is not fair."

"You were stabbed," I say. "You should not be doing anything quickly." I tug my dress. "Do I look all right?" My eyes cut toward Benedict. "I caught a distinct whiff of disapproval. I am not accustomed to the local fashion, so perhaps I am dressed inappropriately."

"Not at all," Jude says. "You look like a proper London lady. Even Aunt Flora will be impressed."

"The dress is too plain," Benedict says.

Jude looks askance at his brother. "I beg your pardon? Was that sartorial criticism from a man who can barely tell silk from muslin?"

"She looks like a peacock in wren's feathers."

Jude's brows rise further. Then he shakes his head sharply and looks at me. "Pay him no mind. He is in a very odd mood."

I turn to face Benedict. "You do not like my gown?"

"Do you?" His gaze meets mine, and the note of challenge there brings a flush of heat to my cheeks.

"Shall I take it off?" I snap.

There's a moment of utter silence. Then Jude bursts into a whoop of laughter, and I realize what I have said. I open my mouth to stammer that was not what I meant, and then . . . I don't. Why bother? The damage is done. Best to just embrace it.

"I doubt your aunt would appreciate me showing up in my underthings," I say. "So the dress stays."

I march toward the coach.

"I was only saying that you should wear what you like," Benedict murmurs as I pass. "I know that is not what you like."

He could say these words in a defensive grumble. That is certainly his style. Instead, they are whispered, an almost gentle private exchange that has me glancing over sharply, expecting to see defensiveness or reproach in his expression. When I don't, I am not certain what to do with that.

"I have two traveling dresses," I say more sharply than I intend. "What else do you expect me to do? Run and find a seamstress before lunch?"

His lips quirk in a semi-smile. "You could wear your nightgown."

It is a wildly inappropriate thing to say, not unlike me offering to take off my dress, but like my comment, I know he does not mean to be inappropriate. I am not certain what to make of this entire line of conversation. He is objecting to my dress because it is not what *I* like? That is akin to chastising a hostess for serving food she does not personally enjoy. It still insults the meal, and he has still insulted my choice of attire.

I remember what he said yesterday.

I am no good at any of this. Not jests. Not comforting. Not saying what I mean. Never saying what I mean.

"My nightgown?" I sniff. "Hardly. It is entirely the wrong color for lunch."

I turn on my heel, and as I walk away, I swear I hear the softest laugh behind me.

15

Lady Flora's house is a grand Elizabethan manor of brown stone, with wings off to both sides. Leaded-glass windows stand open to the moor breeze, and I cannot count the number of those windows, nor imagine how long it takes a servant to open and shut them up again.

A brook dotted with small bridges snakes along the drive. And while the flower gardens have been left covered because of the drought, we pass rows of plum, quince and apple trees, and enough benches and shaded pergolas to host a garden party of two hundred. The view beyond is boundless moors and bright blue skies.

As we head up that endless drive, I decide I do not like Aunt Flora. I know it is wrong to form an opinion without having met a person, and I feel a twinge of guilt, but the fact that it is only a twinge suggests I truly have undergone a metamorphosis in this place. It is as if the wildness of the moor has unfettered me. Or, as I have already speculated, it is the freedom of knowing nothing I do or say here will permanently stain me.

Miranda always says I care too much what others think of me, and I have bristled at that. If I cared so much, I would hardly be sneaking into medical classes, would I? And yet it says much that I sneak in rather than fight against the rules that keep me out. As does the fact that I nearly married a man because marriage was the proper thing to do.

Our world is quick to indelibly brand women—and some men—for perceived offenses against the established order. The shame of my failed engagement has stained me more than I care to admit. I pretend I do not hear the whispers.

She is so pretty and clever and well mannered. What could she have done to frighten him off? Perhaps she is too pretty and she flirted with other men. Perhaps she is too clever—it is not necessarily a desirable trait in a woman. And while she seems well mannered, she is a little . . . Well, odd, isn't she? All the Hastings girls are.

Since that failed engagement, I am even more aware of my every word and action, and Miranda would say I'd been too aware of them already. Too restrained. Too *con*strained.

Here, my actions cannot follow me home, and that is freeing in a way I find disconcerting, as if it reveals a truth I would rather not admit: that when I tell my sisters I am fine with my quiet life, I am lying. Lying horribly, and lying to no one as much as myself.

So when I say I decide I do not like Aunt Flora, I am not racked with guilt for such unfounded condemnation. It is not unfounded. The cause of it is here, all around me, as we head up that drive, surrounded by such beauty and obvious wealth.

Her nephews live in the remains of a ruined castle, chopping wood and shoveling horse dung from their barn. They do not even own a coach she deems worthy enough to travel up her drive.

Benedict and Jude did not lose their family fortune. They inherited their financial woes, and their efforts to resolve them were thwarted by Mother Nature herself. They live in dire circumstances while robbing their father's traitorous friends and using the proceeds to keep their tenants alive during the drought.

And what does their aunt do? Suggests Benedict marry a stranger for her money, and offers to arrange and host the ball herself. Such magnanimity! Truly, I am in awe of her kindness.

I may also be discovering a heretofore unseen capacity for sarcasm.

The driver stops at the front steps. Benedict is first out of the coach, swinging open the door and leaping out before it even stops and then striding off. Jude drops his head dramatically and then puts out his hand to help me from the coach, murmuring, "He really is hopeless."

Jude escorts me up the steps. A butler holds open the door. There is no sign of Benedict until his voice echoes down the hallway.

"That was unacceptable. You do not summon my guests to lunch."

"Good to see you, Ben," a woman's voice says. "You look . . . yourself."

We step inside as a figure walks from a distant room. She is tiny enough that I pause, thinking perhaps this is a young relative or visitor. Then she approaches, and I see my mistake. She is even older than I would expect for the aunt of two men under forty. Her gait is steady, her head held high, but she must be well past seventy, with pure-white hair and a lined face.

"Aunt Flora," Jude says. "May I introduce—"

"No," Benedict says darkly, stalking out after his aunt. "She does not deserve an introduction."

"Perhaps not," Flora says, "but it will be most awkward if I do not have one. What ever would I call her? Excuse me, Ben's mistress, would you pass the salt, please?"

"She is not my mistress," he says.

"Obviously. Look at her."

I stiffen, even more conscious of my dress now that Benedict has commented on it.

"What does that mean?" he says, in a growl.

"She is"—Aunt Flora waves at me—"exquisite, even in that hideous gown. And you introduced her as your mistress? I'm surprised Carleton didn't laugh all the way back to Sterling Hall."

There is a teasing note to her voice, one that makes it clear she is needling Benedict rather than actually insulting him, and it almost makes me sad that I have already decided I don't like her. Almost.

She continues, "However, the fact that he seems to have accepted the fiction will be useful. Most useful."

"What does *that* mean?" Benedict says as his aunt heads into the nearest room.

"Do you really want to know?" Jude murmurs.

Benedict stalks off after his aunt, leaving Jude to sigh and offer his arm to me in escort. We enter a breathtakingly beautiful solarium filled with the lush greenery and flowers that were lacking outside. On a perch, two lovebirds sit uncaged.

Aunt Flora takes a chair by the perch. Jude motions for me to sit on a settee, and then he joins me. Benedict stays standing.

"Would you like us to explain who she actually is?" Jude says.

"A name would be nice, so that I have something to call her. Otherwise, an explanation is only required to satisfy my curiosity. I do not fear that Benedict has taken her captive and locked her in the tower. At least, not while *you* are in residence, Jude."

Jude's lips twitch as he looks at me. "The ruined wing, isn't it? Not the tower." He looks at his aunt. "No, Ben wouldn't dare take this one captive, or he'd more likely end up there himself."

"My name is Portia, ma'am," I say. "I would prefer not to give a surname, but only because it might seem significant when it is not. I am a doctor's daughter from London. I am trained in the medical arts myself. That is how I met Lord and Mr. Sterling. Mr. Sterling had suffered an injury."

"I was stabbed," Jude says.

I expect Aunt Flora to blink in shock—or laugh at the presumed joke. But she only shakes her head. "What were you up to now?"

"Robbing Ward's coach. His son had a knife and decided to use it."

Jude catches my expression, which feels rather slack jawed. "Aunt Flora knows all about our activities. She's the one who discovers when one of our father's enemies is coming through and which route they will take. She is much better connected than we are."

"And much less likely to be questioned if I take an interest," Aunt Flora says. "I am an elderly spinster living along the moors. Starved for news of any sort, poor thing." She pours a drink from a pitcher. "Lemonade?"

Jude leans forward to take the glass and passes it to me. I sip, mostly to cover my confusion.

"So you told Carleton that Miss Portia is your mistress," Aunt Flora says. "That made more sense than saying she was nursing your injured brother?"

"I was caught off guard," Benedict says.

"I see," she murmurs.

"I would agree that the truth might have been unwise," I say. "It would not do for anyone to discover Mr. Sterling had been stabbed . . .

when the story of Georgie Ward stabbing a highwayman may get around."

"Fair point," she says. "As for the fiction, I would suggest we make it a reality."

Jude chokes on a mouthful of lemonade.

"Not like that," Aunt Flora says, pinning him with a look. "I mean that there is some advantage, Ben, to allowing people to think Miss Portia is your mistress."

"I hope that is a joke," Benedict says.

"It is not."

"I do not believe I take your meaning," I say. "Lord Sterling is in need of a bride. Candidates for that position will already be arriving, with the ball tomorrow night. How will they react on hearing that their potential bridegroom is entertaining a mistress at home?"

"Favorably, I suspect," she says.

I can only stare, certain this is indeed a jest.

She continues, "As a potential bridegroom, my nephew lacks two things."

"Only two?" Benedict murmurs.

"I am being kind to you today, Ben." She looks at me. "The first is the most obvious."

"Money," I say.

She nods. "But his bridal candidates are supplying that, so they will not be concerned. The other deficiency is more troubling, and it is the one most likely to frighten off the brides themselves, which is a problem when Ben insists that the brides must willingly accept him."

"Which is only proper," Jude murmurs.

"I agree," Aunt Flora says. "It is absolutely correct. However, it raises the issue of the second deficiency."

"Which is."

"Benedict himself."

"Excuse me?" Benedict says, straightening. "If you are implying—"

"I am implying nothing. I am being bluntly honest, which is a trait we share. You are attractive enough, and you are almost obscenely healthy. Those are positive traits. The problem comes when you open your mouth." When Benedict does just that, she waves him to silence. "No, I misspoke. The problem begins even before that. It comes the moment you fix the poor girls with that scowl, which you will, because it is your natural demeanor."

"Ah," Jude says. "Now I understand."

"Then please educate me," Benedict says. "Because all I understand is that I am being insulted."

"You are not," Aunt Flora says. "I speak in unadorned facts. You come with a very prestigious title. As I said, you are attractive enough and certainly healthy. You are also intelligent, fair minded and good hearted, yet the latter traits will go undetected by your potential brides, who will see only the belligerent scowl and rough manners. Miss Portia will fix that."

"Lord Sterling is not the only one who doesn't understand," I say. "How do I fix any of that?"

"By playing the role of his mistress."

I shake my head. "I still do not understand."

Jude twists toward me. "Aunt Flora means that you are a beautiful widow, who has come all this way to be with Benedict. You are an independent and intelligent woman of grace and manners, who chooses this" —he waves at Benedict—"as your lover."

"*This?*" Benedict says. "I am now *this*?"

"I could be more descriptive, but unlike Aunt Flora, I have to go home with you later. The point is that Portia will reflect well on you. Exceptionally well. You have no money, so she cannot be with you for that. You have a title, but you are marrying another—and she knows it—so she cannot be with you in hopes of winning that. Ergo, you must have hidden charms. Many hidden charms."

"But is it not an insult to the young ladies?" I say. "Their future bridegroom openly consorting with his mistress."

"No," Aunt Flora says firmly. "We have been clear to the parents that the marriage is a business arrangement. Ben does not want the bridal candidates to be under any illusion, either. If they are hoping for a love match, this will set things straight."

Jude nods. "Aunt Flora is right. We should maintain—and even bolster—the fiction that Portia is your mistress."

"That is—" Benedict says. "No. Absolutely not."

"All right then," Jude says. "Well, as I am quite recovered, and Portia has other matters to attend to, I suppose it is time for her to leave—"

"You are not recovered."

"Oh, but I am." Jude makes a show of stretching his arms. "I am very well, thanks to Portia's excellent ministrations. There is a coach leaving Ravensford this afternoon—"

"She would arrive in York at too late an hour. Also, I have sent word to her sister. What if her sister arrives while Portia is heading in the other direction?"

Jude glances at Aunt Flora, whose brows rise as she looks from me to Benedict.

"Is anyone going to ask me what I think?" I say. "As the one whose immediate future is being discussed?"

"It makes no sense for you to leave." Benedict walks over, leaning so that his aunt cannot hear. "I will ensure you are not bothered by the spirit tonight." He straightens, voice returning to normal. "However, I would never ask you to risk your reputation more than you already have."

"My reputation is not a concern," I say. "There is absolutely no chance that anyone coming to the ball will recognize me. I do not move in their circles, nor would they be among my patients. I presume that this arrangement would involve me being seen in Lord Sterling's company while perhaps meeting a few people who can give a good account of me. I can manage that."

Benedict paces along the windows and runs his hands through his hair. "It is a lot to ask," he says, without turning.

I smile. "Risking my reputation? Or being seen in your company while pretending to find you good natured and charming?"

Jude snorts. "No one will ask you to go that far."

"If you must wed," I say to Benedict, "then it should be to the most suitable candidate, which means you cannot afford to frighten off the best of the young ladies, leaving you to choose between the most desperate. You are correct that I should wait an extra day in case Miranda is already on the way. You are also correct that the afternoon coach travels too late. I wouldn't want to be set upon by highwaymen. Once this week was quite enough."

"I can imagine," Aunt Flora says dryly. "Ben makes far too convincing a highwayman. Miss Portia will stay until tomorrow, whereupon I will have my personal coachman drive her to York or wherever else she needs to be."

"Yes," Benedict says before I can answer. "That seems wise." He looks toward the door. "Now, is that lunch I smell?"

"It is," Aunt Flora says as she rises.

Jude stands and takes my arm to escort me. I have not yet agreed to stay, but apparently, I am.

16

Lunch is exquisite. A watercress bisque. Lamb pie with a perfect crust. Cheese, bread, nuts, roasted vegetables . . . The men dig in heartily, after days of their simple fare at home. I do the same, realizing I am hungrier than I thought.

As we dine, Jude and Flora plot the "false mistress" subterfuge, while both parties to that actual subterfuge—Benedict and I—eat in silence, apparently not needed in the conversation.

I keep sneaking glances at Benedict, who looks exceedingly uncomfortable. I want to take him aside and tell him I really am fine with this. I could not agree to a true deception, but this feels more akin to a white lie, a falsehood with a positive intention.

Benedict will not be a poor husband. Yes, that may seem like damning with faint praise, but in light of my post-broken-engagement reflection, I do not think one can be a good *husband* without love. One can only be a good *partner*, and I have not known Benedict long enough to gauge that. From what I have seen, though, once past that prickly exterior, he is a good man, and he is considerate of others, and so he should be a better husband than most.

If this ruse is designed to convey that, then it is not a lie. And if it is also designed to remind a young woman that Benedict is looking for a partnership, not romantic love, then it is also beneficial—parents might be willing to marry off a daughter for a title, but that young woman *must* understand the true nature of the transaction.

His true worry, though, seems to be for my reputation. How do I assure him that I am untouchable without telling the truth? I cannot tell the truth, either. I am still not completely convinced he believes me about the ghost, and I dare not add time travel to my story.

He might also be concerned about my motives. Why would I do this for him? Why would I care whether he makes a good match? Why would I care whether his lands are saved, his tenants remaining under his kinder authority? I have known him two days, and I know his tenants not at all. How do I say, "I barely know you, but I think you deserve better than you are likely to get"?

If he needs to talk about it, we will. Otherwise, I only want him to accept that I am willing to do this. It is the right thing to do . . . even if it benefits me not at all.

"Do you have another gown?" Lady Flora asks, and it takes a moment to realize she is addressing me.

"Yes, but if you are hoping for something more fashionable, this is the better of the two. They are traveling dresses. I had no need of more."

"She's fine," Benedict says with a warning rumble in his voice.

I glance over sharply. Was he not complaining about my gown mere hours ago?

"She *is* fine," Lady Flora says as she spears a pickled beet slice on her fork. "But it would be better if she shone a little more brightly, particularly as others may be seeing her at a remove. A more flattering dress would properly convey the message that your mistress is a fashionable widow with taste—which will reflect well on you—and also with means, allowing her to choose a lover for his own qualities rather than his pocketbook."

"She's staying in the one semi-habitable section of my crumbling keep," he mutters. "Clearly, she did not choose me for my money. Which any prospective bride would also know."

Lady Flora flutters her fingers. "We are fashioning a story, and we cannot rely on our audience being clever enough to read between the lines."

I sink a little at that. It is a reminder of what Benedict can expect. A girl with money and nothing more.

Why does that bother me so?

For the same reason I am doing this.

I hate the thought of him marrying some girl too dull to carry on a conversation. Or a girl who shrieks at the thought of a dog on the bed. Or a girl who would recoil in horror if asked to fix her own meals.

Perhaps he'll get lucky, and she'll be pleasant and intelligent and kind, and he will grow to love her.

That would be better, wouldn't it?

Of course it would. So why does my stomach twist at the thought?

"As luck would have it," Lady Flora says, "my modiste is coming by this afternoon with my gown for the ball. I happen to know she is traveling with other dresses that could be quickly altered to fit, should one of the young ladies find herself in sudden need. There will be something to suit Miss Portia."

"Thank you," I say. "But I am not certain I have enough to pay—"

"My treat," she says with a smile.

I try to smile back, but something in me sours at the reminder. She sees nothing wrong with paying for a stranger's dress or hosting a lavish ball, and yet she cannot spare a few hundred pounds to get her nephews through this drought?

"I believe Miss Portia and I will take our dessert in the drawing room." She sets down her napkin and rises. "Come along, dear."

Benedict nearly leaps to his feet. "If you are taking your dessert elsewhere, so shall I. Jude and I hardly need time for men's conversation."

"No, but *we* need time for women's. Dress details." She lowers her voice. "And since you are not actually her lover, you should not be party to some of them."

Benedict still hesitates. I have no idea what details of dresses are too intimate for a man to hear, which means I suspect she wishes to speak to me in private for another reason. I want to know what she has to say. I only hope I can manage to keep from saying anything myself.

꧁꧂

WE ARE IN THE DRAWING ROOM WITH TEA AND CAKE. IT'S COZY, LADY Flora having had the fire started before we entered.

"That is why I prefer the solarium," she said. "At my age, I need the heat, even when the weather is pleasant."

"The moors are lovely," I say, "but they can be chilly even in summer." I stir my tea. "Do you go down to London at all?"

"A bit in the winter," she says. "But while the warmer weather is more appealing to my old bones, I am terribly fond of the moors. And terribly fond of my nephews."

"Ah."

I keep stirring, afraid to lift my gaze for fear she'll see reproval in it.

"That surprises you, I'm sure," she says. "After all, if I truly cared for them, I would do more than host a ball to marry my nephew to the highest bidder, like a stallion auctioned off for stud."

I stop stirring.

She gives a low laugh. "That was rather crude, wasn't it? It is the truth, though. That is what these girls' parents will see. A strong stallion with a fine bloodline to pass to their grandchildren."

My cheeks flame, and I quickly raise the teacup to cover the blush. That was a part of Benedict's arrangement I had not considered.

Had not considered? Or had understood and avoided considering? This is not purely a business arrangement. Benedict will be expected to sire children. That is what the girl and her parents are paying for. He is strong and healthy and comes with a lineage his children will share.

He truly is being sold like a stud at auction.

"If there were another way, I would leap at it," she says, her voice seeming to crackle around the edges. "It was his idea. Marrying, that is. The ball is my idea, in the vain hope that a wider selection might mean he has some faint chance of . . ." She clears her throat and takes a sip of her tea.

"There is nothing else to be done," she says firmly, as if to convince herself. "I know you must think me a monster, living like this while they suffer. I presume they have not explained the situation?"

I glance up.

"Of course not," she says with a sigh. "Jude is unwell, and Ben would not think to do so, even if it does leave me looking like a gargoyle." She sets her cup down. "As I prefer not to be cast in that stony visage, I will explain. I am their mother's older sister, as you may have heard. You may also have heard that Margaret was an invalid. My parents did not wish her to marry. They absolutely did not wish her to marry Lord Sterling. They did not trust him to care for her properly, and they feared children would weaken her. Yet it was a love match. My sister might have been physically weak, but she had the willpower of a Titan. When they threatened to disown her, she eloped. They gave her one last chance—do not have children. Otherwise, you shall never see a dime."

"And she had them."

"She did, and if they affected her health, it was only positive, bringing her great joy, as did her husband. She made her choices, and she never regretted them. My parents could not see that. They willed everything to me. This house and the property and the money. Every shilling either in their coffers or generated by this estate. If I give one of those shillings to Margaret's husband or sons, it all goes to my cousin, an odious man with an equally odious family. I have tried every way around it, from giving the boys expensive gifts to sending them money through a third party. My cousin finds out—I am convinced he has spies in the area—and the boys must repay every shilling, and I am given a very stern warning that if I try it again, I am in breach of the terms of my parents' will, and my poor nephews will need to make room for me in their keep."

I do not know what to say. It is horrific to imagine a parent doing such a thing to their child. Even worse, I believe, to do it to the grand-children who played no role in the drama except to be born. I cannot say that. They are still Lady Flora's parents.

"I am sorry if I seemed to be judging you," I murmur. "You ought not to have needed to explain a private family matter."

"Oh, in this case, I explain it to whoever needs it explained, lest I am cast in that role of stone-hearted gargoyle, feasting in her fine mansion while her nephews scrape mold off old bread." She glances over. "Tell me it is not that bad."

I manage a smile. "It is not."

She exhales dramatically. "Good. Still, it is an ugly situation, with only one possible solution." Her lips twitch. "My parents locked the estate tight, but they did not think far enough ahead. I cannot give the boys anything for themselves, but if Ben has children of his own . . ." That lip twitch widens to a smile. "My lawyers have assured me that is what they call a *loophole*, and I may bequeath everything to any children of Ben's as well as support those children while I am alive."

"That is an excellent loophole," I say and try not to remember that it requires Benedict to first have a child. "All the more reason for him to marry then."

"Yes, unfortunately."

"You said you can give money to Benedict's children. But not Jude's?"

Her eyes meet mine, a quietly searching look that has me pulling back.

"That was rude," I say. "It is none of my business."

"No, it is a fair question. Why Benedict? Why not Jude? For this whole marriage strategy."

"Because Lord Sterling has the title," I say. "It could go to Jude's children if his brother has no offspring, but that isn't a guarantee. Parents will want the guarantee."

"True, but I am certain there would be many young women happy to take the earl's younger brother. Handsome, charming, good natured. He is, on the surface, the better match."

"On the surface?" I frown as I try—and fail—to imagine Jude having some dark secret side.

"Jude would do whatever was needed of him, for his family's sake. He has offered. Stridently offered. Ben won't hear of it, and I agree. Asking Ben to marry a woman he does not love is wrong. Asking Jude to marry a woman would be even more wrong."

It takes me a moment to parse out what she said.

Asking Ben to marry a woman he does not love . . .

Asking Jude to marry a woman . . .

"Oh," I say, and I feel my eyes widen even as I struggle to keep my expression neutral. "He is . . . That is to say . . ." My cheeks heat, and I inwardly curse myself for my fumbling.

"I said nothing." Lady Flora cuts off a piece of cake with her fork. "Whatever you deciphered is your own interpretation, and I would hope you would keep it to yourself. As I do not wish to be cast in the role of gargoyle, nor do I wish Jude to be cast as the inconsiderate gadabout young brother, content to see his brother unhappily wed without a thought of taking his place. He *would* take his place."

"But he should not," I said, my voice firm. "You are correct. That would be more wrong."

Her eyes meet mine, and she nods, relaxing.

"I am glad you understand that," she says.

"I do."

"Now to the next order of business. You have agreed to play the role of Ben's mistress. Why?"

My mouth opens. I am about to say that I only wish to help, when I realize why she might be asking. Not curiosity but concern.

"If you think I have an ulterior motive, I do not," I say levelly. "I am not angling to become Lord Sterling's mistress."

She lets out a sharp laugh. "Of course you are not." She reaches to pat my knee. "That is no insult to either of you. If I did not think you worthy of Ben, I would not have devised this scheme. As for Ben himself . . ."

She glances toward the window, and I get the impression she looks away to hide her reaction, but those crackles in her voice betray it. "I would be delighted if he came to have a mistress, and I would wish the same for his future wife, that they might both discreetly find happiness elsewhere while respecting one another." She looks back. "But you are not looking for that. You seem to have family and a profession in London."

"I do."

"And no interest in living in a ruined castle as a countess . . ."

I lower my gaze as I catch her meaning. "I do not have what Lord Sterling needs in the way of money. And yes, I have my own life. As for why I am doing this? I came to Ravensford following my sister, who came to help a family. They have left, and so has she. I will follow soon enough, if she does not receive Lord Sterling's message. I can spare another day or two, and if I have no need to leave . . . There is no reason to hurry if staying would benefit others."

"Because that is what you do. As a doctor's assistant. You said you did not fear those coming to the ball would be among your former patients. I presume that means you minister to the poor?"

"Some, but also some of greater means. I do need to pay my bills, as I am not independently wealthy. But none would come from the circles of those attending the ball."

"You are staying because you can, and because it is the right thing to do."

"Yes."

"Good." She waves her cake fork my way. "That was what I suspected, and it was what I hoped to hear. You hardly seem a young chit who might have designs on my nephews, but I must be sure."

"I do not. I am in no need of a husband. Nor would I be seeking a lover hundreds of miles from home."

Her eyes dance. "But you would seek a lover if he were closer to home?" She raises her hands against my answer. "I am only teasing you, dear. There is nothing wrong with that. I did not spend my life alone. I simply did not find anyone worth giving up the independence this brings." She waves around the room. "My modiste will be here soon. Let us get you a proper dress."

17

"**N**o," Benedict says as he strides into the dressing room. "That will not do. Find another."

I glower at him and then rearrange my features before the modiste sees my reaction. If we are to play at being lovers, we must begin now, in front of everyone we cannot trust to keep our secret.

"While I do wish to look lovely for you, Lord Sterling," I say with practiced patience, "I do believe I still dress to please myself."

"Which is precisely the problem. You *do not* dress to please yourself. You admitted as much last night."

The modiste abruptly stops her pinning. I swear Lady Flora bites her lip to hold in a laugh.

"Perhaps, my lord," I say, "as you are in the market for a bride, you ought not to be mentioning what we discuss at night?"

He opens his mouth, brows gathering in annoyance before realizing clarification would not help in this situation.

"I believe I can still mention anything we discussed that is not of an intimate nature," he says. "Which clothing is not."

"No? Depends on the clothing, I suppose."

Now the modiste makes no pretense of returning to work, drinking in our conversation.

I continue, "But as we are discussing *outer* clothing"—I have to pause as Lady Flora chokes on a barely suppressed laugh—"I believe you are entitled to voice an opinion. An opinion sounds like this. 'I do not think that quite flatters you, dearest.' There. Now you try it."

"Find her something else," he says to the modiste. "Show me the options."

"Change my dress while you stand there watching?" I raise my brows in mock horror. "What ever do you take me for, sir?"

"I take you for a woman who is overly amused by this conversation. I did not ask to see you *in* the options. I can judge them for myself. They must be to your taste."

"Bow-y?"

"Yes, bow-y." He looks at the modiste. "She is fond of bows and frills and lace and color." He strides over to where more dresses are arranged. One sweep, and he points. "That one."

The one he's indicating is delightful. Truly. Colors in this time are far more muted than my own. That is not a matter of fashion but necessity. This period lacks the bright colors slowly appearing in my own world. Colors which—as Bronwyn points out from her twenty-first-century history-professor perspective—may contain heavy doses of poison. I now sadly find myself avoiding green.

This dress *is* green, but not in the brilliant shade provided by arsenic. It's green washed silk with bows. Many, many bows. Also, lace trim and fripperies aplenty.

"That . . ." the modiste says carefully.

"It's a girl's dress," I say. "Intended for someone nearly half my age."

"So?" He lifts the dress. "Try it on."

"Are you certain, my lord? I will, if you do not mind being spotted together at a distance and someone thinking your 'friend' is a girl of fifteen."

He drops the dress as if it has burst into flames. Then he eyes it again. "But if you like it . . ."

"It might be a bit much even for me."

"Excessively bow-y?"

I smile. "Too much of a good thing is still too much."

He waves at the dress. "Can it be altered? Would it fit otherwise, if some of the bows and such could be removed?"

The modiste eyes me. "It would fit. It is made a little large so that it can be taken in, as it is intended for a younger girl who might be less . . . womanly in her figure."

"That one then." He meets my gaze. "Yes?"

I resist some sharp comment about whether my opinion matters. It obviously does, or he wouldn't ask.

"Yes," I say.

⚜

I HAVE TWO NEW DRESSES, COURTESY OF LADY FLORA. SHE HAS ALSO LOANED me jewelry to wear, from her mother's collection. We composed a note detailing what she lent me and that it will be returned within the fortnight. That should appease her cousin, if he realizes Benedict's mistress is wearing family jewels. I insist that we also add the dresses. Yes, they will do her no good after I am done with them, but I do not wish to give that cousin any ammunition in this battle.

We are about to leave when a boy rides in on a horse. He is about fourteen, on the cusp between child and man, and when he sees me, he straightens and runs a hand through his hair, to Jude's amusement.

"Hello, Tom," Jude says. "Bringing a message for our aunt?"

The young man shakes his head and motions for Benedict. Jude and I stay where we are, to give them privacy, but I cannot help overhearing the conversation.

"I have sent the messages you asked for, sir," he says. "To York, in search of the Booth family."

"Thank you." Benedict tries to pass over a coin, but the young man steps back. "It was easily done, sir, and you already paid for the messages."

I cannot see Benedict's face, but the tightening of his shoulders tells me he is uncomfortable with this. I murmur for Jude to excuse me and walk over.

"Did I hear something about York?" I say. "You were delivering the messages about the Booths for me?"

"Yes, ma'am."

I hold out a coin of my own. "Thank you."

Now he takes the money with a grin and a thanks before returning to his horse. When Benedict tries to give me his coin, I fix him with a look, which he returns, and we have a standoff until Jude intercedes, taking the coin from his brother and pocketing it.

"I understand it is uncomfortable to have your own tenants refuse to take your money," I murmur to Ben as Jude walks to the coach. "But I was the one who wished to find the Booths. I appreciate that you undertook that for me."

"Are you going to pay me for it, too?" he grumbles.

"Of course. That is only polite." I rise to whisper in his ear and say, "Thank you, Ben." Then I brush my lips across his cheek.

I don't stay to see his expression. I am already walking to the coach and, perhaps, smiling, just a little.

⁂

WHEN WE ARRIVE BACK AT THE CASTLE, JUDE IS SUDDENLY EXHAUSTED, FACE drooping as he rubs his cheek.

"You overdid it," I say as Benedict helps him from the coach.

"Yes, I fear I did. However, it is nothing a little rest cannot fix. I will retire to my room for the rest of the afternoon. Do not count on me for dinner. A small tray would be nice, but I also overdid it at Aunt Flora's luncheon."

"It was a most excellent lunch," I say.

"It was, and if I were feeling better, I should like to take a long walk, but I must leave that to you two. I am certain the puppy would appreciate joining you both on one of Ben's rambles."

"Rambles?" I say.

"Through the moors. Endless walks as he daydreams and wanders."

"I am neither daydreaming nor wandering," Benedict says, eyes narrow. "I am surveying the state of the countryside, as I must."

"Excuses," Jude whispers loudly to me. "He used to say Juno needed the exercise, but now that she is gone, he still does it, always alone because, apparently, having me there disturbs his daydreaming."

"Your chatter disturbs the point of a walk in the moors, which is to enjoy the *silence*."

"If you prefer to walk alone—" I begin.

"You are not Jude. You don't chatter. You talk. He is right that Lyta needs the exercise."

"You can stop at the pub for dinner," Jude says. "That would be an opportunity to be seen together."

"Does that suit?" Benedict asks me. "A walk and dinner."

"It suits very well, thank you."

⊗⊗⊗

WE ARE ON OUR RAMBLE. I LET BENEDICT TAKE THE LEAD. ALL RIGHT, "LET" him might overstate the matter. He walks and presumes I will follow. On the other hand, if I did not wish to follow, I would not, so perhaps "let" is still correct.

Lyta trots along with us, dogging our heels or surging ahead or lagging behind, whichever most interests her puppy brain. I mention the possibility of a lead, only to get a look that suggests I am very much a city person, accustomed to city-person things, such as dogs on leads. If Lyta seemed in danger of wandering off, I would still insist on one—for her own safety—but she never gets out of sight, and if she realizes she's fallen behind, she races up with yips of alarm.

It is remarkable how quickly a dog can adapt to—and even embrace —a new situation. Yesterday, she was with her mother and siblings. Today, she is with strangers, and as happy as can be, without a thought for running off and trying to find her first family.

Perhaps I should not confine that adaptability to canines. I have been with the Sterling brothers for two days, and I am equally comfortable, living in their home, wandering the moors alone with Benedict as if I have known him for years.

We walk mostly in silence. He is correct about that—though I would not admit it. Rambles like this, through landscape like this, are best done in silence, where we can fully enjoy the beauty.

We do talk a bit, at Benedict's instigation, as he points out this or that, and sometimes at mine, if I have questions about things that he has decided would not interest me.

The walk seems as if it could go on forever, over hill and dale, without us ever seeing another person.

"What do you dream about?" I ask as we head through a field. "When you ramble alone?"

I get a fierce look for that.

"I am *not* dreaming. I am assessing and surveying."

"Is dreaming such a bad thing?" I say. "Unbecoming of a gentleman?"

"It makes me sound like a starry-eyed boy," he grumbles.

"Is that such a bad thing?" When he doesn't answer, I say, "Forget dreams. Plans then. When you walk out here, you must be thinking of the land. Not only assessing but planning what you would like to see someday."

"Green," he mutters. "I would like to see green hills and dales again. Fat sheep and healthy children and clean running water."

All right. That was not quite the casual conversation I had in mind. My fault, I suppose, for thinking I might prod him into some glimpse of his hopes and desires beyond the dire situation he faces.

"Do you want to know what I envision?" he says. "Once the drought is done, presuming I am still Lord Sterling of Ravensford?"

"Yes, please," I say, a little too eagerly.

"Then you must go first."

"What?"

He glances over at me. "What do you dream of, Portia from London? What do you wish for your own future?"

"I . . ." I blink. Then I clear my throat. "I am not the one facing anything so dire as a drought."

"Then you have all the more cause to dream, as you have nothing to overcome first."

"If there is nothing to overcome, then they aren't dreams, are they? They're goals."

He tilts his head, considering, and not seeming to notice the sharpness in my tone. "True, but where do goals end and dreams begin? If I say I should like to walk another mile before dinner, that is clearly a goal. If I say I wish I could fly, that is clearly a dream. What lies in the middle?"

"Hopes, I guess. Hopes and aspirations."

"Then what do you hope or aspire to, Portia of London? A country manor? Eight children and a cat? A doting husband to bring you tea in the morning and brandy in the eve?"

His tone is lighter than I have heard it, and I want to seize on that. He is in a fine mood. So I want to keep him there. But the questions set something scraping along my spine.

"Is that what I should want?" I say. "Domestic dreams of happiness?"

I expect he'll snap back that he was only teasing me. That is the way of things, isn't it? Take mild offense and the other party will claim to have been teasing, a defense one cannot rail against without seeming waspish.

Instead, his voice softens. "You are correct. I was making light—I cannot see you with a cat—but I was also being presumptuous."

"You were, indeed. I happen to like cats. The eight children would be more of a problem. In my position, I have seen what that does to a woman, particularly when it might take a dozen or more births to achieve." I shudder. "Three or four seems reasonable."

"And a cat?"

"Perhaps a dog or two instead," I allow. "And, yes, perhaps a country manor, though I find myself torn between the advantages of the city and the country. As for a husband to bring tea and brandy, that seems quite a waste of a husband. A maid could do that."

He makes a sound that I realize is a laugh, a bark of one. "True, and probably with less bother. Forget domesticity. What are your professional hopes and aspirations?"

"Dreams," I say.

He slows, brow furrowing as he slows.

I continue walking. "We have established that dreams come with an obstacle. In my case, it is insurmountable. I wish to be a doctor."

"Then what is stopping you?"

I stop and turn to stare at him.

When he still seems confused, I say, "Have you ever met a woman doctor?"

"No, which means you can be the first."

"Do you think that there are no women doctors because no women *wish* to be doctors?"

His mouth opens. It shuts, and he pulls back, hand running over his face. "That was a foolish thing for me to say, wasn't it? Of course there must be women who wish to become doctors, which means if there are none, it is because there is an obstacle."

"We are not permitted to"—I am about to say we are not permitted to enroll in medical school, when I realize the first official one in London will not open for another fifty years—"study medicine."

"Oh. Yes." He shoves his hands into his pockets. "That . . . is important."

"Quite."

"Is there any way around it?" he says. "Training? Apprenticeship?"

I am not certain of the rules in this time, but I presume they are laxer. "It is possible, if you can find a man who would take on a female student. I have enough training to qualify as a doctor, but the only way I could practice would be to find some remote corner so desperate for medical care that they would accept me."

"We are very remote," he says. "And our local doctor is only marginally better than none at all."

"Yes, that is exactly what I want. A village that would grudgingly accept me until a decent male doctor came along." I wave it off and resume walking. "Well, this conversation has taken a darker turn than I expected when I spoke of dreams. Please tell me you can do better."

When he falls silent, I tap his forearm. "Even after you made me go first to give yourself time to think of an answer?"

"I *let* you go first out of *chivalry*."

I snort.

"That was a most unladylike response," he says.

"Then I am as ladylike as you are chivalrous."

He shakes his head and looks around for Lyta, calling her when she doesn't immediately appear. The dog's head pops up, and she races to us.

"You do not need to tell me anything," I say. "I truly was just trying to make light conversation."

He gives Lyta one final pat and stands. With a nod, he continues on our way, and I think that is my answer. He has accepted my offer to avoid a response.

It takes at least ten steps before he says, "I always thought of this as an obligation."

When I frown, he waves down the valley, dotted with sheep and thatched houses as far as the eye can see.

"Being Earl of Ravensford. I grew up being told that, one day, all this would be mine. When I was young, I'd puff up with importance. I would be earl. All this land would belong to me. All these people would bow and call me lord." He glances over. "I was insufferable at that age."

When I don't respond, he slants me a glance. "You are supposed to say you cannot imagine it."

"I have been sarcastic enough for one day."

A sound that might be a half laugh. "Fine. I can still be insufferable. But one day, I went too far, gloating in front of Jude, and he ran to our mother. I felt bad, and so I followed to apologize, and I heard our mother talking to him. She said that what I was gaining was not a chest of gold but a job. I would be responsible for this land. For these people. If I did it correctly, I would live in comfort—not only materially but by earning the respect of my tenants. Whenever Jude felt he had lost something, by dint of being born second, he must always remember he had gained something, too. His freedom."

"The freedom to do as he wished, beholden to none."

Benedict nods. "After that, I did not see a great treasure I would inherit. I saw only the yoke that came with it. That was not my mother's fault. Had she any idea I'd overheard the conversation, she would have focused my attention on the rewards I might reap and the benefits of my birthright. But I was young, and all I could see was this obligation looming in my future. So when I turned twenty-one, I left, vowing to live my life to the fullest before my sentence of servitude began."

"And did you?"

He goes quiet, and I am uncertain of an answer until he says, "It started off that way. I sought whatever adventures I could find. I earned enough so that I would not need to burden my parents with demands for money. I could not take on an occupation, nor could I marry, and at first, that was freeing. I could do what I wanted, with no obligations. Perhaps, for some men, that would be enough. It wasn't for me. I kept finding new diversions, but soon nothing quieted the restlessness that ate away more of me each year. Then my father died, and I came home to the mess of his finances, and I had what I realized I'd needed all along: a goal. I threw myself into it, and it wasn't an obligation. It was a purpose."

"Then came the drought."

He goes silent again, but after a few steps, he says, "It *is* added pressure. Added fear." He stops abruptly. "I do not mean it frightens me."

"Doesn't it? It would terrify me."

He walks a few steps before his voice drops, and he says, "Yes, it is frightening, in its way. Possibly even terrifying. Everyone is relying on me, and I need to act as if I have it all under control. Which I do. With the bridal-hunt ball. I just . . ." He looks out over the fields. "There has been no time for wishes or aspirations, much less dreams. My attention is entirely on fixing this. After that, I can do more. But what if, in fixing this, I irreparably change my life in a way I will regret for the rest—"

He shoves his hands in his pockets and says, gruffly, "I am growing maudlin. You are right. This is a light conversation determined to become anything but."

"The drought will end," I say.

"Hmph."

"Do you think you might need another plan?" I say. "In case the ball does not go as you hope?"

"If I knew of one, I would pounce on it like a starving cat on a mouse."

"There's the clock. Or is that too implausible to be a real plan?"

He's quiet for a moment. Then he says, "I have been thinking of it. Too much for comfort, as it is rather implausible. And yet . . ." He shrugs and looks away. "I find myself in the mood to indulge implausible dreams."

"I think, if I'm not being too forward, that neither of us is the type to normally indulge impossible dreams, which would suggest that this particular scheme might not be as implausible to others as it seems to us. Merely far-fetched."

He looks over, lips twitching. "There is a difference there, too?"

"*Implausible* suggests a fool's errand. Something one cannot hope to achieve. *Far-fetched* simply means unlikely. *Unlikely* means that we would need to work particularly hard and accept that it might all be for naught. Neither of which, I believe, will be a problem for us."

"Laboring endlessly while knowing I may end up getting nowhere? That has been my life for the past two years."

"Then let us discuss it."

18

We come up with a plan. First, we need to know whether Colin Booth's comrades still scavenge the road to Edinburgh. Colin thought he was turning them in to Scarlet Jack. Was he truly communicating with Scarlet Jack? Or could his compatriots have suspected him of disloyalty, set it up themselves and killed him? Even if he *had* been communicating with Scarlet Jack, it might still have been his fellow highwaymen who murdered him.

Jude knows more about the local highwaymen than Benedict. Apparently, the Sterlings' own scheme was hatched between Jude and their aunt. Lady Flora could find their targets and the schedules of those targets. Jude had already been in charge of coordinating with their militia to free their own county of land pirates, and in undertaking that, he'd learned enough about highwaymen for the brothers to successfully portray the thieves themselves.

We will speak to Jude about that later. For now, we have worked our way around to the pub, which stands just outside the village. It is a country roadside inn, offering both food and lodgings, as well as being the coach stop. When we arrive, it is bustling. A sign in the window says they have neither rooms nor stalls for horses.

Benedict frowns at the sign. "Something must be going on."

I laugh and then realize he is serious. "Your bridal-hunt ball?"

He blanches. "Yes. Of course," he says a little sharply. "Do you wish to go elsewhere, presuming patrons may be coming to the ball?"

"Only if you do. Otherwise, I believe this is what we are supposed to be doing. Being seen together."

His shoulders relax. "Of course. Yes."

I step to the side, away from the road. "Do I look presentable?"

He surveys me. I am wearing the second dress from his aunt's modiste, one with fewer frills, but when the dusky-blue skirt is tied up at the sides and back, it shows an underskirt with gold embroidery. *Gold.* I would not dare wear such a thing in my day, but I think I am in love.

"There is a small paw print on your bodice." He shoots a look at Lyta, slurping from a bowl of water near the stable. "I have no idea where that came from."

I find and knock the dust away.

"Also, some on your cheek."

I lift my hand to my face.

"No, over here." He pulls off his glove and runs a finger over my cheek.

"Lord Sterling," a voice says.

Benedict does not leap back. He does not even startle. He only glowers over his shoulder as if we have been most rudely interrupted.

A ruddy-faced man of middling age puts out a hand. "It is you, is it not? Frederick Lancer. We met briefly in London once. At a"—he clears his throat—"sporting establishment."

Benedict's eyes darken. "It was a gaming hall, sir. When you word it like that, it sounds like something else entirely."

I bite back a laugh as the older man colors more. "Yes, of course." His gaze goes to me. "Ah, so this must be your . . . friend. I heard something of that." His gaze rakes over me. "My lord, you *are* lovely."

Benedict bristles and moves between us, as if the poor man had reached to paw at me.

"Yes, this is my good friend and my guest," Benedict says.

The man keeps eyeing me, and maybe that should be uncomfortable, but it is oddly fascinating. I am accustomed to more discreet looks of appraisal. He is devouring me like a custard cake, and if anything, my dress is more modest than it would be at home. The difference is that he knows—or thinks he knows—my status in the world. I am not some virgin spinster but Benedict's mistress. Is he looking at me and imagining . . . ?

Dear lord.

Again, I should be dismayed. Even horrified. But I am almost amused. It is an intriguing insight into a world I have never entered before.

"If you will excuse us—" Benedict begins.

"First, let me introduce my daughter, Evie, who will be at your ball."

Lancer tugs over a young woman. Dear lord, indeed. He is going to introduce his daughter as a potential bride with Benedict's mistress right there? I make a move to step aside, but Benedict's hand on my arm stops me. I want to pull free of that intimate grasp. Let the poor child at least have some doubt as to what role I play in his life.

But this is the point, isn't it? One of them anyway. Let the young women know exactly what they can expect—marriage with a man who may take a mistress. Yet this feels insulting. Like slapping them in the face with it.

Everything I have seen about Benedict suggests he is a man of honor. He can be unthinking, but he is not callous. I don't believe he would be the sort to parade a mistress about and humiliate his wife. He will need to say as much to whoever he chooses. Assure them that how he behaved as a single man is not how he will as a married one. And, I suppose, even now, he is behaving with decorum, going to dinner with his mistress modestly attired while referring to her as his "friend."

As I am thinking that, the young woman steps forward, and all those concerns shoot from my head as my gut sinks with dismay.

Please tell me this is not the daughter Mr. Lancer is offering at the ball. Tell me this is her younger sister, who will attend as a guest.

The poor girl barely looks sixteen, and when Benedict sees her, his expression darkens enough for the girl to inch back.

"How old are you?" Benedict says.

Lancer clears his throat. "Lord Sterling, let me introduce my daughter, Miss Ev—"

"I asked her age."

"She is—"

"I asked *her*."

The poor girl stammers, and I move forward to touch her sleeve.

"What a lovely dress, Miss Lancer. I hope the ride was not overly taxing."

"She is eighteen," her father says.

"Bollocks," Benedict says.

The girl's eyes widen as if she has never heard a profanity in the wild.

Benedict turns on her father. "I was very clear. No one under eighteen. She's a child. Young enough to be *my* child. A girl of her age cannot enter into an agreement like this." At my look, he turns stiffly and bows to Evie. "Apologies for my gruffness, Miss Lancer. Your father has made the mistake, and it is no fault of yours. If you wish to attend my aunt's gala, you are more than welcome to partake of the festivities. However . . ." He turns back to her father. "I will consider no one who cannot prove she is eighteen." He tips his head. "Good day to you, sir."

He whistles for Lyta, who scampers over and accompanies us into the pub. We are met at the door by a young woman who says, "No dogs—" Then she sees who it is and beams. "Lord Sterling. You finally have a new pup?"

He grunts something that still does not answer the question of who Lyta belongs to. The woman presumes it's a yes and beams again.

"Let me show you to your table by the fire. I know how much Juno loved the fire."

She takes us to a table at the back where two men drink glasses of ale. Seeing Benedict, they scramble up.

"Yes," the woman says. "His lordship is here, and he will be taking his table."

"I do not need that particular one," Benedict says, in a voice almost soft with resignation, as if he knows the protest will do no good. And it doesn't. The men clear out, and the woman wipes it down before seating us.

"The usual, sir?" she says. Without waiting for a response, she turns to me, "And for you, miss?"

Thus far, she's paid me no mind, but now she struggles to keep doing that, as her eyes sparkle with obvious curiosity.

I smile. "Whatever is the house specialty."

Benedict snorts. "The house specialty is whatever is strongest and cheapest."

"I'll bring you something suitable, miss," she says with a curtsey as she hurries off.

Benedict leans over and taps a spot by the fire, urging Lyta there until she settles in. She's barely lying down before a boy shyly approaches with a bone from his family's table.

"May I, sir?" he asks.

"Of course. She will appreciate that."

As the boy gives Lyta the bone and sneaks in a pat, I notice a young woman with her parents at a neighboring table, all of them watching with interest. Another bridal candidate. The girl's mother elbows her and leans in to whisper something as they slide glances Benedict's way. The girl flushes and nods in obvious agreement, and her gaze, when it falls on Benedict, is soft and warm, and seeing that, something in me . . .

It does not matter. The point is that she is older, perhaps in her mid-twenties, mature enough to make such a decision, and her mien is kind, and she is looking at Benedict as if seeing more than she expected. That's good, is it not?

I'm not sure Lady Flora was right about Benedict needing this mistress ruse to show him in a better light. Yes, he is gruff, even testy. Stubborn, grumpy and downright rude. But it doesn't take much to get past that, and this young woman and her parents can already see the real Lord Sterling in the way his tenants treat him. There's no fear, just a level of respect that he might even be uncomfortable with. He is good to his tenants. He is good to his dog. That does not guarantee he will be good to his wife, but it bodes well. He is not the brute he seems.

As for Benedict, he does not even seem to have noticed the young woman, much less her admiring glances. He's busy watching the boy with Lyta and then taking our drinks from the tavern mistress. Mine appears to be wine, which wouldn't have been my choice—I'd prefer a good ale—but I take it with genuine thanks. Then I sip and realize it is cider, which makes me smile. That will do nicely.

Benedict suggests we order the mutton. We are in sheep country after all. I agree, and the mistress brings a carving board with bread and butter.

"How precisely are we supposed to do this?" Benedict whispers as he passes me a slice of bread. "I feel as if we are on a stage."

I look and see what he means. While no one is staring, they are all sneaking looks our way.

"We should talk," I say. "Carry on what appears to be an intimate conversation."

"To show that I am capable of carrying on a conversation?"

I smile. "That wasn't what I meant, but it cannot hurt. If I were a bridal candidate, it would be one of my primary concerns. Not whether you *can* converse, but whether you would converse with *me*."

He frowns. "Why would I not?"

I lift my brows. "Have you not met husbands and wives of the nobility? Sometimes, I shudder to think what their shared meals must be like. Silence broken only by 'please pass the salt.'"

"Don't be ridiculous." He takes a long drink of his ale. "They have a butler to pass it for them. But yes, I know what you mean. I am not certain how much it applies here, though. I have a feeling your criterion for a husband would be vastly different than . . ."

His gaze sweeps the crowded hall and pauses on a young woman wrinkling her nose as she picks through her dinner.

"Perhaps."

He takes another draft from his ale. "Then I should ask what would be the criterion of a woman like you. What would *your* marital criterion be, Portia of London?"

"I would expect fair treatment."

His brows rise. "That seems rather underwhelming."

"Does it? I wish to be treated as an equal partner, not as a lesser one. I would wish to be a full partner in all aspects of the marriage, including decision-making. Yes, that might sound dull to you, but only because you expect that by dint of being male."

He considers. "True. I also do not have the best of role models."

"Your parents did not have equality in their marriage?"

"What?" He seems surprised. "No, they most certainly did. That is what I meant." A pause. "Which I expressed poorly. I meant that, given my experience, partnership seems natural to me, which is why I did not see why it would be so important to you. I shudder to think where we would have ended up if my mother *hadn't* been an equal partner. Living in worse than a ruined keep, I am sure. So you expect marital equality. What else?"

I do not need to think on the next one. "My husband would need to realize that my career was not a whim, not a diversion until I found a husband to take care of me."

"Again, I would think that obvious. You would hardly have studied so hard if you expected to give it up upon marriage. What else?"

Now I do need to consider. After a moment, I say, "I would need to feel confident that the father of my children would be a good one."

"So you do want children?" He nods. "That is right. You said as much. Children, just not eight." His lips twitch. "Agreed, eight would be . . ." He shudders. "So children and a dog or two, and a husband who would be good to both."

"A husband who would realize that being good to both means more than simply never harming them. I have high expectations there, based on my own experience, both with my own father and my brother-in-law. A good father does more than tolerate his children. He supports and encourages them. He genuinely likes them."

He nods slowly. "My own father and I did not always get on. But now that I am older, I recognize that was more the result of my personality than his. You speak of tolerating one's children. I fear that, as I grew older, I did not always tolerate my father."

"You grew frustrated with him," I say softly, not wanting to pry but also feeling an urge to draw Benedict out.

"Yes. He was much like Jude, and sometimes I grow frustrated with my brother as well, but . . . I hope I am mature enough now to rein that in, and to understand that his heart is always in the right place. I faulted my father for being too generous and too trusting, sometimes at the expense of his own family, but it is not as if he chose others over us. It was only that he had difficulty drawing boundaries."

He gives himself a shake and straightens. "Which is only to say that, despite any friction between us, I recognize that he was a very good father. A good father and a good husband, and I would aspire to be the same."

"Also, dogs," I say with a smile. "Good with dogs. That is important."

"Oh, that is simple enough. Dogs are easier than people. They cannot talk back."

I laugh and shake my head, and he leans toward me.

"Anything else?" he asks, and I am suddenly aware of all the eyes on us, the other patrons making no effort to hide their interest. Benedict is only moving closer to be heard over the din, but it feels as if the fireplace itself has moved, a sudden wave of heat washing over me.

It takes a moment to realize he asked a question, and I nearly stammer in my hurry to answer, lest he think I'm about to swoon.

"Mutual respect," I blurt. "I would want a man I could respect, and one who could—and would—respect me."

"Respect is the keystone of any relationship. And kindness? You would want a husband who is kind."

"Inwardly. I do not require the outward trappings of kindness as much as the heart of it: consideration."

"All very reasonable."

He shifts, and his leg brushes mine, and I wait for him to realize it and pull away. He does not.

He takes a drink of his ale, and I watch him swallow. There is a line down his throat where sweat has run a rivulet through dust, and it runs right over his pulse, and I find myself staring at that, transfixed.

When he moves, I jerk away. Staring at his throat? At his pulse? Truly, that cider must be stronger than it seems, and yet, when his leg moves against mine, I do not jerk or even ease away. I lean into it, the heat and strength of it.

"Anything else?" he says.

"Hmm?"

"Anything else you would require? In a husband? We have . . ." He ticks off on his fingers. "Marital equality. Acknowledgment of your profession. Promising paternal prospects. Mutual respect and considera-tion." He pauses. "Oh, and good with dogs. Anything else?"

Love. That is on the tip of my tongue. All the rest is practical. All the rest reflect the qualities I had seen in Reginald, whether they existed or I merely imagined they did. But I had missed one very important thing in that match.

Love.

I need love.

I am almost about to say it when I remember this isn't about me. He's not truly asking what I need in a husband. He wanted to know what someone like me might require. What a mature and independent woman might expect, if that is what he seeks in a wife.

Love will not be part of that equation.

I shake my head. "Those are the qualities a woman like me might expect, should you wish for someone who is . . ." I struggle for the words. Not *like me*, which would be horribly presumptuous and even conceited. "Someone older, a woman who knows her mind and could accept your proposal with her eyes fully open. Someone who might become a helpmate in the management of your lands."

"Yes," he says. "That *is* what I want, ideally. But also, ideally, what else would *you* want. Surely there is something missing there. Some element critical for your own happiness."

I hesitate. Perhaps I should say the word. I have never admitted that I want love in any future union. Saying the word will make it real.

I open my mouth and—

"Lord *Sterling*."

We glance up to see a young woman striding toward us.

19

The young woman who approaches is definitely over eighteen but still looks far too young to be taking that severe, almost snappish tone with Benedict. I certainly wouldn't have had the confidence to do it myself at her age.

She is very pretty, with dark hair and a beautiful pale dress, skirts lifted as she makes her way to us, her gaze swinging about, as if she is mucking through a stable.

"Miss Carleton," Benedict says, and his voice is remarkably restrained.

She plants herself in front of him. "I need to speak to you."

"I may not be the best-mannered person in Ravensford," he says, and I realize that tone is deceptively mild, "but even I know that the proper way to word that—when coming upon a gentleman with his companion at dinner—is to say that you *wish* to speak to me. Unless a family member lies dying at the doorstep and you desperately need my coach, in which case, I would point out that I do not have it."

Impatience steams off her as he speaks, and when she answers, it is as if he has rebuked her in some incomprehensible language, and she was only waiting for him to finish. "I need to speak to you. Tell her to leave."

His brows rise, and his gaze goes to Lyta, happily chomping on her bone. "Tell the dog to leave? I assure you, she is not at all dangerous. The one you need to worry about is me, if you were referencing my human companion in such a tone."

Her gaze only flicks my way. "Your mistress, you mean."

"She is my companion at dinner, which is all that matters."

"If you think you are going to behave this way once we are wed—"

Benedict's laugh drowns out the rest of that sentence. It is not one of the laughs I have heard from him before, and it sends a chill through me. That laugh is like the snap of a hound's jaws.

"We are not going to wed, Miss Carleton. I have been very clear on that, to both you and your father. Now, if you will excuse us, I am in the middle of dining—"

"With a harlot."

The whole pub drops to a silence so complete I hear only the scratch of Lyta's teeth on the bone as Benedict rises with such care that people around us inch back.

"Get out," he says.

She bristles. "This is not your establishment, sir. You cannot throw me out. I heard you were here with your—"

"Choose that next word with care. If it is the least bit offensive to my dinner companion, I shall—"

"L-Lord Sterling," a voice says, and a young man pushes his way through two tables as he fairly runs over. He is slightly older than the young woman, and as well dressed as she is, but where her face is pure fury, his is horror tinged with fear. He fairly throws himself between Miss Carleton and Benedict.

"Lord Sterling," he says. "I apologize for my sister's behavior. She has had a difficult day, and she is not herself."

Benedict snorts. "She is absolutely herself, Mr. Carleton."

The young man flushes. "I still apologize." He turns to Miss Carleton. "Go wait in the coach."

Her mouth opens.

"Go wait in the coach," he says, hardness creeping in. "And imagine what Father will say about this and whether you wish me to tell him."

She stomps off, only slowing to call back. "Expect to walk home, Martin. The coach shall not wait."

"Good," Martin mutters under his breath. He turns to me. "I am sincerely sorry. I was coming after her when I heard . . ." He swallows, and his gaze drops. "I do apologize."

"One never needs to apologize for another," I say. "She was upset."

"It is no excuse," Martin says. "Whatever your"—a short cough—"relationship with Lord Sterling, he is an unmarried man, and if she had any concerns that such an entanglement might continue beyond a marriage, that is a topic for discussion, not an excuse to fling insults." He looks over quickly at Benedict. "Not that I believe my sister will be your choice. I know you have been clear that she will not."

"She will not," Benedict says stiffly. "I will not align myself further with your family."

Martin looks so uncomfortable that I understand Jude's need to act as interpreter, and I suppress my own urge to soften the blow.

"Would you join us for a drink," Benedict says. "As you are apparently walking home?"

This is his way of apologizing for being harsh. Or perhaps that misstates the matter. Benedict does not realize he was harsh. He did not intend insult to this young man, which is clear by the fact he is asking him to join us.

"That is kind," Martin murmurs. "But I would not wish to impose."

"I am never kind. I have a purpose, as always. Miss Portia and I were discussing something that concerns your family, and she has questions."

"If it is about my sister . . ." Martin says warily.

"Miss Portia and I would *not* be discussing your sister. It is about the French clock and the mystery of its disappearance." He shoots me a look that is positively indulgent. "My lady cannot resist a mystery."

"Oh." Martin's expression relaxes into a soft smile. "Of course. It is an excellent mystery, and I would not mind a glass of ale. It will be a long and dusty walk."

"I would offer you a coach ride, but we walked ourselves." Benedict waves for the tavern mistress and then pushes out a chair. "Sit and prepare to be interrogated for the sake of a lady's curiosity."

◈

MARTIN'S ALE ARRIVES ALONG WITH OUR MEALS, AND THE HOSTESS BRINGS him bread with butter and a thick slice of mutton, served with a smile that tells me—if Benedict's demeanor did not—that this is the most popular of the Carleton clan. Martin earns that smile with genuine and effusive thanks.

"The clock," Benedict says as we begin to eat.

"Mmm, yes," Martin says after taking a bite of his meal. "It is a fine mystery, though I would not say so to my father, who becomes quite apoplectic at the mention of it. Do you know the history, ma'am?"

"I know what I have heard. That it allegedly belonged to a French queen, whose lady-in-waiting absconded to England with it, whereupon it disappeared."

"Disappeared would be an exaggeration. That is the story told to keep any Frenchman from demanding its return. The lady-in-waiting seems to have sold it to the first Englishman who offered a fair price, and even then, she had no idea what it was worth. From there it passed through the hands of a few people who also did not understand its value. That is how it came into my father's possession."

"He *did* understand the value."

"Very well. He also had it on excellent authority that the former owner was uninterested in its return . . . because they had obtained it through questionable means themselves. That meant Father did not expect any trouble buying and even displaying it, at least not way out here in our . . ." He glances quickly at Benedict. "At the house we currently occupy."

Sterling Hall. The estate where Benedict grew up. The family home he lost.

Martin hurries on. "So my father made the purchase and had it transported here. But it never arrived. The coach was beset by highwaymen."

That is not the official story Miranda saw in the museum, which claimed a Scotsman had bought it and was planning to sell it back to the French when it was stolen on the way to London. Proof that, with an object like this, even those who made history their business sometimes fell prey to rumor.

"Someone knew the clock was coming to Yorkshire," I say.

"*No,*" Martin says, his blue eyes glinting. "That is what makes it such a fine mystery. My father was very shrewd. He hired a coach that is said to be impenetrable, even to musket fire. He also hired six men to accompany it, all crack shots. It was the talk of the town—well, in certain circles. But that was all for show. While my father was personally trans-porting the supposed clock crate to the coach, it was already on its way here, snuck onto a wagon."

"The wagon was what the highwaymen robbed."

"Precisely, and to hear the poor wagon driver tell it, the thieves were as ragged a bunch as ever trolled the highway. They were only hoping for a few trade goods. Instead . . ." He throws up his hands, his face gleaming in the childlike delight of a good story.

"They struck it rich," I say.

"And my poor father has been searching ever since, furious at his inability to find them. They were not even proper highwaymen. Surely a bribe in the right place would loosen a tongue."

"It has not."

"Silent as the grave."

I glance at Benedict, but he seems lost in thought, leaving the ques-tions to me for now.

"What do *you* think happened?" I ask.

"They made for parts unknown with their treasure."

"Would it not have been noticed? Several men disappearing right after the clock was stolen?"

He shrugs. "It is a drought, my lady. Young men—and old—are disappearing by the day. Leaving to find work elsewhere."

"They did not seem terribly adept criminals," I say. "I would think, if they fled with the clock, one would have wagged his tongue somewhere. And would they not have attempted to sell it by now?"

His face falls. "That is exactly what my father says." He sighs. "I like to think that these poor ruffians made their fortune and ran off to Amer-ica. But yes, it is unlikely they would have the sense to do so in silence, or that they would know where to sell the clock without word getting back to my father. He believes they are dead. Most of them, at least."

"Dead?"

"Fighting over the clock. We did catch a whisper of it, at one time. Have you ever heard of a man called Scarlet Jack?"

I school my features. "Briefly. A highwayman? You think he is involved?"

"No, no. He haunts the highways bringing such men to justice. But the rumor was that he was tracking this gang himself. They found out about it, which led to bitter fighting among the thieves, and the gang broke apart, possibly with only one survivor, who took the clock."

"This is what your father thinks happened?" I ask.

Martin shifts in his seat. "Well, no. I . . . can be a little more fanciful than my father."

I smile. "Nothing wrong with that. An imagination is a wonderful thing."

"It is not entirely my imagination, though." He looks at Benedict. "Did you hear that a man's body was found north of Ravensford six months ago? A man who could not be identified."

Benedict's nose wrinkles in distaste. "A gruesome affair." He looks at me. "It was well away from here, and my reeve did not recognize the . . . remains. The only person who had disappeared around that time was a young man named Colin Booth, and it was most certainly not him." His eyes meet mine, his voice firm, to ensure I do not imagine this was poor Colin.

"But Colin Booth did leave a few weeks before the man was found," Martin says. "And there was a rumor . . ." He trails off and pulls at his collar. "Apologies, sir. I know the Booths were once your tenants."

"And are no more." There's a low growl in Benedict's voice. "They became your father's, and now, from what I hear, he has taken advantage of their situation—with the boy gone—to evict Widow Booth and her daughters from their cottage."

Martin shifts in obvious discomfort, voice lowering as he says, "I played no part in that, sir, and I was most aggrieved to hear about it. I was in London at the time."

"What was this rumor about young Colin?" I say. "If I might ask."

Martin casts a nervous glance at Benedict, who grunts. "Go on. The lady asked you a question."

"Only that he might have become involved with something criminal. After . . ." Another tug at his collar. "After my father became his landlord, instead of Lord Sterling."

Martin's gaze ducks away, but he needn't bother. There's no accusing glare from Benedict. Only a sharp pain in Benedict's eyes.

He blames himself.

He lost the land, and the boy turned to thieving to help his family.

Turned to thieving and was murdered for it.

"I'm sure it is but a rumor," Martin says. "The boy is probably alive and well, making money to send to his family. Perhaps he has gone to America. Owen certainly seems happy there."

"Owen?" I say.

"My elder brother. He went to America a couple of years ago. He writes every few months. Father still won't accept his letters . . ." Martin trails off. Then he says, a little too brightly. "But Mother and I have seen them, and Owen seems well. I am certain he will return soon."

"Your father doesn't seem to think so," Benedict says. "That is why he is so eager to marry his daughter to me. His heir is gone, and he wishes to produce another, preferably with an earl's title. Particularly since *you* don't want to inherit," he says to Martin with a touch of accusation.

"I am heading into the clergy," Martin says to me, almost apologetically. "It is my calling."

"And a fine one at that," I say. "Tell me more about it."

Martin relaxes with a smile and does just that.

❦

AFTER MARTIN CARLETON LEAVES US TO OUR MEAL, WE DO NOT LINGER IN the tavern. I had hoped the conversation might lighten Benedict's mood, but I suppose, to provide a true distraction, it would need to be a particularly rousing account of one's decision to take the cloth.

Well, you see, after sailing the high seas and nearly losing my life—on multiple occasions—to the sword, I decided to return home and join the clergy, particularly in hopes that there might be some divine intervention that will heal this disease . . . of an intimate nature that I procured in my travels.

Sadly, Martin's story contains none of that. Well, not sadly for him, I suppose. But it is a rather dull tale, as such things usually are. A younger son feels the call of the cloth . . . or has that call impressed upon him. In his case, if there is any interesting point, it is that it seems the cloth was impressed upon him at first by his father, but now that the eldest son has traipsed off to America, Mr. Carleton regrets his choice for Martin . . . after the young man has come to embrace it.

Ironic, and I'll admit to a twinge of malicious glee at the thought of Carleton's chagrin, forced to lie in the bed he made. It is most unbecoming of me, and yet I feel quite unable to work up the proper sense of guilt over my glee.

After Martin leaves, we finish our supper with only quiet conversation. Then we are off, walking through the gathering dark with Lyta scampering along, her well of energy refilled and brimming over as she chases rabbits through the gloom.

After at least a half mile in silence, I say, "You obviously do not need to confide in me, Lord Sterling, but I hope you are not brooding over Colin."

"Brooding?"

My lips twitch. I knew that would catch his attention. "Feeling any sense of responsibility for his fate."

"He was my tenant."

"Was. Past tense. He was caught up in a situation that you did not cause and that you are trying to resolve. His death is a tragedy, but the only person responsible for it is the one who killed him."

He grunts, which I take as permission to continue.

"Colin was young," I say, "but he was an adult and capable of making his own decisions. Did he feel this was his only option? Or did he think it was a way to make easy money? Was he lured in by the prospect of adventure? We cannot know, and I doubt he could even answer the question himself. The fact remains that your roads are not overrun with former tenants taking up thievery as the only solution to their plight. Colin made a choice. A dangerous one. And still, the fault lies with whoever murdered him."

More silent walking. Then he says, "Thank you."

"For being blunt instead of kind?"

His lips twitch. "Jude would have said the same but in a very different way, and I would have felt he was only trying to make me feel better. You speak a language I understand." He glances over. "Thank you."

I nod, ducking his gaze, and we continue, now in a comfortable silence, through the moors.

W hen we reach the castle, the candles and lanterns are all out, and Jude's door is closed, suggesting he is abed. I am about to tell Benedict we ought to proceed quietly, when he marches past and throws open Jude's door.

I stay in the hall, where I hear a groggy, "Ben?"

"We need to discuss sleeping arrangements," Benedict says.

A low groan. "Well, as I was already sleeping, perhaps you could do so without me."

"There is a ghost."

A scramble, as if Jude is sitting upright. "Where?"

"In the keep."

"I know that. I mean where is it right now?"

"I have no idea. Cowed into silence, I hope. My point is that there is a ghost, and it may attempt to forcibly communicate with Portia again, which is unacceptable."

"Agreed . . . Still not sure why I'm awake."

"Because she cannot sleep alone. You are unwell, so I will watch over both of you."

Silence. Then, "I hope you're not suggesting we all squeeze into this room."

"There is space. I shall bring a—"

"Portia is not sleeping on a cot, and I am not sleeping on one, either, having been recently stabbed. You can both sleep in your room."

Now the silence comes from Benedict.

"Well, go on," Jude says. "Off with you."

"That would be most inappropriate."

"Portia!" Jude calls.

"Here," I say.

"Do you mind sharing a room with my brother, if his intention is to keep you safe?"

"I do not wish to inconvenience either—"

"Let me reword that. If his intentions are not unseemly, do you object to sharing sleeping quarters with my brother?"

"No."

"There," Jude says, and there's an odd note in his voice. Satisfaction and . . . amusement? Being unable to see his expression, I must be misinterpreting his tone. He simply wants to return to sleep.

Except he isn't talking like someone roused from sleep. There were only those first few moments, which in retrospect, seemed a little overdone.

Is it possible Jude *wasn't* actually asleep? Yes, but if he said so, then he'd have no excuse to refuse his brother access, and I can't blame Jude for not wanting to host a slumbering party in his quarters. He is, after all, still recuperating.

"Go," Jude says. "Sleep in your room, and please don't disturb me again. I need my rest." He pauses. "Unless there is a ghost. You may disturb me if you see a ghost." Another pause. "Which does not mean I hope you encounter our ghost, Portia. I do not. I wish you sleep and sound sleep. Now, close the door on your way out."

❦

WE ARE STANDING IN BENEDICT'S BEDROOM. ONLY NOW DO WE BOTH SEE THE problem. It is small. Very small. The bed takes up nearly all the space, and there is none for a cot.

"I will sleep on the floor," Benedict says.

"Don't be silly. It's your bed. I will sleep on the floor."

"Absolutely not." He looks around, as if expecting one of the walls to magically roll aside, revealing additional space. "Perhaps if I moved the table . . ."

"We can share the bed."

His "What?" comes with such alarm that I need to bite the inside of my cheek to keep from laughing.

"We are both practical people, yes?" I say.

"Yes, but—"

"It is a large bed. Suited for two people. It makes no sense for one of us to sleep on the floor."

His mouth works.

"Fine," I say. "If you are uncomfortable with sharing a bed, I shall take the floor."

"Certainly not. I . . ."

He trails off, and I note that he does not offer to take the floor instead.

Lyta scrambles up onto the bed and barks, as if telling me she is ready to sleep.

"There," I say. "It will not be only two of us in the bed. We have a chaperone."

He slants me a look. I march over and tap the center of the bed. Lyta stretches out there.

"She will sleep in the middle," I say. "We shall each take a side, alleviating any impropriety. Yes?"

He looks at the dog. "I suppose so."

"Then it is settled. Go into the hall, please, and I will prepare for bed. I will call when I am under the covers, and I will keep my eyes closed—and my head averted—while you prepare for sleep."

🙢🙠

WE DO AS I SUGGESTED, AND LYTA SNUGGLES DOWN BETWEEN US, AND I AM asleep within minutes. Hours pass before I wake to the sensation of something resting on my hip, something that does not feel like any part of a puppy.

I lift my head to see Lyta has moved to our feet. The covers are still pulled over us, but I can distinctly feel Benedict's hand on my hip. I am facing the far wall, and he is facing my back, his breath warm against my neck.

Should I remove his hand?

That seems rude. I don't want to disturb his sleep, and it is not inconveniencing me at all. In fact, it is rather pleasant, warm and solid against my hip.

Is this what it is like to lie with a man? Sleep with a man, I mean, as my cheeks heat. Either way, it is not within my realm of experience. Reginald wanted to save all that for marriage, and I hadn't felt any urge to disagree. Miranda would say that should have been a warning sign, but I'd been naive enough to think that once the ring went on my finger, I'd be overcome with desire. I was just restraining myself, that was all.

That was *not* all. If I doubt that, I know it now, lying here in Benedict's bed. Last night, his smell on the sheets was enough to keep me restless. Now that smell is twice as strong. It is the scent of the moors, of heather and dew and moonlight and endless rambles and endless possibilities. It's sharp and woodsy and masculine, and I find myself inching just a little closer to breathe it in. When I do, I feel the heat of his body, that undeniable awareness that he is inches away, lying behind me, clad in very little, his hand on my hip undeniably intimate in its casual touch, as if this is how we sleep every night.

I want to creep closer. Just a little. Nothing overly untoward. But he's asleep, and any movement I make—even that inch I crossed earlier—*is* untoward. Maybe if I leaned . . .

He shifts in sleep, and my heart stops. He is going to pull away. He'll realize where his hand is and—

He presses up against my back, his hand sliding down my hip, his own hips moving against my . . .

Oh.

He is pressed fully against me, even his bent legs curving into mine. His deep breathing tells me he is still asleep. Soundly asleep.

I relax. Of course he is asleep. He would not do this if he were awake, sadly.

Sadly?

What kind of thought is that? I would not want a man who took advantage of my sleeping state to press into me so intimately.

Was that not what I was just wishing I could do with him?

Wishing but not doing. That was the difference. I could not in good conscience slide over against him because I am awake. He is asleep, and so *his* slide is no transgression. No transgression means that I can stop analyzing it.

Stop analyzing and simply enjoy the feeling of his body pressed to mine. Of his hand, now on my thigh, fingers splayed, one brushing the tender inner skin . . .

Brushing *skin*. Not my nightgown. Bare skin.

My nightgown has ridden up to my hips. His hand was on the fabric, and now it is not.

Those fingers move, just a sleepy stretch, and heat rushes through me. Would it be wrong to shift my leg, just a little, letting his fingers slide further down the inside of my thigh?

I'm still wrapped in that predicament when he groans and pushes into my posterior, something pressing hard against it.

If I were not a doctor, I might wonder whether he'd shifted position and that was a bone pressing into me. But I am both a doctor and an avid reader of my sister's novels, and so I do not wonder what it is. Well, yes, I do, but in a very different sense of the word, which is not "to question" but "to marvel."

Oh my. That is . . .

I tentatively press into him, and he lets out an even deeper groan, one that ignites the most delicious ache between my legs.

Desire.

That is desire.

So what do I do with it?

Oh, I know what to do with it. I might not have done more than kiss Reginald—and never even kissed another man—but that doesn't mean I haven't experienced sexual pleasure. Just not with a second party involved.

This time, there is a second party involved. Except he is asleep, and so I can do nothing to him nor expect anything from him, which sets up a quandary. While it *is* a frustrating quandary, it is not the sort to make me endeavor to ignore the situation and return to sleep. No, this is a quandary that requires exploration.

Exploration? My cheeks heat at the word.

No, not that sort. Not while he is right here in bed with me.

And why not? He is deeply asleep.

That's . . .

Wicked?

Perhaps.

Wrong?

Perhaps not.

Benedict presses into me again, his fingers sliding along my bare thigh. He buries his face in my hair, and his other hand slides between my hip and the bed, and he pulls me against him.

Oh my. That feels wonderful.

A little voice whispers, *Do you know what would feel even more wonderful? If that was pressed in another spot, only a few inches away.*

I only need to think that for a gasp to escape me. His fingers tighten.

"Portia . . ." he groans.

I go still.

Did he just say my name?

Is he awake?

I hold my breath, but his breathing stays the same, that deep breathing that tells me he is asleep. Asleep and dreaming.

Dreaming of *me*?

He did say my name.

Am I certain of that?

No, but in my mind, that is exactly what he said. In my mind, he is still saying it, pushing hard and urgent against me. My hand slides down, over my belly and into the opening of my drawers, and I give another little gasp, feeling the spot hot and wet.

I slide my finger in before realizing that I had not decided whether I dared to do this with him in the same bed. Once I start, though, the decision is made. My entire body aches with longing, and I do not think I could pull my hand away even if he woke up. That thought should be like a bucket of frigid water. Instead, it is pure fire, my mind seizing on the thought of him waking to find me touching myself, and I gasp.

I shouldn't be doing this.

It's wicked.

What if he wakes up?

They are all thoughts that should stop me cold, and yet they do the opposite. I bite my lip to hold back my moans, and as soon as I do, Benedict gives one of his own, a long and slow moan of pleasure as he rubs against me.

Am I rubbing against *him*?

Inadvertently moving my hips as I pleasure myself?

I must be. His fingers have tightened on me, his breaths quickening. I hold myself still, but I do not move my hand away. I can't. No, I *won't*. I can do this. Hold myself still, swallow my gasps and moans and—

He pushes against me, pulling me back at the same time, and I feel him, the throb of him, and all I can think about is turning over and straddling him. Feeling that hardness in place of my own hand. Rubbing against him—

I gasp. Pleasure slams through me, and my hips crush back against him, rocking with the waves. I cannot stop. I do not know how to stop.

His face buries in my neck, and he says my name, the word coming on a groan and a gasp as he—

He goes rigid. His entire body goes still so fast it is almost a convulsion.

My own waves of pleasure are subsiding, the after-warmth seeping through me, and I hold my breath, waiting for him to relax so I can curl up against him. That is all I want right now. To feel his warmth and comfort and close my eyes and drift back to sleep.

Instead, he stays completely still, muscles rigid. Then he fairly flings himself backward with a hoarse oath. There's a scramble, as if he's rising from bed, and I hold my breath, heart pounding.

He heard me. Or felt me. He woke to me rubbing against him and gasping, and now he has flung himself up in horror.

He knows I am awake. He knows what I was doing.

I wait for him to speak. Instead, he only draws deep, ragged breaths that scrape through the silence.

I must say something.

I turn my head, ever so slowly, only to see him sitting on the edge of the bed, his back to me as he runs his hands through his hair, his head bowed.

He gives a shudder, and his hands move to grip the edge of the bed. Then he propels himself up as fast as he flung himself off me.

I quickly turn my head back to face the far wall.

He does not know I am awake.

Did he wake to me rubbing against *him*? Or to *him* rubbing against me? Clutching my hips and pressing his hardness against my backside.

From the end of the bed, Lyta hops down, her claws clicking on the stone floor.

"No, pup," he says, his voice hoarse. "Stay here. Watch over her. I will be back soon."

His steps pad from the room, and the door shuts behind him.

B enedict said he would return soon. A distant clock has chimed two quarter hours, and he has not returned.

Has he gone to sleep elsewhere? He must have.

How do I feel about that?

I would understand . . . if the entire reason for this sleeping arrangement hadn't been in case the spirit attacked me in the night.

Benedict must have forgotten that. He woke, realizing he had curled up against me in the night—and more—and stumbled out in embarrassment. Drowsy and forgetting why he was there, he's found another place to sleep.

I understand that, and if anything, I only feel guilt. I should have said something. Feigned that I woke when he got out of bed, sleepily turning over and asking where he was going, whether everything was all right.

If I'd done that, he'd have been assured no harm had been done, and if he still wanted to sleep apart, we could have moved into the library.

That's most likely where he is now.

Should I go and speak to him?

I sit up. Lyta stirs and whines as she clambers onto my lap. I pet her and look around. There's no sign of the ghost. Should I try to sleep?

No. My fingers still hurt from that windowpane. I will not risk enduring that abuse again. I am not some destitute traveler the Sterlings have kindly put up for the night. I am staying to help Benedict, and I understand if he has forgotten why he was sleeping here, but I am not going to spend the night staring fearfully into shadows.

I will not be fearful. It comes down to that. I cannot pretend I'll sleep if left alone in this house, and if I do not sleep, then the ghost has won, as surely as if it attacked me.

I put Lyta on the floor. Then I head into the hall. Yes, I am barefoot and in my nightgown, but it is not as if Benedict hasn't seen this. I won't dress to sleep in a library chair beside him.

I am partway down the hall, Lyta at my heels, when I see moonlight seeping through that barred door at the end of the hall.

It is ajar.

I stop, and the hairs on my neck rise.

The ghost is here. It has opened that door.

I shake myself. No, it has not opened the door. It cannot do that. It can attack me. It can slam a door, but opening this one would require lifting that bar, and I have never encountered any ghost who could do such a thing.

Still, I approach the library door slowly, gaze fixed on that open one at the end of the hall. As I draw near, tendrils of cold air slither around me, and I stop short again, only to pick up the scent of the moors at night.

Heather and moonlight.

The scent of Benedict.

I choke on a laugh, the sound echoing in the corridor. Really? Had I thought that earlier? I truly must have been half asleep. Heather maybe, but what does moonlight smell like?

Soft light in the darkness, an ashy orb swathed in a cloak of cloud.

Not golden sunlight blazing down in joyous rapture, but a pale glow leading one through the shadows.

I give myself another shake. Am I definitely awake? That doesn't sound like me at all.

The point is that I smell the moors, not Benedict, because that scent is coming in on that cool wind. The cold comes from the open door, not a phantom.

I continue on to the library. The door is open.

I rap on it. "Benedict?"

No answer. Has he fallen asleep already?

I step into the room. It's empty. I check both chairs, in case the shadows could somehow mask a man of Benedict's size. Then I take a lantern from the table, light it and head into the hall.

I look down at that open door into the ruined wing.

That seems the most likely place he's gone. It didn't open on its own.

Why would Benedict go into the ruined wing?

Those hairs on my neck prickle again, as all of our jests about imprisoned former wives slide back.

What could be in there?

Something he needed to check.

I squeeze my eyes shut. I am being ridiculous.

He is not there. I don't know why the door is open, but he has obviously gone to stay in his brother's room.

I reverse course and head there. The door to Jude's room is shut. I whisper an apology to Jude—I dare not knock and disturb his much-needed sleep—as I ease open the door and lift the lantern. Jude is facing the other way and well covered with the sheet, so I can safely open the door farther and shine the light in while my foot blocks Lyta.

There is no one else in the room. It is definitely Jude in the bed, and the room is otherwise empty, as are the blankets where Benedict slept the night before.

I close the door.

The kitchen then. Benedict has gone to the kitchen to make himself something to eat. I lift the lantern and walk to the kitchen.

It is empty.

There is no place else for him to go.

Except that ruined wing.

Why ever would he do that?

Because he isn't thinking straight? Roused from slumber and still groggy with it?

Or could there be a room down there where he goes to be alone? Perhaps the tower? I recall climbing the other tower and seeing a chair and book, as if someone found quiet refuge there.

If I owned a castle, where would my most private spot be?

In a tower.

In all the towers, if I could. Little rooms carved out just for me, where I could study and read and gaze over the moors.

Is that like Benedict? Or is it more like Jude?

Either way, it seems apparent now that Benedict is the one who opened that door into the ruined wing.

I return that way. As I near the door, the breeze whistles through, but it is only the breeze, perfumed with the moors. The door is several inches ajar, which strikes me as odd for a heavy door on a slanted floor.

Then I see why it does not shut. Because someone has wedged a piece of wood under the bottom. I adjust the skirt on my nightgown so I might bend and shine the light down. The door has been propped open with a sawed triangle of wood, clearly meant for this purpose.

I smile to myself. My sister might have begun writing novels of detection, but it seems I also have a bit of the detective in me. This scrap of wood is intended to hold the door. That means someone *does* use this door regularly. Someone who wants to be sure it doesn't slam shut behind them. It is something I would do. Ergo, it is something Benedict would do.

I push open the door. Lyta races through before I can stop her. Should I leave her in the library? I wouldn't want her to get hurt. But if I put her on the other side of the door, her barking and whining is sure to wake Jude.

I scoop her up with one hand and set down the lantern on the other side. Then I step in and very carefully close the door, being certain the wedge is in place.

It is not as if I can be trapped in here anyway. If the door shuts and will not reopen, I simply need to climb down through a window opening and go around to the front. Which would mean banging on the door until Jude answered. That is why Benedict keeps it propped. Not to avoid being trapped but simply to avoid the inconvenience of being locked out.

The door catches on the wedge and stays propped. I pick up the lantern. Then I see the next obstacle—that wide crack in the hall floor. Can I cross it with a wriggling puppy, a burning lantern and no free hand to hike my skirts? No. My nightgown is hardly formfitting, but it still binds too much to make such a huge step.

I set Lyta down first, planning to make two trips. Instead, she hops over the gap with ease. I shake my head, lift the lantern and extinguish it for safety. Then I hike my skirt, stretch as far as I can—

Distant footsteps nearly send me tumbling into the gap. I manage to make a shaky hop across and then lift the lantern . . . only to remember the flame is out.

"Benedict?"

As soon as I say his name, I know I won't get a reply. The footsteps are too far away. They do come from down the hall, though. I'm heading in the right direction.

I light the lantern. Lyta trots along at my feet. I do not need to worry about her getting hurt—the doors are all closed. Unable to resist, I open one to find an empty room. It is actually a lovely little room, with a larger window than one would usually find in a castle, as if the stone was chipped out to make a sunnier room. Through the open window, I can see the pasture and the forest beyond.

It would make a wonderful nursery.

I blink and shake my head. Where did that come from?

I obviously thought that's what this room looks like, even unfurnished. A nursery, with a doorway leading to another room beside it. I open the next door—the adjoining room—but the space is filled to the rafters with rolled rugs and tapestries and furniture. If there is a window, it has been boarded over to protect the contents.

A creak up ahead, like a footstep on wood instead of stone. That reminds me of what I am supposed to be doing, which is not snooping through this wing.

Still, the wing is in better condition than I expected. Whatever damage occurred to the hall—from an earthquake or such—it only seems to have affected that. The rest is unused because of the difficulty in reaching it.

The hall could be fixed. The stonework repaired and this wing reopened, the castle becoming a home again. A family home.

Is that what Benedict envisions?

I would. My heart does an odd little skipping dance at the very thought.

I could live in a castle. Fix it up as a home, raise my children in it.

And that is almost certainly not what Benedict's future bride will expect. I'm not even sure it is what he would want. He has done nothing but grumble about living here.

I might consider myself a practical being, but apparently, I have inherited a little of my family's dreaminess.

I set those fancies aside. In another few steps, I reach an open door. I look in. This room is also empty, but it has some sort of balcony attached. Or a terrace, I should say. A half circle of stonework that I suspect was a later addition. A spot to sit in the sunshine, perhaps surrounded by potted plants.

There should be a door going out to it, but the door is gone, the way wide open. When Lyta races through my legs, giving a little yip of delight, I have to smile.

"Agreed," I say. "It is a lovely spot. Or it could be."

That is not what she's thinking, though. She's running for that open doorway. I tear after her, skirts hitched to my knees, and manage to grab her just before she reaches freedom. I scoop her up as she whines and wriggles.

"Do you need a walk?" I say.

While she was very good about not dirtying indoors last night, I suspect that is unusual for puppies.

I squint out through the doorway. Should I take her on a quick walk? I would like to, but while Benedict feels quite confident not using a lead, I am still very much a city person, and when I peer out, I see shadows and predators that could devour a small dog.

If she ran off, how would I tell Benedict? He has not yet clarified whose dog she is, and I suspect the answer is "his." She is a replacement for his beloved hound. I cannot risk losing her.

"Soon," I say. "Let us find Benedict, and then we will all go out together."

I carry her back into the hall and shut the door firmly. She still whines at it, and I'm reconsidering when another board creaks, this one high enough that it can only come from one place.

The tower.

I am correct. Benedict is ascending to the tower.

Then I know where I am going as well.

"**W**e shall fetch Benedict and go out for a walk," I say again, as if Lyta can understand. I have always wondered why people do this. Explain things to their pets as if they are children. It is not me explaining to her—it is me making a promise to her. I am not ignoring her needs, merely postponing them until I can safely take her out.

The hall soon turns and heads down another damaged corridor. Directly in front of me, though, is an open door. Beyond it are wooden stairs to the tower.

I put my head around the doorway. "Ben?"

Footsteps thump in answer. He is still climbing.

I could keep calling, but that would bring him down, when I want to see the tower.

I want to see it with him.

I check my lantern. Still full of oil and burning bright. I begin to climb.

The stairs are worn wood, starting to rot. Yet another thing Benedict cannot afford to fix. He would know these steps well—which ones give underfoot and where it is safe to step. I do not, and so I climb with care and keep Lyta firmly behind me as I check for any spots she might fall through.

It might seem I am being overcautious. The steps are in poor shape but none rotted enough to break under my weight, much less hers. I feel a bit like a clucking mother hen, shooing Lyta back when she tries to pass me. Then, as the stairs round another turn, I am vindicated. There is indeed a dangerous step, one that is not only rotted but cracked.

I set down the lantern, lift Lyta over, hike my skirts and pull myself onto the step above. Then I retrieve the lantern and keep climbing. I find another rotted step and get past it. A third seems questionable, but by this point, I am *not* questioning. I step over it, too.

Then I am at the top.

The stairs crest at an open hatch. I climb through into a tiny room, like at the other tower. There is one key difference, though. This room is empty. Utterly empty. Dust swirls at my movements, moonlight slipping through long, narrow open windows. To the far side, there is what looks like a half-crumbled doorway, the door long gone. Pieces of wood clutter the floor, either the remains of that door or of old furniture.

I turn in a full circle, lantern lifted, as if Benedict might be hiding in the shadows.

There is no doubt. He isn't here.

But I heard him.

I know I did.

Another creak, this one to my left, and I spin so fast that I stumble over Lyta. I set the lantern on a stone windowsill and scoop her up. Then I peer about.

No one is here. The room is barely big enough to fit a chair or two, and there is nothing to hide behind.

The sound came from that open doorway. Beyond it is some sort of landing. Part of the original fortifications, when a wall might have connected the towers? I take a step closer and peer out. It's a stone piece jutting out and then crumbling away, with a partial wall beyond.

I'm backing toward the hatch and stairs when I catch sight of something beyond that ruined stonework. A figure strides through the moors.

Benedict.

He is only about a hundred feet away, heading back toward the castle.

I start to step into the doorway to call out. Lyta wriggles, and if she spots Benedict, she will leap free of my arms . . . and possibly off the tower itself. I glance at the hatch. She will be safer down there for a moment. She is unlikely to run back down the stairs, and even if she did, the rotted ones will support her weight.

I open the hatch and set her down on the other side. "I will only be a moment."

I use a piece of wood to prop the hatch open enough so she can see me. Then I ease onto the landing, one hand holding my lantern, the other gripping the wall.

I can no longer see Benedict. He must be on the other side of those bushes.

I peer down. The landing stretches a few feet out, and it's solid, only the edge crumbling. There are more scraps of old wood on the floor, but none are big enough for me to trip over.

I let go of the wall and take another step. Then a third. I'm still well away from the edge and trying not to look down. The tower soars at least thirty feet in the air. It's a gorgeous view, but I'd rather enjoy that view from inside.

I can see Benedict, though, and that's the main thing, especially since he now seems to be veering from the castle, as if he wasn't coming in after all.

"Benedict!" I call.

He stops and looks around. I lift my lantern.

"Over here!" I call. "On the tower."

He sees me. "Portia?"

"Would you come inside, please?"

I'm about to say that Lyta needs to go out. Then I realize that's not why she'd been whining at that doorway downstairs. Benedict must have left through it. That's why he went into the ruined wing. Not to climb to the tower for privacy, but to go outside for a walk, using an exit that saves him from having to go all the way to the front first.

"I would like to talk," I say. "Will you come in?"

"Will you get off that blasted tower before you fall?"

I huff under my breath. I'm a foot from the edge, with no intention of getting closer. I don't say that. He's striding my way. Good enough.

I turn, and an invisible hand slams into my shoulder. I'm already off-balance, one foot lifted, and the violent shove sends me spinning. One bare foot slips, and the lantern tumbles from my hand, but I manage to start righting myself. Then a blow strikes my right knee, pain exploding.

My left foot has barely had time to touch down, and when my right knee folds, the left cannot support my weight. I scramble for balance. A hand hits my chest. I feel it. The fingers. The palm. The force of the shove.

Somewhere in the night, Benedict yells. He has been yelling since my first stumble, his footfalls thundering across the drought-hardened earth. Now his voice is hoarse with a near-scream as I'm shoved backward off the landing.

My arms windmill. One strikes stone, the crack so sharp that I am certain I have broken a bone, but my fingers find purchase in the crumbling edge of the stonework. My other hand flies up and grabs on, fingers digging in where they can.

Then I am hanging from the edge. It takes a heartbeat to realize that. I have caught the stonework in both hands, and my body is suspended, and while pain rips down my arms, I can hold on, meaning I did not break any bones.

I manage to get one elbow up onto the landing, but when I try to do the same with the other, it scrambles on loose stone, and I nearly fall.

"Don't move!" Benedict shouts from below, his footfalls still thundering. "Stay there!"

"I am not sure where else I can go." I pause. "Except down. I would prefer not to go down."

He makes a sound that says he does not appreciate the jesting. Then the footsteps stop, and he lets out a string of truly remarkable curses.

"Is everything all right?" I call.

"No, you are hanging from a ledge thirty feet in the air. Everything is *not* all right."

"I did not fall. I was pushed. Multiple times."

His voice softens. "I was not blaming you for your predicament, Portia. I saw what happened, and even if you had stumbled, *how* you fell would be the least of my concerns. It is just . . ." A strangled sound of frustration, followed by another curse. "I cannot get closer."

I glance down.

"Don't move!" he bellows, nearly loud enough to startle me into falling.

I see the situation. Below me is a broken wall. If I fall, that is where I will land.

I am not certain what Benedict's plan was—stand below and catch me?—but he cannot get near enough to do even that. He still tries. He places one foot on the stonework as if to climb up, but he cannot get traction.

"You will not be able to reach me," I say. "Even if you could get up there, I would need to drop, and I would knock you over. All you would do is slightly break my fall while being injured yourself."

"Stop being so bloody practical."

"I could scream instead. Would that be better?"

"At least you are calm," he mutters.

"I am calm because I am secure in my hold. Now, you can stand down there and grumble at me, or you can climb up the stairs and haul me in."

He hesitates. Then he says, softer, "I do not want to leave you."

"Then stand there until I fall."

"You are . . ." He seems to struggle for the word.

"Blunt? Honest? Practical to a fault?"

"I was going to say *infuriating*. Even more so because you are correct. Are you certain you have a hold?"

I bite my tongue against asking what he could do if I didn't. He does not need to consider that possibility, particularly as it might slow him down, and he is already lingering longer than I like. My arms have started to shake.

"I have a firm hold," I say. "Please hurry."

"I will be right there."

He takes off at a run, circling the tower. In the quiet night, his footfalls clamber up the stone steps where he'd exited. Once he is inside, I catch Lyta's whines.

Lyta. I'd forgotten she is locked in the stairs. I need to warn Benedict that she is—

Oh no.

There is something else I need to warn Benedict about. Those rotted steps.

"Ben!" I shout.

No answer. Just the distant thump of his feet on stone floors.

"Benedict!" I call again. "Lyta is in the stairwell, and the steps are rotted!"

Nothing.

I keep shouting the same thing, as I tell myself not to panic. He will see the puppy, and even if he breaks a step, it is not as if he could fall through. He will stumble. He might twist his ankle. But he can still get to me.

He *will* get to me.

Footfalls on the wooden stairs. I try shouting again, but now Lyta is howling, hearing Benedict coming, as if he's there to rescue *her*.

Heavy thumps on the stairs as he runs up them. He is fine. He knows those stairs and—

What is that smell?

It's acrid and familiar.

Smoke.

As I think that, tendrils of smoke rise from the platform. The old wood scattered there. My dropped lantern.

It is fine. It is hardly a raging inferno. Benedict can kick it away—

A crack.

A tremendous crack. A shout of alarm. Another crack, and then another, as if the entire staircase is shattering to splinters.

"Ben!" I shout. "Benedict!"

A thud. Then silence.

I scream Benedict's name, but there is no answer except Lyta's frantic barking.

I test my grip while gritting my teeth against the pain of hanging from my arms. I have been trying to ignore that, telling myself this is a pain I can survive and a small price to pay for surviving. But now as I move, that pain rips through me. I force it back and focus on testing my hold. I have one elbow up and the other hand secure. I need to get the other elbow up.

I heave as high as I can to put my weight on the secured forearm. That lets me readjust my grip with the other hand. I find a better spot and ease that forearm and elbow up—

Sudden pain crushes my bruised fingers, as if someone has dropped a rock on them. I am saved only by the fact I have been concentrating too hard to be startled into jumping. When I move my fingers, an unseen foot stomps on them again. I grit my teeth, and that invisible foot grinds down.

I let out a snarled curse worthy of Benedict. Yes, perhaps I should be panicking, and perhaps the fact I am not means I am in shock, but I would like to think it is my stubborn practicality. Panic will not help. Screaming in rage—or agony—would feel lovely, but will not help. What might help . . .

With my free hand, I claw at my attacker. Here, perhaps, that rage does overshadow practicality, because otherwise, I would question what I am doing. Can I hurt a ghost? Can it even feel pain? I don't think of that. I am furious, and I react.

My nails rake down something. It doesn't feel like flesh and bone. There is give, as if I am clawing a pillow. But there is *something* there, and when I claw, the ghost must feel it, because it withdraws long enough for me to shove it off my trapped fingers and heave my bosom onto the platform.

The ghost kicks me in the shoulder. It is not like the earlier kick. Nor like the earlier shoves. There is a tentative quality to it, as if my scratch surprised it, and it is not nearly as confident in its ability to harm me without being harmed.

Good.

I have been powerless to fight these phantoms, and now I am not, and I will kick and scratch and bite if it teaches them to keep their distance.

The shove only unsettles my hold a little and spurs me to heave myself up without pausing to test my hold again. Luckily, my grip is firm, and with one push, my torso is on the platform and—

Smoke fills my lungs. I cough, and if the ghost had picked that moment to strike, it might have shoved me off again, but it is a heartbeat too late. It kicks at my head, and my cough means that my head is no longer where it was.

The blow glances off my cheek, whipping my head to the side but not unseating me from the platform. The blow also enrages me enough that I vault forward with everything I have, landing fully on the platform . . . facedown in fire.

I scramble up, clawing at my face as embers singe it. My sleeve catches fire, and I smack out the flames. The stench of smoke fills my lungs.

Do not breathe it in.

The ghost shoves my shoulder hard, but I'm on my knees, and I only wobble. I glare up where I expect it to be, and then I lower myself to all fours.

Don't stand. If I do, it can push me off the platform.

Not standing means I am crawling through pockets of fire. Again, I tell myself it isn't like crawling through a massive fire. There are pockets. Only pockets. The skin on my hands will grow back. As a doctor, I know that.

Too bloody practical.

Well, that's a good thing, isn't it, Ben? Or I'd be sobbing, hanging over the edge instead of crawling through literal fire to get to you.

Breathing as little as possible, I make it into the small room. There's more fire in here, smoldering bits of that scattered wood. When I can no longer hold my breath, the smoke sends me into a hacking fit of coughs. I need to stand and breathe above the flames, or I will have survived being shoved off a tower to die from smoke instead.

I grab the wall to brace myself as I rise. Once above the smoke, I have to pause and find my breath, as I am heaving more than I dared admit. Another coughing fit strikes, and I spew black sputum.

That is not good.

But it is not fatal. Not yet.

With one hand on the wall, I move toward the hatch far slower than I would like. I am trying to forget that crash I heard. Trying not to imagine what fate has befallen Benedict.

I want to run headlong to that hatch, but that only opens me up to the ghost's assault. I must keep hold of the wall and be braced for attack.

The ghost does not attack. There is little it can do to me here, past the danger of the platform, and I swear I feel it seething in frustration. When it does lash out, it is a mere blow, and yes, that rocks me back on my heels, but it is nothing compared to shoving me off the platform or stomping my hands to make me fall, and so I cannot stifle a derisive snort of laughter.

After that, it stops trying. Stalking off, I would like to think, like a petulant child. Still, I do not trust that it is gone, and so I take care until I reach the hatch. Then I bend, holding my breath again, and take hold of it.

When I open the hatch, Lyta flies through, and I let out a yelp of alarm, imagining the ghost grabbing her. It does not. I have seen no sign that it can touch anyone else. Like the others I have encountered, it seems limited to making physical contact with me.

I lift Lyta under my arm. Below the hatch, it is pitch black. There are slots in the tower, but none let in enough moonlight to see by. For all I know, there is a gaping hole before me.

"Benedict?" I call.

No answer. My heart speeds up. I blink fast to adjust my eyes, and I open the hatch as far as it will go in hopes of a little light. Finally, though, I need to descend and feel the way with my foot.

There is a first step. Good.

I sit and put Lyta on my lap. Then I descend like a child, on my rear. With each step, I stretch my foot down to ensure there is another below me. There is . . . and then there is not.

I have gone five stairs before my legs extend into nothing.

Heart hammering, I wiggle my feet, hoping to touch on a step. When splintered wood stabs my bare heel, I pull back and then explore with my feet again, more careful now.

The step has broken away, leaving splintered wood.

"Benedict?" I say.

Only Lyta's whining answers.

I consider my next move. I cannot continue to feel around with her on my lap. She didn't fall before, suggesting her night vision is significantly better than mine. I set her on the step above me, and then I shuffle around until I can reach down, all the while very aware that the ghost could be lurking, waiting for a chance to shove me down the stairs.

I can feel the ragged edge of the broken step. Beyond it, there is nothing. I creep down another step and stretch out. Still nothing.

When the smell of smoke wafts through the open door above, I go still. Then I curse myself. I need light? That is where I find it.

I scramble up the stairs to the tiny room, where I find a long piece of wood. I light the end on the flames. Once I am back at the stairs, I must pause to deal with the flaming lace trim of my nightgown. Yet even in that, I see opportunity. I tear the lace hem free and wrap it around the stick, which forms a better torch.

I close the hatch, which will hopefully contain the fire and also helps me rest assured that Lyta will not race back up there.

"Stay here, please," I say.

These are words she will know someday, though possibly not the "please" if Benedict keeps her. For now, I only hope that my firm tone tells her what I mean.

Flaming torch in hand, I look out over the broken step, and my breath catches, panic shredding the edges of my heart. I had expected to see Benedict on the other side of a gap. He would have slipped, hit his head and passed out, and I would only need to get past the gap to help him.

He is not on the other side of a gap.

There is no gap.

There are no stairs.

I knew from that tremendous crack that more than one step had broken, but now I see the sickening truth.

They have all broken, and Benedict has plunged into the darkness.

I drop to my knees and lean over the edge, calling, "Ben!" as I shine the light down.

At first, I see only pieces of the shattered steps. Then, I catch the white fabric of a nightshirt. That's what he'd been wearing on the moors —his trousers and nightshirt. He lies in a heap at the bottom, on a pile of broken steps, with more pieces atop him.

I look around frantically. There is a logical answer to this predicament. He is not in a pit. He is on—or near—ground level. I only need to get there . . . except I am still trapped in this damnable tower.

I lift the torch to illuminate the sides. Have enough of the stairs remained for me to creep down along the edge? Are the window slits big enough for me to use them to . . . to what? Climb out and down the tower like a monkey? The answer to both is no. I am trapped near the top of the tower, with nothing but a yawning hole before me.

A yawning hole with Benedict at the bottom. Unconscious.

Only unconscious?

That panic burbles into my throat, choking me.

He is too far down and the hole too dark and my light too feeble for me to even see whether he still breathes.

Do not panic. That is what my best teachers taught me. When faced with a badly injured patient, a doctor cannot afford to panic. If I start down that road, I will be acutely aware that each passing moment could be one moment too long, and I will make mistakes in my haste.

But how do I get down to Benedict? I cannot even lower myself without something to affix a rope onto.

What rope?

I silence the screeching inner voice as my gaze lands on a partly crumbled window opening. There is a chunk missing at the base, which gives me an idea.

I wedge my torch into another window base for light and strip out of my nightgown. Then I begin to tear it on a sharp piece of broken stonework. It is strong fabric, woven wool, my winter nightwear, which seemed suitable for the moors. That also means it does not rip easily, but I manage to get it apart at the seams. Then I tie a knot in one piece and wedge it into that broken window slot. I yank as hard as I can, and the end does not fly free.

Have I constructed the foolproof descent mechanism? I have not. But the alternative is to run back to the platform and scream in hopes someone hears me in the middle of the night, in the middle of the moors.

I tell Lyta again to stay where she is, and then I begin my descent.

When we were young, Miranda loved wild and athletic adventures. These days, she has Nicolas to join her. In our youth, she had a far less enthusiastic companion: me. She never insisted I go along. In fact, she often slipped out on her own, forcing me to catch up and her to feign confusion.

Oh, did I not tell you I was going swimming in the ocean? Leaping off cliffs to dive into the surf? How odd.

I joined her because, otherwise, she'd have been battered on those rocks, leaping before checking the water below. Or that is what I told myself. Miranda needed me there. Yet perhaps I also went because, in spite of myself, I had fun.

All this means that I have scaled rocks and cliff sides more than anyone would think on meeting me. I am no expert—and I have not done it in a decade—but when I lower myself on that nightgown-rope, I am instantly transported back to those days. My bare feet find the wall, and I brace myself with them as I move hand over hand down the rope.

When Lyta lets out a particular whine—one I recognize as fear and uncertainty—I go still. That is the whine she used with the ghost. Every hair on me rises, and my toes curl, as if they can grip the wall.

I brace for a blow. Something that will send me tumbling. I hold as tight as I can.

Nothing happens.

I start to lower myself again, even more carefully now. As long as I am ready for a blow, the ghost cannot startle me into letting go.

Still, nothing happens. Because the specter cannot get down here? As far as I know, ghosts can neither float nor fly. Is it subject to the same constraints I am, only able to get easily down here by stairs? One would think it could jump, but if so, that would take it to the bottom. It could not hover beside me and attack.

I keep going.

And then I reach the end of my nightgown . . . with Benedict still far below.

I knew this would happen. I could hardly fashion a twenty-foot rope out of a single nightgown—not without scissors and time. I dangle my bare foot experimentally as I peer down.

The bottom is at least six feet below.

I have another little bit of nightgown-rope left. Scant inches, and when I reach the end, I'll slide off.

I peer up and look around. Off to my right are the remains of a few steps. The stairs didn't collapse entirely. Just the middle half or so. If I could swing over and grab—

My hands slip. I grip harder. Just swing—

Something strikes my leg, hard enough to swing me in the other direction, and the rope shoots through my hands. I'm grappling at air as I fall. I think to brace myself, but it's too late. I strike down with both feet and yelp as pain shoots through my legs. One knee buckles, and I smack into the stonework and scramble aside to keep from toppling onto Benedict, but I'm not even sure where he is. I landed on what felt like dirt, and the torch is so high above that I cannot see anything below my waist.

I get my balance and wriggle my toes. Yes, it's dirt. I must be at the base. I lower myself down to all fours and feel around. More dirt, along with tumbled rocks and cobwebs and spongy bits I dare not name. Bugs? Dead mice?

I shudder.

"Benedict?" I say.

I do not expect an answer now, but I still say his name as I crawl about the area. When my leg hits something with slightly more give than a stone wall, I slide my hand down and touch fabric. I grip it and feel the hard heat of his leg.

❧ 24 ❧

I follow his leg up seemingly forever, resisting the panicked urge to start flailing about, hoping to find his chest faster. Then I'm there, and even before my hand reaches his heart, his chest rises and falls under my fingers.

I exhale. If I do not exactly crumple in relief, it is only because I have been telling myself he cannot be dead. The fall was not so great; the floor seemed to be dirt rather than stone, and the chance he fatally struck his head was minimal.

"Ben?" I say as my fingers travel up to his shoulder, gripping and giving a sharp shake. "Benedict?"

He lets out a groan.

I lean toward where I presume his ear to be. "Benedict? It is Portia."

He startles awake, gasping, "Portia." Then he claws up, rising under my hands even as I try to hold him down.

"Wait!" I say. "You've had a fall. I need to check you before you stand."

"Fall. Portia. Must get . . ." He trails off. "Portia?"

I smile and squeeze his arm. "Yes. I'm fine. I'm right here."

"You did not fall?" He still sounds confused.

"Well, if I did, then I would be a ghost, and as you do not have the Sight, you would not be able to hear me. Ergo, I did not fall. You did, though. The tower stairs broke. However, you are also not a ghost." I pause. "In case that was a concern, I should clarify."

He makes a wheezing noise, and my breath catches as my hands fly to what I hope is his chest, only to find my fingers on his mouth . . . and realize he is laughing. Then he is not laughing but actually wheezing and gasping in pain.

"Stop that," I say, more forcefully than I intend.

"Stop breathing?" he gasps. "Or stop doing it poorly?"

"Laughing. Moving. Talking. Stop doing anything that could hurt you before I assess your condition."

"And then, after you have assessed, I can do whatever I like?"

"Of course, because by then, I will have advised you of the proper restrictions, and if you ignore me, that is your own fault."

He makes that wheezing sound again.

"Stop laughing," I say as I run my hands around the back of his neck, feeling his spine. "That is an order."

"Marry me, Portia."

"What?" The word bursts out like an expletive.

"Marry me."

Now I am the one sputtering. "Why—why ever would you want to do that?"

More laughing, edged with gasps that tell me it hurts. "Why would I want to do that? Because you make me laugh. Because you drive me mad. Because you are impossible and infuriating and fascinating. Because you can save yourself from deadly tower falls and then save me when I make a royal mess of your rescue. Because you snap at me while I might be on death's door, and I cannot even take offense because I know it means you are concerned."

"You are not on death's door."

"Is that all you heard?"

"It is the part that matters. I am assuring you that you are not dying."

"What are you doing now?"

"Checking your head, because the rest of that declaration means you clearly struck it in your fall. There."

I press a grazed spot, and he sucks in a breath.

"Do you feel dizzy?" I ask.

"I fell through a tower staircase and plunged to my near death. It would be odd if I did not."

"I ask because you have hit your head."

"So you will not marry me?"

"I should say yes, and then when you are feeling yourself, remind you of it and call you a cad for jilting me."

"You could sue me for breach of contract. I must have a few shillings somewhere."

Now I'm the one choking back a laugh as I continue my examination.

"Would light help?" he asks.

"Yes, but shockingly, I could not hold a lantern while descending into the hole to save you."

"Wise. If you would like light, though, I have a tinderbox in my pocket."

"What?"

I feel his shrug under my fingers as he says, "I was going to take a lantern, but it would not light, so I became frustrated and marched out without the lantern but shoved the tinderbox in my pocket."

"May I look for it?"

"You just finished running your hands down my backside. I am not concerned with you reaching into my pockets."

My cheeks heat. "I was checking your spine."

"I know, and I was teasing. Get the tinderbox, Portia."

I do that, and I light a small splinter of wood. I hold it in front of his face, and he grimaces.

"Are you trying to light me on fire?" he says.

"Possibly, if you keep grumbling. I have sacrificed a very fine night-gown for you."

His gaze moves down my chest, which is still demurely covered by the shift I left on last night. "Dare I ask?"

"I needed rope to lower myself down here."

He throws back his head in a laugh, only to wince with pain and shake his head. "Of course you did. I am sorry to hear that. It was a very fine nightgown. Its sacrifice will not be forgotten. I'll buy you a new one for our honeymoon."

I roll my eyes. "With your few shillings?"

His lips curve. "It will have to be a much smaller nightgown, I fear. Far less fabric."

"What else would it be on one's honeymoon?"

His laugh is nearly a bark of surprise, but before he can continue, I say, "Now stop talking and tell me where it hurts."

"That depends. Will you marry me?"

"Absolutely not."

"Then here." He claps his hands to his heart. "It hurts here."

I roll my eyes. "How hard was that blow to the head?"

"Hard enough. Fine, I shall be serious."

Because you were not being serious.

I knew that. Of course I did.

And yet . . .

I shake it off as I search for injuries and obtain his responses. Except for the blow to his head, his injuries seem remarkably slight. I will credit his excellent health and physical condition. He may have bruised his ribs, but none seem broken. His spine appears fine, and I do not see any sign of broken bones.

When I am confident he is not seriously injured, I allow him to sit up. He does, and immediately groans and cradles his head.

"Let me see your eyes again," I say.

I half expect some teasing joke. It would not be unwarranted. I have resisted the urge to stare into those remarkable amber eyes for two days now, and I do not mind the excuse to do so. He makes no jokes. Either he is in too much pain, or he does not realize how striking they are. He only lifts his gaze, and I examine his pupils, which seem fine.

"What is your name?" I ask.

One thick brow rises. "If you do not know it, then I am not the only one who has been struck on the head."

"I am testing your mental faculties."

His lips purse. "They are fair to middling. I was an indifferent student at best. Excellent with numbers. Good at reading, but only because I enjoy it. Otherwise?" He shrugs. "I was quite a dunce at the rest, and only passed because the maths and reading balanced it out."

When I do not answer, he sighs. "Fine. You are not in the mood for jests."

"Oh, I am always in the mood for jests. But failing at science is hardly a joking matter. I was taking a moment to silently mourn your lack of potential."

"As a husband?"

"As a person."

"Ouch."

I smile at him. "Now I am jesting. Fine, forget your name—"

"I thought you wanted me to remember it."

I shake my head. "Enough of this. Your mental faculties are fine. The blow to the head merely put you in a rather silly mood."

"Silly?"

"In a charming way. You could do with a little more silliness, Lord Sterling."

"As could you, Portia of London. And thank you for supplying the rest of my name. Lord Benedict Sterling, Earl of something or other."

My makeshift matchstick goes out—our third so far. I sigh, and this time, he takes the box from my hands in the dark and lights a larger piece of wood from the floor.

"Oh, that reminds me," I say. "The tower is on fire."

Both brows shoot up to his hairline.

"Yes, yes," I say, "perhaps I should have mentioned that, but it is a relatively small fire, contained within a framework of stone."

"We are sitting at the base of a burning tower?"

"Do you smell smoke?"

"No, but I have suffered a blow to the head."

I pluck the burning piece of wood from his hand. "If you are able to walk, we should leave. I must get Lyta. I needed to leave her on the steps, which was less than ideal."

"She is fine. I can hear her whining, but she is being a very patient dog."

"Good. Then you ought to rise. While I do not think the tower is in danger of burning to collapse, either way, it does you no good to be lying in the dirt when you have suffered a fall."

"I do not mind lying in the dirt. It is quite peaceful. I have a lovely doctor in her chemise to tend to me. The sound of crickets in the distance. The gently wafting scent of smoke from the tower above us."

"I thought you couldn't smell it."

"I have a good imagination. I am certain it smells lovely. An evening fire is always a pleasant odor. Portia? Where are you going?"

"Leaving you to your bed of dirt," I call back.

When he grunts with the exertion of rising, I say, "I am jesting. I'm looking for a way out of here. I thought we were at the foot of the tower, but it appears . . ." I shine the light around. "It appears we are about five feet below that."

"Hmm, yes. There is a space under the floor in all the towers. My grandfather claimed they were special hiding places for castle children. He was teasing, but that is what Jude and I used them for. I had the one to the north. He had the one to the south. We shared this one . . . until I accidentally trapped him down here and our mother had it boarded up."

"Accidentally trapped him?"

He sighs. "You know how it is with younger siblings. Sometimes, they are simply too much, and you pretend to trap them under the floorboards to give them a bit of a fright, but then it turns out they can't escape as easily as you expected, and you forget about them until dinner hour, by which time they are in tears and have nightmares for weeks."

"You had me nodding in agreement for the first third of that story."

He sighs again. "I know. I was a terrible brother. I possessed a sliver of boyish malice that was inadvertently widened into a club by a tendency toward youthful forgetfulness. There was also the time I told him to wait for me by the creek and forgot about him. And also the time —" He clears his throat. "I should stop now."

"Poor Jude."

"In my defense, he was a terrible pest."

"Because he adored you and only wanted to spend time in your company."

An even bigger sigh. "You sound like our mother. Fine. I was a terrible brother. Now, why are we discussing Jude again?"

"We weren't. I was commenting on the fact that we appear to be in a hole, which you explained was a storage hold."

"Mmm." He starts rising to his feet, only to nearly bonk his head on the low ceiling.

"Careful!" I say, rushing back to him. I take his hand and lower him back to sitting. "Wait until I have figured out the best exit route."

He jabs a finger. "There is a massive hole in the ceiling right there. Less than five feet above the ground."

"Yes, and yet you chose to stand up over here and hit your head—again—which means you are in no shape to boost me up out of this hole."

"I thought you'd boost me up."

"That seems unwise. I can get out, as I did with the tower platform. I could haul myself up and then go for help from Jude. However, that leaves you and Lyta in here, and while I do not think the tower is likely to collapse, I am not trusting in that. Allow me to survey the area, please, in hopes I will find another way out, one which will accommodate you."

He doesn't answer. He's staring up at me, so long that my heart hammers with worry.

"Benedict? Are you all right?"

"You are so beautiful," he says.

My heart races faster, the worry turning to mild panic. That injury is indeed worse than it seemed. He is losing his grip on reality.

"Benedict?" I grasp his shoulder with my free hand. "Do you know where you are?"

"In a filthy pit, surrounded by pieces of rotting stairs, under a tower that may actually be on fire, with a brilliant woman in a burned and ripped chemise, cobwebs in her wild golden hair, soot on her face, and while she is always beautiful, she has never looked lovelier than she does at this moment."

My hand flies to his forehead. It seems cool, so it is not fever, but only the blow to his head.

"I am fine, Portia." He takes my hand and lowers it. "Yes, I was struck on the head. Yes, I am somewhat dazed. Yes, I am saying foolish things, but the advantage to having a head injury is that I am not pride-bound enough to care that I am being foolish."

He meets my gaze. "Ignore my ramblings. Truly, I am fine, and the more worried you grow about me, the more I will wax rhapsodic on your beauty." He touches my chin. "How can a man resist a woman who is so concerned for his wellbeing? It only proves you are a wonder, to have such excellent taste in men."

I choke on a laugh and lightly rap his arm. "All right. You may continue to be silly, and I will not worry myself on your behalf."

"Mmm, that is not what I want at all. Was that not clear?"

I shake my head and turn with my makeshift torch raised. "As I said, let me have a quick look about. If all else fails, I shall get up top and rouse Jude, and you can pray he does not see this as the perfect opportunity to leave you under the floorboards."

I turn and head past the hole in the ceiling and into the darkness beyond. When I stretch my arm with the torch, I can make out a pile of rags on the floor. Would that help? Could I use the rags to haul Benedict up?

No, that is a foolish enough plan that I fear I am becoming infected by Benedict's nonsensical turn of mind. I cannot haul him out. I should not —his ribs are bruised. Ideally, I would find something for him to step on so I can help him climb out with minimal strain.

There is a boxlike object further in the space. Is that a stool? I blink, certain my mind is as dazed as Benedict's. I was just thinking I need a way to boost him up, and now I see a stool?

Except it does seem to be one. A low footstool, plus a wooden box nearby.

Benedict mentioned that the boys played in here.

"Did you leave a stool down here?" I ask.

"A . . . ? Oh! Actually, yes, I think we did. Jude hated sitting in the dirt, so I brought him a stool."

"You are ruining your reputation as a terrible older brother."

"I know. Balance, that is the key. As with my schoolwork. If I have a defining principle of my life, that would be it. One can be dense in some classes and mean to a younger brother and a complete ass to . . . pretty much everyone else, as long as one strikes the balance. Do well in other classes. Be kind to your brother now and then. Show others that a heart beats beneath your stony exterior. Balance."

I smile. I hate to say there is any advantage to a blow to the skull, but this is a side of Benedict I rather like. The silliness is refreshing, but I also appreciate the insights into his brain, the reflections he would never make if he were feeling more himself.

"Well, I appreciate this particular show of balance," I say. "If this stool is not rotted, it might be the key to getting you out of here."

"It should be fine. It was exceptionally sturdy. It'd been in our family for generations. I probably should have told my parents I brought it down here before they boarded this room up."

"That forgetfulness again?"

"Oh no. I remembered. But if I mentioned it, then I would need to admit that I brought a family heirloom into a dirty crawlspace. I am not entirely a dunce."

I laugh under my breath, light another piece of wood and jam both torches into the dirt. "Let me fetch the stool then. Can you speak to Lyta, please? Reassure her?"

He does that while I move into the cavernous darkness. At first, I only duck my head, but then I realize the floor seems to slope upward, leaving me less than five feet of height. I adjust my shift over my knees so I might hunch and walk. I pass the pile of rags, which give off the most terrible stench. Something has made a nest in them. I suppress a shiver and hurry on.

I reach the stool. I can't see it well—I am blocking the light source—but it feels sturdy. It is taller than most, maybe two feet high. Perfect. I can help Benedict onto it, and he can climb out.

With the stool under one arm, I turn. I take one step and stop. Now that I have turned, the light illuminates my way . . . and it illuminates that pile of rags. Something pokes out from under it. Something bony and pale that I cannot tell myself belongs to a dead rat.

It is a hand. A skeletal hand.

"**B**enedict?" I say.

"Hmm?"

"There is . . . something here."

He leans my way and squints. "Is that a pile of rags?"

"No, it is a dress."

"A dress?"

"There is . . ." I swallow. "Wait."

"Wait?"

I reach and take one of the lit torches. Then I examine the hand. It is only partially skeletonized, which is an important distinction only because it means I am not looking at a decades-old corpse. *Am* I looking at a corpse—an entire body? That is what I am trying to determine. I lean in. The stink hits me.

There is definitely a person-shaped object in that dress.

"Good God," Benedict says at my ear, and I give a small jump before turning to see him beside me.

"Yes, it appears to be a body," I say. "You should stay back. It will doubtless be quite a gruesome sight."

"That is not why I cursed. It is the fact that you are calmly examining it."

I stiffen and try to contain the response, but my voice chills as I say, "I am a scientist. Forgive me if my seeming callousness disturbs you."

"That is not—" He lets out a growl of frustration. "Apparently, my blow to the head is wearing off, as my tongue is no longer as glib. I meant that you never fail to surprise me, Portia. I realized what might lie beneath that dress and hurried over to stop you from getting an unpleasant shock. I should have known you already understood what could be here, and you were making certain of it before you said anything."

"I may not be a doctor in name, but I am one in training. I have seen death."

His voice softens. "I know." He looks down and shivers. "The poor girl. She must have . . ."

He trails off as he realizes what I already have. That this is no accident. The stairs weren't broken until he fell through.

I continue making my way along the body. The woman lies face-down. Her dress is a simple one. The day gown of a maid or a tenant farmer.

The dress is brown with dark stains on the back. I lower the torch to see slices in the fabric surrounding multiple wounds.

"Stabbed in the back." I glance at Benedict. "Were the stairs still sealed when you took up residence in the keep?"

"They were. I have not been in this part for months. I sit in the north tower—the stairs are safer. Jude does not come into this wing, not since —" His voice catches. "Not since I left him here." He looks up sharply, gaze flying to mine. "I did not do this."

"Of course you didn't."

"Thank you. I would not want you to think me a killer."

"Oh, I do not know you well enough to say that. I only know that you are too clever to put the body of your victim in your own castle, and in the same place you once trapped your brother."

"I . . . I am not certain whether to be pleased that you think I am clever or insulted that you think I could be a murderer."

"I would be insulted if you thought I could *not* be a murderer based on a mere three-day acquaintance."

"I . . ."

"In the direst of circumstances, I could take a life. Most people could." I look down at the body. "And if we are being disrespectful to anyone, it is you, poor woman. Forgive us. My lack of obvious distress does not mean I am unaffected by your plight. We will put you to rest."

"Find her family. Bury her properly."

"Yes, of course. I also mean putting her soul to rest."

He goes still and then curses. "She is the ghost. Naturally." He moves back onto his haunches with a wince. "I will not be so concerned for her plight then."

"No," I say. "Do not hold her spirit's behavior against her. We do not know what torment and frustration she has suffered. She was murdered and tethered to a place where no one could hear her." I touch the body. "I am going to turn her over. The sight may prove gruesome."

He nods grimly and moves forward to help, but I wave him back.

"You should not lift anything right now. Your task, if you can bear it, is to see whether you know her."

"I can bear it."

"I would think no less of you if you could not."

I gently turn the body over. The sight is not as horrifying as I might have feared. Most of her face is intact, and her eyes are closed. She looks young, very young, I realize as my heart squeezes. About twenty years of age, with dark hair and freckles.

He lets out a sharp breath. "Oh."

"You know her."

"I do. I was going to say that I doubted I would—we have not had any women go missing. But I did not think of . . . Yes, I ought to have considered her."

He looks at me. "Her name is Pansy. Pansy Miller. She—" He inhales. "As a young girl, she worked for my Aunt Flora as a parlormaid. Then, when the Carletons came, she worked there for a while. She went to work for another family after that. The last I heard, she'd gone to Edinburgh. I only know that because her mother came to me last year, concerned because she had stopped receiving Pansy's letters and money. I had just started investigating when the letters resumed, with extra money and apologies for the delay—Pansy had gone abroad with her new employer."

A moment of silence, then he asks, with reluctance, "Do you have any idea how long she has been dead?"

"At least a couple of years."

"Right around the time she supposedly went to work in Edinburgh."

Using the stool, I manage to get Benedict out of the hole with minimal strain, though by this point, he no longer seems to feel the pain of his injuries. He is too deeply dismayed over the fate of Pansy Miller.

From there, I insist on fetching a ladder from the barn while Benedict waits and reassures Lyta that rescue is imminent. Leaving them there is safe enough. The fire has burned down to a smoldering that doesn't endanger anything. It will need to be left as is and watched in case it reignites.

Once we have Lyta, I escort both Benedict and Lyta back to the castle and rouse Jude, who was still sound asleep. Then I bring Jude to the library, where Benedict is supposed to be waiting. Of course he is not waiting. He has fetched a bottle of brandy and a bowl of water and soap, and he has even gotten the fire started.

I could—and possibly do—grumble at him for not resting, but it is only a half-hearted complaint. Of all the traits I expected to find attractive in a man, domesticity was not one of them. But it is exceptionally attractive. It is caring and forethought from a man who seemed—at first meeting—to possess neither.

He should have been the one resting while I tended to him. Instead, he did that for me. Warm the room. Bring fortifying spirits. Provide soap and water to clean with.

So while I grumble at him not resting, I also thank him—sincerely—as I clean myself and drink the brandy and hope that neither brother mentions the fact I am in my undergarments. If they do, propriety will require me to go and dress, and I really am too tired for that. I needn't have worried. They are both perfect gentlemen, which in this case means that they do not comment on my clothing—or lack thereof.

I have only told Jude that there was an accident, Benedict falling through the stairs. Remarkably, he did not ask why we were in the tower. I could attribute this to drowsiness, but more likely, he knows not to question his brother's behavior. If we were wandering through the ruined wing in the middle of the night, well, Jude is certain we had a good reason.

Now Benedict takes it upon himself to explain that reason. Or a variation on it, where he'd woken, restless, and gone for a walk, and then I woke, went to find him and was lured into the tower by the ghost.

Jude swivels in his chair. "The ghost pushed you off the tower? And you did not see fit to mention this?"

"If her intent was to dash me on the stonework, she failed," I say.

"And so it was not worth mentioning?" He closes his eyes and shakes his head. "You are as bad as he is, do you know that?"

"Worse," Benedict says. "I would have at least been cursing out the ghost who pushed me off the balcony. Portia wants to help her."

"And you would not?" Jude says. "The only reason you are complaining is that *you* were not the one the ghost pushed. You are furious at what she did to Portia. What about the fact that this ghost is responsible for you falling through the tower stairs?"

"That is my own fault," Benedict says. "I knew they were rotted."

"See?" Jude throws up his hands. Then he stops. "Wait. When did our ghost become a she?"

Benedict and I look at each other. I nod to Benedict, and he tells the rest of the story.

⚡

"Pansy Miller," Jude exhales when Benedict is done.

"Her mother was concerned," Benedict said. "I should have done something."

"You did," Jude said. "You started inquiries, and the letters resumed with a plausible explanation that even her mother didn't question. I vaguely remember Pansy from when she worked at Aunt Flora's. She was a girl with her eye on the next rung, which is admirable. She also looked after her family, which is also admirable. But she had to be urged to go home on her half days. She was never inclined to spend time with her family."

"So no one was surprised," I say, "when she left for Edinburgh, sending back only letters and money."

"Precisely," Jude says.

"Obviously, her killer was sending those letters and the money."

Jude pats Lyta's head as the puppy crosses from Benedict to me. "Meaning her killer was a man of means."

"Or a woman," I say, helping Lyta snuggle in at my side. "We would need more to conclude it was a man. But yes, someone of means. They hoped they could taper off the charade and stop sending money. Only her mother went to Benedict."

Jude nods. "Who began asking questions, which prompted the killer to resume the payments."

"Who was her last employer here?" I ask. "You said she went from Aunt Flora to the Carletons to . . ."

Benedict looks at Jude, who shrugs.

"It was up north," he says. "Between here and the Scottish border."

"I'll find out," Benedict says.

"So she went north and allegedly continued on to Edinburgh, yet her body was hidden here? Were you living in the keep at the time she left?"

Benedict shakes his head.

"May we discuss dates?" I say. "So I might understand the timing. When you moved to the keep, when you returned to the area, when Pansy moved from one position to another . . ."

"Our father died four years ago. He was thrown from a horse and lingered for several weeks, during which Jude and I returned home."

Jude says, "The moment he died, his creditors—his former friends— swooped in like vultures. They had quite literally been circling his deathbed, under pretense of helping Benedict. We had barely laid him to rest before Carleton and his cronies dove in with the list of our father's debts, including one which Benedict needed to settle immediately or Sterling Hall—and part of our ancestral lands—was forfeit to Carleton."

"I could not raise the funds in time," Benedict says. "I consulted three legal experts, but there was no loophole to exploit."

"We had to give up Sterling Hall and part of our land," Jude says. "When the Carletons moved in, they wanted to hire their own staff, and Pansy went there. This would have been three and a half years ago."

"And you did not immediately move to the castle, correct?" I say.

"Correct," Benedict says. "I managed to keep us in a rented country house until the drought hit."

"We were living in a comfortable home while our tenants suffered,"

Jude says. "Benedict insisted—rightly—that we give up the house and move here. That was two years ago."

"And Pansy?"

"She lasted less than a year with the Carletons and then less than a year with the next family. She went to Edinburgh . . . ?" He looks at Benedict. "Two-and-a-half years ago?"

"Two autumns before last," he says. "I recall that her mother was upset she didn't return for the holidays. We moved into the keep the following spring."

"So she was most likely murdered the autumn before you moved here."

"Yes, seven or eight months before." Jude looks up sharply. "Which is also shortly before that first report of a ghost. Which would make sense."

"Pansy was murdered and buried here," I say. "Her spirit is trapped here and was spotted by a woman with an inkling of the Sight. That woman fled. Then I come, and Pansy must be able to tell I also have an inkling of the Sight, so she is lashing out in her frustration."

"She tried to kill you," Benedict says. "That is more than 'lashing out in frustration.'"

"Yes, but . . ." I pull Lyta onto my lap. "I do not know how to explain it. My encounters are always negative, and I know from my grandmother and sister that such things are uncommon. A friend's uncle died from being spooked into a fall during a malicious haunting. The friend herself also experienced that malicious haunting. That was an angry spirit, and yet it was still not like this. Whatever happened to suddenly grant me that sliver of Sight, I seem to attract tormented spirits."

"Perhaps spirits who are not in their right mind?" Jude says. "I have read of such things, particularly in Eastern accounts. Tormented spirits lashing out violently."

"Which suggests it does happen," I say. "Whatever the reason, the fact remains that Pansy Miller is dead and murdered, and her ghost haunts your castle."

"We must put her to rest and be rid of her," Benedict says. "Your sister can do that, yes?"

"Miranda can communicate with Pansy. If we can find her killer—or she can tell us who killed her—then we name that person, and she is free."

"It is settled, then." Benedict rises and peers toward the window, where dawn has broken. "I must report her body to the reeve, of course. Pansy's family must be made aware of her fate. Then we must fetch your sister and find Pansy's killer. I will leave for the reeve now and return later to take you to York if your sister does not arrive on her own."

Jude clears his throat.

"I am fine enough to travel," Benedict says. "Portia will be with me, in the event of a turn for the worse, but I do not expect more than soreness and bruises, which will not keep me from this."

"That wasn't what I was going to say. You cannot go to York today, Ben."

"But I must. Portia's sister—"

"The ball?"

"What ball . . . ?" He shakes his head and then scowls. "I hope you are joking, Jude. We cannot possibly have the ball now. A young woman has been murdered."

"Nearly three years ago."

"Her spirit haunts our *home*."

"And does not bother us. She bothers Portia, who will be leaving for York today."

"Yes, with *me*. I cannot possibly attend a ball to pick . . ." His hands wave, annoyance twisting his face.

"A bride," Jude says.

"No." The word comes sharp. "I cannot. I have too much to do."

"You do not actually need to choose a bride tonight, Ben, but you must attend. Unless you have some other reason—some *better* reason— for calling it off."

"Murder is not an adequate reason? A violent spirit who nearly murdered our guest is not an adequate reason?"

I rise, setting Lyta down as I motion for Benedict to stop his thundering. "Jude is right. You cannot embarrass your aunt by skipping your own bridal-hunt ball. Her coach is taking me to York. I will return with Miranda on the morrow."

"What if you cannot find your sister? What if she will not come? You need me—"

"I don't, Ben," I say softly. "I will find her. She will come. You need to attend your ball."

"Unless you no longer require a bride," Jude says. "Unless there is anything—*anything*—that might make you abandon this foolishness and find another way."

Silence. I want to glare at Jude. The ball is not foolishness. It is not a whim. It is the only solution to a problem that affects the entire village. If there was another way, Benedict would have found it.

There is no other . . .

The clock.

I think of the clock, and instead of seizing on it, my stomach twists. It seems a fantasy now, a wild dream of finding a stolen object that will save the day. We have a murdered girl and a vengeful spirit, and neither is going to get us closer to that clock, and yet that is where our attention must move. To Pansy. To her killer.

"I need to go," Benedict says. "I must speak to the reeve."

I step forward. "I can make breakfast before you—"

"If you can make it for Jude, I would appreciate that. He is quite inept in the kitchen." Benedict is already moving toward the door. "I have several things to do this morning, but I will be back before you leave."

26

I t is time for me to leave for York, and there is no sign of Benedict. No, it is *past* time, because I have been dawdling while Jude checks his pocket watch. He has brought their coach around. We are supposed to use it to go to Aunt Flora's—as hers will be in service all day running errands—and then I will head out from there in her coach.

"You will be back on the morrow," Jude says. "You will see Ben then."

"I am not—"

"Not waiting for my brother? Simply finding a dozen reasons why you need to run back inside—oh, did I leave my hairbrush? Did I put out the hearth fire?—and then returning to peer down the lane looking for random visitors? Perhaps another boy selling puppies?"

I glare at him.

"You will see him tomorrow," Jude says.

"I only wished to say goodbye. It is the polite thing to do. Bid him farewell and thank him for his hospitality."

"When you will be enjoying that hospitality again in less than a day?"

"Fine." I tug on the small lead I braided for Lyta. "Come along, girl. We must be off to the city."

Jude offers a hand to help me into the carriage, which is really a one-horse chaise, with two wheels and seating for two.

"There is no room for Benedict anyway," Jude says. "Perhaps he realized that and decided to meet us there."

I try not to fret. I understood why he had to leave early. It would be wrong to enjoy breakfast while Pansy's body lay under the tower. He'd gone to speak to the town reeve. We are in a time that precedes formal law enforcement, and the reeve is Benedict's representative within the village. I presume such offices cover various duties, depending on what the lord requires, which would differ from region to region, lord to lord. I am not familiar enough with the institution to be clear on it, and I can hardly ask and betray my ignorance of this time. I only know that Benedict felt the need to inform the reeve.

The reeve had then sent men to recover the body while Benedict had gone to speak to the Miller family. I am certain he could ask the reeve to do this, but I am not surprised that he wished to do it himself, which strikes me as proper, even if it meant he did not return to the castle.

From there, I do not know what he was doing. I only know that he never returned, and we have eaten lunch and now are on our way to Lady Flora's house, where a coach will whisk me off to York, and Benedict will spend the evening considering candidates for his bride, and I do not know what to do with that. I only know that I want to see him first.

We are heading down the long drive of Lady Flora's home when hooves pound behind us. I clutch Lyta to keep her safe as I lean out. Benedict barrels up beside us.

"You have not gone," he calls, panting slightly as the horse wheezes with exertion.

"I have not." I turn to Jude. "Let me out here, and I will walk."

"The house is right there," Jude says.

"But I wish to speak—"

Jude urges the horse forward, and I have little choice but to continue to the front of the house, where Lady Flora waits. When I get there, Benedict is already off his horse and hurrying over to me.

"I am sorry I was gone so long," he says as he takes Lyta and sets her down. "Do you have a moment before you leave?"

"No," Lady Flora says as she moves forward. "She does not."

Benedict's face darkens. "I was asking Portia."

"And I am telling you she does not have 'a moment' because she is not leaving. I am certain this will be a terrible blow to you both, but I fear Miss Portia must stay with us a while longer."

"Oh?" Benedict and I say in unison.

"Yes. There has been an"—she flutters her hands—"inefficiency in scheduling. Beyond my control, of course. After offering my coach to Miss Portia, I realized I needed to pick up flowers for the ball. That was fine. A hired coach would do. Except the company from which I hired a coach has not delivered it, and it has been hours, so I have given it up for lost."

"You need your own coach to fetch flowers for the ball," Jude says. "I am certain Portia understands."

"Of course," I say. "When will I leave then? After the flowers are delivered?"

"Well, that is the problem. Having hired a coach, I agreed to pick up two groups of guests in the village. Miss Portia will need to stay until morning."

"Until morning?" Thunderclouds drift into Benedict's eyes. "You expect her to stay here, during the ball to select my—"

"Certainly not," Lady Flora says.

"Then what is your plan? For her to return to the keep?"

"That would work," Jude says. "Portia can stay for supper and then return to the keep during the ball. I will likely be too tired—from socializing with my injury—to go back this evening, but Benedict can return. He should be there not long after midnight. He can host Portia until morning."

Benedict turns his glower on his brother.

"What?" Jude says. "Do you object to spending the night with Portia?"

"No, I object to any plan that would see Portia alone in the keep . . . with a spirit that wishes her harm."

I glance over sharply, but Lady Flora gives no sign of surprise, meaning Jude must have already told her of my encounter.

"Oh." Jude glances at Lady Flora. "We—I mean, I had not thought of that."

"That *is* a concern," Lady Flora says. "Dare I hope the spirit was absent last night?"

I look at Jude, but it's Benedict who winces first, his anger dissipating.

"There is something we need to tell you," he says. "I ought to have stopped by this morning to explain. Do you remember your little parlor-maid, Pansy?"

⚜

LADY FLORA IS IN SHOCK AND TRYING VERY HARD TO ACT AS IF SHE IS NOT. I understand the impulse. There is too much to do in preparation for the ball, and she cannot afford to grieve for a girl who was in her employ years ago. I do not get the impression that Pansy was a particularly memorable employee. It doesn't matter. I see much of Benedict in his aunt, stern practicality shadowing a kind heart.

Miranda would say the same about me. I do not see myself as partic-ularly stern or forbidding, and I am baffled when others do. To me, I wear my heart on my sleeve a little too much, and Miranda would say I pull on a chilly cloak to hide it. I fear I will not be taken seriously otherwise.

The discovery of Pansy's body clearly upsets Lady Flora, but she is just as clearly determined not to let it interfere with the evening. She sends Benedict and Jude with the coach to fetch supplies and then enlists my help with decorations.

"You will stay here this evening," she says. "In the library, which has a lovely little garden where you and your puppy can roam with no fear of encountering guests."

The idea of being present during the ball makes me exceptionally uncomfortable. But I have little choice in the matter. Even the local coach is not running to York, having instead been hired to ferry guests for the evening.

I had hoped for a moment to speak to Benedict. Did he learn anything that might help solve Pansy's murder? I presume that was what he'd been doing. Gathering information. Yet he is whisked away by Jude before I can speak to him.

When I hear their coach return, I hurry to the kitchens to speak to Benedict, only to have Lady Flora ask me to fetch her a slice of cake. Once that is done, I swear I hear Benedict in the garden. Lyta races off, seeming to confirm it. But the next thing I know, Jude is carrying the puppy back to me. I ask about Benedict, but Jude does not know where he is. I finish arranging flowers and hear Benedict's voice in the front hall, but before I can get there, Jude cuts me off, asking for my help finding a missing silver service.

I am beginning to get the sense I am being deliberately kept from Benedict.

And it is beginning to annoy me.

The more I am prevented from speaking to him, the more determined I am to do exactly that. Yes, I have nothing critical to discuss, but I do not know why I am being blocked, and it infuriates me.

When I finally hear Benedict's voice, I put Lyta into the library and stride off in that direction. I will speak to him, and no one can tell me he is not here.

He is in the conservatory. Seeing that, I smile. I saw a piano in there, and I remember what Jude said about daring Benedict to play. I'll do that and—

Benedict's voice comes again, now with the clear boom of anger. The thick doors muffle it enough that I can catch only snippets of speech, as if he is pacing past the doors and then away again.

"—not go through with this farce," he is saying.

Lady Flora answers, her voice too quiet for me to hear, but her tone firm.

"Fine," Benedict grumbles. "I apologize. It is not a farce." More that I cannot hear. Then, "But under the circumstances, it cannot proceed."

Lady Flora's voice answers.

"It is an insult to Pansy's family," Benedict says. "To hold a ball on the day her body was discovered."

I move close enough that I can make out Lady Flora's response. "You only just realized this now, Benedict?"

"No, I realized it this morning, but Jude ignored my concerns, and I have decided I will no longer be ignored. I must speak. Holding the ball tonight is wrong."

"All right. How about tomorrow?"

"No. I am sorry, but it must be canceled."

"Must be canceled," Lady Flora says, slowly. "So you are no longer in need of a bride?"

"I have never been in need of a bride. This was a solution to a problem."

"Which you have otherwise resolved?"

"No, but I will."

Silence falls with a weight I feel in my stomach.

Benedict must feel it, too, and he plows on. "There is another solution. There must be. I will find it."

"Why?"

Benedict sputters. "Why? What sort of question is that? So my tenants do not starve. So my land is not forfeit to someone who will let them starve."

"I mean why the sudden need to cancel the ball? Do not tell me it is out of consideration for that poor girl's family. No one here tonight will have known her, and they would be more shocked if we canceled for the death of a former servant."

"I do not care if they are shocked."

"Do you have another reason, Ben? A real reason?"

He blusters, and I don't catch half of it, but soon his aunt interrupts with, "You need a reason, Ben. I did not suggest marriage as a solution to your problem. You did. You came to me, and I tried to dissuade you, but you insisted you had always seen marriage as an eventual duty. A countess for your land, and a mother for your heirs. Nothing more." A long pause. "Has that changed?"

"The point is—"

"The point is that I am asking whether that has changed."

"I have not yet found another way to raise funds, but I will—"

"That is not my question. Is there something that prevents you from marrying? If you have committed yourself to another, while it would take some finagling to avoid scandal, it is a valid reason. You met someone else, who has agreed to marry you, and so you no longer require the ball. Is that the case?"

His answer is more blustering, and in that moment, I realize why Jude and Lady Flora are keeping me from Benedict.

I am a distraction.

A distraction and a temptation.

I could almost laugh at the latter. I am hardly anyone's idea of a temptress. Nor do I think I am the reason Benedict is balking. Instead, I have distracted him with the mystery of the clock and the mystery of Pansy's death. He does not want this ball or this marriage, and I have provided mysteries he hopes he can use to extricate himself from the situation. Either he finds the clock and no longer needs a bride, or he must find a killer and does not have time for a bridal hunt.

Lady Flora mistakenly thinks I am the actual distraction. The actual temptation. She's keeping me from him with Jude's help so that we do not . . . What? Run off and elope? I could laugh at the thought if it didn't set butterflies alight in my heart.

I want that.

Want what? Benedict to declare he cannot bear to wed another and beg me to run away with him and elope?

Yes.

Am I mad?

Am I the one hit on the head?

No.

I have fallen in love. This is what it is like. To meet someone and barely know them and be seized by a sort of madness where wild fantasies set your heart dancing with hope.

This is all my fault.

Jude or Lady Flora have seen the way I must look at Benedict, and they've decided I am a threat. Which I am, only not in the way they think. I have given Benedict excuses to do a thing he does not want to do.

A thing he must do.

Unless . . .

Is there another way? As Jude pointed out, it is not as if there will be a wedding tonight. What if I can come up with a way for Benedict to get the money he needs? Forget fantasies about stolen clocks. Think realistically.

I do not have the money he needs, and I am almost glad of that. Otherwise, I might indeed put myself forward as a bridal candidate, too caught up in this infatuation to realize I'd be falling into the same trap as before, wed to a man who does not love me.

The alternative would be to simply gift Benedict the money, and that is equally wrong. If I had an overflowing bank account, I would happily donate to this worthy cause, but I would not want to face a situation where I would need to decide between helping another and protecting my own financial independence.

While I could give Benedict a few hundred pounds, that is a fraction of what he needs.

Is there anything I can do? Any way I can postpone this, even a little? What if . . . ?

I try to banish the slowly forming thought, but it pushes through. If Benedict has a child, Lady Flora can funnel part of her family wealth to that child. What if . . . ?

No. If that were the easy solution, Benedict would take it. Marry whomever he wants and gamble on a child solving his financial woes. But the drought means he cannot wait a year or more in hopes of a quickly conceived child. He must help his people, and he must buy back the land before that time runs out.

There has to be another way.

I will think on it.

In the meantime, I will respect Jude and Lady Flora, understanding that while they are mistaken about the cause of his distraction, they are correct to fear he is distracted. I am, however subconsciously, sabotaging a vital plan to save their lands. I cannot do that.

I will think on this, and when I am ready—if I have anything to share —I will speak to Benedict. Until then, I will stay out of his way.

27

I do not join the others for supper. I make excuses, and I expect Benedict to come and check on me. When he does not, I am torn between presuming his aunt and brother prevented it . . . and wondering whether I am being silly for imagining he is even thinking of me on this momentous night.

It does not matter. Whatever plan I come up with, it is for Benedict and Jude and their tenants, and it will never be contingent on feelings Benedict may or may not have for me.

The library is, thankfully, as far from the ball as one can get, and even in the garden, playing with Lyta, I barely hear the guests arriving. Strains of distant music reach me, but nothing more. I am alone to think, and I appreciate that.

I have several ideas, possible ways to help Benedict.

A loan from William Thorne or August Courtenay? To be repaid when the drought ends? That presumes Miranda could return to collect on it, and I would never ask either man for money otherwise.

Does Benedict have anything that could be sold in the future? Those moth-eaten tapestries would not be enough, but there'd been more in storage. Could anything be taken forward and sold, the money returned? That would require, again, knowing someone could return. It would also require telling Benedict the truth.

I set these thoughts aside for a while. My mind needs time to clear before attacking the problem from a fresh angle.

While neither solution is ideal, they settle my fears, and the bridal-hunt ball unfurling beyond no longer seems like some fanged beast waiting to devour Benedict. I begin to grow curious to see it. Not to see him. Not even to see the young women. Just to see what a ball in this period might be like.

There are people outside. The party is in full swing, and guests have spilled out onto the lawn. I put Lyta in the library. Then I make my way from the gardens along the side of the house.

The manor is a sprawling affair, all a single-level building. From the library gardens, I cannot simply peek around the corner and see the front lawn. That is an advantage, because it means no one can see me when I slip past that corner. I can make my way along the irregular walls, getting ever closer, with no danger of being spotted.

I am nearly close enough for a look when a laugh tinkles past and my heart gives a little leap. I instinctively pick up my pace, feeling myself smiling as I hurry to see—

Miranda?

I stop short. The laugh sounded like my sister's, and my mind is such a jumble that I forgot where I was. Not in a place where I am ever likely to hear my sister.

Or could I?

She is in this time period. In this region.

In York, chasing down the Booth family. She is never going to be at a bridal-hunt ball for the Earl of Ravensford.

The laugh comes again.

It *does* sound like Miranda.

I ease to the corner and peer around. A cluster of people stand partly out of my view. The laugh sounds, and I follow it to a young woman with her back to me.

A dark-haired woman with a handspan of a waist . . . who is absolutely not my plump blond sister.

I pull back, trying not to be disappointed. I will find Miranda tomorrow and enlist her help in solving Benedict's problem.

I am so deep in these thoughts that I start back toward the garden without fully realizing I have not gotten my look at the ball. Halfway there, a voice behind me says, "Miss Portia."

I wheel to see Miss Carleton. My breath catches. She is stunning tonight, dressed in a black-and-gold dress that sets her apart from the florals and pastels of the younger girls. Part of me wants to see that dress and calculate how many poor tenants it could feed, but I know from experience that if I start doing that, I shall never stop. Everything I see, from the fancy coaches to my own pretty baubles and bows, will be reduced to money that could feed the poor. I am not ready to take a vow of poverty, and so I cannot foist it on others.

"That is your name, yes?" she says. "Miss Portia? I did not get a last name."

"I have not given one," I murmur. "But may I say that dress is truly—"

"Yes, it's very pretty. Mama's idea. Not that it matters. I am quite certain we could parade naked in front of Lord Sterling tonight and he wouldn't notice."

Her eyes flash, and I read a sort of challenge there that almost makes me smile. It is like a child uttering a profanity for the purpose of eliciting shock.

When I cannot resist a twitch of the lips, I say, "I am quite certain he would notice *that*. However, if you are looking for his lordship, I have not seen him since this afternoon."

"I am not looking for him. I am looking for you. I overheard him instruct one of the staff to take you a plate from the banquet. He said you were in the library."

"Yes, it is rather awkward. I was supposed to depart before the ball began—"

"I do not care."

"All right," I say slowly. "Then you have sought me out to say . . . ?"

"Exactly that. I do not care. It is obvious you are no mere dalliance. He is in love with you."

"Lord Sterling is not—"

"I. Do. Not. Care." She enunciates each word as she moves toward me. "All I ask for is honesty. The other girls are atwitter about you, saying that as long as you are gone before the wedding day, that is fine. They do not wish to look foolish." She snorts. "They already look foolish, but that is another matter. As far as I am concerned, I only look the fool if my husband says he has no mistress when he does."

"I see."

"I was angry last night, and I spoke in haste. I have given it a great deal of thought, and I have decided I do not care if he keeps you, so long as he does not lie to me or expect me to sleep alone myself. What is good for the gander is good for the goose."

"Agreed. However—"

"Let me speak plainly, Miss Portia."

I bite my tongue against pointing out that it seems she is doing exactly that already. Not that I take issue with it. I'm actually rather impressed.

"Do you know my family situation? With my brothers?"

I nod. "Your elder brother is temporarily in America, and Martin is joining the clergy."

"Owen is not 'temporarily' anywhere. He is gone there for good, and my father is too willful to see it. Owen took off in the middle of the night rather than tell my father his plans. He sends letters every few months with not a word about returning. Owen is free. That is what he wanted, and it is what he got. As for Martin, I believe he clings to the clergy out of fear that, if he drops his plans and my father still does not appoint him heir, he will have no excuse for being overlooked."

"I see."

"Do you? Owen has abandoned his post, and Martin will never earn it. That means I am effectively my father's heir. I will want for nothing. Nor will my husband and children. That is what I bring to Lord Sterling. My father's wealth, piled at his feet, in return for a title for my children and me. A title and entrance to proper society."

I do not answer. I barely hear her. My mind is still caught on the first part of what she said, about how Owen left.

She mistakes my silence for rapt attention and continues. "I will be a good wife to Lord Sterling. I have a head for business, and I might not be the warmest hostess, but I will do him proud. I will respect and honor him, in return for the same. He may keep you, discreetly, if I might also take a lover with equal discretion. It is the perfect business arrangement."

When I still don't answer, her voice crackles with impatience. "Do you not see that?"

"I do. You are being very fair, Miss Carleton."

"And you will take my offer to Lord Sterling? Persuade him to speak to me himself?"

"I will." I say the words she wants to hear. I was not lying when I said her offer seemed fair. It is. While I cannot imagine Benedict aligning himself with the Carletons, this is not the time to point that out. Something else occupies my thoughts, and so I give her what she wants to end this conversation.

"Good," she says. "I will await his missive. You may join us at the meeting, as it concerns you as well."

"Thank you."

I wait until she starts to leave. Then I say, "You have heard about Pansy Miller, I presume?"

Her shoulders flinch as she turns back, her expression unreadable. "Yes."

"Then I only wanted to offer my condolences to you as someone who knew her."

A thin smile. "That would not be me. I would grieve over any young woman murdered in such circumstances, but we were hardly close. I fear I made the mistake of thinking so at one time."

"Oh? Did she betray your trust?"

"Nothing so dramatic. I only discovered that it was not me she wanted to get to know."

"Ah, someone else in your family."

"Owen," she says. "There are many things I could say about my eldest brother, but at least he was not fool enough to dally with the servants. When he discovered her interest, he arranged her new position for her."

"That is wise. I still offer condolences, and I will ensure Lord Sterling receives your message."

As she leaves, I watch her go.

Owen Carleton.

My elder brother. He went to America a couple of years ago. He writes every few months.

Owen is not 'temporarily' anywhere. He is gone there for good, and my father is too willful to see it. He took off in the middle of the night rather than tell my father his plans. Sends letters every few months with not a word about returning.

Pansy Miller had her eye on Owen. According to his sister, he rebuffed her and found her a new position.

But what if that isn't the whole story? What if Owen accepted her invitation to a tryst and found her a new job to conduct their affair out from under his parents' watchful eyes?

What if they'd been meeting at the abandoned castle?

He took off in the middle of the night.

They meet, and something goes awry. Owen kills Pansy. He hides her body, but then realizes what he's done and flees in the dead of night, sending only letters to his family.

While someone is also sending letters and money to Pansy's family.

I don't think Owen fled the country at all. I think he's still in England, sending those letters while he fashions himself a new life.

A new life under a new identity, making money as best he can, however he can.

A life as Scarlet Jack? The gentleman thief supposedly clearing the roads of land pirates . . . while actually filling his own pockets with plunder?

It is a theory. One I must think on some more before I share it with Benedict.

28

I 'm back in the library garden. Time has passed, but I am too lost in my thoughts to notice. I'd slipped inside to find Lyta sound asleep and a tray of sweets left for me. I took the sweets and went back outside to let the puppy doze. Then I found a place to sit and think.

I am still sitting and thinking when a noise across the garden startles me. I push up quickly, expecting some guest has lost their way. Instead, Benedict stands hidden in shadows.

"Ben?" I peer at him. "How long have you been there?"

He steps forward. "I did not wish to disturb you. You seemed lost in thought."

I start to say yes, I was, and to tell him why. Then I see his face, drawn and pale, and his hair, wild and half-pulled from the tie that had neatly bound it at the base of his neck.

"Ben?" I say, hurrying over. "Are you well?"

He lets out a strangled half laugh. "Well? No, I would not say I am well at all. But I am not ill, if that is what you mean."

"Should you be here?" I glance anxiously behind him. "If anyone sees you—"

"I do not care."

"But you must," I say, trying for what I hope is gentle patience. "This ball is for you, and whatever may come of it, you are its host. You must return—"

"I cannot."

"Why?"

He takes another step, coming to stand right in front of me, close enough that I feel the heat of him.

"Because you are not there. Because I am supposed to be choosing a bride, and the only woman I want is hidden away in the library."

My breath catches.

He leans down to tuck a lock of hair behind my ear. "I tried. For the sake of my aunt and out of respect for the guests, I tried. No matter what does or does not come of the ball, I should play the role of a bride-seeker for one evening. How hard could that be? Dance and talk to the young women and pretend I am considering my options. But it is like trying to see distant stars after staring into the sun." He lowers his face over mine. "Even when you are not there, Portia, all I see is you."

I open my mouth to speak, but his lips lower to mine. He kisses me, and it's sweet and tentative, even as I feel him thrumming with more, a dam holding back the flood. I put my arms around him and open my mouth under his, and the dam breaks. He pulls me roughly to him, that kiss equally rough and urgent.

One heartbeat of instinctive panic pulses through me. I have never been kissed like this, but I know where it leads. Is that where I want to follow?

Yes.

In this world, I am not Portia Hastings, respectable and proper. I am whatever I want to be, unconstrained by anything that might hold me back, beholden only to one simple question.

Do I want this?

Yes.

Absolutely yes.

I kiss Benedict back, just as hard and as urgent, my body molding against his, my breasts pushing into his chest. His hands grip my hips, pulling me against him as he did last night, and I do not have to worry about taking undue advantage. I press against his hardness, and his hands hike up my skirts as he moves me back onto a low wall. Before I know it, my skirts are around my hips, and part of me says that is fine—better than fine—while another part panics again.

Is this what I had in mind?

A coupling that will be over nearly as soon as it starts?

"Ben?" I say, catching my breath as I pull back. "Can we . . . go slower? Please?"

He practically drops me and then dives to help me keep my balance, before quickly backing away and wiping his mouth, his gaze shunted to the side. "My apologies. I did not mean . . . That is to say I got carried away. Of course you would not wish . . . That is much too fast and presumptuous, and I am sorry."

He thinks I was trying to stop him. That by saying "go slower," I meant I do not want the inevitable conclusion of having my skirts around my hips.

I do not know what will happen tomorrow. Will Benedict realize that what he felt for me was lust, now sated? Will he wish for more, but of a temporary nature? A torrid affair before he must wed a more suitable bride? Or does he wish this to end with a wedding vow, if such a thing is possible?

I will not say the answer is irrelevant. But it is irrelevant in making this decision.

I want this. I want him.

I am past the stage in life where I might have fretted that a potential husband would reject me if I did not come to his bed a virgin. I certainly would not expect him to be one, and so, as Miss Carleton said, what is good for the gander is indeed good for the goose. Any man who would fault me for being twenty-nine and not a virgin isn't a man I would wish to marry.

I do not know what will happen after tonight. But I do know this much: if I walk away, I will regret it infinitely more than if I stay.

I step toward Benedict and put my hand on his chest. Part of me is amazed at my brazenness, and part of me is amazed I have never been this brazen before. The truth is that I have never *wanted* to be this brazen before. And now I do.

I look up at him. "It is not the destination I object to, Lord Sterling, but the speed at which we are getting there."

I smile when I say it, and the use of his title should confirm that I am teasing. I expect him to smile back. Maybe even to pull me into a kiss. At the very least, he should be relieved that I am saying yes, I want this. Instead, he stares as if parsing out what I have said.

Should I have spoken more clearly? I am about to do so when he says, "You mean you wish me to go slower?"

I smile. "Yes. That is all. A little slower."

Again, this should invoke a response of relief. *Ah, yes, slower. Is that all? Whew.*

And again, he stares at me in what can only be described as trepidation mingled with terror.

"Slower," he says.

Is that not a word in this time? It must be, and yet he stares as if . . .

Not as if he doesn't recognize it. As if he doesn't know what to do with it. As if I am asking him to reach up and pluck a star from the sky for me.

All right. Perhaps the look doesn't convey *that* much trepidation. As if, then, I am asking him to perform a minor surgical procedure with no training.

Asking him to do something he is not accustomed to doing and does not know whether he can. He is indeed trying to parse out my meaning. Not the meaning of *slower* but what it implies for lovemaking. What exactly am I asking him to do?

I move my fingers to his silk solitaire and make a move to unknot it.

"Yes?" I say.

He nods mutely, and I continue. I unfasten his solitaire and then the top button on his shirt.

"Tell me if I do anything you do not like," I say as my fingers trace down his bare chest, undoing buttons as I go.

His voice comes ragged. "I do not think that is possible."

I spread his shirt and trace my fingertips over the muscles of his chest. When I run my fingers over the erect nubs of his nipples, he lets out a hiss, and a thrill jolts through me.

"You like that?" I say.

"I like everything right now. Too much, which is the problem."

I kiss him and then let my mouth continue downward, my tongue flicking over his salty skin. When I run my tongue over his nipples, he inhales sharply, but I only pause for a moment before continuing down.

"Portia . . ." His voice holds a touch of warning.

I lift my face to look up at him. "Yes?"

He lets out a hiss and puts his hands under my armpits as if to draw me up.

I remove his grip. "I promise to do nothing that will bring a quick end to this."

"Just . . . come up here."

"Why?" I look up at him. "I am doing nothing."

"You are gazing up at me from— Blast it, just come up here."

"I am gazing up at you from . . . ?" I look down. "Ah, I see the problem. I am crouching most awkwardly." I turn to seat him on the low wall. Then I move his knees apart, lift my skirts and kneel between them before looking up again. "Is that better?"

"No, it is most decidedly not."

"What if I were naked?"

"Portia . . ."

"Naked and kneeling between your legs, gazing up at you, as if I am ready to—"

"Stop."

I stand, and he exhales in relief. Then he stops.

"What are you doing?"

"Unfastening my dress. I believe we are going to require that."

"Yes, but—"

I let the dress fall, leaving on my chemise and petticoats, and push his knees apart as I kneel between them. "There. I am not entirely naked, so this is better, yes?" I flick my tongue over his nipples and begin kissing down the middle of his chest, heading for—

He stops me.

I gaze up at him through my lashes, and he groans. "Portia . . ."

"I promise I am not going to do what you think I am. Does that make it better?"

"No."

"Ah. So I *should* do what—"

"*No.* Did you not tell me to go slower? And now you are trying to end it as quickly as possible? You are the most perverse creature—"

"Will it end it if I do not touch you . . ." I slide my hands along the sides of his groin, avoiding the protuberance down the middle. Then I start easing them toward the center, before stopping, my hands just barely touching him through his trousers. "There?"

"Portia . . ."

"It does look in most urgent need of relief," I say. I slide my tongue between my teeth, and he groans. "It felt in need of it, last night."

He goes still. "What?"

I smile up at him, feeling as wicked as I did then. "Last night, when I woke to you pressed against me, hard and—"

"I . . . I was asleep, and I did not know what I was doing."

I sigh. "I know. Which is why I could not do what I would like to do now." I run one finger down him, my touch feather soft. "Touch it. Press myself against the length of it, rub myself against it—"

He cuts me off with a hiss of breath, half swallowed by a groan.

"That would have been wrong," I say.

"Dear God."

"So I had no choice but to let my hand slide down, with you pressed in behind me and—"

"Dear *God*."

I rise up, bringing my face to his. "Should I stop?"

"Yes. No. I mean, yes. Tell me the rest of that story, and I fear I will throw you on the ground and take you."

"Ah, well, then . . ."

I move my mouth to his ear, and I tell him the rest, and I have barely finished before he grabs me around the waist and tumbles me to the ground.

29

I'm wrapped in Benedict, his arms around me, our legs entwined, my head on his chest. I listen to his even breathing, and I am about to decide he has fallen asleep when he kisses the top of my head.

I look up at him, and he kisses my forehead, and I shift until I am able to see him.

"Was that slow enough?" he asks, and while he smiles, there's a hint of actual question in his eyes. Before I can answer, the smile grows. "Yes, I suppose *slow* was not the word one might use, but I will do better next time."

He catches my look, and his brows arch. Clearly, he wishes an answer to this question.

"I was going to say it was well paced," I say. "Too slow would imply a lack of enthusiasm. However, if I say it was fine, does that mean I do not get a 'next' time?"

"Yes, I fear it does. If I have achieved perfection, I am done forever. Best to quit while I am ahead." He lowers his lips to nuzzle my neck. "And that might be the greatest lie I have ever told. No, even if that was indeed perfect—which I know it was not—I will want as many 'next' times as I can get. The only question now is whether we slip into a guest room before the 'next' time or attempt to get back to the keep first."

"I get a 'next' time tonight?"

"Is that a problem?"

"If you think so, Lord Sterling, then you really are very bad at deciphering tone."

His lips quirk. "I am bad at deciphering most things, but I will presume that means you want a 'next' time soon."

"As soon as possible." I lift my head to peer around. "Although you are right to consider other options for a bed and increased privacy. Could we slip back to the keep? That would be ideal."

"We can. We'll take the chaise and leave my horse for Jude." He rises, looks down and makes a face. "I fear, in my haste, I did not remove all your undergarments. We may have left them a bit of a mess."

Apparently, I am still wearing my petticoats. I feel dampness beneath me and tug off the bottom layer of my petticoats. "No matter. They will come clean."

I rise, and he does the same. Then he stops.

"Portia?"

I turn. He's staring down at my discarded petticoat. The wet spot is tinged with red.

"Blood," I say.

He turns that stare to me.

"Do not alarm yourself," I say as I tug on my drawers. "I am not hurt. I presume you have not lain with a virgin before?"

He continues to stare.

"Or perhaps you have and there was no blood," I say, reaching for my chemise. "It is a misconception that the hymen is always intact prior to intercourse. Also a misconception that rupturing it always causes bleeding."

Still more staring.

I turn to look at him. "If I am speaking too plainly for your comfort, Ben, please remember that I am trained in medicine. These things are matter-of-fact for me."

"You are—were—a virgin?"

"Yes." I almost add "of course," but that would imply that an unmarried woman of my background *should* be one, which would be very hypocritical of me to say right now.

"You are not a widow?"

Now I am the one staring at him before I say, "When did I ever claim such? You are the one who told Mr. Carleton I was a widow. It was *your* fiction."

"I . . ."

I shake my head sharply. "It does not matter. I did not mislead you. I was a virgin, and now I am not. If your concern is that you would have taken more care, it is not necessary. I was in no discomfort, and the onus was on me to disclose it if I were."

"You were a virgin."

I reach for my dress. I shall need to check his head once we are at the castle. His confusion from last night appears to have returned.

He straightens suddenly enough for me to look over sharply.

"Then I must marry you," he says.

I laugh.

He glowers at me. "That is not funny, Portia. You were a virgin, and I have compromised you, and so we must wed."

"You are not joking."

He stiffens. "Certainly not. I am a man of honor—"

"Fine. I was not a virgin. That blood was from a cut on my thigh." I yank on my dress with more force than necessary. "There. You are free from any *obligation* to marry me."

"You were a virgin. You said as much. Therefore, we must wed. Quickly. In case you are with child."

When I turn my look on him, he has the sense to recoil, just a little. "And if I *were* a widow, getting me with child would not be a concern?"

He blusters and then straightens again. "You are correct. Virgin or not, I must marry you. In case you are with child."

"Oh, Lord Sterling." I bat my lashes at him. "Take care, or I might swoon. It is my fondest dream come true. A man who will marry me because he feels he must."

"I am—"

"A man of honor? Well, that will prove a pretty puzzle for you to solve. You wish to marry me for honor. Yet I will not marry you, and forcing the matter would be decidedly"—I step up and look into his face —"dishonorable."

He has the grace to flush. "I would never—"

"You asked what I wished for in a husband."

His chin jerks up, his features relaxing. "Yes. Precisely so. You told me what you needed, and I would be all of that. You have my word."

"I lied."

He blinks. "What?"

"You thought my list was missing something. I said it was not. I lied. It was missing something." I meet his gaze. "Love. I will not marry a man who does not offer me love."

He goes completely still, and that is all the answer I need.

"That is what I thought," I say.

I turn on my heel and start marching away. He calls after me, his voice sharp. Something crashes—a garden vase or pot he must knock over—and he lets out a curse and calls again.

But he does not come after me.

I leave, and he does not come after me.

※

I HAVE MADE A FOOL OF MYSELF.

I am so careful about that, so endlessly careful, and now I see why. Because when I lower my guard, I say foolish things that shame me.

There was a reason I did not initially tell Benedict that I required love in a marriage. It sounded foolish. Yet it would not have been nearly so foolish to mention it back then, as a hypothetical. How much worse to admit after he offered to marry me? It implied that I would not marry him unless he loved me. Which is true. Yet only a foolish girl would expect a man to love her on so short an acquaintance.

Benedict has admitted he does not always say what he means. Now I am guilty of the same. What I said sounded like a desperate plea for him to claim he loved me. What I meant was that I would not marry a man— him or any other—who did not love me, and therefore I would not marry him, who had not known me long enough to develop such feelings.

I could have explained that. Instead, I'd been so humiliated by his reaction that I fled, which only confirmed that I am a foolish woman who mistook lust for love. A woman who burst into tears on discovering that a man she has known only a few days has not fallen madly in love with her.

What if he *had* said he loved me? If he'd claimed to fulfill all my criteria, including that?

I would not have believed him. He was so absurdly determined to "make this right" by marrying me that he might have said anything, and if I am being honest, I must allow him credit for not lying.

What if he had said, instead, that he was falling in love with me? That he *could* love me? That he felt what I did for him, a stirring of something that whispered the name of love.

I care for you, Portia. I like you very, very much, and I want to see where this might lead.

If he had said that . . . ?

I shake off the thought.

He did not, and perhaps that is for the best, as I would never know whether he meant it or was only using it to get me to agree to marry him after he'd "ruined" me.

Ruined me. What an absolutely ridiculous concept, one I have never fully considered before. How am I ruined? If a child quickens in my belly, that is indeed cause for concern in a world where my child would suffer the brand of *bastard*. But if I am not with child, am I ruined because a man has bedded me? Yet an unwed man would not be ruined if a woman bedded him? What is the difference?

I know well what the difference is. I am property. I might pretend otherwise, but in the eyes of the law, a married couple becomes one, and that one is the husband. God forbid another man might have stuck his penis in me for a few minutes. I might even have found pleasure in it, and that will not do.

Are men really creatures of such low confidence in themselves?

I am not ruined, and I am furious with Benedict for implying it. That is the action I cannot forgive. He behaves as if he has gone to a tailor, accidentally spilled wine on a shirt and then felt obligated to purchase it. I am not a shirt. I am not soiled. I do not want his bloody obligation.

I am disgusted by it. I expected better. That is the worst of this. I expected better. Which proves I did not know him at all.

"Miss Portia?"

I wheel.

Martin Carleton stands a few feet away, his hands raised. "My deepest apologies, ma'am. I spoke so that I would not startle you, and it seems I have done exactly that."

I catch my breath as I shake my head. "No apology needed. I am skittish with the late hour." I peer toward the front of the house. The music has stopped, and there is the sound of the final carriages being loaded, people saying their farewells.

"Yes, the ball is almost at an end," Martin says. "My parents realized it was over when Lord Sterling excused himself and disappeared. They whisked my sister off in such a hurry that they forgot I was here." His lips twist in a smile. "Not the first time, I fear."

"Will they return for you?"

"Hardly. Oh, they will realize the oversight, but I have two good legs and can get myself home. I was just doing that, cutting through to Sterling Hall." He waves toward the darkness behind the house. "Again, I am sorry for startling you."

He starts to turn away and then pulls himself back. "Is everything all right, Miss Portia? I was trying to be gentlemanly and not comment, but it feels ruder to say nothing. You look distraught." Before I can answer, his eyes widen. "Oh! I do beg your pardon. I was not thinking. Tonight's events . . . of course they would be distressing."

I manage a wan smile. "It was not entirely comfortable. I was supposed to leave before the festivities began. I appreciate your concern, but I am quite all right. Please do not let me keep you . . ."

I trail off. My talk with his sister comes back. What she'd said about their older brother.

Was there anything I could ask Martin while he was here, on his own, being solicitous and perhaps in a mood to talk?

But what do I ask?

"Miss Portia?" He steps closer. "You do not seem well."

"I am. I only wondered—"

"Is that your pup?" He's looking behind me, frowning.

Oh no. I forgot about Lyta. Did Benedict open the library door to go inside and accidentally let her out?

I turn. A hand grabs my hair. I go to yelp, and all my mind can think is, *the ghost!* but another hand slaps over my mouth. A flesh-and-blood hand encased in a glove.

I do not have time to do anything. My hair is yanked, a hand cuts off my cry, and then there is a cord around my throat. My mind screams for me to bite, to fight, but before I can, a knee in my back knocks me to my knees, and then there is no hand covering my mouth, nothing to bite. I go to cry out. My scream is a strangled, garbled gasp as the cord digs in.

My hands fly to the cord. I try to wedge my fingers under it. I cannot. I'm clawing at my own throat, gasping and choking as the cord tightens.

And then . . .

Nothing.

30

I wake . . . somewhere. I do not know where. I do not even immediately care. I wake, and that is all that matters. But it is amazing how quickly one can become dissatisfied with being "merely" alive. At first, the relief shudders through me, and my eyes brim with tears. I thought I had died. I did not.

Praise the angels.

I am alive.

Except . . .

Yes, it takes only heartbeats for the "except" to slink in. It is lovely to be alive, but that matters little if one is not certain one will remain so for long.

As soon as the tears of gratitude fall, I feel them soaking a blindfold. I instinctively lift a hand to remove it and discover my hands are firmly bound behind my back. I twist, and my feet bind—telling me they, too, are bound—and my shoulder knocks against wood. I try the other shoulder. It, too, hits wood. I pull up my knees. They strike wood. I open my mouth . . . and taste the cloth of a gag.

There is more twisting and wriggling after that while I determine that I am not able to easily free myself and that I seem to be in some sort of box.

Like a coffin.

Buried alive in—

No. I will not allow myself to think that is what has happened. A coffin-sized box is not necessarily a coffin, and even a coffin does not necessarily mean buried.

But it could. What if—

Then I die. Truly, there is no other option. If I am buried alive, no amount of panic and terror will change that.

You are ridiculously practical, Portia.

I hear Miranda saying that, and tears well again, but I blink them back. Ridiculously practical or not, I must face the reality that if I am buried alive, there is nothing I can do. However, if I am not buried alive, that is another thing altogether, and therefore it is helpful—and not at all delusional—for me to entertain the possibility of escape.

Buried alive means dead.

Not buried alive means hope.

I yank my knees up, sharper now. They hit the wood with a dull *thwack.*

Would that sound be duller if there were six feet of dirt on it? Did I feel a bit of give, which I would not feel if the box were buried?

I bang my shoulder. Yes, there's a hollow sound. When I press harder, I feel movement, and I tell myself—right or wrong—this proves I am not buried alive.

I twist my hands so I can feel what's under them. Smooth wood.

Like a coffin.

No, in this period—and given the fact I am hardly being laid to rest in a proper grave—my coffin would be a rough box. This feels more like . . .

I am not even certain what it *could* be. It is a polished wood box. Too narrow, now that I think of it, to be a coffin. My shoulders are pressed into the sides.

Does it matter what it is?

Only if it is of poor enough quality that I could break it at the joints. I slam my foot into the side. My bare foot, I realize now. Because I'd fled into the gardens in my bare feet. No wonder Martin questioned what was wrong.

No, Martin only questioned because it gave him an excuse to get close to me. My distress also gave him an opportunity.

He did not happen to come upon me with a length of cord in his pocket. He'd seen me. He must have been lurking about, knowing from his sister that I was at the ball, possibly in the gardens.

Was his sister part of it?

Had our meeting in the garden been part of it, too?

Distract me, pretend to be fine with my "relationship" with Benedict and lower my guard so her brother could attack?

They must have realized it wouldn't work that time. I was too alert, and people were too close. Later, though? When I was so distracted, I was wandering the outer gardens barefoot, the guests almost gone, Benedict nowhere in sight, not even my dog with me?

I continue pressing and poking until I hear—

Are those footsteps? I go still, muscles tensed.

To do what? Fling myself a half inch in the air?

The scrape of something metal, like a key in a lock. Then the creak of a lid opening. Opening on hinges? If I'm held in by a lid with hinges and a lock, I have a chance of getting out.

I try to talk and make only grunting noises. When fingers touch my cheek, moving my gag, my heart leaps. This is not my captor. It is someone come to my rescue.

I wait for the gag to come off. The words pile up in my throat.

Thank you. Oh God, thank you. It's Martin Carleton. He trapped me—

The gag doesn't lower. Instead, something pushed under it presses against my lips. I resist, twisting.

A muffled voice says, "Drink."

It is as if a piece of straw pushes at my lips under the gag. I hesitate, but practicality wins out. I take the tiniest sip. Then I pause, tasting the liquid. Metallic, but clearly water.

I drink more. After a few long sips, the piece of straw disappears. Then the hinges creak.

"Wait!" I say against the gag. The word is indistinct but obviously an attempt at communication. "What do you want? Why—?"

The lid clanks closed. The lock squeaks. I continue to try talking, getting louder, more urgent.

Footsteps retreat. A door shuts. And I am alone.

I take a moment to calm myself. I am not buried alive. Someone is caring for me. They do not wish me dead.

Is this about Benedict?

Miss Carleton wants him as her husband. The entire family wants that. A title for her means they all step up the social ladder. It would be a mistake to think that societal status matters little to a man of the cloth like Martin. Also a mistake—a grave one—to believe that taking the cloth implies a moral character.

This is about Benedict, and I have stumbled . . .

My train of thought fades. I blink. I feel lightheaded. I shouldn't. I certainly slept long enough.

What was I thinking?

Something about stumbling . . . ?

My mind swims now, and a sick dread balls in my gut as I remember sipping that water.

It wasn't just water.

I struggle against my bonds, but my muscles feel like lead, and then I cannot remember why I am struggling. Then I do remember, struggle again and . . .

Nothing.

※

I AM MOVING. DRIFTING THROUGH THE AIR. A SUDDEN THUMP. I START TO slide. A word that sounds like a curse, but it is not in English. Hands catch and steady me. A quick exchange of words. Is that . . . ? That voice . . . I know that . . .

Nothing.

※

I AM IN A CART, JOSTLING ALONG. SOMEONE HAS PUT MY COFFIN INTO THE back of a cart, and I am being taken to the churchyard and—

The smell of the moors at night.

Benedict?

Rain? Do I smell rain?

Benedict! It is raining!

Benedict—

You were a virgin, and I have compromised you, and so we must wed.

Virgin or not, I must marry you. In case you are with child.

My eyes fill with tears.

Benedict.

I try to blink and lift my head, but I cannot even open my eyes. I hear a noise. A whimper. Is that me?

"Portia?" a voice says.

Is that . . . ?

Miranda?

Is that Miranda?

I cannot open my eyes. I cannot speak. I float somewhere, trapped just below waking.

"We have you," she whispers. "He cannot hurt you."

"The bastard." Nicolas? There is a French twist on *bastard* landing the word halfway between the languages.

Nicolas. Miranda.

That laugh I'd heard at the party. The one I thought came from a girl who was definitely not my sister.

My sister *had* been there.

My sister is *here*.

"Shh," Miranda says, smoothing my hair. "You're all right."

"And we will take care of Lord Sterling," Nicolas says. "He will pay for this."

Pay for this? For bedding me?

No, the thought of Miranda or Nicolas raising a sword to protect my "honor" is ridiculous. They are far more forward thinking in such matters than I have dared to be.

Which means . . .

They think Benedict kidnapped me. That he was the one holding me captive.

No!

I need to get back to him. Need to warn him about the Carletons. Need to—

I slide back into darkness and silence.

☙❧

IT IS NIGHT WHEN I AWAKE. I BOLT UPRIGHT AND FIND MYSELF IN THE MAIN bedroom at Thorne Manor. In William and Bronwyn's bed. In the nineteenth century.

Oh, no. Oh, no, no, no!

I try to leap out of bed, but my knees fold. My throat aches, and it hurts to swallow. I steady myself. At a whisper of breath, I look to see Miranda in the bed with me, and Nicolas collapsed in a chair beside her. They are both fast asleep.

I begin the slow journey from the bedroom to the office. There, I pen a letter, as brief as I can make the story. It was not Benedict who captured me, and I must return to warn him of the danger. When they are able, if they could follow me, I would very much appreciate that, as we need their help with a ghost.

I leave the note and toddle to the middle of the room where the stitch waits. I step into it and . . .

Nothing happens.

I blink and give my head a shake, pushing off the haze of whatever made me sleep. I must not be in the right spot.

I try again.

Still nothing.

I try again and again and again, and nothing in the room changes.

The stitch is closed.

৩৯৩

HOURS LATER, MIRANDA AND NICOLAS FIND ME STILL TRYING TO GET through the stitch. By then, I am in a state of high agitation, near panic. Anyone else would tell me to rest before I explained. This is one of the many reasons I love my sister. She understands two things in this situation. One, that explaining is what will relieve my agitation, and two, that there are few things worse than telling a woman, however obliquely, to calm down.

I tell her my story—the important parts, at least. That I went after her and found the Sterlings instead, and there was a ghost and a body, and neither had anything to do with the Sterlings. Nor did my kidnapping. Now I must return to warn Benedict and Jude about their neighbors.

Here is another reason I love my sister—and her husband. Neither even gently questions whether I could have misinterpreted events. Am I certain the Sterlings did not murder Pansy? Am I certain neither brother knocked me out or held me captive? After all, I did not actually see my attacker, nor recognize the voice from that single command, "Drink."

They could point out the holes in my story. They do not, because they trust me, and they know I have already questioned everything myself.

Is it possible either Sterling murdered Pansy? Yes, but I have said so and estimated the likelihood at five percent. Am I certain one or both could not have worked with Martin to attack and capture me? Again, I place the odds at five percent. Both of those five percents are not proof of honest suspicion but the acknowledgment that I could never say I truly know anyone on such a short acquaintance.

It is, I suspect, my agitation that convinces them the most. I am in a state, desperate to get back and warn the Sterlings. I do not get "in a state" with any regularity. The last time Miranda would have seen this was when Rosalind disappeared.

They know I am speaking *my* truth, whether it is *the* truth or not. As for how they found me, they had indeed followed the Booths to York. They'd repaid Mrs. Booth and then promised to speak to Lord Sterling on her behalf. That's who Mrs. Booth told them to talk to, because Benedict is the one who will care, but they mistakenly thought it meant Benedict was the one who'd thrown her off the land.

Benedict's letter never found them. They returned to Ravensford, only to hear delicious gossip circulating about Lord Sterling. He has a mistress at the castle. A woman whose description Miranda thought oddly resembled her sister, which must be a coincidence . . . until they heard the mistress's name. Portia is hardly like Mary or Anna. There was little doubt who it was, and they presumed that I followed them through the stitch when they were late returning.

That was the day of the ball. The Sterlings were already at their aunt's, and "Miss Portia from London" was reported to be with them. I *had* heard Miranda that night. She'd snuck in as a guest to find me. When the ball ended with no sign of me, Miranda and Nicolas began skulking about, trying to peek in windows. They'd heard what was unmistakably my voice speaking to a man, yet they arrived to find no sign of me. Then they'd caught a distant glimpse of a man loading a blond woman into a cart.

They'd given chase, but being on foot, they lost the cart. They spent the next day searching, before finding the cart at a hunting lodge bearing the Sterling crest—which I can presume is on Carleton's land and therefore now his, or else the brothers would be living there instead of the castle.

Miranda and Nicolas were not able to determine who held me captive, but that was hardly important. I *was* there. They got me out and spirited me away in the cart. They'd brought me straight to Thorne Manor and through the stitch. I'd been deeply asleep, aided by whatever sedative I'd been given, and therefore I'd been unable to stop them.

Now I need to get back, and I cannot. They will go through for me. That is what they decide. If I cannot go through, they will.

Why can they do what I cannot? I have no idea. Nor do they. Nor does anyone. We do not know how the stitch works. It brought Bronwyn to William when they were children, and again as adults. It also temporarily kept them apart. Now they can pass, but only between his time and hers. Then it took Rosalind to Bronwyn's world and trapped her there for four years. Now she can also pass freely—with her family—between the two times. Miranda and Nicolas are different. The stitch transports them between their times *and* elsewhere, sometimes taking them where they wish to go, and sometimes taking them where the stitch has decided they need to be.

Is that the criteria? Take people where they need to be? It did for Bronwyn and William. It did for Miranda and Nicolas—and continues to. And Rosalind? Trapped in the twenty-first century for four years? Did some cosmic force decide that was what she needed to save her marriage and, ultimately, bring her and August both peace and happiness? If so, then the stitch is not a kindly force, but a brutally honest—even cruel—one.

Did it send me to Benedict because he needed me? Because I needed him? Finding our way to each other over the centuries? It seems dreadfully romantic, and it might make the end to a lovely story . . . if that was the end.

We found each other. I can help him save his estate and avoid a loveless marriage. My experience in his world taught me that I wanted more than my constricted life—that I *deserved* more. That is all lovely. Truly lovely. Except that the same stitch is now saying, "No."

No, you may not go back to him.

No, you may not help him save his lands.

No, you may not warn him of the danger he and his brother face.

I do not understand the logic, and I can only despair that I am attempting to ascribe logic to a capricious force. Like expecting the wind to carry your boat to shore because it has done so before.

What matters now is that I have Miranda and Nicolas, and they will do what I cannot.

What I cannot.

Cannot help the Sterlings.

Cannot warn the Sterlings.

Cannot see Benedict again.

31

I t is evening, and Miranda and Nicolas are preparing to head into the stitch. I will remain here—the Thornes are in Canada, visiting relatives in the twenty-first century. I will have the house to myself, and I am already steeling myself against the loneliness of that, trapped here with my thoughts.

Miranda and Nicolas will leave at night because that is the easiest time for them to travel. They are simply waiting for the sun to drop further before they go.

"Is there anything else you wish to tell me?" Miranda says as I shake out sheets that do not need shaking, remake a bed that does not need remaking.

"I do not think so."

"Any message to convey to Lord Sterling?"

I stiffen and then shake the sheet more. "Give him and his brother my regards. Please explain that I did not leave of my own accord and wish them the best."

Her voice softens. "And if you never get the chance to see Benedict Sterling again, that will be all you wished to say?"

I look over sharply.

She settles onto the mattress. "Something happened between you two. I can tell, because you speak of his brother with affection and speak of Benedict himself with annoyance. From anyone else, that would suggest you had feelings for Jude. I know better. What happened, Portia?"

"Lord Sterling rid me of my pesky virginity."

Silence. Then she bursts out laughing, so hard she doubles over. "I told Nicolas you seemed different. Not from *that* obviously. But the Portia I knew a few weeks ago would never have been so frank about it." She sobers. "Was it a disappointment? I know it can be."

"Certainly not. It was marvelous."

"And you regret it?"

"Not at all. It showed me what I will want in a husband. Or a lover. I appreciate that. What I did not appreciate . . ."

She rises and moves toward me. "Was he unkind afterward? I know, too, that can happen. A man gets what he wants, and then his words of love turn to ash."

I tense.

Her arms go around me. "Oh, Port. I am so sorry."

"He wanted to marry me."

She stops the embrace and steps back. "What?"

I take another sheet to shake out. "No, *want* is entirely the wrong word. He realized I'd been a virgin and insisted on marrying me."

Her lips tighten. I think it is anger, but then the sparkle in her eyes tells me she is holding back a laugh.

My own eyes narrow. "It was not funny, Miranda. He insisted on marrying me out of honor. The more I refused, the more he insisted. It was the right thing to do, he said. He'd taken my virtue. What if I were with child? We must marry."

"Immediately?" she says, her lips twitching.

"I do not know what you find so amusing."

She sits back on the mattress. "Let me see if I understand this. Lord Sterling was preparing to marry for money. Before you arrived, he was the one pushing for that solution. He would be clear in his intentions, as to not deceive a bride. He was openly trading his title for money—not for himself or gambling debts or such—but out of obligation to his tenants."

"Yes, but I don't see what—"

"Then you appear, and he can hardly bear to attend his own bridal-hunt ball. I was there. I heard the grumbling and barely caught sight of Lord Sterling. He was there in body only, and eventually, he did not even bother with that. Did he go straight to you?"

"Yes, but—"

"Did he say why?"

I shake the sheet more violently. "Some nonsense about only wanting to be with me."

"And afterward, when he realized you had been a virgin, he pounced on that."

"Pounced?" I sniff. "For a writer, you have a poor way with words today, Miranda."

"Not at all. He pounced. Leaped at the excuse. You were a virgin! Oh no! There is nothing to be done but to marry you. Such a shame. Ah, well. Honor and all."

I peer over the sheet at her. "I do not understand."

She smiles, rises and squeezes my arm. "Do not worry yourself about it, Port. I will handle this."

I turn as she walks toward the door. "What does that mean?"

"Nothing at all, dear sister. Nothing at all."

⚜

MY SISTER AND HER HUSBAND ARE GONE, AND I CANNOT SLEEP. THE CLOCK below strikes one, and I am staring at the dark ceiling, watching the play of moonlight dancing as the breeze blows the draperies.

I spend the first hour figuring out what my sister thought she'd deduced from my story about Benedict. Then I spend the next rolling my eyes at her.

She thinks Benedict "pounced" on an excuse to marry me because it is what he wants. Having "ruined" me, he must do the honorable thing and wed me, which is what he wants anyway.

That might be true, but not for the reason she thinks. And if it is true for the reason I think, then it only sinks him lower in my opinion.

Did Benedict see marrying me as an escape from his obligation? None of the prospects caught his attention, and he likes me well enough, so he decided he'd rather marry me? Not that he really wants to, but it's better than the alternative. I am attractive, capable and reasonable . . . and I must surely have funds somewhere. A bit of money to tide us over until I have a child Lady Flora can use to give us the money Benedict needs. Good enough!

Miranda thinks he "pounced" because he is in love with me, which only proves that my sister has the most ridiculously perfect experience of love, with the most ridiculously perfect man. All right, Nicolas has flaws. Everyone does. But he is perfect for *her*, and their courtship proceeded with barely a frisson of conflict. I swear, in the past year, they have argued less than Benedict and I have in the past few days.

They met, they realized how perfect the other was for them, and that was the end of it.

Admittedly, they did not rush off to marry. They wisely courted for a year first, but still . . . It was perfect, and not realizing how rare that is, Miranda expects to see the same in others. Clearly, Benedict Sterling fell madly in love with me on a few days' acquaintance.

I could be worried about her promise to "set things right." I'm not. Once she meets Benedict, she will see her mistake.

For now, I am lying in bed, being stubborn. I should get up and go to the library. Find a book and take it downstairs and read until I am ready for sleep. I can't because I am annoyed at not being able to sleep. I'm back in my own time, in a warm room with all the comforts of the nineteenth century. There is no reason why I shouldn't be snuggled down in sheets that are not nearly threadbare, on a mattress that is not lumpy and coarse, in a room that is not made of cold stone. Did I really envision a life in that castle? What a ridiculous thought. I am a Victorian woman accustomed to Victorian comforts and *cities*. I am accustomed to cities. I could never live in a castle on the moors.

So why does my mind keep slipping to Ravensford Keep, to what it could be if restored to its glory, to thoughts of small footsteps running down the corridors, childish shrieks echoing—

No. That is a fancy. Nothing but a fancy, one that proves I have read far too many books set in castles, and now that I know the reality, I should shudder at the thought.

I do not shudder.

I do not even shiver at the cool wind coming through the window.

It smells of the moors at night. Of heather and moonlight and shadows and—

"Goddamn it!"

I let out the very non-Victorian-lady curse and shove out of bed. *That* must be why I cannot sleep. That damnable open window bringing that damnable smell.

I'm halfway to the window when a dog barks, and I stop.

It sounds like Lyta.

I shake off the thought and shut the window.

The bark comes again, clearly . . . as if from inside the house.

Lyta.

Inside the house.

The stitch!

I lift my nightgown skirt as I run for that locked room. Dog nails scrabble against the door, punctuated by puppy whines.

I throw open the door, and Lyta launches herself at me.

I bend down to gather her in my arms. "How ever did you find—"

"You forgot your dog," a voice says.

I peer into the darkness. The only light comes from a sliver of moon through nearly closed draperies, but it falls across a man whose figure I could never mistake for another, and I know at that moment I must be dreaming.

Heather and moonlight and shadows.

That's what I'd just thought, and now he stands here, in moonlight and shadow, smelling of damp heather.

"You forgot your dog." The words come sharper. "Did you expect me to care for her?"

I hold Lyta as she wriggles in my arms. She's slightly damp, as if it is raining, and when I lower my face, I smell wet dog, and somehow that breaks the spell.

I'm not dreaming.

Benedict is here.

Here, in the nineteenth century.

I reach and light an oil lamp. As it sputters to life, there is no doubt that I'm still in my time. And no doubt that Benedict is standing there, in the middle of Bronwyn and William's office. Standing there and scowling at me, hair plastered to his face by rain.

"It is raining," I whisper as I smile at him.

For a second, he stares at me. Just stares. Then he shakes it off and blinks. "Yes, it is raining, but it will not be enough." He waves at Lyta. "I brought your damn dog. Now I need to get back home."

He strides toward the door, making a move as if to pass me.

"Benedict?"

He grunts as he reaches for the hall door.

"You . . . cannot get home that way," I say.

"What?" He looks at me in obvious irritation.

"Where . . . do you think you are?"

"Thorne Manor," he snaps. "I know Lord Thorne, and obviously, you do as well. I did not mean to break into his house. The door was open, and the damned dog ran in. Now I will take my leave quickly before Lord Thorne wakes."

I step in front of him and say, slowly, "Does this look like your Lord Thorne's house?"

His brows gather. "I know where I am, Portia. I do not know why you are here, but it hardly concerns me. You got to where you needed to be, which evidently is 'as far from me as possible.'"

"I—"

"You have made yourself perfectly clear," he says, looking to the side, face set, words clipped.

Slow anger rises in me. I did not flee him after our night together, but I am suddenly ill-inclined to correct him. It is not as if I snuck from his bed in the night. He knows why I left him in the garden. Because of his insulting insistence on "saving" me after my "ruin." And because, when I mentioned love, the look he gave me said that was not an option, could never be an option.

"Look around, Lord Sterling," I say, teeth gritted. "You are not in *your* Lord Thorne's house."

He casts a quick glance about the office.

"Does it look like the room you went into?" I ask.

"It was dark. I did not stop to gape about. I only followed your damnable dog—"

"Look *around*," I snap. "Does this seem like your world?"

"My world? What foolishness—"

"Look out the window. You have been in the rain. Is it raining here?"

He barely glances at the window. "It must have stopped."

I grab a week-old newspaper from the desk and slap it into his hand. "Read the date, please, paying particular attention to the year."

"The year?"

"Read it."

He does. Then he blinks. Moves it under the lamp. Reads it again.

"Not your world," I say. "Not *your* Lord Thorne's house." I march to the desk and pick up a photograph of Bronwyn, William and the girls. "Is this your Lord Thorne?"

He frowns, as if he can see familiarity in William's features, but then the frown grows more.

"Lord William Thorne," I say, "with his wife, Bronwyn, and their two daughters, none of whom appear to be wearing anything you would see on the streets in your world."

I hand him another photo. "Does this woman resemble me?"

"Yes, but—"

"It is my elder sister, Rosalind, with her son and daughter. And her husband, August Courtenay, younger brother to the Earl of Tynesford. I presume you know the Earl of Tynesford?"

"Yes, but—"

"Is that his younger brother?"

"No, but—"

"Then you, Lord Sterling, are a hundred years after your own time. You are in *my* time, which means . . ."

I walk behind him and push him toward the center of the room. "The way back is over there."

"I—"

"You do not understand? It's a time stitch. I don't pretend to fully understand it, either, but I do know that you cannot return home through the front door." I keep pushing him. "Off you go."

He digs in his heels. "I'm not . . ." He trails off.

I step back, arms crossing. "Not what?"

He hesitates. Then his jaw sets, and he scoops up Lyta. "I am not leaving without my dog."

"*Your*—?" I sputter. "You brought her back to me, and now you are taking her?"

His chin lifts. "I have changed my mind. You left, and since you clearly did not want either of us, neither of us is staying."

"Benedict." I soften my voice and lift my gaze to his. "That is untrue." I step closer and reach out my arms. "I *do* want Lyta."

His jaw sets so hard I fear for his teeth. I ignore it and place Lyta outside the office and then shut the door so she cannot accidentally run into the stitch. Then I turn to Benedict.

"As for you," I say. "I do not want a man who thinks he must marry me because I am ruined. Are *you* ruined after our night together?"

He wisely doesn't answer.

"No," I say. "And so I am not, either, and I will not be insulted by the insinuation—"

"I misspoke." He grinds out the words. "I believe I have said—on several occasions—that I do that."

"Oh, there was no misunderstanding. You said, multiple times—"

"I was offering to marry you, if you wished it."

"Offering? You were insisting. An obligation, as if insisting on buying a shirt you spoiled."

"That is not—" He sighs and runs a hand through his hair. "I do not see you as a ruined shirt, Portia. Nor a ruined woman. I was asking . . ." He clears his throat and seems to need to push the words out. "I was asking you to marry me."

I could keep arguing, insist that there was no way to interpret his words as *asking*. But my will to argue slips away, replaced by an odd exhaustion.

"I told you my criteria for marriage," I say softly.

"Love."

"And there, I am the one who misspoke. I would not expect that so soon. I meant that, when I marry, I must see the possibility of love, some inkling that my husband could come to love me."

"*Come* to love you?" He steps forward, his gaze meeting mine, a strange sort of anger in his eyes. "Is that all you need, Portia? Do you truly want—*expect*—so little that you'd accept the barest glimmering promise of love? You should not marry a man who does not fall on his knees to declare his love for you. Who does not feel, if he lost you, that he would never find another to replace you, would go to his grave loving you and grieving for the loss of you."

My eyes fill, and I look away. "You mock me, sir."

"Mock you?" That snap of anger, now in his voice. "Who did this to you, Portia? Who made you think you were not worthy of that sort of love?"

I keep my gaze averted. "Can we not speak of this, please? I feel foolish for what I said in the garden. I will accept that you did not mean I am ruined nor that you must marry me, but when I mentioned love . . . I received your answer."

"How?" He strides in front of me. "How did you receive my answer when I did not say a word?"

"That was your answer. That, and your expression."

"My expression?" His voice rises. "My *expression*? That is—" He bites off the rest and struggles to moderate his tone. "I do not know what *expression* I made, but it was the expression of a man who does not know what to say because he is certain—from long experience—that whatever he says, he will say it wrong. It was the expression of a man frantically taking a moment to find the right words. And then you left."

"I walked out into the gardens!" I say, my own voice rising. "I did not leap off the earth. I walked away, and you did not follow."

"Because I was naked! I had to dress first."

Now my own jaw sets.

"Oh, do not give me that," he snaps.

"Give you what?"

"That look. It blames me for dressing. It says you would not have taken time to dress, which is a lie. You would have. If you walked into a wall of flame, I would have leaped after you, Portia. But I thought I could seize a moment or two to collect my thoughts while I dressed, and then I would go after you. You were gone. You left."

"I did not—"

"You left, and I spent a day frantically searching for you, and then someone said they had seen a blond woman in a cart with a dark-skinned man, heading toward York. I followed, and another traveler said they saw the same cart heading to High Thornesbury. I find that cart outside Thorne Manor, and I follow Lyta inside, and I step through time.

Through *time*. Into your world. I followed you across time, and I am *not* going back until you tell me that you do not want me."

"I thought you came to return my dog," I say.

He lets out a low growl. "If you are trying to provoke me—"

"No, I simply want to get the story straight. You said you came here—"

Another growl, and he grabs me, lips going to mine, cutting off my words. I kiss him back, my lips as rough and hungry as his. When I finally pull away, I say. "So that is why you really came here."

His eyes glitter. "Perhaps." His lips go to my ear. "Or perhaps, after our last encounter, I wanted to show you that I can take things slower, if I am not bedeviled by a minx intent on undoing me."

"Bedeviled? Minx?"

"You asked me to go slower, and then you ensured I could not."

"How? By kissing your chest?"

"You know what you did, and you will not be doing it again."

"Never?" I slide my hands down his chest.

He catches them. "Do not put words in my mouth, minx. You will not be doing it again today. Because today I am going to apologize."

I stop short. "You are? For what?"

He gives me a look.

"Well, there is quite a long list of things you might apologize for, starting with feeling the need to dress that night in the garden. No, wait, before that. Starting with feeling the need to marry me—"

Again, he cuts me off with a kiss.

"You are going to keep doing that, aren't you?" I say when I pull back.

His grin sends a thrill through me. "It is most effective. However, I believe I know an even more effective way to quiet you. By apologizing for, yes, a litany of things, including the fact that I went rather quickly that night, because I am accustomed to—" He stops and clears his throat.

"Going quickly?"

"Let's not speak of it."

"I wasn't the one who—"

He scoops me up in his arms so fast I don't have time to protest before I am lying on the floor, and he is over me. When his hands hike my skirt, I cannot help but say, "If you have resolved not to go quickly, you might be doing it wrong."

"Oh, I am doing it very right. I am not undressing you—yet. Believe me, I intend to take off every shred of your clothing, as I have chastised myself for failing to do so the last time. I have bedded you and have not even seen you naked. Which I will remedy, but not yet, or we will start down the same road as last time, where I am on you in seconds."

"I rather liked—"

"Another time. Today, you will begin by staying dressed. Also, you are forbidden to touch me."

"Does that include touching you with my—"

"With anything."

"Hmm. All right then. I will have to use my mouth for something else. I had a dream of you last night, Lord Sterling. You came to me in the night—"

"No."

"I cannot talk?"

"Not like that. Now lie back."

I push up on my elbows.

"That is not lying back, Portia."

"What are you doing?"

"Taking off your underthings. What ever are these?" He holds up my drawers. "They are quite in the way."

"You removed them last time."

"Did I? I do not recall."

"Because you were in a hurry."

He shakes his head and tosses them aside. Then he lowers his lips to the inside of my knee, and kisses me there, and . . . And it is more pleasant than it has any right to be. I lie back and enjoy the sensation of his kisses and his tongue against a surprisingly sensitive spot.

Then his mouth moves up the inside of my thigh, and I discover an even more surprisingly sensitive spot. His tongue and lips move, setting me panting softly, even as he is no higher than mid-thigh. Then he is higher, his tongue between my legs, and before long, I am gripping my skirt in both hands, lifting from the floor as if I can move to his mouth fast, bring him faster to . . .

I arch up, gasping as heat scorches through me, the most incredible heat. His tongue moves, and it is not long before I feel the explosion surging—

I shoot upright. "Wait!"

He lifts his head, and in his eyes, there's concern, but also trepidation, as if he might be doing it wrong, which he absolutely is not.

"I . . . I do not want to be finished so soon," I say. "Can we do other things and come back to this?"

His eyes sparkle in a grin. "You like this?"

"I like it very much. Too much."

"Well, I do hate to school a doctor on the differences between the male and female bodies, but this is one of them. When I am done, I am done for a while. When you are done . . ." That grin sparks a devilish light in those gorgeous amber eyes. "You are not actually *done* in the same way. Not until you are too exhausted to continue."

"Oh. And how long does that take?"

That grin lights his whole face. "I intend to find out. May I continue?"

I flop back onto the floor, and he gives a low chuckle . . . and then makes good on his word.

33

"Now will you marry me?" Benedict says as his arms tighten around me, the two of us locked in an embrace, panting as we catch our breath.

"I barely know you."

"That is all right," he says. "It's better that way."

I laugh against his shoulder and shake my head. "If you are remotely serious—"

"I'm not."

I bite down to stifle my disappointment.

"I am not *remotely* serious," he says, moving my face up to his. "I am absolutely, unreservedly serious."

My cheeks heat.

Before I can speak, he continues, "Do you remember that first night together, after the ghost assaulted you? You were in the library, in your nightgown with Lyta by the fire, and it was like seeing the vision of a future that was indeed remote. So remote I could have no more hope of reaching it than of pulling down a star from the sky."

My brows crease, and he rubs his fingertip between them.

"A vision of what could be," he says softly. "A wife who made my heart race. A wife I wanted to ply with brandy and honey and puppies and see her smile up at me the way you did. A wife I longed to sit with and talk to and *be* with, share a life with. I saw you, sitting on that hearth, your hair hanging down, and you looked like someone's wife, and I wanted that someone to be me."

His lips press to my forehead. "I knew then that I would not be satisfied with a wife chosen for her money. Deep in my soul, I longed for more, and if it could not be you, then someone for whom I felt the same way. That was the first night. By the second, I knew I had been wrong again." He meets my gaze. "Wrong to think I could accept anyone but you."

His fingers graze my cheek. "Yes, you think it isn't possible to love on so short an acquaintance, and you may argue the name of what I feel, but I know this: I only want to be with you. I want what I saw that night, and you are the only woman who can be in that portrait of my life."

His lips come to mine, and he kisses me, a long and sweet kiss. When it breaks, I look him in the eyes and say, "So you did not just come to return Lyta?"

He collapses back to the floor, eyes rolling up as he groans. "You aren't going to let that be, are you?"

"Not until you admit that you came for me."

He slants a look at me. "And you do not see how that admission might cause me some discomfort, when *you* didn't come for *me*?"

"I could not." I glance away, and my voice is barely above a whisper. "The stitch closed to me, and I could not get through. My sister and her husband have gone through in my place, to get back and warn you."

"Warn me that you were unable to return."

"No. That— Oh!" I leap to sit up and twist to face him. "I have not told the whole of the story. I didn't leave, Benedict. I was taken captive. In the gardens, almost immediately after we parted. I met Martin Carleton there, and I spoke to him, and then he attacked me."

Benedict bolts up, storm clouds gathering in his eyes. "Martin Carleton laid hands on you?"

"On my neck to be precise." I pull back my hair to show the bruises. "He choked me unconscious, and I woke in a box. My sister says I was in what seemed to be the former Sterling hunting lodge. In any event, they found me—my sister and her husband, that is—and brought me here. I'd been given some sort of drug to make me sleep, and so it was not until I woke here that I could tell them I did not wish to be here."

Benedict's expression is positively thunderous now. "And you did not think to tell me this before now?"

"I— Oh! Jude! Of course. I was thinking that I did not need to immediately warn you, as you were already here, but I forgot about Jude. Yes, we must get to him, in case he is in danger."

"My brother can look after himself. I am talking about what happened to you. You were choked half to death and held captive and did not see to mention it until now."

"It *was* an ordeal. But I am quite fine."

He drops his head and groans. Then he lays his hands on my shoulders. "Portia? I adore your practicality. I am in awe of your resilience. But please, if you have ever been harmed in any manner, tell me immediately."

"I wanted to when you first arrived so that you understood I did not leave you. But you were so angry about it, and you *had* behaved rather poorly, that I thought that if I explained the situation too quickly, you might not see that if I *had* left, I'd have had fair reason."

He groans again. "You are going to drive me to madness, aren't you? And yet, I still want to marry you."

"Oh, that is such a sweet thing to say. So terribly romantic. You *still* want to marry me, despite the fact that I do not let you get away with your nonsense."

His eyes narrow. "Have you always had such a gift for sarcasm?"

"Oddly, no. You seem to bring it out of me. But in answer to your question, before you forget that I have not answered it and start setting the bans, I will not agree to marry you, Lord Sterling."

He tenses, and his face begins to shutter, hands releasing my shoulders.

"We have known each other three days," I say. "To marry anyone on such a short acquaintance would be madness. I am not mad. Neither are you. If you sincerely wish to marry me, it is only because you want to seal the deal, so to speak. So that I do not traipse off back to my own world. You wish a promise of commitment, yes?"

"You make my head hurt, Portia."

"I cannot promise to marry you, Benedict. I am not from your world, in any sense. I can promise that I would very much like to marry you, if the rest can be worked out. And if we take proper time to get to know one another. Otherwise, I fear that every time I disagree with you, you will storm about, growling about marrying in haste, repenting at leisure."

"I would never think that, Portia."

"But would you say it? When you get in a mood?"

He meets my gaze. "You claim to not know me well enough to marry me, and yet you know me perfectly."

"Which is why I will not marry you. Yet. Now get dressed. Whether Jude can fend for himself or not, he should be warned." I reach for my nightgown.

"I shall need to dress properly . . ." I begin, and then I look about, frowning, as I realize we are no longer in Bronwyn and William's office.

"I believe we have fallen through time again," Benedict says. "Perhaps we ought to have moved further from the trigger spot before we began tumbling about."

"Blast it. Am I doomed to wander the world in a nightgown?"

"It is another very lovely nightgown."

I snort. "It will have to do as it seems we are not in my time, and I do not dare briefly return." I pause. "Oh! Lyta! We . . ."

"Should leave her where she is. Both because you could be trapped there if you return and because she is safer there for now."

I do hate to leave her, but both points are valid.

"All right. Dress quickly, please. If I must travel in a nightdress, at least let it still be night." I glance over to see him sitting there. "Well?"

He waves around the room. "My clothing seems to be . . . elsewhere."

"Oh." I peer into the near darkness and pick up his solitaire. "This made it through. That will be enough. You are far too fine to wear clothing anyway. Just tie this around your neck, and you will be formally attired."

He chokes on a laugh. "Indeed. Wait. Did you say I am too fine to wear clothing? That sounds like a compliment."

"No, it is an objective assessment. You are a handsome enough man in clothing, but you look much better without it." I finish pulling on my nightgown. "When we are wed, we will need to keep the fires blazing so you can walk around the castle naked, for my viewing pleasure."

"*When* we are wed?"

"Of course. I fully expect we will be. Just not now."

He catches my face in his hands. "I love you, Portia from London."

"Portia Hastings," I say. "That will be important for the wedding bans."

"It will be. I should write that down, as I am certain I will be needing it soon."

"And that, Lord Sterling, might be what I love most about you."

"My resolute self-confidence?"

"No, your optimism."

He bursts into a laugh and then looks around. "I should find something to wear, and swiftly, lest *my* Lord Thorne return."

"I thought you knew him."

"Not well enough to be found naked in his house."

"Well enough to borrow clothing from his wardrobe? And perhaps from his wife's for me?"

"I guess we will find out."

❦

WE HAVE FOUND CLOTHING. IT DOES NOT QUITE FIT—THAT WOULD BE beyond lucky. In truth, I wish we'd ended up back in my time, where William Thorne's clothing would fit Benedict nicely, and while Bronwyn is taller and broader than me, hers would be preferable to that of Lady Thorne, who is apparently tiny, more akin to Rosalind in size.

We are both left with clothing that is rather, well, tight. Is it wrong to say I do not mind seeing Benedict in a shirt and trousers that leave not one inch of his form to the imagination? From the looks he keeps sneaking me, he does not mind seeing me nearly bursting out of my bodice.

When I pluck at that bodice, he says, "If it is too uncomfortable, you ought to change back into your nightdress. It will still be dark when we return, and I do not plan to stop."

"The way you are looking at me says you like this gown significantly more."

"Then you are, again, a very poor judge of my expressions. I am very fond of your nightdresses."

"Why?"

He shrugs. "Because they make you happy."

And that might be the nicest thing a man has ever said to me. I decide that I would, indeed, be much more comfortable in the nightgown, and so I change into it, while borrowing a pair of boots and a shawl to make it more appropriate, lest we be spotted.

When I get outside, Benedict is in the chaise. As he helps me in, he whispers at my ear. "I am glad to see you changed into the nightdress."

"Do I look all right?" I ask as he gets up into the seat beside me.

"If we see anyone, I will tell them you are from the city. It excuses every eccentricity of fashion."

"Excellent. While fashion in your world is somewhat less colorful than my preference, I do like that women are not expected to wear quite so many layers of skirts and underthings."

"How many would you wear in your world?"

I tell him, as the coach pulls from Thorne Manor, and we continue in that way, discussing his world and mine, until we have been traveling for hours, talking the entire way. It is a beautiful night. The roads are empty, and the rain has faded to a mist over the moors, shrouding them in fog.

Benedict seems to have readily accepted the idea that I come from another time. I can understand why he didn't question it overly much earlier—he'd been intent on arguing with me on other matters. But he does not question it now. He has seen proof with his own eyes, between the newspaper and his changing surroundings, and he is a practical man. If I have proven that I come from the next century and that he visited it briefly himself, then it must be so.

When the conversation peters out, I tentatively lay my head on his shoulder, and he transfers the reins to his other hand, putting his arm around my waist and pulling me closer. I cuddle into him, delightfully warm and relaxed and . . . happy. I am happy.

Benedict said he watched me at the hearth and saw a vision of what could be. In this moment, I *feel* what could be. I am relaxed in a way I never am with anyone except my sisters. I am myself, completely and utterly myself, snuggling against a man. I have never seen myself in such a vision, and yet it feels perfect. A sense of what could be.

"I know . . ." Benedict begins, and then tries again. "While comparing your world to mine is fascinating, there is a deeper matter at the heart of it." His fingers rub at my hip. "We are from different worlds. Different times."

"Yes."

"And that is a problem."

My voice quiets. "Yes."

"I knew it was, even before I understood . . . Well, I am still trying to fully understand it, but I accept it as truth, as unimaginable as it might be. Before that, I still knew you were from London, with a life and a family in London."

"Yes."

"But it is not just London, miles away. It is London, over a hundred years from now."

"Yes."

"Yet if you speak of marriage, might I presume . . . we could . . . find a solution?" Before I can answer, he hurries on, "A solution for both of us, that is not me assuming you would come here and live with me." He looks down at me. "I would never ask you to give up your life, Portia."

"Thank you. If that is how you feel—that you expect compromise rather than capitulation—then we *will* find a way."

He exhales. "Good. Then there is only one question remaining, and this is the one that could truly rend a future together impossible."

"All right . . ."

He looks down at me, all solemnity. "As much as I adore your night-dresses, I really must insist you do not wear them to bed."

I frown. "Then what will I wear?"

He leans to my ear and whispers, "Nothing."

"Hmm. I can see the appeal."

"Good."

"But you may need to invest in more blankets."

"Done. Then there is another question."

"Wait. You said *one*."

"I lied. Now the question. Two children? Or three?"

I shake my head. "Two or three, it hardly matters. You are missing the far more important numerical answer we must determine."

"Which is?"

"Sexual congress. How often a day can I expect it? At least once, I hope."

He grins. "Why else do you think I asked you to forgo the nightdress?"

"So we are going to do it in a bed? What a novel idea."

His grin grows. "Where else would you like it, my lady?"

"Where else *can* we have it?" I say. "That is the question, and I believe we need to discover the answer to that. I would like to start with the rain." I peer up at the sky. "Yes, I would very much like to have it in the rain. On the moors. Under the moonlight. In the sun, too, but I will start with the rain and the moonlight."

He reaches down and kisses my lips, firm and even a little rough, a teasing taste of passion before he pulls back.

"Then let us hope we have plenty of rain, my lady. And sunshine." He glances over. "How do you feel about snow?"

"Cold. But also, yes, we must have it in the snow. And in front of the fire. And atop the tower. And in the barn. And—"

A horse and rider appear on the road ahead.

34

W e are passing through a narrow gap in a copse of trees, and
Benedict's gaze casts about those trees as he lets out a curse.
"Ben?" I say, and then I see the problem.

We have entered the perfect spot to be set upon by highwaymen.
Benedict would know that better than anyone, and I presume he would
normally be more careful, but we'd been engrossed in our
conversation.

"It is a single rider," I say, peering at the horse coming our way. It is
too shrouded in darkness for me to see more than a figure with a pale
face.

Benedict only grunts.

"I am certain it is but a fellow traveler," I say.

Another grunt. Then he calls, his voice echoing, "Give way, sir. We
cannot both fit through here."

"The trees ought to have been cleared," I murmur. "This is an unnecessarily dangerous spot."

"On my lands, they would be cleared. Others are not so careful. The
trees are pretty, are they not?" His snort says what he thinks of
picturesque beauty at the expense of safety.

At first, it seems the rider is going to give way, but he was only
turning his horse . . . to walk straight down the center.

"We cannot back out," Benedict calls with a growl. "If you continue, I must presume your intentions are cause for concern."

"Then you would presume correctly, Lord Sterling."

The voice comes hoarse and muffled, and in another step, I see that the "pale face" is actually a pale scarf covering the lower half of the man's face. He wears a hood of some sort under his hat, so all we can see is a sliver of eyes shaded into obscurity by the hat's brim.

"You know who I am," Benedict says. "But I do not know you. Care to remedy that?"

The man lets out a laugh. "I think you know who I am. If not by name, then by reputation." He fingers his neckcloth. It's red. Scarlet red.

"What do you want?" Benedict grinds out the words. "If you know who I am, then you know I have a ha'penny in my pocket and nothing more. I've long since sold any jewels of note. In short, I have nothing to give."

"Nor do I," I say. "We left in a hurry, and as you can see . . ." I lift my arms. "I am wearing my nightdress."

"Perhaps I will take that," Scarlet Jack says.

"Do not even jest—" Benedict begins.

"I do not want your whore, Sterling. I am certain she's quite well used by now."

Benedict rocks to his feet, but before he can speak, I say, "We have nothing of value. You know that. So why did you stop us?"

The man lifts his hand. At first, I think he is raising a knife. It is too short to be a musket or a sword, and pistols have not yet been invent—

And then I see my mistake. It is indeed a pistol.

The gun barrel swings up. That is all I see. No, I see two things. It swings up, and it is pointed at Benedict.

I knock Benedict out of the way just as the gun fires. Something hits my hip. Impact and then pain. There is a scream. My scream? Benedict roars. Then I am falling, and there is another scream, and this time, I know it is not me. It's the horse. The chaise lurches forward, and I catch a glimpse of our horse rearing in panic.

An oath from Scarlet Jack. The chaise lurches again. Benedict is crouched on the carriage floor with me, and the chaise itself is jumping forward, the horse starting to run.

"Horse," I pant through the pain. "The reins!"

I catch another glimpse, this time of Benedict's face and the moment where he understands what I am saying, but he does not care. He's reaching for me, lips parting in my name.

"Bloody hell," I manage. "Reins!" I grit my teeth. "Our chance. Get away. Before he reloads."

Benedict finally understands my meaning. The shot has panicked the horse, which is barreling forward, and I am not nearly as concerned about Benedict taking control of the chaise as I am about him using the opportunity to get past the man intent on shooting him.

Benedict grabs the reins. "Hie!" he shouts. "Hie!"

Scarlet Jack fires another shot, but it goes wild.

"Go!" I say. "He must reload!"

"I know that," he says. "I am familiar with— Why the hell am I arguing with you?"

"Good question. Don't."

"Stay down."

"I am."

We must shout to be heard. The chaise is rocketing forward. There'd been a bump earlier, as if we'd grazed Scarlet Jack's horse, but now we are past him, and the horse is running as fast as she can, which is faster than she should with the chaise bouncing along behind her.

I touch my hand to my hip. The fabric there is soaked with blood, and my hip burns, but I can move my legs.

I have treated pistol wounds in my time. While I have no idea what guns are like in this time—I did not even think pistols existed—it seems that it shot a ball that seared past my hip, scraping a deep furrow but doing—I hope—no lasting damage. Except for the bleeding. Bleeding is always a concern . . . unless one is in a runaway chaise fleeing a highwayman bent on murder, and then bleeding is a thing that must be considered later.

I inch along the floor. Benedict doesn't seem to notice me until I lift my head to peek behind us.

"Portia!"

I wave him to silence, which only makes him let out a string of curses.

"He is pursuing," I say, loudly enough to be heard.

"Really? I had not noticed."

I let the sarcasm pass without comment.

"We cannot outrun him," I say. "He is on a horse, and we are slowed by—"

The chaise goes airborne, and when it lands, I clip my tongue with my teeth, tasting blood.

"We are going too fast," I say.

"Too fast or too slow?" he snaps.

"Both," I snap back. "Too fast for the chaise to handle. Too slow to outpace him."

Benedict does not answer, which means he already knows this. Of course he does. He just does not know what to do about it. Keep going, and we will crash and be at Scarlet Jack's mercy. Slow down, and we will be overtaken and at Scarlet Jack's mercy.

"You would not have a pistol, would you?" I ask.

His snort is loud enough to hear over the cracking of the chaise's bouncing wheels.

"That is no," I say. I lift my head again.

"Portia . . ."

"There!" I say, pointing. "The trees to the right. He is on the left. We must jump out at the trees."

"I hope you are joking."

I pull myself into a crouch on the right side of the chaise.

"Of course you are not," he grumbles.

"Do you have a better idea?"

More grumbling, most of it swallowed by the clacking of the wheels. Then he says, "We go on my signal."

He does not wait for my response. Instead, he pulls the reins, slowing the galloping horse just a little. Letting Scarlet Jack catch up. I wonder what Benedict is doing, and then I understand. The rain hasn't been enough to soak the road, and Benedict is getting Jack into the dust thrown up by our chaise, so he will not see us leap.

"Go!" he says with a wave. "Be care—"

I am already leaping. Pain blasts through me as I hit the ground, and for a moment, I am blinded by it. Then I recover and scramble through what I realize—too late—are brambles. It does not matter. I scramble as if my life depends on it.

That is when I realize Benedict has not jumped.

My heart jams into my throat. Benedict has not jumped. He has tricked me into getting to safety while he shouts for the horse to go faster.

No, please, no. Do not be a fool, Benedict.

He is not a fool. He urges the mare faster so that he can get Scarlet Jack into his dust again. Then he leaps.

Scarlet Jack keeps riding, trying to catch up to the runaway chaise, giving no sign that he has seen us vacate it. I force myself to duck deeper into the trees and brambles, lest he look back. Then I crawl until my hip screams for me to stop. I'm past the brambles now and in amongst the trees. At a crackle of dried undergrowth, I look up to see Benedict hunched over and running toward me.

"That worked," I say.

"Do not sound so pleased," he mutters. "If jumping from the chaise injured you further—"

"It is still better than being shot again."

His fingers tighten on my shoulder as he crouches beside me. "He meant to shoot *me*. And he shot you."

"It does not matter."

"It does. That is why he ambushed us. To kill me. And you are the one who was shot."

"I would have been shot eventually anyway."

When he looks at me, I shrug. "He would hardly shoot you and leave me alive. He was only getting the greater threat out of the way first. His plan, I presume, was to leave us both dead, murdered by highwaymen at a dangerous spot on the road."

He grunts and leans over to peer at my injury. "How bad is it?"

"I can move, and it does not seem to be gushing blood, so it will hold for now. Which it must. It will not be long before he realizes—"

"Lord Sterling!" Scarlet Jack shouts, his voice echoing over the clatter of the disappearing chaise.

Benedict's head shoots up, his gaze veering that way.

"We must go," I whisper.

"Go where?" he says.

"To . . ." I trail off as I look about.

We are in a small line of trees, maybe fifty feet long by ten feet wide.

Once we leave these trees, we will be running across open moor, where Scarlet Jack can shoot us.

"Do not worry," Benedict whispers against my ear. "I have thought of this part."

I exhale in relief.

He continues, "But it is going to require you doing something very, very difficult."

I nod and steel myself. "I am ready."

"I am not certain of that," he murmurs. "We shall try anyway."

"What do you need me to do?"

"Nothing."

I blink.

His hands squeeze my shoulders as his face lowers to mine. "I need you to do nothing, Portia. Nothing except hide."

I let out a sound uncomfortably akin to a squeak.

"Yes," he says. "You will not want to, but being absurdly practical, you *will* do it. Because you know it is the best thing to do. You are injured. I need you to hide and let me take care of him."

"But—"

His gaze meets mine. "I do not want to lose the opportunity to spend my life with you, Portia, which means that I do not want to lose you . . . but I also do not want to lose my own life, which is an equally important part of that future. I will be careful."

I hesitate. He is correct, of course. I am injured. I should hide.

I trust him. That is the most important thing. I trust that he is capable and will handle this as best it can be handled.

I nod.

He presses a kiss to my forehead. Then he strips off his jacket and lays it over the white skirt of my nightgown, hiding me in the undergrowth.

35

As Benedict crawls away, I move, and he looks back sharply, but then he sees that I am only adjusting my shawl to hide my face. He nods and continues crawling. Then I do something so difficult I can scarcely believe I manage it: I close my eyes and lie still and listen.

"I know you are in here!" Scarlet Jack shouts. "There is no place else for you to be."

When there is a noise I cannot place, it takes all my willpower to keep from looking. I cannot open my eyes and see what is happening. If I do, I might react, however involuntarily.

A curse follows the noise, and then the thump of boots hitting the earth. I realize then what I heard. Scarlet Jack had attempted to ride his horse into the trees and realized they were too thick. He's now on foot. Good.

"Do you really think I will not find you?" Jack says. He has reverted to his disguised voice, now that he is no longer shouting loud enough to hide it.

Disguising his voice because Benedict would recognize it.

Because it is Owen Carleton.

I had already considered that the most likely identity of Scarlet Jack. Now I realize I am correct. He might be hiding his voice, but he is not hiding his accent or his diction. A true highwayman of the moors would have a broad Yorkshire accent. I realized this when Benedict and Jude stopped the Wards' coach. They were clearly from the region, but their accents were lighter, and their diction was high enough to mark them as educated men.

Scarlet Jack speaks with a London accent and the same diction level as the Sterlings.

That is what makes me decide this is one of two people: Owen Carleton . . . or his brother, Martin. I will allow it could be Martin. The younger Carleton certainly is not innocent. At the very least, he set me up in that garden for his brother to attack. At the worst, he did it himself. But aligning all the information—Pansy's murder, Owen's disappearance, Scarlet Jack and the murder of Colin Booth—I heavily lean toward this being Owen Carleton.

Scarlet Jack continues walking into the small forest, his head turning this way and that as he scans his surroundings. The moonlight barely penetrates the tree cover, and when I peek, all I can see is that pale scarf around his face, yet he strides forward, confident that he will spot Benedict. Or confident he will spot me, in my white gown, with Benedict close at hand?

"Come now, Sterling," he says. "Hiding hardly befits the Earl of Ravensford, the boorish brute who is quicker with his fists than his words. Words are not really your weapons, are they? Nor wits. So let me help you with that. You will want to die a fighter. You will want to die protecting your lady love. You will not want to perish cowering behind a tree."

"True."

Scarlet Jack spins, and Benedict is right behind him, a hulking shadow in the darkness. Benedict's fist slams into Scarlet Jack's jaw.

"I *am* better with my fists," Benedict says.

Scarlet Jack reels back, the gun rising, and I go to cry out, but here Scarlet Jack is very wrong. Benedict's wits are just fine. His attention is fully on that gun . . . and getting it away. The pistol fires, but Benedict has his hand on the barrel, thrusting up. He hisses with pain—presumably from the heat of the gunpowder blast—but he does not release his hold.

Scarlet Jack's free hand swings back, silver winking.

"Knife!" I shout.

Benedict leaps aside just in time, the blade catching his jacket. He wrenches the pistol from Scarlet Jack's hand and pitches it away. The gun is useless to Benedict—he has nothing to reload it with.

It is an excellent pitch, the pistol landing deep in the forest, too far for Scarlet Jack to run after it. But Scarlet Jack still has his knife, and he dives at Benedict. This time, Benedict cannot get out of the way fast enough—he is *not* fast on his feet. The blade catches his arm, slicing through his sleeves, and he hisses in pain again.

Scarlet Jack flies in again. Benedict's fist catches his jaw, and Scarlet Jack falls back but catches himself and stays upright. When Benedict comes at him again, he dances out of his reach and then ducks in and slashes at him again, this time catching him in the shoulder. Benedict stays back, assessing, only to have Scarlet Jack lunge, his blade ramming toward Benedict's chest.

Benedict gets out of the way just in time, but when he tries to land another blow, he catches the blade again instead. Benedict is bigger and more powerful, but also slower. In a bare-knuckle fight, Benedict would simply charge and take Scarlet Jack down. But the smaller man has a knife, and Benedict cannot get close enough without giving Scarlet Jack the advantage.

When Scarlet Jack lunges again, I leap from my spot and shout, "Owen!"

He swings toward me. Benedict charges in, hitting him with a blow that nearly knocks Scarlet Jack off his feet before he slashes.

"Owen Carleton!" I shout. "I know that is you behind the mask."

Scarlet Jack dances back, his attention divided, unable to keep himself from listening to me. Good.

I wait until he seems to recover. Then I shout, "Pansy Miller," just as he swings again. He pauses, and Benedict hits, staggering him. This time, Scarlet Jack doesn't attack. He only raises the knife as he backs away from Benedict. Defensive posture. Warning Benedict off. Good.

"I know you murdered Pansy," I say. "You stabbed her in the back and hid her body in the tower. Then you pretended to flee to America while sending letters home and to Pansy's family."

"It was not my fault," Scarlet Jack says. "She threatened to expose our affair. Said if I did not marry her, she would tell everyone she was with child and I was the father."

"A heart-wrenching story," Benedict says. "It may even be true. But not for Owen Carleton."

Benedict steps toward Scarlet Jack. "Two days ago, before my ball, I sought information on Pansy Miller. I found someone who knew she had a beau. He liked to meet at Ravensford Keep, as he knew a way inside from when he was a boy. The girl thought that meant Pansy was seeing my brother, Jude. I knew that was untrue. Yet I recalled Jude saying that when they were boys, Owen never went with him to the old keep. The mold gave him sneezing fits. Someone else always wanted to go in Owen's place. Do you remember that"— Benedict steps closer still—"Martin?"

Benedict reaches to yank the scarf and manages to get it partway down before Martin Carleton slashes him.

"Ben!" I shout, and there is fear in my voice but also a touch of anger.

Really, Benedict? Really?

Yes, you had realized it was not Owen. You were right, and I was wrong, but my mistake gave Martin a chance to blame his brother, lest one of us escape to tell the tale.

You should have let him have that, and his guard would have been down. Instead, now he is revealed beyond any doubt.

Benedict manages to avoid the slash, but he is in retreat now, with Martin coming at him in a fury, slashing wildly. Benedict is backing out of the way in steps and jumps . . . with a looming tree behind him, about to stop his retreat.

"Martin!" I shout.

My voice gives him pause. I hobble forward.

"Tell me what you want," I say. "Money? I can get you money. Whatever you have done, we will keep your secrets. We can blame Owen."

I'm babbling, but with purpose. I do not think Martin will be swayed by money—even if I had any to offer. Nor does he care about us keeping his secrets. They'll be kept better by our deaths. But I am talking, and he is listening because he cannot help himself. What if I should say something important? He cannot miss that.

I keep hobbling, making it appear that I can barely walk.

"Portia . . ." Benedict says, voice low with warning.

"What do you want, Martin? Tell us— Oh!" I stumble, falling to one knee and panting in pain I do not need to fake.

Martin's gaze darts to me, the wounded dove. He should keep his attention on Benedict. It is not as if I can flee the forest and escape. Benedict is the threat.

Yet here I see the truth of Martin Carleton. He is not a young man who takes the difficult road in life. I do not know whether his story about Pansy is true, but he did kill her. I am certain of that, and he killed her because it was the easy way out.

I am the easy prey, and he cannot help but focus on me. I am wounded, unable to fight or flee. Kill me first, and then he can take care of Benedict.

Martin takes a step my way.

"Martin . . ." Benedict rumbles.

I catch Benedict's gaze, my own expression hard. He understands. He can see by my look that I am faking the extent of my injuries. He knows I am luring Martin away. Luring him from the real threat. Giving Benedict both room and opportunity to attack.

Benedict still glares at me, his jaw setting, and I cannot tell whether I have won this silent war of wills. I do not think I have.

"You murdered Pansy," I say when Martin hesitates, as if reconsidering his choice. "You were the lover she was threatening."

"Because I had been tricked. She wanted Owen. Always Owen."

"She did not insist you marry her, did she? Nor did she threaten to claim she was pregnant."

His lip curls. "She wanted me to help her seduce Owen. Yes, we dallied together, she and I. That is why Owen had her sent away. But it was nothing more than dallying, for which I paid her as well as I would any whore. It was not the money she wanted, though. It was the blackmail. In the aftermath of passion, I had confided secrets to her, and she threatened to tell my father unless I helped her seduce Owen. The silly chit. What did she expect? That Owen would be forced to marry a mere maid? I told her that, and she would not listen to reason, swore she would tell my father things I had done."

While Martin talks, Benedict takes slow and silent steps in his direction. But then he fails to notice a twig underfoot. It snaps, and Martin wheels. He sees Benedict and charges, knife raised, snarling with animal rage.

Benedict lunges out of the way, but Martin keeps coming, and if he seemed in a fury before, it is nothing compared to his rage now, as he slashes and stabs.

"Martin!" I shout.

He does not seem to hear me. I push to my feet and stagger as fast as I can toward the two men.

"Martin!" I shout again. "I know where Owen is. I know what you did to him."

That gives him just enough pause for Benedict to swing out of the way. I continue moving forward.

As Martin was talking, I saw my mistake. I've been looking at this entirely wrong, working on the presumption that the angry ghost was Pansy.

We found her body and knew she'd died shortly before the ghost was first seen. She'd died at the time Owen allegedly left for America. Therefore, Owen must have murdered her and fled, and her ghost haunted the keep.

But if Martin killed Pansy, then why did Owen leave at the same time?

Why did both Owen and Pansy start sending letters home, letters that acted as the only proof they were alive?

It could not be a coincidence.

And what is more likely to enrage a ghost beyond reason? Being murdered by the lover she was trying to blackmail? Or being murdered by one's own brother?

"You killed Owen," I say. "You murdered your—"

Martin spins and rushes at me. Benedict charges after him, but I am too close, and Martin is right there, and I am falling back, hands raised to shield myself from his knife when my hip really does give way. I start to fall and—

A whistle slices through the air. Martin staggers, an arrow piercing his shoulder. Then another slams in next to it, making him scream and drop the knife.

Benedict runs for me. Before I quite understand what is happening, Benedict has me in his arms, and he is running full out for the road. He breaks through the brambles without even a wince of pain. Then there's a snort. The snort of a horse.

"Can you ride?" he says.

"I—"

"Can you *ride*?"

I nod, and again, I am still not quite certain what is happening, but then Benedict is lifting me onto an unfamiliar horse. Martin's horse. When I am steady, he turns and looks back toward the forest.

"I must stop Martin," Benedict says. "He will flee."

"But—"

"He is injured. He cannot find his pistol. I must—"

"No."

That word does not come from me. We follow the deep, raspy voice to a figure standing in the shadows. A figure with a bow, arrow notched and pointing at Benedict.

"No," the archer says again.

Benedict takes a step in that direction. The archer pulls back the string on the bow. Benedict slows.

"I must stop—" Benedict says.

"Leave," the figure says.

"He cannot get away with it."

"He won't. Go."

Benedict still hesitates. Then the clouds shift, and the moon illuminates the figure better. It is a person of middling height and boyishly slender. The figure is dressed in a long black coat, tall black boots and black trousers. A black hood shadows the top of the face. And the lower part? It is covered by a bright-red silk scarf.

"Scarlet Jack, I presume," Benedict says, his voice a deep rumble.

No answer from the figure.

"The real Scarlet Jack," I say.

The figure's hood turns my way. Still no answer.

"We know Colin Booth is dead," I say. "Murdered by Scarlet Jack."

The figure finally speaks. "Not by me."

"Martin Carleton then?" I say. "Appropriating your role when it suits him? Using it to murder a young man and steal his father's clock back? Or did he hire Colin's band of thieves to steal it for him . . . and young Colin knew too much?"

Silence. We are not getting more than a few words from this Scarlet Jack, and I think I know why.

"I don't suppose you know where that clock is?" I say.

A snort, as if Scarlet Jack realizes I do not expect an answer.

"Well, if you find it, we would like it," I say. "A little rain is not enough to undo the damage done to the people of Ravensford. The sale of that clock would let Lord Sterling help them and buy back his land, putting the people under much more benevolent management. If you *are* Scarlet Jack, and if you are truly concerned about justice then . . ." I shrug. "Using Mr. Carleton's clock to help the tenants he ignores seems like justice, does it not?"

Scarlet Jack points at the horse.

"Yes, yes, we're going. But Martin cannot escape what he has done. I presume you mean to see him punished. If you do not, we must take matters into our own hands."

Another point toward the horse. Benedict looks at me. I reach my hand down. He ignores it and climbs up behind me, and we leave the hawk to its prey.

36

We find the mare and chaise. Thankfully, the mare is fine. The chaise is in worse shape, but it is of far less concern than the horse. We decide to leave the small carriage for now, as we each have a horse to ride. Or, I decide this. Benedict wants to find a way to use the chaise because I am injured and should not ride a horse for another hour or more.

I agree to take a moment to examine my injury, which is—as expected —only a deep graze where the ball shot past. It will require cleaning and bandaging, and I will be in some temporary discomfort when walking, but I can ride, and that is the most expedient way of getting to the castle.

On the way, we discuss what we have learned, both during the forest encounter and before that. I hadn't had a chance to tell Benedict what Miss Carleton said about Owen, and he hadn't had a chance to tell me what he'd learned the day of the ball. That led to me pinpointing Owen as the killer, while Benedict knew Pansy's lover was more likely to be Martin. And that isn't simply because her lover met Pansy at the castle, which Owen never visited.

"My aunt says she . . . spoke to you about Jude," he says, "and you seemed to take her meaning."

"That he . . ." I am not certain of the present terminology, so I say, "Prefers the romantic company of men."

Benedict does not answer, and I look to see him watching me closely. Watching for my reaction.

"That is why you knew Pansy's lover could not be Jude," I say, "as your informant presumed."

"Yes."

He keeps looking at me.

I sigh. "I do not care whether your brother prefers men or women. I only care which *you* prefer, as that would be a matter of importance to me."

His shoulders relax. "All right. I presume my brother's preference is better accepted in your time?"

"Sadly, no. But I was raised to care about *who* people are. The rest is none of my business."

"Yes, that is how I knew it was not Jude, but it is also how I knew it was not Owen."

I remember what Miss Carleton said, that she knew Pansy's attentions were in vain. "Because Owen shared the same preference. Were he and Jude . . . ?"

"Briefly, but they did not suit. They had been friends after a fashion, being thrown together by our families' acquaintance. But they were not close friends, nor did they become more for any significant period of time. Yet it was enough for me to be sure that Owen was not Pansy's lover."

"Do you think I am correct? That Owen is dead?"

"Yes."

"And that his brother murdered him?"

A heaviness comes into Benedict's voice as he says, "Yes."

☙❧

It's morning when we arrive at the castle to find Miranda and Nicolas there. I had been trying not to worry about why Benedict hadn't seen them. It seems their paths simply had not crossed. Miranda and Nicolas headed for Ravensford to speak to Benedict, who was at that moment already searching for me, drawing close to Thorne Manor but along a different route.

Miranda had gone straight to the castle to warn the Sterlings. Jude was there—Benedict having insisted he stay behind in case I returned—and so they've spoken to him. We find them in the library, deep in urgent conversation. On hearing us, they leap up. Jude is out of the room first, greeting his brother. Then he sees me and pulls me into an embrace. Physical contact is yet another thing that is different in this world. I am not convinced I'll ever be comfortable in a world of easy embraces, but I'll make exceptions for Jude.

"Is that . . . blood?" Miranda says as she appears.

"It is nothing," I say. "A powder-ball graze, that is all."

"A powder-ball graze?" Miranda's voice rises.

"Do not attempt to reason with her on it," Benedict says. "She will tend to it after the rest is sorted, and not a moment sooner." He spots Nicolas and thrusts out his hand. "Benedict Sterling."

"Nicolas Dupuis."

I introduce my sister, and then we move back into the library as I say to Miranda, "Have you encountered the ghost yet?"

"Introductions done, time for business," Jude teases.

Benedict shoots him a glare. "Portia has returned to a place where a ghost nearly knocked her to her death. Of course that is her immediate concern."

"Knocked her . . . ?" Miranda spins on me. "What is this?"

"Oh, did she leave that out of her story?" Jude says. "Shocking. Benedict, you can explain."

I bristle. "I am quite capable of speaking for myself."

"No, dear Port," Miranda says. "Capable of speaking in general, yes. About yourself? No. Lord Sterling, I would prefer to hear your version of events."

Benedict tells Miranda and Nicolas about the two attacks while I bite my tongue against every urge to minimize it.

When he finishes, Miranda says, "I am so sorry, Portia. That must have been terribly upsetting. To have such a thing happen, when it has never happened before." She meets my eyes. "Because it never has happened before, correct?"

I do not answer. Her look and her tone tell me she suspects the truth.

"Portia . . . ?" she says. "If this is indeed the first time it has happened, that is important."

"It is not," Benedict says.

I glare at him. He only glares back.

"I *can* speak for myself," I say.

"Then do it."

More glaring, and I swear Miranda bites her cheek to keep from laughing.

"Fine." I turn to Miranda and tell her the truth about what has been happening to me. As I do, the sadness on her face reminds me why I *didn't* tell her. This is not her experience, and it is not one she can help with. It feels like unburdening myself on her unnecessarily.

When I say something to that effect, she gives me a hard look. "I may not know the solution to your situation, Portia, but I still want to know you are experiencing it."

"I wish I could communicate with these spirits," I say. "I believe that is the problem. I cannot communicate, and it angers them."

"To the point of attacking you? If you are ignoring them, how would attacking you help?"

"They might hope to bully her into communicating," Nicolas says.

"Perhaps, but she is saying that she cannot see them or hear their words. Either they can hear her saying that—and believe she is lying—or they cannot hear her and ought to know that indicates a problem."

"In which case," Nicolas says, "it is still bullying. They do not care whether she can communicate. They can hurt her, and that is enough." He looks at his wife. "Sometimes, for some people, that *is* enough."

Miranda nods, acknowledging his point. "Still, I suspect there is more to it. You asked whether I've made contact with this ghost. I have. In a fashion."

"And it is not Pansy," Jude says.

"It is Owen," I say.

He looks surprised.

"I am sorry," I say. "I know you were close, at a time."

Jude shrugs. "We were friends in happenstance. Of an age, with fathers who often brought their families together. I am not certain Owen and I were ever truly friends, and I have not spoken to him in nearly a decade, but I will still mourn his passing."

"And we shall set him free," I say.

"If we can," Miranda murmurs. "I said that I made contact *in a fashion*. He is not your typical spirit, and I think that might explain why he is attacking you."

"When ghosts do not normally attack."

Miranda goes silent. Then she catches her husband's eye and sighs. "All right, Portia. Perhaps you are not the only one who has kept things from her sister. Particularly angry ghosts *can* lash out. What Owen is doing to you—physically touching you—is different, but ghosts can be vindictive, particularly if they think a living person is responsible for their death. However, in those cases, I can make contact. With Owen, it is like trying to speak to a seething whirlwind of rage. I caught glimpses of him—enough to know it was a young man—but he cannot speak to me."

"Or he refuses to," Nicolas says.

"Yes, that is also possible."

"Possible that the anger comes *first*," Jude muses. "Not that Owen hurt Portia because he is angry that she will not speak to him. He hurt her because he is already angry."

"That is a very good point." Miranda looks at me. "I am going to try again to contact him. We were discussing that when you arrived. Perhaps you should not be near while we do so."

"Agreed," Benedict says. "I will take—"

"No," I say. "If I have even a little of the Sight, I should be here to help."

Nicolas looks over at me. "Will you leave if you are under threat?"

I hesitate and then say, "Yes. Now, Miranda, tell us what you need."

"Ideally, we should find Owen's body. That ought to help."

"Oh!" Jude says. "Perhaps we can enlist the puppy to use her nose. Where is she?"

"I fear I accidentally shut her up in the nineteenth century," I say. "I trust she will be well there. I did not dare return in case I could not get back to this timeline again."

"Nineteenth . . . ?" Jude gives his head a sharp shake. "What?"

I turn to Miranda. "I presume you did not tell him?"

"I was avoiding that until necessary. It rather derails everything else, and it did not seem immediately pertinent." Her eyes cut toward Benedict. "I take it *you* know, Lord Sterling?"

"Do I know that Portia is from a hundred years in the future and came here through a magical spot in Thorne Manor? Yes."

"Wait," Jude says. "What?"

"We will explain later," I say.

"Later? No. I think I need this explained . . . Where are you all going?"

"To find a body," I say.

"But what about—?"

"Not immediately pertinent," Benedict says, echoing Miranda.

"The hell it's not. Get back here and . . ."

Jude's voice fades as we head down the hall, in search of either a ghost or the corpse of one.

37

B enedict makes me tend to my injury before we actually search. I would have refused, but he had everyone's annoyingly vocal support. Also, it gives me the excuse to examine his own injuries. He has said they are "merely scrapes," but if he insists on tending to my scrapes, then I can insist on tending to his. And the fact that we are in a castle with an angry ghost means that even the act of undressing for that mutual wound-tending does not delay our return to the others. I will not say I don't notice every part of his body as he unclothes it. I will only say that I am very pleased that—despite noticing —I am able to keep my mind *mostly* on the task at hand.

Benedict has divided the castle and grounds into sections for our search. Miranda and Nicolas took the outside, where her Sight might allow Owen to lead her to his buried body. Jude took the main part of the castle, poking into any place where one could hide a corpse. That leaves Benedict and me with the smallest but most likely place: the ruined wing.

We start in the newly opened room under the tower. Pansy's body is gone, but the smell permeates the area even more now, as if intensified by its disturbance.

We have brought lanterns, and we use them to scour the dirt floor for signs of disturbance. Yes, it has been two years since her murder, but I would expect to see some sign where the ground has been dug and repacked. There is none. Nor is there any place where a body might hide —it is a fully open space.

"I do not understand," Benedict says as he boosts me from the hole. "If Martin hid Pansy here, why not Owen? Does it not make sense for a single killer to hide both bodies in the same place?"

I dust off my skirts. "If I were a killer—"

"I do not think I like how easily you put yourself in the mind of one," he says as he hauls himself out.

"Take it as fair warning." I head back into the ruined wing. "If I had killed both Pansy and Owen, I would not hide them together. Pansy is— in my killer's mind—a mere housemaid. I am not overly troubled if she is found. I might even find it advantageous to lead people to her body if I wished to blame my brother. I could not, in that case, also hide him there. He is the one they will care about. He must be very well concealed."

"That does make sense."

"Do not sound so surprised."

"I mean that I will accept it as a sensible answer rather than one that suggests you possess an alarmingly murderous mind."

"Excellent. Then Owen Carleton's body is not the only thing kept well concealed."

Benedict only shakes his head. "All right then. If you do have a murderously inclined mind, where would you hide him?"

"It is not my mind we must consider. It's Martin's. More than his mind. His physique also plays a role. How far could he carry Owen's body? How high could he lift it? How deep could he bury it? For our purposes, the first question is how well he knew the castle. The fact that Owen haunts the castle means he is unlikely to be buried far away. He is here. Either in the keep or close by."

"What hiding spots did he know?" Benedict muses. "Besides the one under the tower, which he would have known from his visits here as a boy."

"Did you have other hiding spots?"

"Martin is ten years my junior. When he accompanied Jude, I was no longer at the age for such things. We told him about the one under the tower. Otherwise, I would have been poking about or riding or reading.

The pursuits of a boy on the cusp of being a man. I did not play—" His chin jerks up. "Hiding games."

"You did not play hiding games?" I say. "That is a shame."

"No." He walks faster, calling back, "I *did* play such games with Jude. We did it mostly as a way to keep Martin busy."

"He'd hide, and you wouldn't seek."

"We never left him for long. But one time, we could not find him and spent an hour searching. We finally discovered him in the last place we would have looked."

He realizes I have fallen behind, hobbling as I am, and waits for me. "You really ought not to be walking."

"And yet I am. Walk on ahead. I will catch up."

He shakes his head. "Owen's body is not going anywhere. Here." He reaches down, and before I can protest, he scoops me up into his arms.

"Lie still," he says. "The corridor is narrow, and if you struggle, you will bash your head."

He picks his way along the hall of the ruined wing. I feel rather silly, draped over his arms, but my hip does burn from walking.

"You said it was the last place you would look?" I say.

"Yes."

"Which is . . . ?"

"The privy."

At my look, he gives a quirk of a devilish grin. "What, my lady? Have you never hidden in the privy?"

"I have never been so desperate to win any game."

"In Martin's defense, it was not as repulsive as it might seem. It is the old castle privy—a seat placed high over a deep hole. It has not been used as a privy in hundreds of years."

"Meaning any waste matter has long since turned to soil."

"Rich soil, which was dug out by my forefathers for their gardens."

"And Martin climbed down into the hole and could not climb out?"

"Hardly. There are the remains of rungs for retrieving the soil. He could get out again. He was waiting to be found. When we did find him, our mother insisted that this hole—like that under the tower—be boarded over, as it proved too great a temptation for small boys."

"Small boys so desperate to win a game that they would hide in an old privy."

"At the time, I dismissed it as childhood foolishness, but Martin has always been rather desperate. For attention, mostly. He is neither the male heir nor the daughter destined to win the family a title." Benedict pushes open a broken door with his foot. "Jude might be the younger son, but he never lacked our parents' love and attention."

"Martin did." I remember how Martin let on that he didn't want to be heir, when his sister suggested that was not an option.

"Yes."

Benedict sets me down. We are in a tiny room that is empty save for a raised platform.

"The privy?" I say, nodding toward it.

"Indeed. We are earls with our own castle. No expense is too great to ensure our comfort."

"You can laugh," I say, "but I have seen your chamber pots, and I am not certain they are much of an improvement. In fact, given that you need to empty them yourselves, I might prefer this to be repaired."

"I shall make that a wedding gift to you. I will even sand the wood myself, so you do not get splinters in your lovely bottom."

"So you are planning to live in the castle?"

"So you are planning to marry me?"

"Heavens, no. I only want to live with you most scandalously."

He shakes his head and begins to pull the boards nailed over the privy seat. "As tempting as that is, I must insist that we wed. We may still live scandalously, of course."

"In the castle?"

He heaves again, the old wood cracking. "You might change your mind about that in the midst of winter. Or summer."

"I will manage. I can be quite stubborn."

"I had not noticed." He wrenches again. "Speaking of stubborn . . ."

"I do not think you are supposed to do that with your bare hands."

"I will manage."

"Speaking of stubborn . . ."

He is about to say something when another yank breaks the board, and he stumbles back. He catches himself and sets the board aside. Then he lifts a second board, this one seeming to have been a seat. Once it is raised and secured, the hole below is significantly larger. That must be how men were able to climb down into it to fetch soil.

Benedict peers into the hole.

"As charming as you remember?" I say.

When he does not answer, I frown. "Ben?"

"There is . . . a smell," he says, his voice going solemn.

I do not joke that it is a privy pit. One might expect there to be a smell. He doesn't mean that.

"A body?" I say.

He nods grimly. "I'll fetch a lantern. There's one in the next room."

As he steps out, I move up to the ancient privy hole. It truly is a piece of wood over a raised box. In my world, outdoor privies are common enough, and for those who cannot afford a maid to empty a chamber pot, they would be the usual substitute. Still, it seems odd to have one in the house. The advantage to owning a castle, I suppose, where every effort will be made to ensure the earl and countess's comfort.

I peer into the hole. There is no smell of waste. As Benedict said, that would have long turned to soil. Instead, I catch the same odor we'd encountered with Pansy. The stink of a long-dead body.

A crumbled piece of the wall allows in moonlight. I shift to let the light fall on the hole and lean over. The black hole below seems bottomless. I start to rise—

A hand shoves my head down, the push so brutal that I crumple forward, hands flying out to brace on either side of the privy hole. Hands clamp down on my hips. I let out a yelp of pain as fingers dig into my gunshot injury. The attacker hauls my hips up, shoving my head toward the privy hole.

Here is where being overly practical is indeed a flaw. All I can think is that I am clearly in no danger of being dropped into a privy hole. It's too narrow. Yet this is a service hole, big enough for a man to climb, and that invisible force now has me by the shoulders, forcing me down.

I will fall in headfirst. Headfirst into a very deep hole.

"Ben!" I shout. "Benedict!"

I thrash and struggle. I'm still holding the edge, but my arms are twisting, and there is nothing to grip. One slips free.

A roar from behind me. Hands grab my legs. Hands that I know belong to Benedict even before he snarls, "Let her go!"

Benedict's hands move to my hips and get them tight in his grasp, and I bite my lip against the pain of that. He gives a mighty yank, and we both fly backward. I try to rise, but Benedict is scrabbling to grab me in both hands. He lifts me up and backs into the wall, with me in his arms.

"Owen!" he shouts. "This woman has done nothing to you. Stop!"

Fingers grab my hair again. They yank, and I howl. My hands fly up to claw at them. Benedict tries to run with me, but Owen still has my hair tight in his grip, and I'm wrenched by my hair, the pain sudden and excruciating. When I shriek for Benedict to stop, he holds me tight and resumes shouting at Owen, which is not terribly helpful, although I am certain it makes him feel better.

I take hold of my hair, holding it fast. Then I pull hard myself, ripping it from Owen's grip.

Before Owen can lash out again, Benedict is running. He carries me into the hall. I realize he is racing toward the tower, and I do not know why, but then he veers into the sunny room I'd marveled at before. He races through it and out the door into the long-gone gardens.

"Miranda!" he shouts. "Nicolas!"

I try to add my own shouts, but Benedict's bellows are ten times louder. Soon Nicolas calls back.

"They are coming," Benedict says. "I will take you to my tower. That should be far enough from Owen—"

"I must stay and help Miranda."

"No, you must not. You *must* get to safety."

I struggle against his arms. "I am helping my sister."

"Bloody hell, woman," he says as he puts me down. "You will be the death of me."

From the doorway, a voice says, "At least you will die happy."

I look over at Jude. "Of course he will. He is never so happy as when he is grumbling and thundering."

Benedict scowls. "And you are never so happy as when you are making me grumble and thunder."

I reach up to kiss his cheek. "No, I am even happier when I make you —" I whisper the rest into his ear, and I am rewarded with a dark blush that sets Jude laughing.

"Are you all right, Portia?" Jude says. "You act none the worse for wear, but I have learned that means nothing."

"You are correct," Benedict says. "Her mood is not indicative of what she has endured. I believe we have found Owen's body. And he attacked her for it."

"I am fine," I say. "Benedict will whisk me out of range if needed."

"I can do that more easily if I am carrying you."

I sigh. "If you must."

He lifts me again, and I resist the urge to curl into him, my body relaxing as he draws me tight in his arms.

"Now that is a portrait for one of my novels," Miranda says as she appears with Nicolas. "You must lean backward more, Port. Let your hair fall free and look into his eyes."

Now my own cheeks heat.

"Or you could start struggling and tell him to put you down right now," Miranda says. "Stab him if he refuses. That works for my stories, too."

"It seems murderous minds run in the family," Benedict murmurs.

"Remember that," I say. "You may carry me as long as I am in danger of otherwise being dragged off by Owen. After that, you must—"

"Drop you?"

"Put me down."

"Drop you most unceremoniously on your pretty bottom," he says. "Understood. Now, let us go back in there and get this over with."

38

We are all crammed in the privy, which is just barely big enough for the five of us, especially with me still being in Benedict's arms. He stays by the door, ready to get me out of there. For now, Owen has gone silent.

"Can you hear me?" Miranda says. "I am able to communicate with you. My sister is not. If you hurt her again, I will leave."

I glance at Miranda, who shakes her head, meaning Owen is not replying.

"We have found your body," she says. "We know what happened to you. I can set you at peace. You only need to make contact with me. Confirm you are here."

Still nothing.

"Finding his body is not enough, I believe," Nicolas says. "He may want to be assured that we will put his remains to rest. The problem . . ."

"Is that someone needs to climb down there," Jude says with a shudder.

"I'll do it," Miranda says. "The location does not bother me."

Jude raises a hand. "I will. It *does* bother me, but I have been down there before."

"Were you not injured recently?" Nicolas says. "Please, allow me to descend."

"I would rather do it myself, as I knew Owen. I can hope that will help." Jude speaks aloud to the room. "We did not part on the best of terms, Owen, but I still care for you. You know that I do. I will bring you up and see that you are put to rest."

Jude glances at Miranda and whispers, "Dare I hope that was enough, and you can now see him?"

She shakes her head.

Jude sighs and reaches for the lantern. "I will investigate, confirm it is Owen and determine how he was killed."

Jude descends with one lantern. Nicolas holds a second light at the top. It seems to take forever before Jude's hollow voice wafts up.

"You were correct, Ben. Owen is down here. There is . . . not much remaining, but there is what seems to be blood on his back, as with Pansy."

"Stabbed in the back," I say. "Martin stabbed him—"

The blow comes from nowhere. It strikes me in the jaw, slamming my head back. Benedict lets out a snarl of rage and gathers me to him. Then he begins retreating from the room, but Owen grabs my hair before I remember to cover it.

"Owen!" Miranda shouts. "Enough of this!"

Owen only pulls harder.

"Owen!" she shouts. "I will not help you if you harm—"

A blow to my stomach. Benedict is getting me out of there as fast as he can, but when he turns around, he bashes my legs into the wall and then pulls back too fast, staggering.

"Put me down," I say.

Benedict is still recovering from the stagger. I have just enough time to wriggle free, and I do, getting onto my feet and backing away, hands raised.

"Let me do this, Ben," I say. "Please. I do not know why he is fixated on me, but he is."

"I think he can only see you," Miranda says. "I do not know why, but he seems unable to hear me. I *can* see him. He is beside Benedict, watching you."

"Tell me if he goes after her," Benedict rumbles.

"I will," Miranda promises. "For now, he is watching you, Portia.

He's seething with rage. I can barely make him out. His anger is like electricity sparking around him."

Electricity? This must be some term from the future. It hardly matters. I understand what she means.

"Owen!" I shout. "Can you hear me?"

"He isn't reacting," Miranda says. "But he is staying where he is and watching you."

"Is there another way to communicate?"

Benedict grabs something from the floor. It's a piece of stone. He scrapes it against the wall, where it leaves a chalky line. Then he hands it to me.

I nod my thanks, and I am already writing. Four letters.

Owen.

"Any response?" Benedict says.

"I can see him better. The sparks have faded."

I write another word.

Murder.

"Yes!" Miranda says. "He looked at me. Can you hear me, Owen?"

I write one last word.

Martin.

A noise like a sigh echoes through the stone corridor.

"He is here," Miranda says. "Fully here. Owen? You can hear me, yes?"

She nods, and then she turns to us. "He's here. Whatever madness seized him has passed, at least temporarily. I can speak to him now."

❧

MIRANDA OBTAINS OWEN'S STORY AND RELAYS IT TO US. HE WAS INDEED murdered by his brother. He had heard rumors that Pansy Miller was meeting someone at the old castle, and he had cause to believe it was Martin. He'd followed Martin, intending to talk sense into him. When he'd witnessed the argument, he'd stayed back, not wanting to embarrass his brother in front of Pansy.

He'd seen Martin murder Pansy. That's when he'd rushed forward, hoping to intercede. He'd bent over Pansy's body . . . and Martin stabbed him.

It is indeed rage that seems to have transformed Owen into a seething, mindless spirit. The rage of being murdered by his brother. The rage, too, of realizing why.

While Martin might tell himself he killed Owen because he witnessed Pansy's murder, Owen believes he also saw an opportunity. The chance to become the heir.

Owen's torment was more than anger. It was guilt, too. Had he interceded before the fight, Pansy would have lived. He'd seen Martin's mounting anger and frustration, and he did not rush forward until the knife came out, and by then, it was too late.

Once we have Owen's story, Miranda sets him free, formally naming Martin as his killer.

Owen is gone. His body will be recovered. And his murderer? Well, that is another matter. Scarlet Jack seemed to promise that Martin would be dealt with, but . . . I have a feeling, if my hunch is right, that the resolution may not be the sort of justice we'd like to see.

⚜

IT HAS BEEN THREE DAYS SINCE MIRANDA FREED OWEN'S GHOST. MARTIN has apparently gone to America to look for his brother. In his case, rather than disappear, he told his parents of his plan. That means he is still alive. Alive and beyond the reach of the law.

Benedict had Owen's body retrieved, but by then, Martin was long gone, having departed that morning while we were searching for Owen's body.

Martin will not return. His actions have cast him into exile. If he ever comes back, Benedict will accuse him of the two murders. So he will stay overseas, and the family fortune will fall to his sister, who . . . Well, that's a matter for another day.

I was not there to witness the retrieving of the body. I'd returned to Thorne Manor. Not only was Lyta on the other side, but my life is there. My old life? That is . . . complicated. Benedict knew he had to let me return, and if he could not be there to see me do it, perhaps that was for the best.

To my immense relief, I found I could both cross to my own time and back again. I tried a few more times—all successfully—before Miranda and Nicolas escorted Lyta and me back to Benedict.

I'd found Benedict on the road, as if he'd heard the clatter of hooves. Had he been waiting? Checking each passing coach? I did not ask. I was too busy enjoying that moment when he saw me and caught me up in his arms, and we clung together, shuddering with relief.

Despite my apparent ability to freely cross between the two times, we are not getting married. Not yet. I have been very firm on that, and when I explained my reasoning, Benedict stopped his grumbling.

It is not only a practical matter of becoming more acquainted. I do not need that. I know what I want as much as he does. But we must make decisions first.

Benedict suggested the possibility of coming to my time and making Jude the earl. I wouldn't hear of it. First, Jude does not want the title. Second, I would not deprive Ravensford of Benedict. Third, I would not deprive Benedict of Ravensford.

This is his home in a way London is not mine. I enjoy the city, but if it were not for Miranda, I'd have moved wherever my career took me. Now Miranda is married, and while I will miss my medical practice in London, I can more easily build a new one here. I *want* to build a new one here. That is equally important. I am not sacrificing my livelihood for Benedict's. I have sensibly selected the more fitting location for us.

What I *will* miss is my family. I am not gone forever, naturally. I think of it as I would moving to the Continent to marry. I cannot pop in to join my sisters for afternoon tea, but I could not do that before, either. Rosalind is in Yorkshire, and Miranda is off on her endless adventures. I will make a new life, but they shall always be part of it.

How different will it be living a hundred years in the past? So far, the change has not been overly difficult, and I think that is because I have only been in the countryside, where life is not so much dictated by current fashions and foibles. But I do not fool myself—it will be an adjustment.

We will wait to marry because I must return to London and settle my affairs there. Benedict also has much to do here. He no longer has hopes of a wealthy wife. We could borrow money from August, but I know Benedict would see that as a last resort. It is the trap his father fell into, and so I will not suggest it unless absolutely necessary.

There was a light rain the night we returned, but nothing since. It was not enough, yet it gave us hope that the drought could end. We cannot count on that, though. Ending the drought only helps his remaining tenants. Nor can we count on any eventual children to solve the problem —that should never be the point of having children. Benedict needs money, soon, if he hopes to recover the remainder of his land before the Carletons evict more tenants.

To that end, we are in the room where the tapestries are stored. We have been opening them and setting aside those in the best condition to take into the future and sell. I am certain they will fetch an excellent price, particularly if Bronwyn and William can get them through to the twenty-first century. My concern is that anyone willing to pay that excellent price will insist on them being authenticated as true medieval tapestries, which will take time. Benedict does not have time.

"We could sell some cheaply," I say. "Without waiting for authentication. Allow the buyers to take a chance and later realize they got them at a bargain. I would like to keep some, if we can, for the walls."

"You are intent on living here, aren't you?"

"Only if you agree. Compromise is critical."

"To the marriage you have not yet agreed to?"

"Precisely." I walk across the room, surveying it. "I would like to turn the room beside this one into a playroom. It is nice and bright, with a garden, where I might sit with the children and Lyta. Would that suit?"

I look back, and he is staring at me with that look, the one I'd first seen in the library that night. I understand what it is now. It is as if I have given him a glimpse through a time stitch of his own, one into a possible future.

"I . . ." He swallows. "Yes. That . . . that sounds . . ." He gives his head a shake and wags a finger at me. "You are doing that on purpose."

"Doing what?"

"Painting pictures so I cannot refuse your ridiculous notion to live here."

I walk over and put my arms around his neck. "If you truly do not want to . . ."

He sighs. "It is old and drafty and falling to ruin."

"And you love it." I lift my face to his. "Just as I will love you when you are old and drafty and falling to ruin."

He laughs and kisses me, pulling me into his arms and—

He pulls back, gaze narrowing as it goes toward the front of the castle. "Did you hear that?"

"Hooves? It sounds as if Jude has returned."

"Damn him. He promised to be gone until evening."

"Promised?"

Benedict doesn't respond to that. He's already in the adjoining room and out the one into the old gardens. I follow, and we see a rider departing.

"That's not Jude," I say. "Also, whoever it was is leaving."

Benedict is already striding toward the front of the castle. I follow. Lyta comes charging from wherever she's been, yipping as if we are going for a walk without her. We continue until we can see the front steps. At the base sits a wooden box.

I hike my skirts and hurry over. "Oh, I do hope it is another puppy."

"What?"

"Another puppy. I have been thinking we need two."

"We are not even wed yet, woman. More dogs should wait until we are actually living together, as man and wife."

I ignore him and keep running to the crate. It has a lid, and I pull it off to see—

"Oh!" I say.

"Another puppy?"

I turn to him, grinning. "Better."

My grin seems to slow his step. He stares at me, and I shake my head at his foolishness. Then I reach into the box and take out a small card with writing in block letters.

I read it aloud. *"Lord Sterling. I heard you were looking for this. I trust you will put it to good use."*

"What the devil?" Benedict says, striding closer.

I bend into the box and lift the contents from the cushioning straw.

Then I turn, lifting it for him to see.

It is the clock.

39

I have been haunting this path for three days now. I spent the last week settling my affairs in London, with Benedict, who was able to cross with me. We've sold the clock. August bought it. That was not charity but a legitimate investment. He paid very handsomely for it, and then will find a way to resell it in the twenty-first century, where he will certainly make money on the deal . . . and will insist on giving us part of the excess, but that is an issue to be handled when the time comes. What matters is that August paid what is, in Benedict's day, a small fortune. Enough to buy back his lands. Enough to keep his tenants fed through the drought. Enough to even begin repairing the castle.

Now I am home again. Home. Ravensford. Benedict.

I am walking with Lyta. I have heard a rumor that someone likes to ride along this path, so I am here. Three days now of coming here. Three days of seeing nothing.

And then I hear it. The patter of a horse galloping.

"Watch there!" a woman's voice shouts.

I keep Lyta off the path, but I turn around myself and block it.

She shouts again. I stand my ground.

"Are you trying to get yourself killed, Lady Sterling?" she snarls as she pulls her horse to a halt.

"It is not Lady Sterling yet," I say placidly. "Good afternoon, Miss Carleton. By the by, I do believe I have never heard your given name."

"Sabrina," she snaps. "Now get out of my—"

"I believe you dropped this."

I lift a square of red silk. I searched through a half-dozen London shops to find exactly the right color. Seeing it, there is a flash of horror in her eyes, enough to confirm my suspicion before she douses it and finds her scowl.

"That is hardly my style," she says. "A vulgar shade suitable only for . . ."

"Vulgar women?" I finish. "Do not hold back now, Miss Carleton. I know what you think of me. It is only odd that you cannot say the words. Perhaps you are not quite the harridan you seem."

Her lips curve in a humorless smile. "Oh, I am every bit a harridan, Lady Sterling. Do not think otherwise."

"Perhaps. A harridan, and yet one who struggles to fully condemn another woman for her scandalous actions."

"I do not condemn you. I applaud you. You have won yourself an earl. And saved me the trouble of marrying that brute myself. If anything, I owe you."

"Oh, you have repaid me. With the clock."

Her brows furrow in a pretty show of confusion. "The what?"

I walk over and lay the scarlet silk on her saddle. "Condolences on the death of your brother, Owen."

She gives a stiff nod, but genuine grief fills her eyes. She says nothing. Nor does she look down at the red silk. She knows what I am saying, and I do not expect her to confirm it.

"I trust we will not see your brother Martin again soon?" I say.

"He is gone to America. He will not return."

Her gaze lands on mine, and her jaw sets. She is waiting for me to comment. Waiting for me to remark that, with both her brothers gone, she is the sole heir to her family's fortune. That is true, but it is also true that she had nothing to do with those circumstances. Yes, I'm sure Martin fled at the toe of her boot, but if he'd stayed and gone to prison, the end result would be the same. She did not kill Owen. She played no role in Martin's actions. He murdered at least three people—Owen, Pansy and Colin Booth—and he likely did more while stealing her persona as Scarlet Jack. Did he know he was stealing from his own sister? I doubt it.

Sabrina Carleton was the proper Scarlet Jack. The one ridding the roads of bandits. Any evil was done by her brother, in the same guise.

Also, she will not inherit her family's fortune. It will pass to her husband and to her sons. She might have said she's happy not to marry Benedict, but I doubt that is true. Oh, she didn't want *him*, per se, but she would have recognized he was a good man who would have been good to her.

Now . . . ?

"I am sorry," I say. "For anything I might have unwittingly taken from you."

She sniffs. "You have taken nothing. I will be fine. Now, if you will step aside, Lady Sterling?"

I do that, and she rides off without another word.

"Goodbye, Sabrina," I say. "Goodbye and good luck."

❦

I AM WALKING HOME WHEN A RUMBLE STOPS ME SHORT. I LOOK INTO THE SKY. It has turned nearly black, and I have been so lost in my thoughts I did not notice it. The rumble comes again. Thunder.

"Portia!"

I look up to see Benedict. He is on his horse, riding toward me.

He swings off, breathing a little hard. "I saw Miss Carleton head this way. Are you all right?"

"Quite fine. I do believe we need to speak about Miss Carleton, though."

He strides over, face darkening. "What has she done now?"

I smile at him. "Nothing bad. We will talk later. For now . . . ?"

I point up.

He barely glances at the sky and then says, a little impatiently, "Yes?"

I shake my head and hold up my arms. Then I tilt my head back.

"What the devil are you—?"

The sky opens, the rain sluicing down.

I look over at him. He's staring into the sky with the same look he

gives me. The wonder and joy of a man catching a glimpse of the future.
A grand future.

"Did you call for rain, Lord Sterling?" I shout, raising my voice to be
heard over the storm.

He grins, scoops me up and swirls me around. Then, with the rain
gloriously pelting around us, he kisses me.

MORE STORIES

I hope you enjoyed **A Castle in the Air**!

If you're looking for more time-travel by me, consider my new series. **A Rip Through Time** stars Mallory Atkinson as a Vancouver detective who flies to Edinburgh to be with her dying grandmother. When she's attacked one night, she wakes up in the body of a stranger . . . in 1869. Mallory finds herself the housemaid to Duncan Gray, an early forensic scientist . . . who just happens to be investigating a murder.

A Rip Through Time is now available. You can read the first chapters on my website: KelleyArmstrong.com

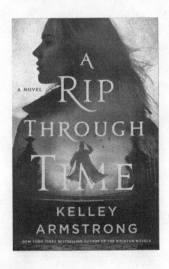

ABOUT THE AUTHOR

Kelley Armstrong believes experience is the best teacher, though she's been told this shouldn't apply to writing her murder scenes. To craft her books, she has studied aikido, archery and fencing. She sucks at all of them. She has also crawled through very shallow cave systems and climbed half a mountain before chickening out. She is however an expert coffee drinker and a true connoisseur of chocolate-chip cookies.

Visit her online:
www.KelleyArmstrong.com
mail@kelleyarmstrong.com

f facebook.com/KelleyArmstrongAuthor
🐦 twitter.com/KelleyArmstrong
📷 instagram.com/KelleyArmstrongAuthor

9 781989 046739